BLINDSIDE

Also by Catherine Coulter
in Large Print:

Afterglow
The Aristocrat
Calypso Magic
The Countess
The Courtship
The Deception
Earth Song
The Edge
Fire Song
The Heir
Midsummer Magic
Moonspun Magic
Riptide
The Scottish Bride
Secret Song

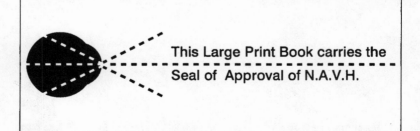

This Large Print Book carries the
Seal of Approval of N.A.V.H.

BLINDSIDE

An FBI Thriller

CATHERINE COULTER

Thorndike Press • Waterville, Maine

Published in 2003 by arrangement with G. P. Putnam's Sons, a member of Penguin Group (USA) Inc.

Thorndike Press® Large Print Basic.

The tree indicium is a trademark of Thorndike Press.

The text of this Large Print edition is unabridged.
Other aspects of the book may vary from the original edition.

Set in 16 pt. Plantin.

Printed in the United States on permanent paper.

Library of Congress Cataloging-in-Publication Data

Coulter, Catherine.
    Blindside : an FBI thriller / Catherine Coulter.
      p. cm.
    ISBN 0-7862-5625-7 (lg. print : hc : alk. paper)
    1. United States. Federal Bureau of Investigation —
Fiction. 2. Sherlock, Lacey (Fictitious character) — Fiction.
3. Savitch, Dillon (Fictitious character) — Fiction.
4. Government investigators — Fiction. 5. Large type
books. I. Title.
PS3553.O843B58 2003b
   811'.54—dc22
                                    2003060734

TO MY MOTHER
ELIZABETH COULTER

As the Founder/CEO of NAVH, the only national health agency solely devoted to those who, although not totally blind, have an eye disease which could lead to serious visual impairment, I am pleased to recognize Thorndike Press★ as one of the leading publishers in the large print field.

Founded in 1954 in San Francisco to prepare large print textbooks for partially seeing children, NAVH became the pioneer and standard setting agency in the preparation of large type.

Today, those publishers who meet our standards carry the prestigious "Seal of Approval" indicating high quality large print. We are delighted that Thorndike Press is one of the publishers whose titles meet these standards. We are also pleased to recognize the significant contribution Thorndike Press is making in this important and growing field.

Lorraine H. Marchi, L.H.D.
Founder/CEO
NAVH

★ Thorndike Press encompasses the following imprints: Thorndike, Wheeler, Walker and Large Print Press.

1

It was pitch black.

There was no moon, no stars, just low-lying rain-bloated clouds, as black as the sky. Dillon Savich was sweating in his Kevlar vest even though it was fifty degrees.

He dropped to his knees, raised his hand to stop the agents behind him, and carefully slid into position so he could see into the room.

The window was dirty, the tattered draperies a vomit-brown, with only one lamp in the corner throwing off sixty watts. The rest of the living room was dark, but he could clearly see the teacher, James Marple, tied to a chair, gagged, his head dropped forward. Was he asleep or unconscious? Or dead?

Savich couldn't tell.

He didn't see Marvin Phelps, the sixty-seven-year-old man who owned this run-down little 1950s tract house on the outskirts of the tiny town of Mount Pleasant, Virginia. From what they'd found out in the hour before they'd converged on this small house, Phelps was a retired math teacher and owned the old Buick sitting in the patched drive. Savich knew from his driver's license that Phelps was tall, skinny, and had a head covered with thick white hair. And for some reason, he was killing other math teachers. Two, to date. No one knew why. There was no connection between the first two murdered teachers.

Savich wanted Phelps alive. He wanted the man to tell him why he'd caused all this misery and destroyed two families. For what? He needed to know, for the future. The behavioral science people hadn't ever suggested that the killer could possibly be a math teacher himself.

Savich saw James Marple's head jerk. At least he was alive. There was a zigzagging line of blood coming over the top of Mr. Marple's bald head from a blow Phelps must have dealt him. The blood had dried just short of his mouth.

Where was Marvin Phelps?

They were here only because one of Agent Ruth Warnecki's snitches had come through. Ruth, in the CAU — the Criminal Apprehension Unit — for only a year, had previously spent eight years with the Washington, D.C., police department. Not only had she brought her great street skills to the unit, she'd also brought her snitches. "A woman can never be too rich, too thin, or have too many snitches" was her motto.

The snitch had seen Marvin Phelps pull a gun on a guy in the parking lot of a small strip mall, pull him out of his Volvo station wagon, and shove him into an old Buick. The snitch had called Ruth as he was tailing them to this house, and told her he'd give her the whole enchilada for five hundred bucks, including the license plate number of the man taken. Savich didn't want to think about what would have happened to Mr. Marple if the snitch hadn't come through.

But Savich shook his head as he looked at the scene through the window. It didn't fit. The other two math teachers had been shot in the forehead at close range, dying instantly. There'd been no kidnapping, no overnight stays tied to a chair with a sixty-watt bulb chasing the shadows. Why change the way he did things now? Why take such a risk by bringing the victim to his own home? No, something wasn't right.

Savich suddenly saw a movement, a shadow that rippled over the far wall in the living room. He raised his hand and made a fist, signaling Dane Carver, Ruth Warnecki, and Sherlock that he wanted everyone to stay put and keep silent. They would hold the local Virginia law enforcement personnel in check, at least for a while. Everyone was in place, including five men from the Washington field office SWAT team who were ready to take this place apart if given the word. Every corner of the property was covered. The marksman, Cooper, was in his place, some twenty feet behind Savich, with a clear view into the shadowy living room.

Savich saw another ripple in the dim light. A dark figure rose up from behind a worn sofa. It was Marvin Phelps, the man whose photo he'd first seen just an hour ago. He was walking toward John Marple, no, swaggering was more like it. What was he doing behind the sofa?

When Phelps wasn't more than a foot from Marple, he said, his voice oddly deep and pleasant, "Are you awake, Jimbo? Come on, I didn't hit you that hard, you pathetic wuss."

Jimbo? Savich turned up the volume on his directional receiver.

"Do you know it will be dawn in another thirty-seven minutes? I've decided to kill you at dawn."

10

Mr. Marple slowly raised his head. His glasses had slipped down his nose, and with his hands tied behind him, he couldn't do anything about it. He licked at the dried blood beside his mouth.

"Yes, I'm awake. What do you want, Philly? What the hell is going on here? Why are you doing this?"

Philly? The two men knew each other well enough for nicknames.

Phelps laughed, and Savich felt his skin crawl. It was a mad old laugh, scratchy and black, not at all pleasant and deep like his voice. Phelps pulled a knife from inside his flannel shirt, a long hunting knife that gleamed even in the dull light.

Savich had expected a gun, not a knife. It wasn't supposed to go down like this. Two dead high school math teachers, and now this. Not in pattern. What was going on here?

"You ready to die, Jimbo, you little prick?"

"I'm not a prick. What the hell are you doing? Are you insane? Jesus, Philly, it's been over five years! Put down that knife!"

But Mr. Phelps tossed the knife from one hand to the other with easy movements that bespoke great familiarity.

"Why should I, Jimbo? I think I'm going

to cut out your brain. I've always hated your brain, do you know that? I've always despised you for the way you wanted everyone to see how smart you were, how fast you could jigger out magic solutions, you little bastard —" He was laughing as he slowly raised the knife.

"It's not dawn yet!"

"Yeah, but I'm old, and who knows? By dawn I might drop dead of a heart attack. I really do want you dead before me, Jimbo."

Savich had already aimed his SIG Sauer, his mouth open to yell, when Jimbo screamed, kicked out wildly, and flung the chair over backward. Phelps dove forward after him, cursing, stabbing the knife through the air.

Savich fired right at the long silver blade. At nearly the same moment there was another shot — the loud, sharp sound of a rifle, fired from a distance.

The long knife exploded, shattering Phelps's hand; the next thing to go flying was Phelps's brains as his head exploded. Savich saw his bloody fingers spiraling upward, spewing blood, and shards of silver raining down, but Phelps wouldn't miss his hand or his fingers. Savich whipped around, not wanting to believe what had just happened.

The sniper, Kurt Cooper, had fired.

Savich yelled "No," but of course it was way too late. Savich ran to the front door and slammed through, agents and local cops behind him.

James Marple was lying on his back, white-faced, whimpering. By going over backward he'd saved himself from being splattered by Mr. Phelps's brains.

Marvin Phelps's body lay on its side, his head nearly severed from his neck, sharp points of the silver knife blade embedded in his face and chest, his right wrist a bloody stump.

Savich was on his knees, untying Jimbo's ankles and arms, trying to calm him down. "You're all right, Mr. Marple. You're all right, just breathe in and out, that's good. Stay with me here, you're all right."

"Phelps, he was going to kill me, kill me — oh, God."

"Not any longer. He's dead. You're all right." Savich got him free and helped him to his feet, keeping himself between James Marple and the corpse.

Jimbo looked up, his eyes glassy, spit dribbling from his mouth. "I never liked the cops before, always thought you were a bunch of fascists, but you saved me. You actually saved my life."

"Yeah, well, we do try to do that occasionally. Now, let's just get you out of here. Here's Agent Sherlock and Agent Warnecki. They're going to take you out to the medics for a once-over. You're okay, Mr. Marple. Everything is okay."

Savich stood there a moment, listening to Sherlock talk to James Marple in that wonderful soothing voice of hers, the one she had used at Sean's first birthday party. One terrified math teacher wouldn't be a problem compared to a roomful of one-year-olds.

Agent Dane Carver helped support James Marple, a slight smile on his face until Sherlock stepped back, and then he and Agent Warnecki escorted Marple to the waiting paramedics.

Savich turned back to the body of Marvin Phelps. Cooper had nearly blown the guy's head off. A great shot, very precise, no chance of his knifing Marple in a reactive move, no chance for him to even know what was happening before he died.

It wasn't supposed to have happened that way, but Cooper had standing orders to fire if there was imminent danger.

He saw Police Chief Halloran trotting toward him, followed by a half-dozen excited local cops, all of them hyped, all of them smiling. That would change when they saw Phelps's body.

At least they'd saved a guy's life.

But it wasn't the killer they were after, Savich was sure of that. Theirs had killed two women, both high school math teachers. And in a sense, that maniac was responsible for this mess as well. It was probably why Cooper had jumped the gun and taken Phelps out. He saw himself saving James Marple's life and taking out the math teacher killer at the same time. In all fairness, Coop was only twenty-four, loaded with testosterone, and still out to save the world. Not good enough. Savich would see to it that he had his butt drop-kicked and then sentenced to scrubbing out the SWAT team's bathroom, the cruelest penalty anyone could devise.

The media initially ignored the fact that this killing had nothing to do with the two math teacher killings. The early evening headlines read: SERIAL KILLER DEAD? And underneath, in smaller letters, because math teachers weren't very sexy: MATH TEACHERS TARGETED. The first two murders were detailed yet again. Only way down the page was it mentioned that the kidnapping and attempted murder of James Marple by Marvin Phelps of Mount

15

Pleasant, Virginia, had nothing to do with the two other math teacher killings.

Par for the course.

2

Savich wasn't stupid. He knew it when he saw it, and the gorgeous woman with the long black hair pinned up with a big clip, wearing a hot pink leotard, was coming on to him.

He didn't know her name, but he'd seen her around the gym a couple of times, both times in the last week, now that he thought about it. She was strong, supple, and fit, all qualities he admired in anyone, male or female.

He nodded to her, pressed the incline pad higher on the treadmill, and went back to reading the report Dane Carver, one of his CAU agents, had slipped under his arm as he'd walked out of the office that evening.

Bernice Ward, murdered six days before, was shot in the forehead at close range as she was walking out of the 7-Eleven on Grand Street in Oxford, Maryland, at ten o'clock at night, carrying a bag that held a half-gallon of nonfat milk and two packages of rice cakes, something Savich believed should be used for packing boxes, not eating.

There had been no witnesses, nothing captured on the 7-Eleven video camera or the United Maryland Bank ATM camera diagonally across the street. The 7-Eleven clerk heard the shot, found Mrs. Ward, and called it in. It was a .38 caliber bullet, directly between Bernice Ward's eyes. She'd been married, no children. As yet, there was no motive in sight. The police were all over the husband.

And just three days ago, the second victim, Leslie Fowler, another high school math teacher, was shot at close range coming out of the Alselm Cleaners on High Street, in Paulette, Virginia, just before closing at 9 p.m. Again, there were no witnesses, no evident motive as of yet for the husband, and the police were sucking him dry. Leslie Fowler had left no children, two dogs, and a seemingly distraught husband and family.

Savich sighed. When the story of the second shooting broke, everyone in the Washington, D.C., area was on edge, thanks to the media's coverage. Nobody wanted another serial killer in the area, but this second murder didn't look good.

Dane Carver had found no evidence that

either woman had known the other. No tie at all between the two had yet been found. Both head shots, close range, with the same gun, a .38.

And as of today, the FBI was involved, the Criminal Apprehension Unit specifically, because there was a chance that a serial killer was on the loose, and the Oxford P.D. and the Paulette P.D. had failed to turn up anything that would bring the killers close to home. Bottom line, they knew they needed help and that meant they were ready to have the Feds in their faces rather than let more killings rebound on them.

One murder in Maryland, one murder in Virginia.

Would the next one be in D.C.?

If the shootings were random, Dane wrote, finding high school math teachers was easy for the killer — just a quick visit to a local library and a look through the high school yearbooks.

Savich stretched a moment, and upped his speed. He ran hard for ten minutes, then cooled down again. He'd already read everything in the report about the two women, but he read it all again. There was no evidence of much value yet, something the media didn't know about, thank God.

The department had started by setting up a hot line just this morning, and calls were flooding in. Many of them, naturally, had to be checked out, but so far there was nothing helpful. He kept reading. Both women were in their thirties, both married for over ten years to the same spouses, and both were childless — something a little odd and he made a mental note of that — did the killer not want to leave any motherless children? Both husbands had been closely scrutinized and appeared, so far, to be in the clear. Troy Ward, the first victim's husband, was the announcer for the Baltimore Ravens, a placid overweight man who wore thick glasses and began sobbing the moment anyone said his dead wife's name. He wasn't dealing well with his loss.

Gifford Fowler was the owner of a successful Chevrolet car dealership in Paulette, right on Main Street. He was something of a womanizer, but he had no record of violence. He was tall, as gaunt as Troy Ward was heavy, beetle-browed, with a voice so low it was mesmerizing. Savich wondered how many Chevy pickups that deep voice had sold. Everything known about both husbands was carefully detailed, all the way down to where they had their dry cleaning done and what brand of toothpaste they used.

The two men didn't know each other, and neither had ever met the other. They apparently had no friends in common.

In short, it appeared that a serial killer was at work who had no particular math teacher in mind to target. Any math teacher would do.

As for the women, both appeared to be genuinely nice people, their friends devastated by their murders. Both were responsible adults, one active in her local church, the other in local politics and charities. They'd never met each other, as far as anyone knew. They were nearly perfect citizens.

What was wrong with this picture?

Was there anything he wasn't seeing? Was this really a serial killer? Savich paused a moment in his reading.

Was it just some mutt who hated math teachers? Savich knew that the killer was a man, just knew it in his gut. But why math teachers? What could the motive possibly be? Rage over failing grades? Beatings or abuse by a math teacher? Or, maybe, a parent, friend, or lover he hated who was a math teacher? Or maybe it was a motive that no sane person could even comprehend. Well, Steve's group over in behavioral sciences at Quantico would come up with every possible motive in the universe of twisted minds.

Two dead so far and Steve said he'd bet his breakfast Cheerios there'd be more. Not good.

He wanted to meet the two widowers.

Savich remembered what his friend Miles Kettering had said about the two math teacher killings just a couple of nights before, when he and Sam had come over for barbecue. Six-year-old Sam was the image of his father, down to the way he chewed the corn off the cob. Miles had thought about it a moment, then said, "It's nuts. But you know, Savich, I'll bet the motive will be something you can't even begin to imagine." Savich was thinking now that Miles could be right, he frequently had been back when he and Miles had been agents together, until five years before.

Savich saw a flash of hot-pink leotard from the corner of his eye. She started up on the treadmill next to his, vacated by an ATF guy who'd gotten divorced and was telling Bobby Curling, the gym manager, that he couldn't wait to get into the action again. Given how many single women there were in Washington, D.C., old muscle-bound Arnie shouldn't have any problem.

Savich finished reading Dane's report and looked out over the gym, not really seeing all the sweaty bodies, but poking around deep inside his own head. The thing about this killer was that he was in their own backyard — Virginia and Maryland. Would he look farther afield?

Savich had to keep positive. Even though it had been unrelated, they'd saved James Marple from having a knife shoved in his chest or his head. It had come out last night that Jimbo had had an affair with Marvin Phelps's wife, who'd then divorced Phelps and married Marple — five years before. But Savich knew it wasn't just the infidelity that was Phelps's motive. He'd heard it right out of Phelps's mouth — jealousy, pure and simple jealousy that had grown into rage. The last time Savich had seen James Marple, his wife, Liz, was there hovering, hugging and kissing him.

"Hello, I've seen you here before. My name's Valerie. Valerie Rapper, and no, I don't like Eminem." She smiled at him, a really lovely white-toothed smile. A long piece of black hair had come loose from the clip and was curved around her cheek.

He nodded. "My name's Savich. Dillon Savich."

"Bobby told me you were an FBI agent."

Savich wanted to get back to Dane's report. He wanted to figure out how he was going to catch this nut case before math teachers in the area became terrified for the foreseeable future. Again, he only nodded.

"Is it true that Louie Freeh was a technophobe?"

"What?" Savich jerked around to look at her.

She just smiled, a dark eyebrow arched up.

Savich shrugged. "People will say anything about anyone."

Standard FBI spew, of course, but it was ingrained in him to turn away insults aimed at the Bureau. And, as a matter of fact, what could he say? Besides, the truth was that Director Freeh had always been fascinated with MAX, Savich's laptop.

"He was sure sexy," she said.

Savich blinked at that and said, "He has six or seven kids. Maybe more now that he has more time."

"Maybe that proves that his wife thinks he's sexy, too."

Savich just smiled and pointedly returned to Dane's report. He read: *Ruth Warnecki says she's kept three snitches happy since she left the Washington, D.C., Police Department, including bottles of bubbly at Christmas. She gave a bottle of Dom Perignon to the snitch who saved James Marple's life, only to have him give it back, saying he preferred malt liquor.*

The booze Ruth usually gave to her snitches would probably burn a hole in a normal person's stomach. They'd been very lucky this time, but what could a snitch know about some nut killing high school math teachers? They weren't talking low-life drug dealers here. On the other hand, most cases were solved by informants of one sort or another, and that was a fact.

He tried to imagine again why this person felt that his mission was to commit cold-blooded murder of math teachers. Randomly shooting company CEOs — that was a maybe. Judges — sometimes. Politicians — good idea. Lawyers — hands down, a top-notch idea. But math teachers? Even the profilers were amused about how off-the-wall crazy nuts it was, something that no one could ever remember happening before.

He was inside his brain once more when

she spoke again. He nearly fell off the treadmill at her words. "Is it true that Congress, way back when, was responsible for shutting off any communication between the FBI and the CIA? And that's why no one shared any information before nine-eleven?"

"I've heard that" was all he said.

She leaned close and he smelled her perfume, mixed with a light coating of sweat. He didn't like Valerie Rapper looking at him like she wanted to pull his gym shorts off.

She asked, "How often do you work out?"

He had only seven minutes to go on the treadmill. He decided to cut it to thirty seconds. He was warmed up enough, loose, and a little winded. "I try to come three or four times a week," he said, and pressed the cool-down pad. He knew he was being a jerk. Just because he was anxious about this killer, just because a woman was interested in him, it didn't mean he should be rude.

And so he asked, "How often do you come here?"

She shrugged. "Just like you — three or four times a week."

Without thinking, he said, "It shows."

Stupid thing to say, really stupid. Now she was smiling, telling him so clearly how pleased she was that he liked her body.

He was an idiot. When he got home he'd tell Sherlock how he'd managed to stick his foot all the way down his throat and kick his tonsils.

He pressed the stop pad and stepped off the treadmill. "See you," he said, and pointedly walked to the weights on the other side of the room.

He worked out hard for the next forty-five minutes, pushing himself, but aware that she was always near him, sometimes standing not two feet away, watching him while she worked her triceps with ten-pound weights.

Sherlock, much smaller, her once skinny little arms now sleek with muscle, had worked up to twelve-pound weights.

Thirty minutes later he forgot all about the math teacher killer and Valerie Rapper as he opened the front door of his house to hear his son yell "Papa! Here comes an airplane!" and got it right in the chest.

Two evenings later at the gym, while Sherlock was showering in the women's locker room after a hard workout, and Savich was stretching his tired muscles in a corner, he nearly tripped on a free weight when Valerie Rapper said, not six inches from his ear, "Hello, Dillon. I heard that you saved a math teacher from a crazy man a couple of days ago. Congratulations."

He straightened so fast he nearly hit her with his elbow. "Yeah," he said, "it happens like that sometimes."

"The media is making it sound like the FBI messed up, what with that old man getting his head blown off."

Savich shrugged, as if to say what else is new? He said again, "That happens, too."

"Maybe you'd like to have a cup of coffee after you've finished working out?"

He smiled at her and said, "No, thank you. I'm waiting for my wife. Our little boy is waiting for us at home. He's learning how to make paper airplanes."

"How delightful."

"See you."

Valerie Rapper watched him as he made his way through the crowded gym to the men's locker room. She watched him again when he came out of the locker room fifteen minutes later, showered and dressed, shrugging into his suit coat. He wished there were more men in Washington, D.C. Maybe he should introduce her to old Arnie. He found Sherlock talking to Bobby

Curling. He grabbed her and hustled her out before she could say a word.

She asked as she got into the Porsche, "What was all that about?"

"I'd rather tell you when we get home."

Savich brushed out a thick hank of Sherlock's curly hair and carefully wrapped it around a big roller. "I'm glad you're feeling better. I'm glad you were at the gym tonight."

She watched him in the mirror, concentrating on getting her hair perfectly smooth around the roller. He was nearly done. He really liked doing this ever since they'd met an actress who'd had a particularly sexy way with hair rollers. Of course, the rollers didn't stay in her hair all that long. "Why? What happened?"

He paused a moment, smoothed down her hair on another roller, and slowly turned it. Sherlock shoved in a clip to hold it. "There's this woman. She's not taking the hint."

Sherlock leaned her head back until she was looking up at her husband's face. "You want me to go kick her butt?"

Savich didn't speak for a good thirty seconds. He was too busy untangling the final thick hank of hair for the last roller.

"There, done. Now, be quiet. I just want to look at you. You can't imagine how that turns me on, Sherlock."

She now had a headful of fat rollers, perfectly placed, and she was laughing. She turned and held out her arms. "Now what, you pervert?"

He stroked his long fingers over his chin. "Hmmm, maybe I can think of something."

"What about this woman?"

"Forget her. She'll lose interest."

Sherlock did forget all about the woman during the removal of the rollers in the next hour. She fell asleep with a big roller pressed against the back of her knee.

It was just after six-thirty on Friday morning when the phone rang.

Savich, Sean under one arm while Sherlock was pouring Cheerios into a bowl, picked it up. He listened. Finally, he hung up the phone.

"What's wrong?"

"That was Miles. Sam's been kidnapped."

3

Don't give up, don't give up. Never, never give up.

Okay, so he wouldn't give up, but it was hard. He'd cried until he was hiccupping, but that sure hadn't done him any good. He didn't want to give up. Only thing was, Sam didn't have a clue where he was and he was so scared he'd already peed in his jeans.

Be scared, it's okay, just keep trying to get away. Never give up.

Sam nodded. He heard his mama's voice every now and again, but this time it was different. She was trying to help him because he was in big trouble.

Don't give up, Sam. Look around you. You can do something.

Her voice always sounded soft and kind; she didn't sound like she was scared. Sam tried to slow his breathing down.

The men are in the other room eating. They're watching TV. You've got to move, Sam.

He'd been as quiet as he could, lying on

that stinky mattress, getting colder and colder, and he listened as hard as he could, his eyes on that keyhole, wishing he was free so he could scrunch down and try to see what the men were doing. He heard the TV; it was on the Weather Channel. The weather guy said, "Violent thunderstorms are expected locally and throughout eastern Tennessee."

He heard that clearly: *eastern Tennessee.*

He was in Tennessee?

That couldn't be right. He lived in Virginia, in Colfax, with his father. Where was Tennessee?

Sam thought about his father. How much time had passed since they'd put that cloth over his face and he'd breathed in that sick sweet smell and not really waked up until just a while ago, tied to this bed in this small bedroom that looked older than anything, older even than his father's ancient Camaro? Maybe it was more than hours, maybe it was days now. He didn't know how long he'd been asleep. He kept praying that his father would find him. But there was one big problem, and he knew it even while he was praying the words — his father wasn't in Tennessee; as far as Sam could see, there was no way his father could find him.

I'm really scared, Mom.

Forget about being scared. Move, Sam, move. Get your hands free.

He knew he probably wasn't really hearing his mama's voice in his head, or maybe he really was, and he was dead, too, just like she was.

He could feel that his pants were wet. It was cold and it itched so that must mean he really wasn't dead. He was lying flat on his back, his head on a flattened smelly pillow, his hands tied in front of him. He'd pulled on the rope, but it hadn't done anything. Then he'd felt sick to his stomach. He didn't want to throw up, so he'd just laid there, breathing in and out, until finally his stomach calmed down. His mom wanted him to pull on the rope and so he began jerking and working it again. His wrists weren't tied real tight, and that was good. He hadn't talked to the two men when he woke up. He was so scared that he'd just stared up at them, hadn't said a single thing, just stared, tears swimming in his eyes, making his nose run. They'd given him some water, and he'd drunk that, but when the tall skinny guy offered him a hamburger, he knew he couldn't eat it.

Then one of the men — Fatso, that's

what Sam called him in his head — tied his hands in front of him, but not too tight. Fatso looked like he felt sorry for him.

Sam raised his wrists to his mouth and started chewing.

"Damned friggin' rain!"

Sam froze. It was Fatso's voice, loud and angry. Sam was so scared he started shaking, and it wasn't just the damp chill air in this busted-down old room that caused it. He had to keep chewing, had to get his hands free. He had to keep moving and not freeze. He couldn't die, not like Mama had. His father would hate that almost as much as Sam would.

Sam chewed.

There weren't any more loud voices from the other room, but he could still hear the TV announcer, talking more about really bad weather coming, and then he heard the two men arguing about something. Was it about him?

Sam pulled his hands up, looked closely, and then began working the knotted rope, sliding his hands first this way, then that. The rope felt looser.

Oh boy, his hands did feel looser, he knew it. Sam chewed until his jaws ached. He felt a give in the rope, then more give, and then the knot just came loose. He couldn't believe it. He twisted his wrists and the rope fell off.

Unbelievable. He was free.

He sat up and rubbed his hands. They were pretty numb, and he felt pins and needles running through them, but at least they didn't hurt.

He stood up beside the mangy bed with its awful smells, wondering how long it had been since anyone had slept in that bed before him. It was then he saw a high, narrow, dirty window on the other side of the room.

He could fit through that window. He could.

How would he get up there?

If he tried to pull the bed to the window they were sure to hear him. And then they'd come in and tie him even tighter.

Or they'd kill him.

Sam knew he'd been taken right out of his own bed, right out of his own house, his father sleeping not thirty feet away. He knew, too, that anything those men had in mind to do to him wasn't any good.

The window . . . how could he get up to that window?

And then Sam saw an old, deep-drawered dresser in the corner. He pulled out the first drawer, nearly choking on fear when the drawer creaked and groaned.

He got it out. It was heavy, but he managed to pull it onto his back. He staggered over to the wall and, as quietly as he could, laid the drawer down, toeing it against the damp wall. He stacked another drawer on top of that first one, then another, carefully, one upside down on top of another.

He had to lift the sixth drawer really high to fit it on top of the others. He knew he had to do it and so he did.

Hurry, Sam, hurry.

He was hurrying. He didn't want to die even though he knew he'd probably be able to speak to his mama again all the time. No, she didn't want him to die, she didn't want him to leave his father.

When he got the last drawer balanced on the very top, he stood back, and saw that he had done a good job putting them on top of each other. Now he just had to climb up on top and reach the window.

He eyed the drawers, and shoved the third one over just a bit to create a toehold. He did the same with the fourth.

He knew if he fell it would be all over. He couldn't fall. He heard Fatso scream, "No matter what you say, we can't stay here, Beau. It's going to start raining any minute now. You saw that creek out back.

A thunderstorm'll make it rise fast as bat shit in a witch's brew!"

Drown? The thunderstorms he'd heard on the Weather Channel, that must be what Fatso was yelling about. He didn't want to drown either.

Sam was finally on the top. He pulled himself upright very slowly, feeling the drawer wobbling and unable to do anything about it. He froze, his hands flat against the damp wall, then his fingers crept up and he touched the bottom of the windowsill.

Things were unsteady beneath his feet, but that was okay. It felt just like the bridge in the park when he walked across it, just like that. He could work with a swing, even a wobble, he just couldn't fall.

He pushed at the window but it didn't budge. Then he saw the latch, so covered with dirt that it was hard to make out. He grabbed it and pulled upward.

He heard Fatso yell, "Beau, listen to me, we gotta take the kid somewhere else. That rain's going to start any minute."

So that was his name, Beau. Beau said something back, but Sam couldn't make out what it was. He wasn't a screamer like Fatso.

Sam had the latch pushed up as far as it

would go. Slowly, so slowly he nearly stopped breathing, he pushed at the window.

It creaked, loud.

Sam jerked around and the drawers teetered, swaying more than ever. He knew he was going to fall. The drawers were sliding apart like earth plates before an earthquake. He remembered Mrs. Mildrake crunching together real dinner plates to show the class how earthquakes happened.

He shoved on the window as hard as he could and it creaked all the way out.

The drawers shuddered and moved and Sam, almost crying he was so afraid, grabbed the windowsill. With all the strength he had, he pulled himself headfirst through that skinny window. He got stuck, wiggled free, and then fell outside.

He landed on the ground, nearly headfirst.

He lay there, breathing, wanting to move, but afraid that his head was split open and his brains might start spilling out. He lay listening to the wind pick up, whipping through the trees. There were a lot of trees around him, and the sky was almost dark. Was it nighttime?

No, it was just the storm coming closer, the thunderstorm the Weather Channel had talked about for eastern Tennessee. How could he be in Tennessee?

He had to get up. Fatso and Beau could come out at any moment. The drawers had fallen over, no doubt about that, and the loud noise would bring them into the bedroom fast. They'd see he was gone and they'd be out here with guns and poison and more rope and get him again.

Sam came up on his knees. He felt something sticky on his face and touched it. He'd cut himself with the fall. He turned to look up at the window. It was way far off the ground.

Sam managed to stand up, weaved a bit, then locked his knees. He was okay. Everything was cool. He just had to get out of there.

He starting running. He heard Fatso scream the same instant a bolt of lightning struck real close and a boom of thunder rattled his brains. They knew he was gone.

Sam ran into the thick trees, all gold and red and yellow. He didn't know what kind of trees they were, but there were a lot of them and he was small and could easily weave in and out of them. If they got too close he'd climb one, he was good at that, too good, his father always said.

He heard the men yelling, not far behind

him, maybe just a little off to the left. He kept running, panting now, a stitch in his side, but he just kept his legs pumping.

Lightning flashed through the trees, and the thunder was coming so close it sounded like drums playing real loud rock 'n' roll, like his father did when he thought Sam was outside playing.

Sam heard Fatso yell, and stopped, just for a second. Fatso wasn't even close. But what about Beau? Beau didn't have the belly Fatso had, so maybe he could slither through the trees really fast. He could come out from behind a tree and jump Sam, cut his throat.

Sam's heart was pounding so loud he could hear it. He crouched down behind one of the big trees, made himself as skinny as a shadow, and waited. He got his breath back, pressed his cheek to the bark, and listened. He didn't hear anything, just the thunder that kept rumbling through the sky. He rubbed his side and the stitch faded. The air felt thick, actually felt like it was raining before the first drop found its way through the thick canopy of leaves and hit him on the jaw.

They'd never see him in the rain. Fatso would probably slip on some mud and land on his fat belly. Sam smiled.

You did it, Sam, you did it.

He'd done it all right. Only thing was he didn't know where he was.

Where was Tennessee?

Even with the thick tree cover, the rain came down hard. He wondered if the forest was so big he'd come out in Ohio, wherever that was.

4

It was Saturday afternoon, her day off, but with the storm coming, anything could happen. Katie Benedict was driving slowly, listening to the rain slam against the roof of her Silverado. It was hard to see through the thick gray rain even with the windshield wipers working overtime. The mountains were shrouded in fog, thick, heavy, and cold. And now this storm, a vicious one, the weather people were calling it, was on the way. An interesting choice of words, but she bet it was apt. She realized now that she shouldn't have chanced taking Keely to her piano lesson given the forecast, but she had. At least it had only just started raining, and they were close to home. She just hoped there wouldn't be any accidents on the road. If there were, she'd be up to her eyebrows in work.

She hunched forward, peering through the thick sheets of rain, Keely quiet beside her. Too quiet.

"Keely, you all right?"

"I'd like to find a rainbow, Mama."

"Not for a while yet, sweetie, but you keep looking. Hey, I heard you playing your C major scale before. It sounded really good."

"I've worked hard on getting it right, Mama."

Katie grinned. "I know, but it's worth it."

Suddenly, Keely bounced up on the seat, straining against her seat belt, and began waving through the windshield. "Mama, what's that? Look, it's a little boy and he's running!"

Katie saw him. The boy was sopping wet, running out of the woods to her left, not more than fifty feet onto the road in front of her. Then she saw two men burst out of the trees. It was obvious they were after him.

Katie said, even as she reached over and quickly released Keely's seat belt, "I want you to get down and stay there. Do you understand?"

Keely knew that tone of voice, her mama's sheriff voice, and nodded, slipping down to the floor.

"Cover your head with your arms. Everything will be fine. Just don't move, okay?"

"Okay, Mama."

Katie pulled to a stop, quickly leaned over the front seat and punched in the two numbers to her lock box beneath the back bench. She pulled out her Remington rifle, loaded, ready to go. By the time she opened the door, the men weren't more than a long arm's reach from the boy. Thank God he'd seen her and was running toward her. He was yelling, but the wind and rain wiped any sound he made right out.

The big man, his beer gut pounded by the rain, had a gun. Not good. Despite his size he moved quickly. He turned toward her, away from the boy, and raised the gun.

Katie brought up her rifle, cool and fast, and fired, kicking up muddy water not a foot from the fat man's feet, splattering him to his waist. "I'm the sheriff! Stop right there! Don't move!"

The skinny man behind him yelled something. The idiot was wearing a long black leather coat that was soaked from the rain. Katie calmly raised her Remington again and fired. This time the shot dug up a huge clod of dirt, spraying the leather coat.

The man in the coat yelled something and grabbed at the fat man's shirt. The fat man jerked away, yelled something toward the boy, and fired from his hip, a lucky shot in the fog and rain that very nearly hit her.

"You idiot!" she yelled. "I'm Sheriff Benedict. Drop your weapon! Both of you, don't move a single muscle!" But the fat guy pulled the trigger again, another hip shot, this one nowhere near her. Katie didn't hesitate, she pulled the trigger and the guy flinched and grabbed his upper arm. She'd wanted to hit him high on the shoulder, wanted to bring him down, but the rain and fog were hard on her aim.

He managed to keep his gun. She had hoped he'd drop it.

She shouted, "Come forward, both of you, slowly!"

But neither of them took a single step toward her, not that she'd expected them to. Both men ran back into the thick trees. She fired after them, once, twice, then a final time. She thought she heard a yell. Good.

The little boy, panting so hard he was heaving, was on her the next instant. He grabbed her arm and shook it.

"You can't let them go, ma'am! You've gotta shoot them again, you gotta kick their butts!"

Katie laid her rife alongside her leg, and

pulled the boy against her. "I got the fat one in the arm. Maybe I got the other one, too, while they were running back into the forest. You can count on it — the fat one's hurting bad. Now, it's going to be all right. I'm Sheriff Benedict. I'll get right on my cell phone and call for some help with those guys. Come into the truck and tell me what's going on."

Sam looked up at the tall woman who could have shot Fatso right in his big gut, but had only shot him in the arm instead. "Why didn't you kill him?"

Katie smiled at the boy as she quickly herded him back to the truck. She didn't want to hang around here. No telling if those guys would pop back out of the woods. "I try not to kill every bad guy I run into," she said. "Sometimes I like to bring them in front of a judge." She squeezed him hard. "You're okay and that's all that matters. Now let's move out of here."

The narrow bench in the back could hold no more than a couple of skinny kids. What it did have was a stack of blankets, not usually for warmth, but to soften the ride.

She grabbed the blankets and lifted the boy up onto the front seat. "Keely, we're going to make room for —"

"My name's Sam."

"We're going to make room for Sam. He's cold and he's wet." She settled him between her and Keely and covered him with five blankets. "Sweetie, don't worry about your seat belt. You just press close to him to help him warm up, okay?"

"Okay, Mama." Keely pressed against his back. Her little face was white, her voice a thin thread.

"It's going to be all right, baby. I don't want you to worry. I want you to be real brave for Sam here. He needs you to watch over him now. He's been through something bad. Can you do that?"

Keely nodded, the tears that were near to brimming over nearly gone now. To Katie's surprise, she shook Sam's arm. "Hey, who were those guys? What were they doing to you?"

Sam was shuddering.

"Not now, Keely. Let's just let Sam warm up a bit before we grill him."

Sam managed to get his mouth working, but it was hard. "What's your name, ma'am?"

"I'm Sheriff Benedict and that little girl next to you is my daughter, Keely. Did those men kidnap you?"

Sam managed to nod. He wasn't going to cry. "I squeezed through a window and fell on my head. But I got away."

"My goodness, you're really brave, Sam. Now, let's get you over to Doc Flint's. Keely, you press close to Sam and try to get him warm."

"I call him Doc Flintstone," Keely said, watched her mom frown, then grab one of the towels to dry off the little boy's head.

Sam said from behind the towel, "My mama used to give me Flintstones vitamins every morning with my toast."

"I like marmalade on my toast. I don't think smashed vitamins would taste very good."

Sam thought that was funny, but he was just too cold and too scared to laugh. He burrowed under the blankets; all he wanted to do was get warm. He pressed himself as hard as he could against Sheriff Benedict's leg. He felt the little girl squeezing against his back. He wondered if he was going to die now that he'd gotten away from those men. The little girl was pressed so hard against him, he'd bet she was going to get her clothes as wet as his.

Katie slid her rifle onto the floor behind the driver's seat. She turned the heater on high. "Okay, kids, I cranked up the heat so it'll be roasting you both in a minute. I know you're wet clear through, Sam, but the blankets should help a little bit."

"I don't like marmalade," Sam said as Katie was looking at him closely.

"You'll like my mom's. It's the best." Good, the boy wasn't in shock, at least not yet. Katie put the truck in gear and started up. She had to watch her speed; the heavy rain made the road a river. As they passed where the men had disappeared into the trees, she looked carefully, but saw no sign of them.

She picked her cell phone out of her breast pocket and called Wade at the station house.

"Hello, Wade, it's Katie. No, don't tell me anything about the storm just yet. This is urgent." She told him about Sam and his kidnappers, the two men who'd been chasing him, and how she'd shot the fat one in the arm. "I'm on the south end of Delaware. Sam came out of the woods in nearly a straight line from the road to Bleaker's cabin — I'll bet that's where they were holding him. They're armed, they tried to kill me. Take three deputies and get out there fast." She gave them descriptions, then said, one eye on Sam's white face, the other on the woods, "Get out here fast, Wade. I'm taking Sam to Doc Flint's. I'm on my cell. Let me know what you find. Did you hear any names, Sam?"

"Fatso and Beau." Just saying their names made Sam so afraid he had to concentrate not to pee again in his jeans.

"The one in the black leather coat is Beau, the other one is Fatso, that's Sam's name for him. Put out an APB on them, Wade. The one with the bullet in his arm — chances are he'll need some medical attention. Maybe the other one, too. Alert all medical facilities in the area. I'll tell Doc Flint. I'll bet he'll be putting in some calls himself. I'll check in again after I make sure the boy's all right."

She looked one last time toward the woods. No sign of either man. She pressed harder on the gas. She couldn't go any faster, it was just too dangerous. "Sam, you keep bundled up. Don't worry about talking right now. Just get yourself warm, that's right. You can tell me everything in a little while. Right now, you just think about how you saved yourself. My goodness, you're a hero."

Sam nodded. It made him feel woozy. A hero? He didn't feel like much of a hero. His teeth were chattering and that made him feel like a baby. He hadn't been a baby for longer than he could remember. And there was that little girl Keely pressed against him, two fat braids the color of wheat toast hanging over her shoulders, touching his face she was so close. He closed his eyes. He wasn't about to cry in front of the little girl. He wanted his father.

It took them nearly twenty minutes to get to Doc Flint's office in the rain. Katie kept talking to both children, keeping her voice calm and low, telling Sam about how the weather was going to be really bad until some time tomorrow, telling him how Keely was five, not as old as he was, and about how Keely could play "When You Wish Upon a Star" on the piano. Keely chimed in and told Sam she'd teach him how to play it, too, and the C scale.

Sam looked bad, Katie thought, worrying now as she pulled in front of the small Victorian house that stood at the corner of Pine and Maple, two blocks off Main Street. It was tall, skinny, and painted cream with dark blue trim. Jonah Flint lived upstairs and had his examination rooms and office downstairs. She said, "Keely, I want you to stay put until I get Sam into the office. Don't move, don't even think about moving. I'll come back for you with the umbrella."

She and Sam were already soaked, steam rising off their clothes because of the hot air gushing out of the truck heater. The little boy's face was sheet-white and his dark pupils were dilated. There was blood oozing down his cheek from a cut on his head.

She eased him across the front seat, raised the umbrella, and whispered against his small ear, "Grab me around the neck, Sam, it'll make it easier." When she straightened, he wrapped his legs around her waist. "That's good, Sam. Now, it's going to be all right, I promise you. You're with me now and I'm as tough as an old boot and meaner than my father, who was meaner than anybody before he died. You know something else, Sam? Since you're a hero, I'm not the only one who's really proud of you. Your folks will be proud, too. Don't worry now, everything's going to be all right."

She kept talking, hoping she was distracting the boy as she carried him into the empty waiting room. Katie wasn't surprised there wasn't anybody there, not even Heidi Johns, Dr. Flint's receptionist and nurse. Who would want to be out in weather like this except for Monroe Cuddy, who might have shot himself in the foot again, or Marilee Baskim, who was close to having a baby.

She called out, "Jonah!"

No answer. What if he wasn't here? She didn't want to take Sam to the emergency room.

"Jonah!"

5

Jonah Flint, just turned forty and very proud of his full head of blacker-than-sin hair, came running out of the back room, the stethoscope nearly falling out of the pocket of his white coat.

"Jesus, Katie, what's going on? Who's this?"

"This," Katie said, carrying Sam into the first examination room, "is Sam and he just escaped kidnappers, believe it or not. There's a cut on his head and I think he's going into shock. I was afraid you weren't here."

"I was doing some research in the back. Now, let's see what we've got here." Dr. Flint smiled at the boy even as he peeled him off Katie and removed all the blankets, taking in all the signs and talking to Sam all the while.

"How do you feel, Sam?" He sat the boy on the edge of the examining table. "Do you take any medications? No?" He began to check him over. "Does your head hurt? I know the cut does, but do you have a headache? No, okay, that's good. I'll give you something to cut the pain. You got away from kidnappers? That's something now, isn't it? Okay, Sam, let me get you out of those wet clothes. You can just call me Doc Flintstone, okay? That's right, you help me. Now, do you hurt anywhere else? No? Good. Katie, you can step out, please, just men in here. You going to call the kid's parents?"

Sam looked shell-shocked.

Katie said, "I'll call his parents in just a bit, when you're through examining him. First things first. He's the most important thing right now." She took one last long look at the little boy who'd run out of a wilderness of maples and oaks. She picked up the huge office umbrella, lots bigger than hers, and fetched Keely from the truck.

She sat Keely on a chair, handed her the huge black waiting room bear, and called Wade again. "What's the word, Wade? You see anything out there?"

"Not yet. Where are you?"

"I'm in Jonah's waiting room. He's with Sam — that's the little boy. I don't know his last name yet. Making sure he's okay is the first priority. I've got Keely with me, too. With the two kids, there was no way I could do anything but get out of there.

Have you checked out the old Bleaker place yet? That's bound to be where they were keeping him. It's hidden and nobody can hear anything for all the trees."

"I think so, too. Me and Jeffrey are out here on the road, and even with the fog and the rain, we found where the guys had come out of the woods. We found several shells, probably from your rifle. You also dropped a blanket. We're fixing to go into the woods now."

Katie wanted to be the one to go to the Bleaker cabin. It was tough, but there was just no way she could leave the kids, not yet. "Listen, Wade, you and Jeffrey be really careful. Anyone else with you? Good, glad that Conrad and Danny got there. Don't forget, these guys are dangerous. If they're still at the Bleaker cabin, it could get dicey. If they're not there, I want you to secure the place. Be real careful not to destroy any possible evidence."

"You got it, Sheriff," Wade said. "Over and out."

Over and out? Katie shook her head. Wade sounded pleased as punch that he was the lead on this. She just hoped he'd be careful. She disconnected and said to Keely, "I sure hope Jeffrey wears his glasses."

Keely said, not looking up from the bear, "Jeffrey has to wear his glasses or he'd step in the toilet. Millie likes him without his glasses, but she says it's just too dangerous."

Millie was Jeffrey's girlfriend. Katie smiled and felt her tension lessen just a bit. She fully intended to keep the boy with her as long as it took to get him safe. She hardly knew anything about him. She hated to wait before talking with him, but the child needed Jonah a lot more than he needed to answer questions right now.

Sam's parents. She'd get their names and phone number as soon as Jonah said Sam was okay. She knew they had to be frantic.

Jonah came out from the examination room twenty minutes later, smiling, holding the little boy's hand. "Sam's been telling me how his mama kept talking in his head, telling him what to do, how to get himself free."

How could Sam be okay? He looked white and exhausted, a big Flintstones bandage on his head. Katie said, "You did great, Sam, you didn't give up."

"No, ma'am, I didn't." There was a flash of pride in that exhausted little voice, and that was good. Sam looked like the little boy he was, wrapped in two very big blue blankets, a pair of Jonah's black socks on his small feet. Sam looked up at Jonah. "I want to go home, Doctor."

Katie patted Keely's head, and walked swiftly to where the boy stood. She picked him up and held him close to her. "You're just fine, Sam, just fine. Now, if Jonah is through torturing you, I'm taking you home with me. You'll be safe there until I can get your folks here."

"We're in Tennessee?"

"Yes, we are. Eastern Tennessee, Jessborough is the name of the town."

"Where's Tennessee?"

"We're sandwiched among lots of states. Where do you live, Sam?"

"I'm from Colfax, Virginia."

"A nice state, Virginia," Katie said and turned to Jonah. "It's not too far away from here. He's okay?"

"Yep, he might come down with a cold from his run in the rain, but he's a strong kid. He'll be just fine. Give him a nice big glass of juice. He needs the sugar. I don't want to take any chances that he'll crash." He patted Sam's head, ran his fingers through his damp black hair. "His clothes are still wet. What do you want to do?"

"If you could wrap his clothes up in a towel, I'll wash and dry them."

Katie realized she was rocking Sam, sort of stepping from one foot to the other, swaying, just like she did with Keely. She smiled, "I'm going to squeeze him in next to Keely and take both of them home. You like hot chicken noodle soup, Sam?"

He didn't say anything, but she felt him nod. She and Jonah looked at each other. Neither of them knew what the kid had been through, at least not yet.

"You be careful, Katie, it's coming down thicker than confetti on New Year's," Jonah said. "Take good care of my patient. Keely, you keep a close eye on Sam, too, okay?"

Keely allowed Sam to sit next to her mother, his head on Katie's leg. She pressed close to his other side. "I'll keep him warm, Mama."

"Sam," Katie said, lightly touching her fingers to his pale cheek, "you're a very lucky boy."

Sam, who felt dopey and stupid, said, "That's what my mama was always telling my dad."

"I'll call your daddy right now if you'll just tell me his name and phone number."

Sam said against the wet denim on her leg, "My dad's name is Miles Kettering. He's really cool. He can fix anything. He fixes helicopters for the government."

His father was a government contractor? Could that be why he was kidnapped?

"What's your home phone number, Sam?"

He was silent, thinking, but he couldn't get it together, and she knew his brain was closing down. "It's okay. I'll call information. Colfax, Virginia, right?"

Sam managed to nod before he closed his eyes. He felt her strong leg supporting his head. She still felt wet through the blanket she'd put under his head, felt the sway of the truck and the little girl's body pressed close against him. He was warm. He was safe. He was asleep in the next minute.

Katie pulled the blanket more closely around his shoulders, and whispered to Keely, "He'll be okay, sweetie. You just stay there, keep him really warm."

After a moment, Keely said, "I would have saved myself, too, Mama."

"I know you would have, Keely. Now, let me get information in Virginia and find Sam's daddy."

When the phone rang, Miles jumped nearly three feet. He'd been telling the agents again how the government contracts worked, who his competitors were, and how much money was involved. Agent Butch Ashburn, the lead on Sam's kidnapping, nodded to the other agent, Todd Morton, who'd just swallowed a doughnut too fast and was choking.

"Showtime," Agent Ashburn said.

Savich, who'd just gotten to the Kettering house, laid his hand on his friend's arm and said, "Everything's set, Miles. Just answer the phone. Keep calm, that's more important than I can say."

Miles Kettering forced his hand to reach for the phone. He didn't want to touch it, didn't want to because he was afraid that Sam was dead. So many children were kidnapped and so few survived. He could hardly bear it.

It had been a day and a half. This was the first word. His hand shook as he lifted the phone.

"Hello? This is Miles Kettering."

"Hello, Mr. Kettering, my name is Sheriff K. C. Benedict from Washington County, Tennessee. Don't worry, I have your boy, Sam. He's just fine. He managed to escape his kidnappers. He's with me. Mr. Kettering? I promise you, he's okay."

Miles couldn't speak. His throat worked. "I don't believe you. You're the kidnapper, right? What do you want?"

Butch Ashburn and Todd Morton were standing there staring at the phone, trying to look both calm and competent. Savich took the phone from Miles's hands. "Who is this?"

Katie understood. She said again, "This is Sheriff K. C. Benedict from Washington County, Tennessee. Sam is just fine. He managed to save himself. I've got him with me. Tell his parents not to worry, he's okay."

"This is Dillon Savich with the FBI, Sheriff. Thank you very much. Give me your exact location and we'll be there as quickly as we can."

Katie gave the man directions. She'd never before met a special agent with the Federal Bureau of Investigation. She patted Sam's shoulder, whispered, "Your daddy's going to be here soon now, Sam," but Sam didn't hear her. He was asleep.

She heard Mr. Kettering say in the background, "I want to talk to Sam."

She said to Agent Savich, "Sam's asleep. Do you want me to wake him?"

Miles Kettering came on the line. "No, let him sleep. I'll see him soon. Please, Sheriff, tell him I love him. What about the people who took him? Did you get them?"

"I'm very sorry, but they escaped. But we've got a group of my deputies in the field and they'll do their best."

When Katie hung up the phone, Keely said, nearly asleep herself, "What about his mama?"

"She'll probably come, too. If I were her, I'd beat his daddy here to get him."

"Stealing Sam was a bad thing, Mama."

"You're right." And she thought, *I should have just brought the bastard down, not given him a kiss in the arm. I should have kicked his butt like Sam said.*

6

Katie's phone rang at a quarter of seven that evening. It was Alice Hewett from Hewett's Pharmacy, and she was out-of-breath excited.

"Oh, Katie, that man who kidnapped the little boy — I think it was him. He just left. I called the station house and Linnie told me to call you at home."

Katie's heart started to pound, deep and hard.

"Was he the fat one, Alice?"

"No, he was the other one, tall, almost sick-looking thin, but he wasn't wearing that long black leather coat Wade told everyone about, just a white shirt and jeans, and some scarred black boots. But he had a ponytail, like you said. And he was shivering, which means he left that leather coat in his car because he was afraid to be seen in it. He bought bandages and antibiotic cream and some Aleve. And when he was leaving I saw blood on the back of his sleeve."

"He was in his forties?"

"Yes, I'd say so."

"And he had a ponytail."

"Yeah, wet and stringy-looking. He didn't say anything, just brought the stuff up to me at the register, and paid cash. He had a really big roll. I saw a couple of hundreds, lots of fifties."

"Did he just leave the pharmacy?"

"Yes."

"Did you see his car?"

"Yes, Katie, the instant I saw that blood I knew. When I heard his car, I peeked out the front window. He was driving an old van, light gray I think, but it was hard to tell with all the rain."

Katie nearly held her breath. "License number?"

"I just got part of it. He screeched out of here pretty fast. It was a Virginia plate, the first three letters were LTD — you know, like that old Ford sedan — LTD. I think the next one was a 'three' but I can't be sure."

Katie wanted to leap through the phone line and kiss Alice. "That's just great," she said. "Now, was there anything about the man that was unusual, something that would make you remember him as opposed to another man?"

Silence, then, "He was wearing a necklace, you know, a gold chain with some sort of pendant or stone hanging off the end of it. I've never seen anything like it before. Oh yes, his two front teeth overlap."

"Alice, do you want to be sheriff when my term is over?"

Alice Hewett laughed. "No, Katie, it's all yours. Just looking at that guy made my stomach cramp up. Besides, I'm too young to be sheriff, I just turned twenty last week."

Katie was pleased, as was the rest of the town, that Alice was no longer a teenager, particularly since Abe Hewett was fifty-four years old and had three grown boys all older than their stepmama. "Well done, Alice. Thank you."

"Let me know, won't you, Katie?"

"You bet."

Katie called Wade at home, got him between spoonfuls of his wife's special pork stew. "I'm really sorry about this, Wade, but —"

"I knew you'd call, Katie. I sent Conrad over to talk to Alice, see if she remembered anything else. Man, this stew is the best." A long silence, then Katie heard Wade's wife, Glenda, say something in the background.

"Tell you what," Katie said, "stay put. Just keep close to your phone. Call Jeffrey and have him update the rest of our people, including our three volunteer deputies. Keep an eye out for that van — we've got a partial plate. It's Virginia and it's LTD three something. I'm going to call the FBI, let them check it out."

"You don't want me to go out right this minute?"

"Nah, stay put. I'll call you if something comes up."

She called the Knoxville FBI field office because she knew the Johnson City field office just didn't have the staff for this sort of thing. She got Glen Hodges, the special agent in charge, pretty fast and told him what was going on. Then she dialed Agent Savich's cell phone. He picked up immediately.

"Agent Savich?"

"Yes. Is this Sheriff Benedict? Is Sam all right?"

"Yes, he is, but listen to this, please," and she told him about the kidnapper's visit to the pharmacy. "Alice thinks they're driving a light gray van, Virginia license LTD with a possible next number of three."

"Got it. I'll call Butch Ashburn, he's the agent leading the kidnapping investigation.

He'll find out who the van belongs to."

"I called Agent Hodges from the Knoxville field office, told him what was going on. He's on his way here."

"Good. You have Sam with you?"

"Yes, he's still sleeping. He's just fine." It was then she heard the deep rumbling noise. "You're in an airplane?"

"Yes, it'll take us a couple of hours since we're in a Cessna. Sheriff, I don't like the fact that the kidnappers are still local. What else is happening?"

"Here's the deal, Agent Savich. I don't like the fact that those two guys are still hanging around here either. I'm hoping that Fatso — that's the name Sam gave one of the kidnappers — is hurt bad and that's why they haven't hightailed it out of here. But if he was badly hurt, then why not take him to a doctor? We have two doctors in town. Both of them call me from home every hour so I'll know they're okay."

"Well done," Savich said.

"Yeah, but you know, the truth is, I don't know what to make of it. They've got to know that everyone is looking for them. Why would they stay local?"

"You're basing this on one witness?"

"Yes. Her set of eyes is just fine."

"You shot Fatso in the arm?"

"Yes, that I'm sure of. Then I fired several more times while they were running back into the forest. Maybe I shot him again, I just didn't see, all I heard was a yelp." She drew a deep breath. "I know where they were keeping Sam. Agent Glen Hodges said he and his people will dust the place for prints when they get here."

"I'm not too happy that they're still around, but it sounds like you've got everything under control. We'll be there soon. Be careful, okay?"

Katie pressed the "off" button on her cell. Well, she was being careful. She was keeping Sam with her, the FBI was on the way, and she'd called in all her people — with the exception of Wade, who'd already worked his butt off today. Everyone was out looking for that light gray van now.

Her cell phone played the first bars of "Fly Me to the Moon" a minute later. A man's voice came on the line. "Sheriff Benedict? This is Miles Kettering. I'm with Agent Savich. I'm sorry to bother you, but I just wanted to thank you, and . . . please take care of my boy. Savich told me he was still sleeping?"

"Yes, he's out like a light. Do you want me to wake him up?"

"Oh no, it's just that I'm —" He stalled.

"I understand, Mr. Kettering. If someone had taken my child, I'd be scared out of my mind until I actually had her in my arms. You're flying the Cessna?"

"Yes. It was the best I could do on short notice, but it's a solid little plane."

"It's pretty bad weather here, as I'm sure you know. You're coming in at Ackerman's Air Field?"

"Yes, soon now."

She checked that Miles Kettering had directions from Ackerman's Air Field to her house before disconnecting.

She got a call not five minutes later from Glen Hodges, the SAC of the Knoxville Bureau field office.

"I've got three agents in the car with me. We'll be in Jessborough about two hours from now, give or take because of the weather. Is there any more you can tell me?"

"No. Everyone's out looking for the gray van, and doing general surveillance on anyone looking like either of the two men. I gave Agent Savich the partial license plate of the van. He said he was going to call Agent Butch Ashburn."

"Yeah, Savich just called me. Agent Ashburn will get the owner of that van in no time."

"Agent Savich and Mr. Kettering, the boy's father, will be here soon as well."

"Savich didn't say what he was doing involved in a kidnapping? Last I heard he was in L.A. playing around in one of the Hollywood studios."

"I'm sure I don't know, Agent Hodges. I just assumed he was assigned to the case with Agent Ashburn."

"Oh no, Savich is the unit chief for the Criminal Apprehension Unit at headquarters."

"What's that?"

"He works mostly with computers, setting up databases and data-mining programs to help catch criminals. The Bureau set up this unit for him and that's what he and eight or so other agents do."

"Sounds like something I'd want real simplified."

Glen Hodges laughed. "I'm with you, Sheriff. Oops, we're starting to break up. You get in these mountains, and you're down faster than you can catch a snake. You take care of the boy, ma'am. We're coming as fast as we can."

Katie slipped her cell back into her shirt pocket. She asked herself again what more she could do. She didn't come up with an answer.

At nearly ten o'clock that night the worst fall storm in twenty years — according to the weather folk — seemed to be fizzling out. There was less rain, but the howling winds were still a nice side show, keeping people hunkered down in their homes, hoping their trees wouldn't be uprooted.

She couldn't imagine being up in a small airplane in this wind. She looked out Keely's bedroom window, north, toward Ackerman's Air Field, and said a little prayer.

All in all, they'd lucked out, Katie thought as she closed the window and walked over to Keely's bed and gave her a kiss and smoothed her eyebrows. "I can tell you're awake, sweetie. You just smiled. You love the sound of the rain, don't you?"

"Oh yes, Mama, and the wind howling like banshees — that's what Grandma says. You told me you liked it, too, Mama, when you were my age."

"Yes, I remember pressing my nose against the window, wanting lightning, more lightning, and with it, the boom of thunder — the closer the better."

"Can I go press my nose —"

"No, not tonight. You're going to sleep now, Keely."

"Is Sam okay?"

"Yep, he's just fine." One more kiss and Katie sat by her daughter until her breathing evened into sleep. Then she walked to the window and pressed her nose against the glass. It wasn't the same. Her nose was cold and she wanted to sneeze. She left Keely's bedroom, knowing she'd pass the night easily, the sound of the rain a lullaby to her daughter.

Wade had had only one emergency call some twenty minutes before from Mr. Amos Halley, who'd gotten himself stuck in his garage when the electricity had gone out and the door opener wouldn't work. Even the manual override was stuck. Wade, pulled from his dinner, had nearly cried, but he'd gone over to the Halley house where Mrs. Halley stood in the entryway, arms crossed over her bosom, shaking her head, and told him, "Leave the old man in there, Wade. If you let him out, he'll just go drinking down at the tavern."

Wade had tried his best to get the garage door open, but the sucker hadn't budged. Then the electricity came back on, and he was a hero, at least to Amos, who claimed he was near to croaking of a heart attack it was so black and airless inside the garage.

As Wade downshifted his jeep, he saw

Amos Halley drive off toward the east side of town — that's where the Long Shot Tavern had been hunkered down since just after World War II.

The rain had lightened up considerably, but winds still buffeted the jeep. There would probably be some flooding, but nothing they couldn't handle. All in all, it wasn't bad. He hoped one of the deputies would spot the gray van. He'd told them to call him first.

He made it home in record time and grinned at Glenda.

But something hit him about five minutes later. It was worry, real deep worry, and he didn't know what to do about it.

7

Katie checked on Sam, then sat down with a cup of coffee after putting some more logs in the fireplace. The fire made the living room warm, shadowy, and cozy. It was as if she'd commanded it to happen. Her cell rang. "Sheriff Benedict here."

"This is Agent Hodges, Sheriff. I just got a call from Agent Ashburn. The van is a gunmetal gray Dodge, full license is LTD 3109, registered to Mr. Beauregard Jones of Alexandria, Virginia. Is this one of the men?"

"Sam said his name was Beau, so bingo, Agent Hodges, it sounds like you guys nailed it. Excellent."

"Agent Ashburn said he was heading out to Alexandria himself to check it all out. He'll let us know what he finds."

"Good. How close are you to me?"

"We're only another half-hour, maybe. Unfortunately, Sheriff, we just blew a back tire a few minutes ago. It'll take us a while to get rolling again."

She shut down her cell and leaned back.

Why had Fatso and Beau stayed in the area? Why would Beau go to the local pharmacy? Were they idiots?

~ If bandages from the first-aid section of the pharmacy would take care of Fatso, then she hadn't hurt him very badly. Or maybe it was a bad wound and they were trying anything they could get their hands on.

Where were they holed up? Not at Bleaker's cabin, the place was nailed down tight, police tape over the windows and a deputy outside. But where had they gone? Just stayed in the van? She raised her head, frowned and listened. She heard the rain, nothing but the rain, and the wind battering tree branches against the house.

She got up, checked on Sam and Keely. They were both still sound asleep. She lightly touched her palm to Sam's forehead. No fever.

She stood there, looking down at the boy, thinking there was nothing else to do until everyone arrived. Then her breath caught. She knew why the men were still in town, and it wasn't because Fatso was too badly hurt to be moved. No, they still were after Sam. Was there that much money involved?

She pulled her SIG Sauer out of its holster on the top shelf of her closet, shoved it in the back of her blue jeans, and pulled a loose sweatshirt over it. Then she checked her ankle holster, where her two-shot derringer was held tight. If anything happened, she was ready.

All right, you bastards, come to Mama.

Her heart raced. She could feel her skin, smell the oak trees as the winds whipped through them, even hear the soft crackle of a single ember in the fireplace.

She pulled out her cell to call over some deputies as she walked to the living room window, everything inside her alert and ready, and pulled back the drapes. She very nearly fell over. A man's face was staring in at her. He looked as surprised as she was, but his gloved fist slammed through the window, and in that hand was a gun, pointed right at her chest.

"Don't even think about moving, lady."

She dropped her cell phone. Could she get to her gun before he killed her? No, probably not. "You're Beauregard Jones, I take it?"

"Shit! How do you know who I am?"

"Law enforcement is pretty good nowadays, Mr. Jones. Just about everybody in Jessborough knows who you are. The FBI is already at your place in Alexandria and more agents will be here in about three minutes." She looked behind Beau. "Where's Fatso?"

"You just shut up, lady."

"I'm not a lady, I'm the sheriff. Surely you know that. How'd you find out where I lived? What's the matter? Is Fatso hurt so bad he can't help you anymore?"

"Shut your trap, no, wait, back up, just back up. Nail your ass to that spot and don't move or I'll kill you and that cute little girl won't have a mommy any longer." He kept the gun pointed at her as he broke the rest of the glass in the window. Then he stepped through.

When he stood dripping water on her grandmother's prized Aubusson carpet, he looked her up and down, glanced over at the fireplace and said, "You've given us lots of trouble, Sheriff. And here you are, looking all tousled and frumpy like any good little housewife on a Saturday night."

She was aware of her SIG Sauer nestled against her back, the derringer pressed against the ankle holster. "I haven't begun to give you trouble, Mr. Jones."

He gave her a big grin, all big white crooked teeth, the two front ones overlapping, just like Alice had said. "I like a girl with a big mouth. Fatso's real name is Clancy and he doesn't like people bugging him about that gut of his. But no matter. He's waiting for us in the van. You'll meet him soon enough. Go get the boy."

Beau realized in that instant that it wasn't a good idea to let her go off by herself. She didn't look at all tough, and she looked real young, what with her hair pulled back with a tie and no makeup on her face. But she had to have something going for her, they'd elected her sheriff of this hick town, after all. He'd been watching her through the window, watching her eyes just like his daddy had taught him before he'd gotten himself blown away during a bank robbery down in Atlanta. His daddy would have called those eyes of hers hard, the kind that saw way down deep into you, and he'd never want to drink a beer with her. He hadn't realized how his daddy would have hated her eyes until he'd seen her up really close. He thought she knew things, thought things, that he couldn't.

Beau wasn't about to take any chances with her, not with those eyes. "Wait," he said, "you walk ahead of me, don't make no sudden movements or I'll have to put a bullet in your back. You got that?"

Katie fanned her hands, and said, "I got it."

"Let's go."

"I don't understand something, Mr. Jones."

"Walk, Sheriff, stop trying to slow things down. You might be right about the FBI coming, but hey, they're clowns, everybody knows that."

"I didn't know that. Why do you think they're clowns?"

"Just shut up." He waved the gun. "Move, now."

Katie walked out of the living room into the small front hallway. She said over her shoulder, "I told you that the FBI knows who you are, and they're on their way here right this minute. You also know they're not clowns. If you don't get out of here now, you're going to be in the deepest trouble imaginable. There's really got to be a lot in it for you to make you come here for the boy. Somebody's paying you and Fatso lots of money, right?"

"Shut up, Sheriff. Keep walking, or I'll just shoot you and get him myself. Hey, I just might take the little girl, too. Bet I could get some loot for that cute little button."

"Yes, there must be big bucks in this for

you and Fatso to take this kind of risk." In ten steps, she'd be at the guest room door. And Sam was inside.

Beau grunted. "Keep moving."

She had to do something, had to do it soon. It was up to her, not the FBI, not anybody else. But he was holding what looked like a 10mm Smith & Wesson pistol, a good weapon. Patience; she had to be patient. There was lots of time before he got hold of Sam.

She opened the door of the bedroom slowly.

The room was dark — and cold. It was very cold, she could feel the wind touching her cheek. The light switch flicked on behind her.

"Damn! Where are you, boy? You come out here now or I'll kill the sheriff!"

"The room's cold," Katie said, turning to face Beau, so relieved she wanted to dance. "Don't you see? Sam heard you coming and went out through the window."

"No, that's impossible. He's just a little kid —"

"Yeah, sure, and he went out the window at Bleaker's cabin, too, got away from you and Clancy. He's long gone now, Beau. Just feel how cold it is in here. You'd best get your butt out of here now before the FBI comes and hauls it off to jail."

Beau didn't know what to do. He eyed the open window, the rain whipping the light drapes into the room, the wind making him shiver. "Gonna ruin the floor, all that rain," he said. He waved the pistol at her. "Go close the window."

Katie closed the window, taking her time. She tried to look through the thick rain, but didn't see any movement, any shadow of a little boy. Where was Sam?

She turned, hoping he couldn't see the satisfaction in her eyes. Sam was out of it, at least for now. It was just between the two of them and he was rattled. Just let him get a bit closer.

Beau walked quickly to the door and motioned with the pistol for her to come to him.

"May I suggest that you slink out of here while you still can, Beau? Or better yet, why don't you drop that gun and let me take you to my nice warm facilities?"

"Shut up, you infernal woman. What we're going to do is get that cute little girl. Maybe we can negotiate a trade."

Her heart nearly stopped. "No, take me and leave the little girl alone, do you hear me, Beau? Leave her alone or I'll kill you so slow and so hard you'll scream so loud even the Devil won't want you."

But Beau just laughed, pushed her in front of him until he himself shoved open Keely's bedroom door. "Come on out, kid! I've got your mama!"

There wasn't a sound.

Beau flipped the light switch.

Both of them looked at the lump beneath the bedcovers. Katie's heart nearly dropped to her knees, but then she saw something wasn't right here. Keely had ears as sharp as a dog's. Why was she just lying there? Beau waved Katie to the far side of the room, walked to the bed, and poked the lump with the muzzle of his gun.

"Come on out, little girl. Your uncle Beau's gonna take you for a nice long ride."

8

The lump didn't move. Beau poked his gun harder.

"Not again." He jerked back the covers. There was a pillow molded in the shape of a person, a very little person, underneath the covers.

Both Sam and Keely were gone.

Katie was nearly giddy. "Looks like my kid's pretty smart, doesn't it, Beau?" Thank the good Lord for Katie's favorite climbing tree.

"I hate this job," Beau said. "All right, the little kids aren't dummies. It's you and me now, Sheriff, and we're heading outside. When we're clear of this place, I'm going to whump your ass."

"Okay," she said, so relieved she thought she'd choke on it, "since you put it so nicely."

Where was the FBI?

At that instant, Katie could swear she heard the soft purr of a car motor. She looked at Beau out of the corner of her eyes, realized he hadn't heard a thing.

The rain had picked up again and battered sideways in through the open window Beau had smashed in the living room.

Beau didn't look happy. "You're walking too slow. Move! This is your fault, you bitch! The slower you walk, the more I'm going to hurt you."

He shoved her hard, and then, because he wasn't stupid, he took a quick step back.

"Go! To the front door, now!"

You want a hostage, Beau? That's just fine with me, you bozo.

She walked swiftly to the front door, slid free the dead bolt, and opened it.

She saw a flashlight beam aiming toward her, then a hand quickly covered it. Someone was close.

She wanted to shout that Beau was right behind her with a gun at her back, but she kept her mouth shut. Anyone watching would see him soon enough.

Beau shoved the gun against her back. "Go, move! Get those arms up, clasp your hands behind your neck. Get out there!"

She put her hands behind her neck, walked through the open front door, and stopped on the front porch. The overhang didn't help much since the wind was slapping the rain sideways. Katie shouted,

"You out there, Clancy?"

Not a sound, just another flicker of a flashlight whipping around, cutting through the thick rain, its vague beam a ghostly light. She thought she heard men's voices, low and whispering. Was Agent Savich here? Or had Wade gotten worried and come over? Whoever it was, she hoped they had a good view of her and Beau.

Beau shouted, "Clancy, drive the van up next to the front porch! If you FBI geeks are out there, just stay back or the sheriff's dead. You got that?"

There was no answer, just the wind, rumbling through the trees at the sides of her house.

"You hear me, Clancy? We're taking her with us. Then we'll see about the boy."

A man's voice came out of the night, just off to her right. "In that case, Mr. Jones, why don't you just consider us observers. Do whatever you want to do."

Beau jumped. "Yeah, you guys just stay back. I'm taking her and we're leaving."

Katie recognized Agent Savich's voice, and there was something else in his voice, something meant for her. She wished she could see his face, then she'd know what he wanted her to do.

The big van came hurtling toward the

house, its tires spewing up black mud. Fatso was at the wheel, turning it hard until the front fender scraped against the steps of the front porch. She watched the big man lean across the front seat and push the door open. "Get her in here, Beau, fast!"

Savich's voice, loud and sharp, "Now, Sheriff!"

Katie threw herself off the front porch, jerking her SIG Sauer free even as she crashed against the back tire of the van.

She heard Beau yell, heard two shots. With no hesitation, Fatso gunned the van, but he didn't get far. She saw Agent Savich turn smoothly and shoot out both back tires. Fatso skidded in the mud and crashed hard into an oak tree. She could see him hit the windshield, then bounce back, his head lolling to the side. He wasn't going anywhere.

Katie swung her SIG Sauer around toward Beau just as Savich leapt onto the porch. He was so fast he was a blur, and his leg, smooth, graceful, like a dancer, kicked the gun out of Beau's hand. It went flying across the porch, landing against a rocking chair leg. Beau grunted, grabbed his hand, and turned to run.

Agent Savich just grabbed his collar,

jerked him around, and sent his fist into his belly, then his jaw.

Beau cursed, and tried to fight back. Savich merely belted him again, this time in his kidney. He shoved him down onto the porch and stood over him. He wasn't even breathing hard. "Sometimes I like to fight the old-fashioned way. Now, you just stay real still, Beau, or I just might have to hurt you. You hear me?"

"I hear you, you bastard. I want my lawyer."

Katie, her SIG Sauer still in her hand, walked slowly up onto the porch. She looked down at the man who probably would have killed her, killed Sam and Keely, without a dollop of remorse. She shoved her SIG Sauer back into the waistband of her jeans, lifted her booted foot and slammed it into his ribs.

"Here's one for Sam and Keely," she said, and kicked him again.

"That's police brutality," Beau said, gasping from the pain in his ribs. "I'm gonna sue your ass off!"

"Nah, you're not," she said. "You're in the backwoods now, Beau, and do you know what that means?"

"You marry your brother."

"No, it means *you'll* marry my brother, if

I want you to."

Dillon Savich was laughing as he looked at the bedraggled woman, hair hanging down, pulled free from her ponytail, her mouth pale from cold. "Sheriff Benedict, I presume?"

"Yes," she said, already looking around for Sam and Keely.

"I'm Agent Savich. A pleasure, ma'am. You like excitement, don't you?"

"What I liked best in all of this was the sound of your voice and sight of your face, Agent Savich. Those were some cool moves you made to take down old Beau."

"I tripped, dammit!"

"Yeah, right," Katie said, and looked toward the van again. Clancy was still out of it. She was on the point of going over and pulling him out when Sam shouted "Papa!"

"Mama!"

She heard a man yell "Sam!"

"Mr. Kettering?"

"Yes, that's Miles. I ordered him on pain of death and dismemberment to stay back. And here's your little girl, ma'am."

Keely was wet to the bone, her flannel pajamas plastered to her, her hair hanging in her eyes. Katie swept her up into her arms and held her so tight the little girl squeaked.

"Keely got me, Papa! Keely woke me up and we crawled out the window in Keely's bedroom. We've been hiding just over there, behind that tree. I recognized Beau and knew we had to stay hidden. Did you see Uncle Dillon? He kicked the crap out of skinny old Beau!"

Uncle Dillon? Katie smiled, kissed her daughter's wet hair, and called out, "You wet as Keely, Sam?"

"I'm wetter than a frog buried under a lily pad."

She saw Sam's smile before she saw the rest of his face. He was being carried by a big man who was as wet as he was, and who was smiling even bigger than his boy. She liked the looks of him, liked the way he held his boy.

Miles carried Sam up onto the front porch. He saw Beau lying on his back, not even twitching, and he handed Sam to Savich.

He went down on his hands and knees, closed his fist around Beau's shirt collar, and jerked him up. "Hello, you miserable scum."

"Get off me, you bastard!"

"Oh, I'm lots more than a bastard. I'm your worst nightmare, Beau. I'm meaner than the man who just kicked your ass. I'm

90

Sam's father and do you have any idea what I want to do to you?"

"Get him away from me!"

"Oh, no," Savich said, Sam now hanging about his neck, held real close. "You deserve whatever he wants to do to you. If he wants to, he can kick your tonsils out the back of your neck."

Miles Kettering pulled Beau to his feet and sent his fist into his jaw. Beau went down and stayed down.

Miles gave him one more dispassionate look, then turned to take Sam from Savich.

"You walloped him good, Papa," Sam said, and he patted his father's face, dark with five o'clock shadow. "Can I hit him, too?"

"Nah, he's had enough. You just stay real close to me until I get over being so scared."

Sam hugged his father's neck, really hard. "This is Katie, Papa. She helped me a whole lot."

Katie stuck out her hand even as she held Keely against her with her other arm. "Mr. Kettering, you've got some brave boy here."

In that instant, Katie saw black smoke billowing up around the front of the van. "Oh no — Fatso, I can't even see him through that smoke! I forgot about him! I've got to get him." She pushed Keely into Miles Kettering's arms, and took off running toward the van.

Savich, who saw flames licking up from beneath the van, yelled, "No, wait! No, Sheriff!" He leapt off the porch, and ran after her. He yelled over his shoulder, "Miles, protect the kids!"

Katie was no more than twelve feet from the van when she was tackled from behind, hard, and smashed facedown into the wet ground.

In the next instant there was a loud explosion, and the van blew up in a ball of orange, parts flying everywhere. He was covering all of her, his head on top of hers, his arms covering both their heads. The heat whooshed toward them, sucking the air out of their lungs, heavy, scalding.

She heard him grunt. Oh God, something had hit him. She heard him suck in a breath, then she did the same.

Then it was over. Everything was still again, except she could hear Keely crying, "Mama, Mama."

He'd saved her life. He'd known the van was going to blow, and he'd brought her down.

Katie said, trying to turn over, "Agent

Savich, are you all right?"

He grunted again, then she felt his determination as he pulled himself off her.

She was up in an instant, standing over him as he remained on his knees, head down, breathing hard.

"Your back. Oh God, your back!"

She looked up to see that Miles Kettering had both children pressed against the side of the house, protecting them, just as Agent Savich had told him to. Had he known, too, that the van was going to blow?

"I'm so sorry, I didn't know, I'm so sorry." She was on her knees beside him now. "Just hold still."

But Savich rose slowly, managed to straighten. "I saw the flames, you didn't. We survived it. I'm all right." He could feel the rain hitting his back, feel the pain building and building. He could also feel his blood flowing, and that wasn't good. He looked over at the van, engulfed in bright orange flames, black smoke sizzling into the air, rain mixing with it, making it filthy black soot.

"Yeah, sure you are, Agent Savich. You just come with me." She was leaning down to grasp him under his arm, when she heard Beau yell, "All right, you jerks, it's my turn now!"

She whirled around to see Beau leaning against the porch railing, his own gun in his hand. She should have cuffed him — even if she believed he was dead, she should have cuffed him. "You bastard, you killed Clancy! Ain't nothing left of him but vapor. But now I'm gonna take that boy."

Sam was tucked against his father's leg, Keely against him. Miles pressed the children more firmly against the side of the house, shouted over his shoulder, "Give it up, Beau, just give it up."

"Send the boy over, or I'll have to kill you, Mr. Kettering."

"Then do it," Miles said. "Neither Sam nor Keely is going anywhere."

Katie could tell that Agent Savich was going to go after Beau again. She couldn't let that happen. She watched Beau raise his gun, watched him aim that gun at Miles Kettering. She leaned down, smoothly pulled her derringer from her ankle holster, and fired.

She got him through the neck.

"Ah" was all Beau said, clutched his throat, and turned to face her, the gun swinging her way.

She fired again, this time a death shot, even for a derringer, through his chest.

Beau fell off the porch, landing on his back, his eyes open to the rainy night. The orange ball of flame flickered in his open eyes.

Miles Kettering said, his arms wrapped tight around the children's heads, "Sam, I've got to see to things here. Promise me that you and Keely won't move an inch. Keep your faces against the house, that van just might blow up some more. Do you hear me? Not an inch."

Miles raced down, pulled Savich over his shoulder in a fireman's carry, and went into the house. Both children raced after him. Good, she didn't want them to see Beau.

"Put him on his belly on the sofa. I'll call nine-one-one," Katie said and quickly dialed. She got Marge, who always sounded breathless, told her to get an ambulance out here, and Wade, too, then hung up. "Not more than ten minutes. Now, let's see how bad you're hurt, Agent Savich." But first she'd have to move her daughter aside.

Savich said, "You're Keely?" One of his arms was dangling over the side of the sofa, and his feet hung off the other end.

The little girl gently smoothed her fingertips over his face. "I'm Keely and my mama will take care of you. She takes care of everybody. Do you know they pay her to do that?"

Savich didn't want to laugh, but it came out of him anyway. It died in a gasp. His back was on fire.

"I'm glad they pay her, Keely. How bad is it, Sheriff?"

It was Miles who said, "You've got a long horizontal gash, middle of your back, just above your waist, probably from a piece of flying metal. It doesn't look too deep, Savich, but it's nasty. You just hang on. Here's the sheriff."

"We need to apply some pressure, Agent Savich —"

"Just Savich. Or Dillon, that's what my wife calls me."

"Okay, Dillon, I'll be right back. I'm going to have to put some pressure on this wound and it's going to hurt, I'm sorry."

Savich closed his eyes and willed himself far away, back with Sherlock and Sean, his own little boy.

"Miles?"

"Yes, I'm right here, Savich."

"You sure Sam's okay?"

"I'm here, Uncle Dillon," Sam said, and patted Savich's shoulder. "Keely and I are both just fine. Did you see the sheriff shoot

Beau? Whap! She got him right in the neck, then shot him again when he turned that gun on Papa."

So much for protecting the children, Katie thought as she came back into the living room with a thick towel. She leaned down and pressed the towel hard against the wound.

Savich didn't know where the moan came from, didn't know he had it in him. The woman was very strong.

"Tell me what happened, Sheriff," Savich said.

Keely, her fingers still touching his cheek, said, "I heard that bad man talking to Mama in the living room, and I knew he wanted Sam."

Katie said, "And so you made a lump in your bed with a pillow, and went to wake up Sam."

The little girl nodded. She stuck her hand out to Sam, who took it. "He shoved up the window in my room and we climbed out on my oak tree." She frowned. "Sam wanted to help you but I told him that you're really tough, Mama, and that you would fix Beau's hash. Is that Beau out there?"

"That's his sorry self, yes," Katie said. "Now, Dillon, how are you doing?"

"Okay," he said, and she heard the pain in his voice.

"You don't seem to be bleeding through the pressure. The paramedics should be here any minute. You're going to be okay."

"Make sure you keep the kids with you."

"You can count on that," Miles said, and he knew that all the adults wondered what could possibly motivate those two to come after Sam again. Money, there had to be lots of money in it for them.

Katie looked from Keely to Sam. "Now we've got two heroes. Well done, kids."

They heard the sirens in the distance.

Katie lightly patted his shoulder. "Just another minute. I guess Clancy is dead. I can't get near the van, the flames are just too hot and the smoke's too thick."

"He couldn't have survived that blast," Savich said. "Don't worry about it."

She heard men's voices outside, one she recognized. "It's Wade, one of my deputies."

"Ho! What the hell happened here? You got a dead guy out here drinkin' rain."

Katie walked to the front door. "Bring everyone inside, Wade. The paramedics will be here momentarily. Agent Savich's back was cut by a piece of metal."

9

Mackey and Bueller helped Savich to the ambulance — it felt like a five-mile hike to Savich, who didn't think he'd ever want to walk straight again — then eased him down on his stomach onto the gurney.

"It'll be all right, Special Agent, sir," said Mackey, so impressed with having a federal officer as his patient that he nearly stuttered. "Sheriff, are you coming with us?"

"Oh, yes. Give me a minute, Mackey." She turned to Miles Kettering who was holding Keely in one arm and Sam in the other. "Could you bring the children to the hospital, Mr. Kettering? Oh goodness, they're all wet. Could you change them into dry clothes? As you can see, Sam's wearing my sweats. You'll find another pair in my bedroom, folded in the second drawer of the dresser. They're drawstring, so you can pull them tight enough for Sam. All of Keely's clothes are in her dresser."

"Don't worry, Sheriff, I'll see to both of them. Just go with Savich. And thank you."

She kissed her daughter's cheek, wishing she hadn't witnessed all the violence, and knowing she'd have to deal with it sooner rather than later. As for Sam, at least he was with his father now.

As she walked quickly back to the ambulance, Katie said to Wade, "Glen Hodges, FBI Special Agent in Charge from Knoxville, will be here very soon with a couple of agents. Just secure the scene and if any idiots chance to come out here to stop and gawk, threaten to toss them in jail. Oh yes, Wade, do give the FBI all your cooperation. It's their case since it's a kidnapping, and it happened in Virginia."

"No problem, Sheriff," Wade said, and walked over to where Beau still lay on his back, rain splashing off his face.

"He won't be causing any more trouble. As for that van, we can't get close just yet, it's still burning too hot."

"The guy inside was Clancy," Katie said. "Call the fire department, have Chief Hayes come out here and clean up the mess."

Keely called out, "Mama, you take care of Uncle Dillon."

"What?"

"That's Agent Savich," Miles said.

"I will, Keely, don't worry." So many

new people in her life in a very short time, and one of them hurt because of her. She jumped into the back of the ambulance, closed the doors, and settled herself in. "I'm set. Let's go, guys."

Mackey had Savich propped up on his side and Bueller had unbuttoned his shirt and scissored his undershirt open down the front so he could attach the EKG monitors. He said to Savich, "We'll let the doctor take care of getting the clothes off that wound. Just a moment more, Agent, sir, and you'll be better. It's important to just keep you still now."

Savich grunted.

When they at last settled him on his stomach, Mackey slipped oxygen clips into his nostrils. "That should feel a bit better."

It did, thank the good Lord.

"Just a little nip here in the arm, Agent," Mackey said. "I'm going to start an IV."

Mackey got it on the first try, for which Savich was grateful.

"Now, Agent, sir, we're going to apply a little more pressure to the wound," Mackey said. "You just try breathing as normally as you can and hold still."

When Savich had the pain controlled, he opened his eyes to see the sheriff on her knees beside him, holding his hand, which was hanging off the side of the gurney. Katie saw his control. He was a strong man, not just physically. She said, "Thank you for saving my life, Agent Savich."

"It's Dillon. You're welcome. You didn't have to come in the ambulance. There's lots to do back at your house."

"Oh, yes I did." She smiled at him and kept stroking his hand. She said after a moment, "I should have realized that where there's smoke —"

"Gasoline was leaking out, and the heat was building up fast. I just didn't know how long it would be before it blew. A little more time would have been nice, though."

"I wonder if that could happen with my big Vortec V8 engine."

Savich couldn't help himself, he smiled through the god-awful pain. If she'd come along to distract him she was doing a good job. "Yeah, it could even happen with that engine."

Katie said, seeing that reaction, "She's got three hundred horses at forty-four hundred rpm. Isn't that something?"

"She?"

"My truck. I know she's female. She just doesn't have a name."

"Three hundred horses, yeah, that's something, all right."

His eyes closed a moment; it was time for her to move on, time to get serious here. She said, "My mom told me once that learning lessons always hurt, only this time you took the hit for me. I owe you, Dillon. You saved my life."

"Everything's looking good, Agent, sir," Mackey said. "Your EKG's A-okay, and the bleeding's nearly stopped. I'm sorry we can't give you anything for the pain. You hanging in there?"

"I'm hanging in," Savich said. "Katie, would you please call my wife in Washington, D.C.? She's not much into truck engines, though, so you might not want to go there."

Katie pulled out her cell phone from the T-shirt pocket beneath her wet sweatshirt. "I could teach her."

He smiled. That was good.

"Okay, give me the number."

Savich closed his eyes as he gave her the phone number, to keep the moan in his throat.

"What's her name?"

"Sherlock."

Katie guessed he wasn't kidding about her name. One ring, two, then "Hello? Dillon, is that you? What's going on? Are you all right? What about Sam —"

"I'm calling for your husband, Mrs. Savich," Katie said, and automatically lowered her voice to make it soothing and calm. "I'm Sheriff K. C. Benedict calling from Jessborough, in eastern Tennessee. Your husband asked me to call you, ma'am. Let me assure you that he's all right, Mrs. Savich. He —"

"Put Dillon on, please, Sheriff."

Katie held the phone to his ear.

Savich drew a deep breath, hoping he was wiping all the damnable pain out of his voice. Sherlock could hear the smallest sound; she could even hear Sean's breathing change before he hollered. "Sherlock? It's me. No, no, I'm okay, just a little problem. Yes, we got Sam back. He's just fine. So is Miles. What little problem? Well, you see this van blew up and I was a bit too close to it. I got hit in the back by some flying metal."

He closed his eyes, feeling the pain trying to draw him in. He really wanted to give in to it, but he wasn't about to scare Sherlock out of her wits.

Katie simply took the cell and said, "Mrs. Savich, he's going to be okay. We're on our way to Washington County Hospital, just outside of Johnson City. Your husband will be all right. I'm not lying to you. I will stay with him. Don't worry."

Savich managed to say "Tell her not to come here" before his brain swam away.

He heard the sheriff talking, but he didn't know if she was still speaking to Sherlock. He knew Sherlock was scared. If he'd gotten a call like this about her he would freak himself. He saw the sheriff lift her wet sweatshirt and slip the small bright blue cell phone back into the T-shirt pocket.

He couldn't seem to stop looking at that cell phone even after she'd pulled the sweatshirt back down over it. Blue, it was a bright blue, ridiculous, really, but on the other hand, she'd never lose it. Blue for cops. He liked that. He closed his eyes, wanting very much to control the blasted pain. He could picture the sharp slice in his back, not an appetizing image. He really wished Sherlock were here even though he'd asked her not to come. Of course she'd be here as soon as humanly possible.

He was vaguely aware that Katie was speaking in a slow deep voice. "— my truck also has stainless-steel exhaust manifolds."

Manifolds?

"And a high-capacity crankshaft that's internally balanced. That reduces stress on the crankshaft, don't you know. Did I tell you it was raining so hard this afternoon that I could barely see ten feet in front of me, even though I have the remarkable high-speed and twice-as-thick grade F windshield wipers on my truck?"

He wanted to laugh and she saw it.

But Savich didn't hear any more after that, just sounds that were soothing, as she was used to speaking to someone who was hurt or not quite with it. Like him.

He didn't rouse his brain until they were in the hospital emergency room and a nurse came forward and directed the four men to lift him from the gurney onto one of the narrow beds.

He heard the nurse speaking to the paramedics, heard Bueller give her a report on what had happened, heard the nurse greet the sheriff. She checked his IV and began cutting off his clothes. "Goodness, you're dirty, Agent Savich. Not to worry, we'll clean you up. You just keep holding on to his hand, Sheriff."

"It's too bad," he said. "Sherlock just got me these slacks."

"They're sexy," the nurse said, "but they've got to go, Agent Savich. Just stay

106

still, Dr. Able will be here in a second to examine you."

He heard Katie's voice and focused on it as the nurse checked his blood pressure, took off the old EKG patches, and put on her own.

Katie said, "My truck has two cup holders in her center console, great for the kids."

"My car doesn't have even one cup holder," Savich said. He felt cold wet cloths cleaning the mud from his legs. He wasn't cold even though he was naked, and that was odd. "I'd like to have one," he said, frowning a bit.

He was almost with her again. She said, "What kind of wheels do you have?"

"A Porsche."

"I should have known, a hotshot guy like you."

He wanted to chuckle, but it was beyond him. The nurse was talking to Katie, giving her his wallet and keys, and pulling a sheet up to his waist.

"Did you see Wade, my chief deputy? I just wish he didn't want my job so badly," Katie said, and he heard the frown in her voice. "That means I can't trust him one hundred percent, and that's too bad. But I guess you have to take the good with the bad, don't you?"

"Kick Wade's butt out of Tennessee or one day you'll find yourself sabotaged but good."

"I will surely think about that, Dillon. Thank you."

"Agent Savich? I'm Dr. Able. Don't move now. I see Linda's got you all cleaned up. You've got no other wounds, just the one across your back. The EKG looks fine. You seem to be pretty stable, and that's good. Now, I'm going to give you some morphine for the pain and examine your back."

Savich looked at the dark-faced man with tobacco-stained teeth leaning over him and wondered how a doctor could begin to justify smoking to himself. He wanted to tell him smoking was nuts. He wanted to tell him that he didn't want morphine, that he didn't want to lose himself, but maybe it would be good if he checked out for a while. He felt Dr. Able fiddling with the IV line they'd started in the ambulance. Savich hoped he knew what he was doing.

"Let's wait just a moment for the morphine to kick in," Dr. Able said. "I'm going to draw some blood, see what's going on, okay? Also we need to type and cross you.

I'd say that with this wound you might be a quart low."

Savich wanted to smile because that was funny, but he could only manage a nod. He just couldn't do any more than that. He felt Katie stroking the back of his hand, and he focused on that.

As Dr. Able slipped a needle into his vein to draw blood, he said, "Sheriff, I understand there've been two fatalities?"

"Yes, Clyde. And I was almost the third. The only reason Agent Savich is hurt is because he saved my life. He tackled and flattened me in the mud when the kidnappers' van exploded. I know I look bad, but it's all on the outside. Don't come near me with any of your needles, my innards are just fine."

"Thank you, Agent Savich, for saving her neck. We need Katie. Linda said you were a mess, but not any longer. Nasty weather out there."

Savich didn't answer, didn't ever want to move again. Then the morphine kicked in and it was like someone had pulled the monster's teeth out of his flesh.

"There, we've got the blood." Savich felt a pat on his arm. "Just lie still, Agent Savich. Here's a pillow against your stomach to keep you up on your side.

Another couple minutes, then we'll see what we've got. Katie, how is the little boy?"

"Sam's just fine. He and my daughter are probably out in the waiting room with Sam's father, Miles Kettering. He and Agent Savich flew from Colfax, Virginia, into Ackerman's Air Field. I'll tell you, Clyde, given the winds out there, that's quite an accomplishment."

Everyone speaks so freely. Will she even tell him we flew in a Cessna?

"An accomplishment or just plain stupid. All right now, Agent Savich, let's see just how bad this is."

The pain was a low throb, nothing more, thanks to the morphine. Only thing was, his head was emptying out and he couldn't bring himself to care a great deal about anything, himself included.

He didn't realize he'd been gone until he heard Katie say, "Dr. Able doesn't think it looks too bad. It's a real clean slice but not deep, thank God."

"We're going to take you to the procedure room, Agent Savich, not the OR. It's just on the other side of the emergency room. It's nice and sterile and quiet. Katie, you can stay with him, but first you're going to have to jump in the shower. Then put on scrubs and a mask, and those cute little booties for your feet."

She patted his hand. "Don't worry, Dillon, I'll be right back."

"They'll let you in this procedure room?"

"Since you're special, they'll allow it this time. Now, I'm going to go get hosed down. Until I get back to you, I want you to think about that really neat coolant loss protection on my truck."

Ten minutes later, thoroughly scrubbed, Katie settled herself down beside Savich, and picked up his hand. It was a nice hand, strong and tanned, with short buffed nails. She remembered that Carlo's hands were like that, powerful and strong. A pity that her former husband's character hadn't matched his hands. False advertising all around. Good riddance to him.

Savich heard a mellow baritone singing "Those Were the Days," and saw Dr. Able's face leaning over him.

10

"Here's what we're going to do, Agent Savich," Dr. Able said, his minty breath wafting over Savich's face. "We're not going to put you under. We're going to give you what we call conscious sedation. That means Linda here will inject some morphine and Versed into your IV. It'll keep you comfortable and sleepy. I'm now going to give you some local anesthetic. All right?"

"All right," Savich said. They'd slid him from the gurney onto his stomach on a narrow bed, a sheet to his waist.

Savich didn't feel pain, just Dr. Able's fingers probing the wound. He wanted to hear more about the sheriff's truck or maybe even hear Dr. Able sing some more, but words wouldn't form in his brain, and so he just lay there, enduring. He wished he was with Sherlock, maybe playing with those fat rollers in her hair.

Dr. Able talked as he worked. "Nothing vital seems to be cut, just your skin and a bit of muscle. You're going to hurt a while, not be able to lie on your back for up to a week, but all in all, you're a very lucky man, Agent Savich. It could have been worse, much worse, and I'm sure you know that. Okay, I'm going to set the stitches in layers now — the deep ones, and then the surface stitches. This will take a few minutes."

Savich didn't feel any pain, just the dragging pull of the thread through his flesh, an obscene feeling he hated.

"You married, Agent Savich?"

Savich wasn't up to even a yes or no answer and Katie saw it. "Yes, he is, Clyde. I have a feeling his wife is going to show up here even though he told her not to come."

"Women," said Dr. Able, "if only they were more like trucks — nice and predictable; you floorboard 'em and they just go, right where you tell 'em to."

"Yeah, I can see what you mean, Clyde," Katie said. "Not only that, you buy a truck, pay for it, and that's it. But with women, you gotta pay and pay — and don't forget the interest."

"Oh yeah? What about the maintenance?"

"Lots more than your truck'll ever need."

Dr. Able laughed hard and Savich was very relieved not to hear him say "Oops."

He heard their voices, but still felt no particular pain, just the slow pulling of the thread through his flesh; his mind, what was left of it, drifted back to the two interviews he'd had just yesterday with the husbands of the slain high school math teachers. It was odd, but their faces blurred together, and he had trouble telling them apart. Then his own face blurred over the both of them.

Troy Ward, tears in his voice, said, "My wife has been dead for six days, Agent Savich, the police don't have a clue who did it, so how do you think I feel? I've told them everything I know, including my mother's social security number."

Savich nodded. He didn't particularly like Troy Ward, the overweight sports announcer. "The thing is, Mr. Ward, the FBI is involved now —"

"Yeah, I've heard all about you big boobs waltzing in and taking over. And now the TV's screaming that it's a serial killer. God, we don't need another one. That last one still gives me nightmares."

"No, we don't need another one. But I really need to know . . ."

Savich's brain floated away, and when he managed to snag some of it back again, Troy Ward seemed more overweight now than he had been just an instant before. "Mr. Ward, have you spoken to Mr. Fowler?"

"The other murdered woman's husband? No, I haven't. Two grown men sitting together sobbing, it wouldn't play well in the football locker room, now, would it? Can't you just see the guys laughing their heads off? No, not much point to that."

What did football have to do with grieving? "Did you play football, Mr. Ward? Is that how you got into announcing?"

"You making a joke, Agent Savich? Let me tell you, I wasn't always this big, and I tried out, but I never got past high school ball. They were a bunch of macho assholes anyway." He jumped to his feet, his three chins wobbling, and screamed, "I wanted to get in the locker room!"

Savich said when that scream died away, "I played football."

"Well, yeah, I can tell by looking at you. I'll just bet you had girls hanging off your biceps, didn't you, you brainless jock?"

That wasn't very nice of him to say, Savich was thinking, but then Troy Ward had a microphone in front of his mouth and he was screaming, "Go, you macho jock jerks! Run!" He yelled in Savich's face, "It's a touchdown! You see that, a touchdown!"

Savich said, "You never met Mr. Gifford Fowler or Leslie Fowler, his wife?"

Now Savich wanted to lie down on this big soft sofa and just listen to the soft rain falling against the front windows of Troy Ward's very nice house in an excellent area of Oxford, Maryland. "Nope, I already told the police I'd never heard of them. I don't think my wife, Bernie, knew Leslie Fowler either, never mentioned her name or anything, not that Bernie and I ever talked about other women all that much. She wasn't worried about me playing around on her, said I was a really bad liar and she'd know." He paused, then tears oozed out of his eyes, falling into the deep creases on his double chin. "I want you to catch the maniac who killed Bernie!" Then he threw back his head and yelled to the ceiling, "I want to be a jock asshole!"

Troy Ward was suddenly standing over him, his hand extended. "Do you want a rice cake? I'm trying to lose some weight, gotta get back into shape, you know, because, who knows, the Ravens just might make the playoffs and I'll be all front and center with the players. I may be doing some locker room interviews with the guys." But he wasn't holding a rice cake out to Savich, it was a huge Krispy Kreme the size of an inner-tube swing. Savich backed away from the doughnut and Troy Ward, that officious little sod of an over-weight sports announcer, blurred into the tall gaunt features of Leslie Fowler, the car dealer, who was talking right in his face, "You want to buy one of my Chevys? I've been selling Chevys right here for the last twenty-two years! I'm solid, they're solid. *Like a Rock!* Hey? Just like the commercial. Whatcha think, Agent Savich?"

"Did you kill your wife, Mr. Fowler?"

"Nah, I sell cars, I don't kill wives. You divorce wives, not kill them. I divorced two before Leslie got herself whacked. Cops are stupid, but the fact is it's just not worth the risk. I just know that if I'd knocked off Leslie they'd get me and then I'd only have eighteen good years left before they toasted me in the gas chamber. Whatcha think, Agent Savich?"

"It's a lethal injection now, Mr. Fowler. Sometimes it's even longer than eighteen years. That's only the average. Did you love your wife?"

"Nah, she wasn't a Mercedes anymore, looked more like a real old Chevy Impala. She used to be hot pink, then got too many miles and turned a dirty gray, ready for the junk pile. Glad we didn't have any kids with me and her as parents — they'd be stealing cars off my lot, the little bastards."

"Do you and Troy Ward, that famous Ravens announcer, ever bowl together?"

"Oh yeah, I heard about his bowling — always leaves splits and someone, it was his wife I hear, always had to come in and clean them up." He laughed and laughed, slapping his knees. "Boy, is he fat, or what? None of the players or any of the coaching staff like him. He's gross, you know? Not like me. Want to see my abs?"

"That's all right, Mr. Fowler, leave your shirt on, but those cuff links, now, they really don't go with that shirt."

"Old junk-heap Leslie gave them to me. I'm wearing them to honor her — one more time, I figure she was worth it. Then I'll flush 'em down. Hey, Agent Savich, you sure you don't want to test-drive a Silverado? Cops like Silverados because they got that fancy coolant loss protection. It would fit your image, all hard muscle, really hot for the girls. Hey, let me show you my hard muscles." As he unzipped his dark gray wool slacks he softly sang "When You Wish Upon a Star."

Voices, Savich heard voices, and this

time they were close and he recognized them and could even make sense of them. It was Dr. Able.

"In deference to your wife, Agent Savich, I'm closing your skin real pretty so she'll think your scar's sexy."

His brain wasn't floating anymore, it was hovering, and things made sense now, more or less. He said, "Sherlock thinks everything about me is sexy," and was pleased because it was true. "Another scar'll just give her someplace new to kiss." He'd lost all sense and his tongue had lost its brakes. He heard a laugh, from Katie. Then he saw Troy Ward again, stuffing that huge doughnut into his mouth, and there was Gifford Fowler, dangling Silverado keys in front of him, winking, and then he threw the keys, and they went higher and higher and even though Savich jumped a good three feet in the air, they just kept flying away.

"A woman with great taste," Katie said. She squeezed his hand. "You guys married long?"

"I don't know about long," Savich said. "I knew her before I ever saw her. She says I'm her fantasy."

"I'd sure like to be a woman's fantasy," Dr. Able said.

"She likes to scrub me down when we get home from the gym."

"There, you see, Clyde, she treats him just like a truck — keeps him nice and clean and revved up."

Dr. Able stopped stitching a moment because he was laughing. Savich was grateful he'd stopped.

"We have a little boy, Sean. She says he looks just like me, not fair since she did all the work. All I did was just have fun, and not even think about it."

Dr. Able said, "I had a little boy once. And you know what? The little bugger grew up. Can you beat that? After all I did for him, he had the nerve to grow up on me and leave. There, done, no more needles pulling through your skin."

"Sherlock got knifed once. I watched the doctor put stitches in her skinny white arm. It shouldn't have happened. I wanted to kill her for taking such a chance."

"Did she succeed?" Katie asked.

"Oh yes," Savich said. He sounded so proud and so pissed, with a layer of dopiness over it, that she had to smile.

"I doubt you'll remember any of this when you wake up tomorrow, Agent Savich," Dr. Able said. "But, can you understand me?"

Savich nodded.

"Your antibiotics are in and the wound looks fine. We're going to keep you here tonight so that the drugs wear off, and make sure there aren't any complications, not that I expect any. Your blood tests look okay. Now, I don't want you worrying about anything, just rest. Again, you were very lucky. I know this wasn't a piece of cake for you, but if that metal had sliced your back any deeper, it wouldn't have been any fun at all. Now, I'm going to make sure you get a real good night's sleep. I sure hope you like sleeping on your stomach."

Savich never opened his eyes though he heard everything. He smelled everything, too, including a hint of lemony soap. Maybe he'd said some things that he normally wouldn't have said. Who cared? Now, he thought, he could just let go.

Life was unexpected. You woke up in the morning, fed your little kid some Cheerios with a sliced banana on top, walked out into the sun, everything going along just fine, and then *whap!* — that night you're laid out in an emergency room in Tennessee.

"You got anything to say to Agent Savich, Katie?"

She lightly touched her fingertips to his cheek. "Just that I can't wait to meet Sherlock, and you need to rest," she said as she pulled off the surgical mask. Savich wanted to say something, maybe to thank the doctor, but it just seemed too hard. He sighed, and slept.

Katie asked, "How long will he be out?"

"He could wake up at any time, but I hope not until morning, not all that long a time away. You know that sleep is the best thing for whatever ails you. Like I said, this man was lucky."

"I'm grateful to you, Clyde, and to his luck," she said. "I'll be in the waiting room with Sam, his father, and Keely. Let me know when Agent Savich is settled in. I know Miles will want to see him, not to mention Sam."

"You sure you don't want me to check out Sam?"

"Nah, the kid's fine. Real proud of himself and that's good, it'll help him keep the fear at bay."

She gave him a small salute, thanked the ER personnel she'd known all her life, and went down to the women's room to wrap her wet clothes in a towel she'd pulled out of the hamper.

She went out into the deserted hospital

corridor wearing green scrubs to call in to the station. Wade was still there, just as she'd known he would be. He brought her up to date, then gave her over to Special Agent Hodges.

"We saw the aftermath of all the excitement, Sheriff. I'm really sorry we missed it."

"We're sorry you missed it, too."

"Your house is a crime scene, but we didn't put tape across your front door. Wade and some deputies boarded up the window Beau broke in. My people are finished up inside, so you can go back in. As for the van, it's still smoldering and the fire chief roped it off. Is Savich all right?"

"He will be, but he won't be doing push-ups for a while. Thank God his wound wasn't deep, just really painful. He'll be in the hospital overnight, just to make sure. Give him a week or so, says the doctor, and he'll be able to sleep on his back again."

She listened to Glen Hodges sing Savich's praises, then he laughed. "We've got a three-way bet going here as to what time Sherlock will show up in the morning, if it takes her that long."

"Really," Katie said, "there's no way for her to get here that fast, even driving."

"You'll see, Sheriff. We'll come over and

visit Savich tomorrow. We're just doing paperwork here, and then Deputy Osborne will take us the local B&B — what is it called? Mother's Best?"

"Mother's Very Best," Katie said. "Mrs. Beecham's grandmother named it that back in the forties. It's a nice place — on the frilly side — and the food is to die for. If you've never had grits before, you're in for a real treat."

"Excellent. Oh, Sheriff," Agent Hodges paused a moment, then said, "I'm, er, really sorry, but there's something else that you need to know, something you might not be expecting. You know I told you the truck was roped off? Well, that was after it was checked over real good. We decided not to bother you with it right away, what with your heading off to the hospital with Agent Savich, and Wade agreed with us."

Didn't need to bother me with something?

Keeping her voice mild and easy, she asked, "What didn't you think was important enough to notify me about, Agent Hodges?"

"Well, it's not exactly that it's not important . . . it's like this, Sheriff: There was no body inside the van."

11

"What?"

"It looks like Clancy — big gut and all — got out before the van blew," Agent Hodges said. "Of course, he had lots of motivation. Wade called all the county sheriff's offices and all area police departments, and the state police. He gave them all the particulars and a description of Clancy. We figure he's got to be in bad shape, I mean, he did crash the van hard into that tree, and Wade told me you'd shot him in the arm or shoulder, so he's got to be in pretty bad shape.

"As I said, we've already got a manhunt going. Any stolen cars will be reported directly to us. We'll find Clancy.

"I'm really sorry we've got to add this to the mix, Sheriff. As for Beau, the coroner has his body. There'll be paperwork for you to do, but I guess you know that. And I'm sure you'll be getting a call first thing in the morning from the TBI."

The Tennessee Bureau of Investigation — oh yeah, she'd get lots more than a call.

But that was tomorrow. At this moment, she was so mad at Agent Hodges that if she'd been within arm's reach she would have clouted him in the head, really hard. She told herself keeping calm was her forte and she used that now, her voice still smooth and mild. "Let me see if I've got this straight. You decided not to bother me with this small detail, Agent Hodges? It didn't occur to you that since I'm the sheriff I should be called immediately?"

"Well, ma'am, we've got a lot going on here —"

"You just made a big mistake you will not repeat, Agent Hodges. I'm the sheriff of Jessborough, I run things here, you don't, regardless of anything my deputy might have said."

"Now wait a minute, Sheriff. I'm sorry about the delay, but it is our case."

"I don't need to speak to you any longer, Agent Hodges. Put Wade back on the phone."

"Yo, Katie. Come on now, don't be pissed."

She pictured driving her truck over him, maybe letting the back tires with their cast-aluminum wheels sit on him for a little while, really settle in and get comfortable. Savich was right. She should boot his butt

126

to the Tennessee line and hand him over to North Carolina or Virginia or Georgia — she had lots of choices. Hey, Kentucky sounded good. She said, "You should have called me immediately, Wade, not agreed with the Feds."

"Look, Katie, you were on your way to the hospital with Agent Savich. I didn't want you to have to worry about something else. Everything's being done that should be done."

"Worrying is my job, Wade. We'll talk about this tomorrow. Right now, I want you to bring our people in. Have them go home and sleep, but keep a patrol going near my house, no, that's not enough. I want a couple of deputies sitting out in front of my house. If Clancy is alive, chances are he's hiding in the forest. If he's not badly hurt, he might double back.

"Oh yeah, tell Dicker to bring his dogs over to my house first thing in the morning if Clancy hasn't been found by then. The state police can keep looking tonight, those guys don't deserve much sleep. One other thing, check in with every family within a five-mile radius of my house. Warn them. You got that?"

"I already had Mary Lynn call all the neighbors. I do know what to do, Katie."

"He'll try to steal a car if he's able to."

"Yeah, we know that."

"He's a dangerous man, Wade. Keep reminding everyone just how dangerous."

"Yes, I have, of course. Even though I'm sending out deputies to guard your house, Katie, you be careful, too. No telling what that moron will do."

"There's something else, Wade — something very important — but I think I'll let it wait until tomorrow morning when Agent Savich is back in the land of the living. You don't need to worry about it now, Wade."

"Wait! Whoa, Katie, what do —"

"Nah, you've got enough on your plate tonight, Wade, both you and Agent Hodges." She smiled as she hung up. *That should have him thinking and cursing about me not telling him something.*

She pushed away from the wall and walked to the waiting room. Her brain was fried, or very nearly.

So Fatso had managed to get out of the van and into the forest before the sucker blew. Well, wasn't that just peachy?

Now she had to tell Miles, though she didn't want to. She had to tell him, it was his right to help protect his child.

It was time to herd her daughter and her

128

guests home. Maybe they should just wait and go to Mother's Very Best, just to be on the safe side. No, she was losing it. A headache started to burrow in over her left eye. Home would be safe. Home sounded like heaven right now, even with a boarded up front window and a burned-out van in the front yard.

She walked into the small waiting room that prided itself on having the oldest *Time* magazines anywhere — most of them from the Watergate period in the seventies.

Keely was wearing her pajamas, a robe, and bunny slippers over nice thick socks. Sam had on a pair of Katie's gray sweats, with the legs rolled up more times than she could count, the long sleeves of her shirt pushed up as well, so thick it looked like he had tires around his arms. He had a pair of her socks on his feet. A nurse, Miles told her, had brought them each a couple of blankets and pillows.

That would be Hilda Barnes, she told him. Hilda always took special care of any visiting children.

Katie realized Miles was the only damp one in the waiting room.

Sam was on his feet the instant he saw her. "How's Uncle Dillon, Katie?"

"He's going to be just fine, Sam. He'll be staying here tonight. Dr. Able just wants to make sure everything is okay."

Miles said, "You look sharp in your scrubs, Katie." Actually, she looked rather ridiculous, her hair in a ratty wet ponytail, the scrubs hanging off her. And she looked valiant — a strange thing to think, but it was true. She leaned down to scratch her knee. If only he'd known, he would have offered to do the scratching for her.

"They wouldn't let me in with Dillon unless I got hosed down first. Here are my clothes, wrapped in this towel."

"Mama, I think you look cuter than Dr. Jonah."

"Let's just keep that between us."

"Okay. Who is this man who needs to shave?"

"You mean me, Keely?" Miles said, momentarily distracted. "You know who I am. Your mama needs some aspirin."

How did he know that?

"No," Keely said, "the man in the picture, in the magazine."

"Oh, that was President Nixon," Katie said. "I was born just before he resigned, a very long time ago. When was it?"

"In 1974," Miles said. "I was just a bit younger than Sam."

"Does your head hurt, Katie?" Sam said, and looked up at her.

"Just a little bit. Don't worry about it. Miles, I hear there's a bet on as to how fast Sherlock will get here. Savich told her not to come."

"Doesn't matter," Miles said. "When Sherlock's on a mission, if you don't help, you'd best get out of her way. Now, kids, it's after midnight, time for both of you to be in bed — again."

"I'm not tired," Keely said immediately, and yawned.

"Sure you're not," Katie said and swung her into her arms. She smiled at Miles Kettering, a man she'd not even known existed until she'd come across Sam. His clothes looked damp and itchy, the wool smelled, and his feet squished in his shoes, but no matter, he'd made the kids comfortable.

"You look dead on your feet, Miles. Maybe close to a coma, even." Actually, even with fatigue and worry for Sam etched on his face, those eyes of his were brilliant with relief and just plain happiness. She knew to her toes that he was a strong man, competent, a good man who loved his child more than just about anything.

Miles Kettering was so tired after two days of little sleep and endless worry that a coma didn't sound like a bad thing. "I'm good for a few more miles yet" was all he said. He rose slowly, Sam in his arms, looking like he never wanted to let him go again. And she knew exactly how he felt. He wanted Sam close, he wanted to feel Sam's heartbeat against his palm, to know that he was safe, and with him again.

"Let me take Sam to see Dillon for a moment. He's scared and I want to reassure him. Then we'll be right with you."

At that moment, a nurse came around to let them know Special Agent Savich was in his room, on the medical ward.

"That was good timing," Miles said. "Could you get some aspirin for the sheriff, nurse?"

"Oh, sure. Katie, just a minute, I'll get you some even stronger stuff."

"Not too strong," Katie called after her. "I can't be comatose just yet."

"I want to see Uncle Dillon, too," Keely said.

Katie knew no one was about to keep the kids out at this hour. Almost everybody here had known Keely from the moment she was born, five years before just two floors up. Come to think of it, everybody knew everything about everybody within a ten-mile radius of Jessborough, with updates every couple of hours or so. You'd have to be sick or dead to be out of the loop about what happened today.

The four of them stood by Agent Savich's bed, watching him sleep. Sam lightly patted his shoulder, and looked up to his father. "Uncle Dillon doesn't look so good, Papa. Why's he on his stomach?"

"You remember, he got cut on his back, that's why. He'll be just fine, don't worry, Sam."

"I think he's handsome," Keely said. "Do you think you'd like him, Mama?"

"It's too late for us, pumpkin," Katie told her daughter, "he waited as long as he could, and then he met Sherlock and she proposed to him. She was more in need than we were. What could he do?"

Miles wanted to laugh, but he was just too tired to do more than blink.

By the time Katie walked out of Dillon's hospital room, two Advil in her system, Keely's head rested on her shoulder, and she was sound asleep. Ten minutes later, Katie eased down into the front seat of Miles's rented Ford and settled Keely on her lap. Miles fastened the seat belt. Then he paused, and both of them realized they didn't want Sam to be alone in the back-seat.

It would be a tight fit, but they could do it. Miles said, "Sam, do you think you can hold real still?"

"Sure, Papa," Sam said, so tired his voice slurred like a drunk's.

"Okay, I want you to sit on my lap, but since I'm driving, you can't move a whisker."

Katie had given people tickets for such stupidity, but she didn't say a word. It would work.

Once Miles had the seat belt around both of them, Sam nearly touching the steering wheel even though Miles had pushed the front seat all the way back, Katie said, "Maybe you'd best stay at Mother's Very Best tonight, Miles. The other Feds are staying there."

He was silent for a long moment as he started the car.

"It's not that I won't want you at my house. It's something else entirely."

12

She paused, saw that both children were asleep, then said, her voice low, "Something's happened, Miles."

His hands were fisted around the steering wheel. "Tell me."

"It seems that Fatso/Clancy got out of the van before it blew. They haven't found him yet. The hunt will begin in earnest early tomorrow morning, at first light. If he's still in the forest, he might be dead of his wounds or pneumonia by morning. But I don't think we'll get that lucky."

His right hand thumped the steering wheel. Sam jerked, but didn't awaken. "So there's still danger."

"Well, yes. I felt much better thinking he was dead and accounted for, given what's happened. I'm hoping that he'll run as far and as fast as he can. At least when we catch him, we'll have a chance to get out of him why he and Beau took Sam."

"That would make me feel a whole lot better. There wasn't a ransom note. Everyone was thinking a pedophile had taken him. Now? I don't have a clue." He paused, then added, "I guess you don't think he's dead."

There was such hopefulness in his voice, but she didn't lie. "No, I don't. Life is never that neat and tidy. When you mix criminals in, things really get mucked up."

"So that's why you want me to stay at this B and B in town."

"It might be for the best."

"Wouldn't we be just as safe with you and your deputies, Sheriff?"

"Two deputies will be in front of the house all night and there will be lots of people there tomorrow. Either way, you should be fine, but it's up to you, Miles."

"If you'll have us, Sam and I would like to stay with you. He knows your house, Sheriff, he's comfortable with Keely and with you. I don't want to take him to another strange place unless I'm forced to."

"No, you don't have to. But please remember, Clancy and Beau came back to my house to get Sam again. I'm not really sure Clancy is going to hightail it out of here."

"Ah, I don't think you know this, Katie, but I was in law enforcement myself until five years ago, in the FBI. Savich and I worked together, as a matter of fact, and that's how we became friends. I can handle myself and a gun, if the need arises."

She shook her head at him. "I knew there was something about you, something that made me think you'd been in the military, or something."

"Yeah, I can just imagine how bad-ass dangerous I looked holding two children in my arms."

It took them a good twenty minutes to get there, never going faster than twenty miles an hour. The rain had slowed to a drizzle but a low-lying gray fog blanketed the ground. The air was bone-numbing cold, pregnant with more rain.

The children continued to sleep all the way back to Katie's house, a neat two-story with a wide porch built in the forties. It was just outside Jessborough proper, along a road lined with tulip poplars, set back on five acres that was mostly covered with hardwood trees — beech, red maple, white ash, sassafras.

Miles said, "Do you know, I can't see the mountains, but I know they're there, nearly in your backyard."

"Just wait until morning. Fall is the most glamorous time of the year. So many different trees, so many bright colors, each one distinctive. Come back, say, the end of March and it isn't so pretty."

Miles pulled the Ford in behind the deputies. Katie waved to them, then handed a sleeping Keely to Miles to put on his other shoulder. She watched him pause a moment and stare at the still smoldering van and the boarded-up front window. Then he took the children into the house.

Katie was pleased the car was parked right out in front, as conspicuous as could be. No way Clancy could miss them. They also had a huge thermos of black coffee on the front seat between them, enough, they assured her, to last them until doomsday, or later.

It was nearly 2 a.m. when Katie handed Miles a cup of hot chocolate and pointed to a big easy chair.

"Why don't you drink this. I find hot chocolate always slows me down even if my brain is revving. I'll bet it'll send you right off to sleep."

"Your headache under control?"

"Oh yes. But how did you know?"

He smiled at her. "I just knew."

She couldn't help herself and smiled back. "It's been an eventful day," she said and both of them sipped the hot chocolate.

She closed her eyes in bliss as it warmed her belly.

"An understatement. Both kids were boneless. I just poured them into their beds. It's always amazed me how a kid can do that."

Katie smiled. "Thank you for taking care of Keely. My sweats are warm even if they don't fit Sam very well. I haven't had time to wash his clothes. We can do that first thing in the morning. Sam's a brave kid, Miles."

"Yeah, he is. Obviously it's you who deserves thanks for saving my son's life. I owe you, Katie, I owe you forever."

"You're welcome. Remember, Sam saved himself. It was luck that I was driving really slow and Keely saw him."

Miles said, "When I put Keely to bed while you were drying my clothes, she still had that blanket Hilda gave her at the hospital. She didn't want to give it up."

"She didn't mention Oscar? That's her rabbit. They've been inseparable since she was six months old."

"She sleeps with her rabbit?"

"Oh, sure. Does Sam have a favorite animal he sleeps with?"

"Yes," Miles said. "A big stuffed frog named Ollie. It's really ratty, but Sam refuses to let it go."

"Wait just a second." Katie left the living room only to return a few seconds later, a big green frog under her arm. "Would you look at this sitting in her closet — her grandmother, my mother, gave it to her for Christmas last year. Maybe Sam would let it be a stand-in for Ollie."

He smiled, the first one Katie had seen. "You have a name for the critter?"

"Oh yeah, she's Marie."

"Sam might not want a girl."

"Trust me. Green isn't girly. And you'll make it Martin."

She watched him close his eyes again, saw the tension flooding back over him, and waited. After a minute or so, he said, "Best I can tell, Sam was taken out of his own bed close to dawn, early Friday morning. It's been like an unending nightmare." He swallowed convulsively. Katie just let him talk.

"I went to get him up for school, and he wasn't in his bed. I thought he was in the bathroom and I went yelling for him to hurry up. It took at least five minutes before I realized he was gone, that someone had taken him. My first thought was a sexual predator, and believe me, the FBI checked that out immediately. Then we all wondered if it was some sort of revenge — after all, I'd been in the FBI myself and captured some bad guys. Since I own a good-sized company, it could have been ransom. They spoke to my sister-in-law, to some of my employees, even a couple of friends. It all takes time, so they'd really just gotten started. But no matter what the agents said, no matter what they did, all I could think about was some child molester had gotten him."

His voice broke. He opened his eyes. "I wanted to hope, to believe that the FBI would get him back, but there have been so many kidnappings, and the kids either disappear forever or they're found dead. I've never been so scared in my life."

"I'll bet. I can't imagine how I'd feel if it were Keely." She shook her head. "Did Sam tell you that his mama got him moving when Beau and Clancy had him at the cabin?"

"No, he hasn't had time to tell me everything just yet."

"I hope your wife is all right."

"His mother has been dead for two years now, a car accident."

"Oh, I'm so very sorry; Sam never told me."

He smiled wearily. "It's all right. He

doesn't talk about it yet. His mom speaks to him every so often; funny thing is, sometimes she talks to me, too. Of course it's just in my head, when I'm stressed out or something, and I have a problem that's all muddled in my mind, but if she spoke to Sam to help him get away, good for her." He shrugged. "Maybe, somehow, he needed her to help him help himself. And so he did. Can you tell me what happened, Sheriff?"

"Sure. Let me tell you about Sam's great escape." She spoke for maybe two minutes, then realized her audience had nodded off. She leaned down and lightly shook his shoulder. He came awake instantly, a flash of fear, then relief that Sam was okay.

"It's time for bed, Miles. I don't think my sweats would work for you as well as they do for Sam. We can go shopping tomorrow for both of you. There's a bathroom right beside Sam's room. When my dad was alive he used to visit, so you'll find guy stuff in there."

"Thank you, Katie." She watched him walk from the living room. He was a big man, fit and runner-lean, dark-haired and dark-eyed, looking rather silly with a green frog tucked under his right arm. He looked like exhaustion walking. And the oddest thing was, she felt like she'd known him for a good long time, and it felt good.

After a long hot shower, Katie checked Keely's room. Her daughter was smiling in her sleep, Oscar lying tightly squeezed to her chest, one floppy ear showing above the blanket Hilda had given her.

Katie climbed into bed with one more thing to do before she let her brain go. She opened her laptop and went to the NCIC, the National Crime Information Center, the FBI's national criminal database that could be accessed by local law enforcement. The late Beauregard Jones was a career hood who hailed from Denton, Texas, a three-time loser, with warrants that could have put him in jail for the rest of his miserable life, if it weren't over already. She couldn't find anything about kidnapping or about any family in or near Tennessee.

She had no clue what Clancy's last name was or how he'd gotten connected to Beau. She called Ossining, Beau's place of residence until a couple of years ago. She left a message for the warden to call her as soon as possible. Clancy was the key, she just knew it.

She shut down her laptop, unplugged the modem, and pulled the covers to her neck.

She dreamed that Keely was calling to her, but when Katie got close to her daughter's voice, all she saw was a long line of vans. She watched, horrified, as each of them blew up, one after the other. Then she saw Clancy stuffing Keely into a van that hadn't blown up yet. She woke up, frightened and wheezing, her nightshirt sweated through.

She couldn't help herself. She checked on Keely, then on Sam and Miles. Sam was on his side, his face on his father's shoulder, his father's arm cuddling him close. Martin the frog was sprawled on top of Miles, Sam's arm around him.

She was still shaking from that wretched dream. Beau was dead. As for Clancy, she'd get him and throw his ass in jail.

13

The hospital was quiet at ten o'clock on Sunday morning. Katie, Miles, and the children trooped into Dillon Savich's semi-private room that had only Savich in it.

Leaning over him was a small woman in black slacks, black leather half-boots, and a black denim jacket over a red sweater. She had curly red hair that wasn't really a red red, or not an auburn, just a marvelous mix, and a very nice laugh. She looked up when she heard them coming.

Her eyes lit up. "Hey, Sam, Dillon tells me you're a hero."

Sam shouted as he ran to her, "I did it, Aunt Sherlock, I climbed out that window myself, and it was so skinny that my shoulders didn't want to fit through, but I finally wiggled free and my butt fell right out. I landed on my face in the mud. That was yucky but I ran and ran and then Katie was there — and you know that she shot those bad men?"

He finally took a breath. Sherlock grabbed him up in her arms and danced around the room with him. She kissed him all over his face as she danced.

Sam asked her when she paused to take a breath, "Where's Sean?"

"He's with his grandmother. I'd bet that right now he's sitting in church."

"That could be bad," Sam said to Katie. "Sean doesn't like to sit still."

"You're right about that," Sherlock said, and kissed him one final time. "We bribe him with graham crackers."

Sam immediately turned to Savich. "You're sitting up, Uncle Dillon. Are you better?"

"I'm just fine, Sam, just a bit stiff." Savich hugged Sam against him, doing his best not to wince when the boy's hands brushed against the bandage over his back. "Sherlock's going to spring me today, she promised. Did you and your dad sleep at the sheriff's house last night?"

"Yeah, Papa slept with me. I got hot, but he didn't want to let go of me."

"I wouldn't let go of you either," Sherlock said. "Okay, what else do you have to tell me, Sam?"

"When I woke up there was this strange frog on top of Papa."

"That was Marie," Miles said to Sherlock. "A big green stuffed frog, on loan from Keely."

Sam was outraged. "He isn't a girl frog. He's Martin."

Miles said, "Hey, I thought you were so macho that it wouldn't matter. Isn't that right?"

While Sam looked uncertain, Miles said, "I told Katie that you'd be here this morning, Sherlock. How'd you manage it?"

Savich said, "She called Jimmy Maitland, our boss, told him I was in bad shape in Tennessee, and he sent her over in a Black Bell Jet helicopter."

"Oh wow," Sam said. "Katie, my papa makes parts for helicopters and he can fly them, too. Can we go home in a helicopter, Papa?"

"Very doubtful," Miles said, "particularly an FBI helicopter. Every taxpayer who didn't get to ride in it would be pretty upset. Isn't the Cessna any good anymore, Sam?"

While Sam was trying to explain how much cooler a helicopter was, Katie met Sherlock.

Sherlock took her hands and just held them in hers. "Thank you so very much for saving Sam."

"It was my pleasure. However, Mrs. Savich —"

"No, just call me Sherlock, everyone does."

"I'm the one responsible for your husband being hurt. If I hadn't run toward that van —"

"No, no, that's quite enough. I'll admit I was angry at first, but then Dillon told me how you saved Sam not once but twice, by shooting Beau when it was crunch time. So we can stand here and thank each other or we can get on with things."

Katie looked at each of them in turn. "There's something I've got to tell you two you may not know yet."

Every eye went to her.

"Clancy wasn't in the van. He got out before it blew. We've got a manhunt going on. If he's anywhere near here, we'll get him."

Savich said, "Do you have dogs, Sheriff?"

"Yes, Bud Dicker has four hunting dogs. They've been out since about six o'clock this morning. No word yet."

Sherlock said, frowning, "I can't imagine he'd stay in the area unless he was badly hurt. Okay, Katie, I can see you know something more. Come on, cough it up."

"It isn't all that much just yet. I know you've all probably wondered by now why Beau and Clancy brought Sam here, to

Jessborough, Tennessee, and held him in Bleaker's old cabin. Was his kidnapping connected to someone local? Or was it all just happenstance, as in there was this cabin, and Clancy and Beau knew about it, and just used it?"

Savich sighed, recognizing an excellent performance when he saw it, and didn't say anything.

Katie said, "Miles, do you know anyone local? Anyone at all?"

"No, I don't. Like I told you last night, I've never been in this part of Tennessee before in my life."

"Okay, so I thought the next step was to connect up Beau and Clancy to a local. It was no big shock to find out that neither of them came from around here, and so, no convenient relatives popped up. But they were both lifelong criminals, in and out of prison, and I just knew to my bones that's the answer. Clancy or Beau met someone in prison and that someone is from around here or has friends or relatives here. I found out from NCIC that Beau was at Ossining, so I gave them a call to see if they'd ever had a Clancy in their fine facility.

"Ossining got back to me just a little while ago, and sure enough, Clancy Edens had enjoyed their hospitality until about eight months ago — conspiracy to commit kidnapping. It turns out one of the kidnappers got cold feet and ratted out his friends.

"They faxed me his photo, and he's our boy. I had copies Xeroxed and plastered all over town. Problem is, I just haven't found any connection between Clancy Edens and someone local."

Savich smiled. "You've got a good brain, Katie. No reason to wait. Sherlock, hand me MAX. Let me see what he can find out."

Once the modem was plugged in, Savich booted up MAX. While they waited, Miles told Katie about MAX, sometimes known as MAXINE, the laptop he used to access the data-mining software he'd worked on for years. "Bottom line is that either MAX or MAXINE could probably find out what kind of deodorant the president smears in his armpits if it's on a database somewhere. He's even better with computers than I am," Miles added, "and that bums me, it really does."

"Be quiet, Miles," Savich said, not looking up. "You can do everything else better. I wouldn't know a night guidance system from a bowling ball."

Sherlock said, "I remember you took Dillon down to the mat a couple of weeks ago."

Savich looked up. "That was just an accident, Sherlock. I must have been dehydrated or something."

Katie smiled as she said, "Sam, I can see you're fretting. I don't want you to worry about Fatso. We'll get him, no doubt in my mind. We've got his photo nailed up everywhere and special flyers are being printed up as I speak. But do you know what? Your uncle Dillon is going to find out why they brought you here real soon."

"He's got a big stomach, Uncle Dillon," Sam said as he settled in on his father's lap.

"I know, Sam," Katie said. "His belly nearly fills up the photo we've got out there."

Miles said, "Keely, this is the only chair. You want to climb up here, too?"

Keely didn't hesitate to climb up on his other leg. Miles said, "They're still so excited they can't think straight or talk about anything else. Okay, kiddos, just lean on me and listen for a while, okay?"

Sherlock said, "Sam, I meant to tell you, you look cool. I really like those jeans and your Titans sweatshirt. I wonder what all your Redskins friends are going to say when they see it. Are those Nikes I see on your big feet?"

Katie said as Sam preened, "Mary Lynn Rector — believe it or not her father's the local Presbyterian minister — brought them over about seven o'clock this morning. She'd heard Sam didn't have anything except my sweats, said it was Sunday and even Kmart didn't open until ten. As for Miles, at least his clothes are clean, no new ones yet for him."

Sam said against his father's chest, "I'm cool."

Keely looked at her mother, frowned, and stuck her thumb in her mouth, something Katie hadn't seen her do in at least six months. On the other hand, Keely hadn't seen a van blow up or a man shot not ten feet away from her in the last six months either. She would have to ask Dr. Sheila Raines what do to about this. Sheila, a childhood friend, was the only shrink in Jessborough Katie trusted. She moved to stand beside her daughter when Sherlock said, "Mr. Maitland wanted the other FBI guys to fly here with me, you know, the ones working with us, Miles, but I convinced him to let me come out right away. But I wouldn't be surprised if Butch

Ashburn showed up here today. He's a bulldog, Katie."

"Is he like Glen Hodges?"

"More so," Savich said, still not looking up. "I can just hear her now, Katie, telling Maitland that she'd get things all cleaned up herself, no reason to load the helicopter down with unnecessary personnel."

At that moment, Glen Hodges and two other agents stuck their heads in the door. Two of them had huge grins on their faces, the third looked really down. "We knew you'd be here, Sherlock. Hot-diggity, I just won fifty bucks off Jessie here. The poor stiff said you wouldn't show up until two o'clock this afternoon." There was a boo and hiss from Jessie.

"Well, of course I'm here," Sherlock said to Glen Hodges. "Where else would I be?"

"Jessie here," Savich said to his wife, "just didn't realize that you were perfectly capable of moving a mountain or two to get what you wanted."

There was a bit of laughter, then Agent Hodges said, "Sheriff, Mothers Very Best is just excellent. You wouldn't believe the breakfast she gave us. You're not looking too bad, Savich. The sheriff said you'd just be sore for a week or two. I see you're working on MAX." He eyed Sam and

Keely, then said, "Do you still want to belt me, Sheriff?"

"Agent Hodges," Katie said to the rest of the group, "didn't bother telling me about Clancy not being in the van, just took charge himself. The proverbial Fed with big wing tips."

Sherlock said, "Are you serious, Katie? You're telling me that Glen didn't call you immediately when they found out Clancy wasn't in that van?"

"Well, yeah, I did call her just a bit later."

"Actually, I was the one who called Wade. Nobody called me."

"Do you want me to belt him for you, Sheriff?" Sherlock was standing nearly *en pointe*.

Katie knew Sherlock was thinking Hodges was a sexist jerk, and maybe he was. In the short term, it really hadn't mattered, but she was the sheriff of Jessborough, and yeah, she was still low-level pissed at him. "I'll deal with him, Sherlock, thanks just the same."

"Ah, if neither of you is going to hit me right away, then there's some more stuff you and I need to go over, Sheriff. Then it's out again to look for Clancy. Strange how that guy could move so fast with all that weight on him."

Savich said, "Glen, call Butch Ashburn at home, fill him in if he's still there. He'll get out here right away since he was the lead on the investigation. I know he'll really want to hear from you. Actually, he's probably nearly here by now, but give it a try."

Katie said, "Okay. Dicker is out with his dogs, and we've got a good thirty others hunting him as well. I've had Wade expand the call to all law enforcement offices in a fifty-mile radius. Any reports from them will come immediately to me."

"Er, Sheriff, despite my not telling you about Clancy, despite everything, well, you know, since this is a federal crime, it is in my jurisdiction. Do you think these reports could also come to me?"

"Now he's thinking the way he should," Sherlock said. "There's still hope for you, Glen. Tell your wife to call me."

"Why?"

Sherlock gave him a fat smile. "Just girl stuff."

"You're going to tell her to torture me, aren't you, Sherlock?"

"Good guess," Savich said, and smiled at his wife.

Glen said, "Sheriff, you got Wade all in a

knot last night when you said there was something else and that you wanted to talk it over with everybody this morning. I'm here. What's that about?"

Miles said, "The sheriff started wondering why Beau and Clancy came to Jessborough, which one wouldn't necessarily consider the kidnapping center of the world. Was it a coincidence or was there someone here connected either with Beau and Clancy or just maybe connected to someone in Colfax? Well, I think maybe we've got something."

"Got it!"

Katie stared at Savich. "Not even fifteen minutes and you've got something?"

Savich said, "Sometimes things just pop. Okay, Clancy Edens was in Ossining from 1998 to about eight months ago where he shared a corridor with a Luther Vincent of Kingsport, Tennessee, which is, if I'm not mistaken, only about fifty miles from here, right? To the northeast?"

"Right," Katie said and tapped her knuckles against her forearm.

"Do you know any Vincents?"

Katie frowned, tapped her foot, and finally, shook her head, sighed. "No."

Savich said easily, "No big deal. We'll just make a note of him and I'll keep checking. I should have another one of Clancy's files in a minute."

Savich looked up a few minutes later, grinning like a bandit, and said, "Guess what? Old Clancy Edens changed his name some twenty years ago. Turns out his daddy was a real loser — beat his wife, beat his two kids indiscriminately, from the looks of it. Clancy joined the army when he was eighteen, was dishonorably discharged two years later, changed his name and commenced his life of crime."

Katie said, "Come on, spill the beans. What name did he change from, Dillon?"

Savich smiled at her. "I sure hope you've heard of someone by the name of Bird."

Katie blinked, looked down at Keely's perfect small fingers, then said, "Bird. There aren't any local Birds, at least I don't think there are. But, Bird sounds familiar." Katie smacked her thigh. "Yes! I've got it! I remember now, her name was Elsbeth Bird."

"Elsbeth Bird?" Sherlock was standing on her toes, she was so excited. "Talk, Katie."

"Elsbeth Bird married Sooner McCamy back in the early nineties and moved here. So Clancy Edens is her brother?"

"He's in his forties, so I'd say yes, brother it is."

"Thank you, Dillon. Since you're already taken, maybe I can move in with MAX. Glad to meet you, Sherlock. I'm out of here."

Sherlock said, "Hey, wait a minute, Katie. You're not going to see this Elsbeth Bird who married Sooner McCamy alone, are you?"

"It's Sunday," Katie said patiently.

"What does that have to do with anything?"

"Reverend McCamy just happens to be a local preacher. He has a small congregation who worship him and God, probably in that order. The members pretty much keep to themselves around here. I've never been to one of their services. I wouldn't say they're a cult, but sometimes you wonder. The women are supposed to be subservient and if they're not subservient enough, rumor is the husbands are encouraged to discipline them. His church is called the Sinful Children of God."

"What?"

"Yep, that's what they're called. I know Reverend McCamy will be preaching all morning — and again this afternoon and evening. Just time off for lunch. The reverend has charisma from what I've heard, and can hold an audience in the palm of his hand. I haven't witnessed the charisma when I've seen him around town. He's quiet, pays his bills on time, hasn't ever caused any trouble, and is considered quite respectable.

"Reverend McCamy is very intense — you know, he looks all dark and broody, thin, tall, like he spends a lot of time on his knees conversing with God. I've never heard of him being involved with any of the women in his congregation. Besides, Elsbeth, his wife, is one of the most beautiful women around here — long blond hair, slender, soft-spoken, does whatever he asks. It's sure hard to see either of them being involved in this."

"Hmm," Glen Hodges said, and Katie waited, just waited, for him to make some sexist remark, but he didn't. Indeed, he was frowning. "Doesn't sound true to type," he said finally.

"You're right," Katie said. "He's always polite, always pleasant, but there's just something about him, something that makes you want to take a step back, if you know what I mean."

"How many people in his congregation?" Sherlock asked.

"Maybe fifty, sixty, I'm not really sure. I'm thinking I'll just swing by their house, you know, check it out a bit, see if just maybe Clancy is hanging around out there. He's her brother, after all. Where else would he hide?"

"I'm going with you, Katie," Sherlock said and slung the strap of her purse over her shoulder. "No way are you on this little sightseeing visit by yourself."

"What about me, Mom?"

"You stay here. Oh dear." She stared blankly at Miles, who was giving her a crooked smile.

"Go get 'em, tiger," Miles said. "Keely, you and me and Sam are going to stay and play gin rummy with your uncle Dillon and maybe have some lunch in the cafeteria. Whatcha think?"

"I don't know how to play gin rummy," Keely said.

"I want to go, Papa."

"Sorry kid, not this time. They serve who also wait, or something like that. Keely, you'll learn real fast. Now, say good-bye to your mom."

"Good-bye, Mom."

"I'll see you soon, sweetie."

"Take another pain pill in exactly thirty-one minutes, okay?" Sherlock said as she kissed her husband's whiskered cheek. "And find out if it's at all possible that the McCamys could be behind Sam's kidnapping."

"A preacher wanting Sam?" Miles said as he settled Sam back onto his lap. "I can't begin to imagine why."

Katie shrugged. "I'll bet Clancy has visited Elsbeth here in Jessborough, knew about Bleaker's cabin, and that's why they took Sam there. You ready, Sherlock?"

Could Elsbeth McCamy be involved in this? Katie just didn't think that could be right. Elsbeth was a wuss, a woman who worshiped her husband, and was utterly and completely dominated by him. She never even referred to him by his first name.

Glen Hodges said, "I should go with you, Sheriff. Like I said, this is a federal case and —"

Sherlock said mildly, "I'm a Fed last time I checked, Glen. You keep heading up the search. Welcome Butch Ashburn when he arrives, wing tips polished. The women are going to the preacher's house."

14

As Katie turned onto Boone Street, she said to Sherlock, "That's Town Hall, where Mayor Tommy hangs out. I've got about six messages on my voice mail from him already this morning. And that's the combination Police Department and Fire Station. We're coming up on Main Street, Jessborough's main drag. You're in for a treat."

Sherlock was already craning her neck to see everything. The sky had cleared after the heavy rainstorm of the night before, and the fall leaves were in full color, with spectacular reds, yellows, and golds. Beautiful old buildings lined the brick sidewalks. Sherlock saw half a dozen churches, with spires rising above the brilliant trees. There were antiques stores and galleries, a saddle shop, several gift shops, including a quilt shop that Sherlock would have liked to visit, and an enclosed marketplace. Small restaurants were dotted in among the shops, ranging from burgers and fries to Italian cuisine.

"This is lovely," Sherlock said, turning in

162

her seat to look back down Main Street. "Does one of these churches belong to the Sinful Children of God?"

"No, that one's out on Sycamore Road, in an old church that used to be Lutheran before Reverend McCamy took it over some three or four years ago."

"I see some gift shops. You have a lot of tourists?"

"More during the summer. We're a little off the beaten track."

"And those mountains," Sherlock said, waving her hand at them. "It feels like you could reach out and touch that blue haze. They're solid and eternal, and that's comforting, I suppose."

Katie smiled. "The Appalachians change a lot with the seasons. Fall is the most beautiful time, but they're sort of like a good neighbor who stays put, you can count on them always being there under that blue haze — well, that's why we call them the Smokies. I'll tell you, it still sometimes makes my heart skip a beat when I look up and see them."

"This is a beautiful town, Katie. No exhaust fumes, no gangs of teenagers with bolts through their noses. It's so peaceful."

"You get all those things just up the highway."

"But you're tucked away all safe and sound. Until yesterday, anyway." Sherlock rolled down the truck window and breathed in the clean crisp air.

"Yes, it's always been peaceful, until now."

"I brought my big hair rollers," Sherlock said as she watched a horse-drawn carriage pull onto Main Street.

Katie, who'd been thinking the last thing she needed was this FBI character, Butch Ashburn, trying to out-wing-tip Glen Hodges with his heel on her neck, blinked, turned to look at Sherlock, and said, "What?"

"A while back Dillon and I were in Los Angeles on a case. There was this crazy guy murdering people, copying a TV show —"

"You were involved in those TV show murders?"

"Well, yes. As I was saying, Dillon and I discovered quite by accident that he really likes to roll up my hair on those big hair rollers and then have me pull them out of my hair, one by one, and sort of toss my head and string my fingers through my mane. So I brought them along with me to cheer him up. But I think it's going to have to wait a couple of days before he's up to playing again."

Katie laughed. "Hair rollers. Hmmm, I never thought of that."

"I hadn't either until I met Belinda Gates," Sherlock said. "Boy, could she pull out hair rollers. It was enough to make Dillon sweat."

"She's that actress who starred in *The Consultant*, isn't she?"

"Yep, she's the one, a real piece of work. Actually, I liked her when I didn't want to punch her out. You wouldn't believe some of the people we met in Hollywood. They were so crooked you wondered how they could walk. You've got a cute kid. What is she?"

"Yes, she just turned five last month. She's all mine, thank God."

Sherlock wanted to know what she meant by that, but it was too pushy to ask, at least this soon. "Tell me more about Elsbeth Bird McCamy."

Katie turned her truck off Main Street onto Poplar Drive, checked the old Ford coming up on her left, and said, "The very first thing you notice about Elsbeth is how beautiful she is — she's got this fall of very light blond hair, all the way to her waist. She always wears it loose, tucked behind her ears so you can see her Jesus earrings."

"Her what?"

"I call them Jesus earrings. They're silver — Jesus on the cross — and they hang down about an inch and a half. When she moves, they move. I'll tell you, it makes me shudder. I think she's about thirty-five now, which isn't all that young, but given that Reverend McCamy is well over fifty, it's a bit on the creepy side. Like I told you, he's very intense — his eyes blaze and nearly turn black when he looks at you."

"He's scary?"

"Well, sort of, I guess. It's just that he's so much into his own particular brand of religion. As I said, Elsbeth calls him only by his last name. It's always Reverend McCamy this, Reverend McCamy that."

"I haven't run into that before. You mean like some wives did back in the nineteenth century?"

"Yes. And he calls her Elsbeth. She treats him like he has but to speak and she'll jump to obey. Whatever he wanted, I can see her jumping through hoops to get it for him. I'd say she was close to worshiping him."

Sherlock's left eyebrow climbed up. "Is that part of what he preaches? That wives should be as subservient to their husbands as she is?"

Katie shrugged. "Yes. From what I

understand of the Sinful Children of God, Reverend McCamy preaches that women, in order to do penance for their huge sin of munching on the Eden apple, have got to give their all to another human being and that human being, naturally, is their husband."

"That's really convenient."

"Well, I wouldn't swear to it, but that's what I've heard anyway. People around Jessborough are tolerant of each other. None of the members of the Sinful Children of God who live locally has ever been arrested or disturbed the peace. They're good people, respectable, and tend to keep to themselves. I think most of the members come from neighboring areas. Like you said, it's pretty convenient, at least for all the men in the congregation. Maybe that's why Reverend McCamy has been so successful. He holds up his own wife as the model all the women should try to copy."

"What happens if the wife isn't interested?"

"I guess she could refuse to join, but I know he offers some kind of counseling for wayward wives."

"Just imagine," Sherlock said. "He preaches enslavement of women and it's all tax free."

"You're right. They're a church, so no taxes."

"I wonder if there's some kind of point system here," Sherlock said as she looked at a herd of cows spread over a low green hill. "You know, points for bringing the husband a beer during a football game?"

"Or points for meeting him at the front door at night with a drink?"

Sherlock laughed. "I can't believe they're that many sandwiches short of a picnic."

"I have no idea, really. I've never been to one of their services."

Sherlock shook her head, giggling. "Come on, Katie. You want me to believe a sizable group of women actually buys this stuff? You said the congregation was fifty or sixty people. That means at least twenty-five women?"

"To each his own, I guess. Like I said, people around here are tolerant of other people's beliefs, so long as they're left alone themselves."

Sherlock was silent for a moment, drumming her fingertips on the window. "They're in the middle of a service right now?"

Katie checked the purple big-faced watch that Keely had given her for Christmas. "Yeah, for another half-hour at least.

Then there's a lunch break."

"Good. We've got plenty of time to see if there's any sign of Clancy hanging around their house."

Katie took a left onto Birch Avenue, then a right onto Sassafras Road. "Once off Main Street, all our streets are named after local trees. I live on Red Maple Road."

"Can spring be as gorgeous here as the fall?"

Katie smiled, shook her head. "It's pretty here in April and May, but you're lucky to be here just now. All the colorful trees with the mountains in the background . . . it makes you feel like there's something more than just life and death, something that's endless and beautiful."

"Have you lived here all your life?"

"Oh yes. My father owned the chip mill — Benedict Pulp — until he died two years ago. Now my mom runs the mill for me. We're coming up on Pine Wood Lane where the McCamys live. I'm going to ditch the truck. We'll go in by foot, okay?"

"Sure." Sherlock pulled her SIG Sauer out of her shoulder harness, checked it, and put it on her lap. "You know, Katie, we'd need a warrant to actually go inside the house."

"Yeah, I know that."

Katie pulled off Pine Wood Lane onto a dirt road, more a path really, that went into some thick woods. "This is good enough. The house is just a bit up the road."

Sherlock followed Katie as she wove her way through the pine trees, well away from the road. The air was cold but clear, except for the blue haze forming over the mountains.

They heard a small animal scurrying away from them deeper into the forest. The birds were quiet this morning, with just a few crow calls breaking the silence.

Katie said, "Sooner inherited his house and property from an aunt who passed on not long after he married Elsbeth. It's a nice place."

"Is he from around here?"

Katie shook her head, shoved a branch out of the way. "No, he moved here maybe ten years ago from Nashville. I really don't know his background but I'll make it a point to find out about him now, even whether he puts butter on his popcorn. He went off and married Elsbeth, brought her back here, and then the aunt died."

They walked out of the pine trees and stopped a moment. Katie pointed to a big three-story Victorian that stood in the middle of a huge lot filled with birches, oaks, and maples, some of them right up against the sides of the house. The golds, reds, and yellows of the leaves were incredible. It was an idyllic setting, and the house was a gem, the trim painted three different shades of green. There were no cars in the driveway.

"Just Sooner and Elsbeth live here. Reverend McCamy has money from his aunt, but they don't have anyone cleaning for them as far as I know. There's a gardener who comes by, Mr. Dillard, a really old fellow with no teeth in his mouth, but he's magic with flowers. The place should be empty. Let's just check it out."

Sherlock carried her SIG Sauer pressed downward, next to her leg.

Katie stopped abruptly.

"What is it?"

"I think I saw a flash of light in one of the upstairs windows."

"What kind of flash?"

"Like someone was holding a mirror and it caught the sun."

"Let's just see if our guy's here."

They made their way to the back of the house and watched for a few minutes.

Sherlock said, "Okay, Katie, if you'd just stay here for a little while, I'm going around to the front now and ring the front-door bell. If Clancy is in there, all his interest will be on the front door. You can come around the side and look in, see if you spot him. If he's in there, hey, we've got hot pursuit."

"Let's do it."

Sherlock jogged back into the forest and made her way back around to the road in front of the house, her SIG Sauer safely in her shoulder harness again. She started whistling when she turned into the driveway of 2001 Pine Wood Lane.

Are you there, Clancy?

She walked right up to the front door and rang the bell, whistling Bobby McFerrin's song, "Don't Worry Be Happy."

There wasn't a hint of anyone coming to the front door.

She rang again.

Was that a sound coming from inside?

She called out, "Anybody home? I've got some real great deals to offer you this morning. I know it's Sunday, but do you want a chance to win a trip to Maui? Stay at the Grand Wailea?"

She rang again. She heard something, this time she was sure. She could practically see Clancy hovering near the front door, wondering what he should do.

Open the door, Clancy.

He wasn't going to open the door, or maybe he just wasn't there. Katie should be coming around the side of the house now, looking in through all the windows. *Quiet, Katie, be careful.*

Sherlock called out again, "Hey, I can hear you in there. Why don't you want to talk to me? I'm tired, you know? Could I at least have a glass of water? I've been walking a whole lot this morning."

Suddenly, the door opened.

15

Katie and Sherlock faced each other.

Katie whispered, "I didn't see him. But you know? The back door was open, I kid you not. Let's just take a quick look around."

"We shouldn't be in here, Katie. We're the law and we're supposed to have a warrant."

"I know, but this is personal, Sherlock. This guy threatened me and Keely. Five minutes. Then we can drive the truck up all right and proper into the driveway and wait outside for Sooner and Elsbeth to come home for lunch. This is our best chance, before he knows we're coming."

Sherlock pulled her weapon out of her shoulder holster and the two women searched the downstairs. It took much longer than five minutes because the house was so big, with old-fashioned nooks and crannies.

Katie nodded toward the stairs, wide enough for both of them to go up side by side, but they didn't. Katie motioned for

Sherlock to follow her.

Katie had been in the house a couple of times, knew there were at least six rooms on the second level. They went through each of the rooms. Five were bedrooms and each was empty. There was nothing, not a sign that Clancy had been there.

The last door on the second level was the master bedroom, and it was something else. Katie and Sherlock, after checking every corner, stood in the middle of the room and stared.

"Preacher likes his comfort," Sherlock said.

"I'll say." Katie stared at the huge bed with the white fur cover, and four pure white pillows. The only other color used was black, and that was just a single leather chair and hassock.

Sherlock raised her eyebrow. "White and black — good versus evil?"

"I guess it's an endless struggle, even in the bedroom." Katie checked the closet. It was small, too small, nothing much in it. She stood in front of it, frowning. Then she saw a small, nearly hidden latch on the back wall, and pressed it down.

Another door opened and she stepped into a room that was nearly as big as her dining room. "Sherlock, come take a look."

Katie said, "This is the biggest walk-in closet I've ever seen. And look at that marble slab in the middle — what do they use that for? Look here, Sherlock, there are drawers under it, with underwear, her sweaters. And he's got his shirts piled on top."

"Oh my," Sherlock said, stepping into the room, "you're right. This green marble slab, isn't it gorgeous, looks Italian. You know, this is odd, but I'd say that marble slab looks more like an altar than some place to stack your freshly laundered shirts."

Katie walked around the large six-foot marble slab that was about three and a half feet off the white-carpeted floor. It was a lovely richly veined green, quite expensive. She saw something tucked under one corner of the marble. She easily flipped up an open stainless-steel cuff. A cuff? She found a cuff on each corner.

Katie raised an eyebrow.

Sherlock said, "I'd say they were for wrists and ankles."

"Oh my," Katie said, fingering one of the cuffs. "I'm kind of embarrassed. I was thinking Elsbeth was a regular garden-variety kind of subservient wife, but would you look at these cuffs? I can't imagine it would be very comfortable lying on that hard marble."

"No. I wonder what they do once he cuffs her down?"

Katie shuddered. "You know, maybe that's not any of our business. This is creepy. Let's check the rest of the house for Clancy, then we can come back here. Just maybe I can bust Reverend McCamy for something."

"Nah, forget it, we're actually breaking and entering here, Katie. Hang on just a second. What's this?" Sherlock pulled two tie racks aside. She found a button and pushed it. A cabinet opened up. It was deep, maybe five feet high. On the left, there was an array of whips, artistically displayed. Next came a block of wood topped with thick fur, a netful of small silver balls, nearly a dozen dildoes of different sizes, shapes, and colors.

Near the top of the cabinet was a wide shelf with at least a dozen vials neatly lined up on it. "Illegal drugs?" Katie said, reaching for one. "If so, maybe I can figure out how to get a warrant." She read the label. "Tears."

"Tears? What could that be?" Sherlock reached out for the vial. She unfastened the round top and sniffed the liquid.

"Phew!" Immediately she started to tear up. She swiped her fingers across her eyes. "It makes tears all right, Katie. Essence of onion?"

"Probably, but for what?"

"Well, maybe if she's not crying enough while she's being whipped, he gives her a whiff of this." She refastened the cap and set the vial back on the shelf. She picked up another. "Look at this one. Of all things it's called Man's Instrument. I guess that says it all."

Katie opened the lid and sniffed. "I wonder if a guy drinks it or rubs it on."

Sherlock said, "Probably drinks it. Here's one called Woman's Gift. Pills, big red pills. I wonder what they're for?"

"Maybe these pills assist the Man's Instrument?"

"Viagra?"

"Could be."

Katie said, "Well, it looks like there's more to this than I'd ever imagined. Nothing illegal, though."

"Even if we'd found a ton of cocaine, we couldn't arrest him for it. Let's go, Katie. I'd just as soon not be caught here by either the reverend or his wife."

"There's a thought that makes me shudder."

Sherlock said as she closed the cabinet doors and rearranged the tie racks, "I guess everybody has their own version of hair rollers."

They checked the third floor — former servants' quarters, what looked like an old schoolroom, and an unfinished attic, filled with enough old stuff for a garage sale, but no Clancy.

As they let themselves out the back door, Katie said, "Whatever I saw in that window, I guess it wasn't Clancy. I was just hoping for a sign of him, anything."

"I know. I wonder what you did see."

Katie shrugged. "Thanks for breaking the law with me, Sherlock."

"No problem. Let's just keep it between the two of us."

They were back in Katie's truck and in the McCamy driveway a good ten minutes before they saw Sooner and his wife drive by in their white Lincoln Town Car.

Sherlock said, "You'll note that the car's white, not black."

"These people," Katie said slowly, "aren't exactly your garden-variety preacher and spouse."

"You're right about that. Savich isn't going to believe this."

"I hope he doesn't laugh so hard he

bursts his stitches. Okay, you up for a chat with Reverend McCamy and his sex slave?"

16

Sherlock was fully prepared to greet Rasputin. She wasn't far off, except that Rasputin had been ill-kempt with long black matted hair, and evidently didn't bathe often. Reverend Sooner McCamy was dark, those eyes of his nearly black as a matter of fact. He was charming, if on the aloof side, and that was a surprise to Sherlock. He made eye contact, shook her hand firmly. He was courteous, offering coffee and some cheesecake his wife had made that morning, before church. But somehow he just didn't seem to be quite all there with them. He was away somewhere, in his head. And what was he thinking? He had a smooth deep voice — charismatic, that voice, it compelled you to listen. It was hypnotic, almost, and after hearing him speak for a few minutes, Sherlock understood his power over people.

This man appeared to have boiled himself down to the very essence of what a man of God should be. He frightened her for the simple reason that she could imagine some people hanging on his every word, maybe doing things they wouldn't normally do. Or maybe he gave them permission to do things they shouldn't want to do. Did disobedient wives listen to that voice and jump back on the straight and narrow?

Or was she over the top here? Sherlock didn't know. But he sure didn't seem like a man who would open any of those vials and apply the contents to either his wife or himself. He didn't look like a man who would whip his wife with one of those riding crops with their beautifully braided handles. If he was a Rasputin, if he was evil on the inside, he kept it hidden real deep. Sherlock had to remind herself that there were more layers to people than you could ever guess.

As for his looks, she could only say that if one believed in a handsome Satan, then Reverend McCamy would fit the bill. He was dark, his black hair a bit on the long side, a bit curly, and he had a heavy growth of beard, noticeable in the early afternoon.

He looked like a monk whose thoughts were so different from hers that they weren't even in the same world. He was in his fifties, but there was no white in his hair. Did he dye it? She didn't think so. He was slender, but that was all she could tell about his body. He was wearing a black suit, a very white shirt, and a black tie. He had good teeth, straight and white.

Elsbeth was very pretty, just as Katie had told her, and that hair of hers was glorious. Thick, rich natural blond, in loose waves down her back. She was wearing her Jesus earrings, as Katie called them. When she walked the crosses swung. She was tall and slender, but big-breasted. What made alarm bells go off for Sherlock was that the woman seemed to look at her husband as if he were a god. She looked like she'd jump up onto that marble slab and offer her wrists and ankles for the cuffs, and yell as loud as he wished when he applied a whip. Sherlock couldn't help wondering how she used that block of wood with one side padded with thick fur.

"I've heard that you've had some excitement, Sheriff. The little boy who was kidnapped, you rescued him?"

"Yes," Katie said as she sipped on Elsbeth's delicious coffee. "He's just fine now. How were morning services, Reverend McCamy?"

He said nothing, merely nodded, obviously pleased with how the morning services had gone. He took a cup of coffee from his wife, not looking away from Katie. Elsbeth said, barely above a whisper, "Two new parishioners found God this morning. Two."

Not by so much as a flick of his eyelids did Reverend McCamy acknowledge his wife's words. He then turned his attention to Sherlock, "I've never met an FBI agent before, Agent Sherlock. Why are you here?" He kept his eyes on Sherlock now, all his attention focused on her. When Sherlock purposefully nodded toward Elsbeth, he said, "You asked how services went this morning, Katie. I was pleased and gratified. I'd been counseling this couple for three weeks now. With encouragement and the endless love and understanding of God, they have found their way. By God's grace, they gave their souls to Him this morning."

He sipped his coffee. He looked out of place in this lovely living room with its human beings drinking coffee. Rasputin, Sherlock thought, he was a twenty-first-century Rasputin.

"Now, Agent Sherlock, Katie," Reverend McCamy said, "tell me why you're here. How may I help you?"

"Actually," Katie said, smiling toward Elsbeth, who was sitting demurely, her knees pressed together, her face utterly beautiful in the light shining in on her from the tall front windows, her Jesus earrings still and shiny, "we're here because of Elsbeth."

Elsbeth McCamy flinched, and the dreamy look fell right off her face. Just an instant, so fast Katie wasn't certain she'd even seen it. Fear. Her fingers fluttered. "Me? I don't understand, Katie. What could I possibly know that would help you? Surely, Reverend McCamy —"

Katie pulled out a fax with Clancy's photo. "Is this your brother, Elsbeth?"

Elsbeth shook her head, back and forth, sending the Jesus earrings dancing.

"Is he, Elsbeth?"

"Yes," she said, "that's Clancy. But I don't understand —"

"We've just found out this morning that one of the kidnappers is your brother, Elsbeth — Clancy Bird, now Clancy Edens. We found out he legally changed his name when he was younger. If you have any idea where he is, please tell us."

Elsbeth didn't move, didn't blink, didn't betray anything at all. She seemed to be waiting for Reverend McCamy to speak.

And he did. He took the photo from Katie and studied it. He nodded. "No one

185

in Jessborough knows that Elsbeth is cursed with such a worthless brother," Reverend McCamy said. "Naturally she hasn't seen him in years now."

Katie said, "That's too bad. We hoped you'd heard from him. He's badly hurt. He could die if we don't find him quickly."

"My husband is right, I haven't seen my brother in a very long time, Katie. I know he turned away from God when he was young, but he was always a support to me when I was a little girl."

"He protected you from your father?"

Elsbeth only nodded, looking down at her shoes. "He was a very bad man. Clancy protected me as best as he could. It was so many years ago." She raised pale blue eyes to Sherlock's face and touched her fingertips to a Jesus earring.

Sherlock said, "When did you last see Clancy?"

"He'd just been released from one of his stays in prison, some six years ago, I think. Naturally he was back in prison for something else after that. When I heard there were two men, one of them named Clancy, I never thought it could be my brother."

Elsbeth said, "Are you certain he kidnapped that little boy, Katie?"

Katie nodded. "Yes. We are certain that

186

your brother and a man named Beau Jones kidnapped Sam Kettering and brought him here. They kept him in Bleaker's cabin until the boy managed to escape."

Elsbeth's eyes dropped to her hands, now even more tightly clasped in her lap. "I heard about it, of course. Everyone in the congregation was talking about it. We stopped at the pharmacy this morning and Alice Hewett couldn't talk of anything else, particularly since she'd sold that other man some bandages."

Katie said, "He hasn't contacted either of you for help?"

"Oh no," Elsbeth said. "Why would he do that? Surely he must know that Reverend McCamy wouldn't help him. Why, he's a devout man of God. He feels deep pain at the actions of sinners."

Sherlock said, "All right, Mrs. McCamy. I can certainly understand wanting to help a brother just as I can understand a sister not wanting to help the police find him."

"Oh no! Lying is a sin. I wouldn't do that, ever. Just ask Reverend McCamy. I don't ever lie."

Reverend Sooner McCamy said, "I assure you, my wife doesn't lie. Now, Agent Sherlock, Clancy hasn't called either of us. If he's guilty of kidnapping that little boy, both Elsbeth and I hope that you catch him and send him back to prison."

Sherlock said, "If he wouldn't call you, Mrs. McCamy, then do you have any idea whom he might contact? Does he have any friends close by? Family?"

Elsbeth shook her head. "Clancy doesn't know anyone in these parts."

Except you, Sherlock thought. *Only you.*

"How do you think he knew about Bleaker's cabin?"

"I don't know, Katie."

Katie said, "Thank you for speaking with us. If Clancy does contact you, Elsbeth, if he does ask you to hide him, if he does ask you for money, I hope you will call me immediately. You heard, I know, that his partner, Beau Jones, died last night."

"We heard that you shot him, Katie," Reverend McCamy said. "You killed him."

Sherlock heard the cold disapproval in his voice, no chance of missing it. Why?

"Hurting a man, actually killing a man, it's very bad," Elsbeth said, clearly distressed.

Katie said, "There wasn't a choice, Elsbeth. He would have killed someone else if I hadn't stopped him. Now it's Clancy who's in danger. There's a huge manhunt going on right now for him, as I'm sure both of you know. I really don't see this ending well for Clancy if you don't help us find him."

Elsbeth said, her voice shaking, nearly on the verge of tears, "I'm sorry, Katie. I don't have any idea where Clancy could be. I don't understand why he would kidnap a little boy and bring him here to Jessborough."

Sherlock said, "Obviously Bleaker's cabin is a good out-of-the-way place to store a kidnap victim. But it has to be more than that. Most likely someone locally wanted Sam Kettering brought here."

Katie said, "It's all quite a mystery. There was no ransom note left, no calls made in the two days he was gone from his home in Virginia."

Sherlock said, "Do you have any idea at all why your brother would bring Sam here, Mrs. McCamy? Other than to use Bleaker's cabin?"

Elsbeth looked from Katie to Sherlock. Then she said to her husband, "Reverend McCamy, you know that I know nothing about any of this. Could you make them believe me, please?"

"Well, the thing is, Elsbeth," Katie said before the reverend could jump in, although, truth be told, he didn't look like he was even very interested. No, fact was, he looked like he wasn't really here. "You're the only one Clancy knows in the area. Someone also reported seeing a man who looked like him near your house. I think that's enough to have a judge issue a warrant to search your house, unless, of course, you give us permission to look around right now?"

Sherlock saw that Reverend McCamy was back, all of his focus, all of his brain was back in the living room, and he knew he had a problem. He stood, looking like an avenging prophet. "You may not search my house, Agent, Sheriff. Get your godless warrant, but I really doubt you'll be able to talk a judge into it." Of course, he realized that any search would turn up his party room, and the good Lord knew that would never do.

Their chances were about nil for getting a warrant and the good reverend knew it.

For just an instant, Katie was reminded of Carlo Silvestri, her ex-husband, standing there all arrogant and righteous, just like Reverend McCamy, looking at her like she wasn't worthy to polish his shoes.

"You mean," Katie said, rising as well, "that Benson Carlysle won't grant a warrant. His brother's a member of your church, isn't he?"

"Yes. He's a good man, a fair man. He and his wife are devout members. His brother won't allow you to harass my wife and me just because someone thought he saw her brother near here."

Elsbeth said, every muscle tensed, desperate to convince them, "Even if Clancy was here, hiding, naturally, he's certainly not here now, and we knew nothing about it in any case. He's got to know that I can't have anything to do with him."

"I see," Sherlock said, and rose to stand beside Katie.

Reverend McCamy said, "Good day, Agent Sherlock, Sheriff Benedict. You do not believe what I believe. You do not behave as women should behave. I would like you to leave. I don't want my wife tainted with your presence, your suspicions, your lack of grace. However, if Clancy does contact Elsbeth, rest assured that I will call you."

Katie dug a card out of her shirt pocket and gave it to Elsbeth. "Good. Understand, Elsbeth, if Clancy does call you, you might be able to save his life. If he doesn't turn himself in he probably won't survive. You don't want him dead."

Elsbeth's eyes filled with tears, beautiful

sparkling tears. She began to moan and rock back and forth on her chair. "Of course I don't want him dead. It's a sin to want somebody dead. And he's my brother."

Katie fanned her hands in front of her, so impatient she snapped out, "Elsbeth, I'm not planning on gunning for Clancy at high noon, but I'll do what I have to do to bring him in. Now, thank you for the coffee. Remember, the chances of Clancy living through this decrease by the minute."

Sherlock and Katie walked themselves to the door, Elsbeth's sobs echoing behind them. Sherlock couldn't help herself. She turned a moment to see Reverend Sooner McCamy standing in the middle of the light-filled living room, a portrait in black and white, his face impassive, his dark eyes burning.

Sherlock said to Katie as she started up her truck, "He never asked who it was claiming to see Clancy near his house."

"No, he didn't, did he?"

17

"He's Rasputin."

Savich had popped a pain pill ten minutes before so he was easily able to smile at his wife.

"Yes, but what did you really think?"

"He's scary."

"In what way?"

"He's not quite here. It's like he's into an inner self where there's only his God and what he owes his God and what he can do to get other people to worship his God. The thing is, I'm not sure he includes women or if it's just men's souls that interest him."

Savich said, "An otherworldly sexist. He sounds too preoccupied with himself to be a kidnapper."

"Yeah, you're right, he does. But I haven't heard much condemnation about his ideas out of you yet."

"Hmmm."

"Why don't you yell and holler that it isn't fair, that you denounce it, that you spit upon such notions?"

"It's not fair," Savich said. "I can't spit because it would hurt my back. This guy sounds very strange, sweetheart."

"Yes, he is. He's very intense, as I said, like Rasputin or, more to the point, some descendant of Rasputin. Now, since Katie and I didn't have a warrant, we just sort of wandered around outside their big Victorian house, which is really quite beautiful, and would you just look at what fell out of a window."

"Fell out of a window? Yes, if I close my eyes I can see it falling right at your feet. Come on, what have you got?"

Sherlock tossed him a vial and told him about the hidden room off the small bedroom closet.

He read the label. Salvation. He blinked, unscrewed the top and sniffed the liquid, which had a faint almond scent. "Sex with a religious theme? Are you planning on drinking this, Sherlock? Have things gotten this bad?"

She laughed, hugged him very carefully, kissed his mouth. He fastened the cap back on the vial and handed it back to her. "When all this dies down, let's send it to the lab and see what's in this salvation stuff."

"Maybe we can find out if it's manufactured or if the reverend makes it himself. There were about a dozen other vials, all with charming names like this one. I know I shouldn't have taken it but I just couldn't resist." When she finished telling him about the whips and the green marble altar and the wooden block, he said as he looked down at his fingernails, "You wonder what that wooden block with the fur on top is for?"

"Well, I'm not going to chew off my fingernails if I don't find out, but yeah, I'd like to know."

"It's to pad your stomach."

"What? To pad . . . oh goodness, I see now. You know, Dillon, big hair rollers are one thing, but being propped up on a wooden block is quite another. No, I don't think so. Has Dr. Able been around to see you? I want to get you out of here."

"Yes, he has. I'm fine, just need to sit forward for the next year or so. Stitches come out next week. You ready to break me out of this place? I was just waiting for you to get here."

Sherlock said over her shoulder as she fetched him the clothes she'd brought from home, "Yes, but we're in a bit of a pickle, aren't we? We have no idea why Sam was brought to Jessborough and we don't know yet who hired Clancy and Beau to bring him here. The investigation is just starting. Clancy's still out there and we need to help. I think, too, that Sam and Miles probably need to remain with us. It's dangerous for Sam and Miles to go back home alone, don't you think?"

"Yes, we'll stay," Savich said, and got himself dressed. "Don't worry about a few more days. Mr. Maitland called a little while ago, told me to take it easy, not to worry about the math teacher killings."

He looked big and tough, much more like himself with his leather jacket slung over his arm. Sherlock beamed him a brilliant smile. "Can I kiss you?"

"Yeah, but don't tease me, Sherlock." He carefully put his arms around her, nuzzled her neck. "You know, I just might be ready for some hair rollers tonight. I wish we had time to check out what's in that vial, just maybe it's something we can use."

At five minutes after three o'clock that afternoon, five FBI agents, one former FBI agent, one sheriff, and two children congregated in Sheriff Benedict's living room.

If Butch Ashburn wondered why two young children were present during a meeting, he didn't say anything, just watched the little girl for a moment — the sheriff's kid — playing with a big-eared rabbit named Ollie. His own kid was now nearly twenty, but he could remember when she'd have been on the floor playing with a stuffed animal. The years just swept over you too fast, he thought, leaving you older and slower, and your little kid a grown-up.

"I'm thinking," Savich said, "that I want to go to church. Does Reverend McCamy have a service this evening, Katie?"

"Yes, he goes all day on Sunday. The church is really nice, sort of like Paul Revere's church in Boston. Sooner also does tent revivals — every June, out in Grossley's pasture, about three miles west of Jessborough."

Katie glanced over at Miles, who still looked dead on his feet. All his attention was on his boy. After she'd dropped Sherlock off at the hospital a couple of hours before, she'd taken Miles and the kids out to Kmart to buy some clothes. Miles was wearing the black jeans, boots, and plaid flannel shirt he'd bought. He looked, she realized, really good. As for Sam, he looked like a miniature copy of his father, down to the black boots.

"Papa forgot to pack clothes for us,"

Sam had confided to her earlier in the truck. "He didn't think about anything else, he just wanted to get to me as fast as he could."

"I wouldn't have packed anything either," Katie said, smiling at Miles. "Not with a Kmart in the neighborhood."

Of course, Keely had to have black jeans and black boots, and her mother, knowing when to throw in the towel, had given in.

Butch Ashburn said to Savich, "If you and Sherlock plan on staying in Jessbborough for a while, I think Jody and I will head back to Washington. We're still running checks and interviewing all neighbors and employees, and I want to check Beau Jones's apartment myself. If there's a tie-in to Jessborough, we'll find it. Also, since Miles is former FBI, we're checking particularly violent cases he was involved in. I don't buy the idea of revenge myself, but we're checking everything." He looked over at Sam, who'd just taken a big bite of fried chicken. "I'm more pleased than I can say, Miles, that you've got such a brave, smart boy."

Miles swallowed, then nodded, and said sharply, "Sam, don't wipe your greasy fingers on your new jeans. Use the napkin."

Life, Butch thought, was always unexpected and even, sometimes, like now, not bad at all. He said, "You guys work on a connection from this end and, like I said, I'll work the other end. Hopefully, we'll meet in the middle real soon."

Katie smiled at Special Agent Butch Ashburn — *no wing tips on my neck from this guy.*

Fifteen minutes after a telephone call, Katie's mother, Minna Bushnell Benedict, arrived to take charge of the children. She won Sam over with a chocolate chip cookie the size of Manhattan, and assured both Miles and Katie that she'd keep both Sam and Keely safe, with the help of the two deputies seated in their cruiser just outside the house.

"Butch, you have a safe trip back to Washington. Miles, Katie, we're off to meet the Sinful Children of God," Savich said, and took Sherlock's hand. "Maybe we can talk to some of the congregation before the service starts."

"Find Fatso," Sam called after his father as they went out the front door. "Shoot him."

The church of the Sinful Children of God was on Sycamore Road. Katie was right, it looked like the Old North Church in Boston — a tall wooden spire, painted all white, the roof sharply raked with shingles, the windows small and traditional.

There were maybe twenty cars parked in the paved lot behind the church, which was set back from the road, at the edge of a thick stand of maple and oak trees. And Miles found himself marveling yet again at how many trees there were in this part of the country.

The church was nearly full, maybe as many as fifty, sixty people. Men were in suits, women in dresses, hats on their heads. Children sat quietly beside their parents. The four of them sat down in the back. A couple Katie didn't recognize scooted farther down the bench, not speaking to them.

Katie realized, as she looked around at all those well-dressed people, that she didn't know very many of them. She wondered from how far away they came. It took her a while to recognize Thomas Boone, the postman, because he looked different in a suit. There was Bea Hipple, an expert quilter, sitting only shoulder high to her husband, Benny, a local mechanic. For the life of her, Katie couldn't imagine Bea being all that submissive.

She knew maybe twenty-five of the adults in the congregation, no more than that. The organist finished "Amazing Grace." Throats cleared, papers rustled, and then the church fell quiet. Hearing "Amazing Grace" played in church always made Katie, hard-assed sheriff or not, get tears in her eyes.

Reverend Sooner McCamy rose from his high-backed chair to walk up the winding stairs to the pulpit that was set on a six-foot-high dais. He stood there for a few seconds, looking out. He was wearing a lovely white robe over a black suit and white shirt.

Reverend McCamy wrapped his large hands around the corners of the beautifully worked pulpit. They were strong hands, nicely formed, with short buffed nails, black hair visible on the backs even from a distance. When he spoke, his voice reached to every corner of the room, forceful and deep. Katie was aware that people were sitting at attention now, leaning forward a bit so as to not miss a word.

"I welcome all of you back again for our evening service. It has been a full, rewarding day, and a very unusual one as well. My wife and I spoke with Sheriff

Benedict and an FBI agent at our home at noon. It seems that Elsbeth's brother, Clancy, is wanted for questioning in the kidnapping of the little boy who managed to escape. Yes, Clancy Edens is indeed my wife's brother. I would ask that if any of you know of this very man's whereabouts to call the sheriff. I've been told there are posters of him all over Jessborough."

He never broke eye contact with Katie while he spoke. She found herself nodding as one by one, the congregation turned to look at her.

Reverend McCamy paused a moment, looking, it seemed, at each of his congregation. He said finally, "Our spirits need constant nourishment, just as our bodies do. We recognize this need even if we don't understand how to bring deep into ourselves the nourishment our souls require. We must pray that Clancy Edens finds the nourishment tonight."

"Amen. Amen."

"We must all first realize there is a common bond among right-thinking men, men who recognize there is something more to living than being a part of the human herd, something beyond us. It is something more precious than life itself, something that can bring us all infinite understanding and peace. And these men know that this something is our beloved God, and that it is He who is our spiritual nourishment, He who brings value to our lives, He who makes us know the path we must tread. Let us pray for him tonight, brothers, pray that he seeks this path with us."

"Amen . . . amen . . . amen."

"It is we men who must lead, who must show these sinners, as we show our precious helpmates, the way to grace and salvation, ensuring God's forgiveness for their eternal sin. All of you seated before God and His messenger here this evening know that we each have a role in this life, some of leadership and some of submission. Both will free us. I exhort all of you: Seek always to understand what it is you must be and what you must do. Let nothing stop you from attaining what it is God wants you to have, what God wants of you."

Only men can understand God? Sherlock felt Dillon lightly touching his fingertips to her arm. When she turned, he was smiling. Then he winked at her.

"There are special graces that God grants a few men on this earth that allow them to be special victims of God's grace, to actually experience his own sacrifice for all of our sins."

Victims of God's grace? What did that mean? Sherlock tuned him out until some five minutes later, when Reverend Mc-Camy said suddenly, "Now it's time for us to divide into our Sunday evening study groups. Our topic for discussion this evening will be 'Submitting to the Path of God's Grace.'"

Katie looked at Miles, her head cocked to one side. His dark eyes were glittering, narrowed on Reverend McCamy's face. His hands were fisted, one on his thigh. She smoothed his fisted hand with her own, feeling the tension slowly ease. She would ask him what he was thinking later. It had been smart of the reverend to be up front about Elsbeth McCamy's brother, very smart indeed. She wondered if the good reverend would have said a word about Sam's kidnapping if the four of them hadn't trooped into his service.

After the congregation split into groups, Sherlock made a request to join them. Reverend McCamy looked infinitely patient. "I'm sorry, Agent Sherlock, but you must be a believer and member of this church before you can attend our study groups. Why did you come?" He looked at all of them in turn, one very black eyebrow arched up, a bit of a satyr's look, if he but knew.

Katie introduced Savich and Miles Kettering.

Reverend McCamy said nothing, merely nodded at them. He gave Miles a long look, then he looked down at the ring on his third finger — an odd ring, thick, heavy-looking, silver with some sort of carving on top. The carving was deep black. Sherlock couldn't make out what it was. Surely this monstrosity couldn't be his wedding ring.

Reverend McCamy said, "Special Agent Savich. You appear to be hurt."

How had he known that? No, that was easy, Savich thought, likely everyone in town was talking about how the federal agent got his back sliced open by a flying piece of van. Savich removed his hand from the reverend's. "Just a bit."

Reverend McCamy said, "I will direct all our congregation to include you in their prayers. Sheriff, you've known some of these folk all your life. You know they'll help if they can. Now, if you'll excuse me, I must attend to my children."

Katie looked over toward Thomas Boone and remembered a scene in the post office between him and a Mr. Phelan.

They'd been arguing about the church and Reverend McCamy. She wanted to speak to Mr. Phelan.

After Katie dropped Savich and Sherlock off at Mother's Very Best, Savich looking like he was nearly ready to drop in his tracks, she and Miles went for a cup of coffee at Maude's Burgers. Maude herself, tall, skinny as a post, with big white teeth, served them. Bless her heart, she didn't say a word about the kidnapping.

"It's an amazing thing," Miles said as he sipped his black coffee. "In the space of a day and a half, I went from absolute despair to euphoria to something like dread. Do you think Clancy is still here?"

Katie nodded as she stirred some cream into her coffee. "He's hiding somewhere."

"You think the reverend and his wife know where he is?"

"I wish I could say yes, but actually I haven't the slightest idea if they do. You're a former FBI agent. What do you think?"

"As I said, I've only been here for a day."

"What field office were you assigned to?"

"Actually, I stayed in Washington along with Savich after we met at the academy. I was in the Information and Evidence Management Unit."

"You dealt with forensics."

He nodded as he looked through the big front windows out onto Main Street. "My father wasn't pleased with my choice of career, but to his credit, he encouraged me endlessly. When he died, I realized that it was time to make a change. Fact is, I was getting burned out. I remember reading John Douglas's book and being struck to my gut when he wrote about his wife cutting her finger. He wrote that what he paid attention to was the way the blood splattered, not his wife's injury. It could have been me. So, when my father died, I resigned and took over my father's business. I've been doing it now for five years." He paused a moment, sipped his coffee, closed his eyes, and said, "Fact is, I like it, and I'm good at it."

"What is it?"

"We design and build parts for helicopters, like guidance systems, primarily for the army, but we've built components for all the other branches of the military as well. I'll tell you though, after some of our negotiations with the military agencies, I thought life was easier at the Bureau."

She laughed, and realized she liked this man. It had been so very long since she'd even looked at a man and actually saw that he was male, a male to admire and make her laugh. It felt rather good, actually. Carlo had burned her to the ground, the bastard.

18

The house was quiet. All was well. Katie had made coffee for the deputies, double-checked all the locks, and looked in on Keely before sinking down beneath three blankets on a bed so soft she was convinced her mother had ordered it for her from heaven. Miles was with Sam, who had on his new, spiffy red Mickey Mouse pajamas. Miles hadn't bought anything so she guessed he was sleeping in his shorts. Now, that was a strange thought. She hadn't thought about a man's shorts in a very long time. Boxers? Katie grinned and nodded. Yeah, she'd bet he wore boxers.

Miles lay on his back, feeling Sam's heartbeat against his side, and his soft hair smooth against his neck. He still wasn't over the debilitating fear he'd felt for those endless hours before Katie had called. He wondered if he'd ever be over it. They'd been lucky, so damned lucky. He pulled Sam tighter and felt him wheeze a bit in his sleep. No nightmares, so far. He'd have to keep a real close eye on that.

Miles was so tired he felt like his skin was inside out and his brain was in a fog bank. Yet he couldn't seem to shut down and sleep. So he lay there, listening to his boy breathe.

He closed his eyes and thanked Alicia yet again for encouraging Sam to get himself out of that cabin window. He'd wondered many times if she really was keeping a close eye on her son from the other side, if there was an other side, but if there wasn't, how had Sam heard her voice? Miles knew it was Sam's subconscious that had prodded him, but it was still somehow reassuring to believe, if even for a moment, that her love for her son overcame the silence and separation of death.

The air was soft, warm. He would swear he felt a brief touch of fingertips on his cheek. He smiled as he closed his eyes.

He had no idea how much time had passed. But one moment he was thinking about the problems with the new rotor blade design on the army's new Proto A587 helicopter, and the next he was alert, ready to move. He lay there, listening.

There was a scraping sound.

It stopped. Then nothing.

Surely Clancy wouldn't come back to try yet again to get Sam. There were two cops sitting just around at the front of the house.

It was probably just a branch whispering against the side of the house in the night wind.

No different sounds now, nothing at all.

Miles drew a deep breath, and settled in again. He imagined he'd be hearing things for many years to come.

"Hold yourself real still, Mr. Kettering."

Miles's heart nearly seized. His eyes flew open. He looked up into Clancy's shadowed face, and pulled Sam closer.

"Yeah, I saw you wake up. Then I decided to wait just another minute, and sure enough, you were out again."

Miles didn't want to wake Sam. He whispered to that round white face above him, "What the hell are you doing here? How did you get past the cops outside?"

Clancy grinned, and Miles saw he hadn't escaped scot free from the van. He had a split lip with some dried blood on it, his cheek was swollen and covered with three Band-Aids. There was another cut over his left eyebrow, a Band-Aid patched vertically over it. His right arm wasn't in a sling, but he was holding it stiffly against his side.

Miles felt the muzzle of the gun, sharp and cold against his neck. Clancy leaned his face real close to Miles's, and he smelled Clancy's breath — salami and beer. He said, real low, "It was easy as kicking dirt. They were nearly unconscious last time I checked. By now, they might be dead, the morons. I've worked enough on cars to know about what not to do with a car exhaust. Pretty dangerous things, if you don't know what you're doing. Yep, nothing so easy as the car exhaust. Easy as cooking a hot dog. You see, the bozos kept the car turned on because they were too wussy to take the cold. That was when I knew exactly what to do."

"You murdered two people just to get to Sam?"

"That's right, Mr. Kettering. What's your point?"

"Who's paying you to do this? Who?"

"Well now, Mr. Kettering, that just isn't any of your business, now, is it?"

"You have to know this is insane, Clancy. Half the state is looking for you. There's no way you'll get away with Sam, no way at all."

"You know, Mr. Kettering, with all your yapping, I'm wondering if I shouldn't just pop you now." The muzzle dug in. Miles didn't move, barely breathed, and he thought, *I can't die, I can't. I have to protect*

Sam. He thought of Katie just down the hall, asleep. If Sam could hear his mother, then why the hell couldn't he talk to Katie? He did, and then focused himself again. He was an idiot, a desperate idiot. Sam was too close for him to try to make a move. And it appeared that Clancy had nothing at all to lose. Who was paying him so much money that he just couldn't give up? He felt the muzzle stroking his neck now.

"You don't look too good, Clancy. I'm surprised you're even walking around. I saw the van explode. It was a burning hell."

"When the sheriff fired I slammed into that tree and knocked myself silly, but just for a minute. I saw the sheriff kill Beau and got the hell out of the van. Yeah, I wanted to pop all of you, destroying my van like that."

But Clancy didn't pull the trigger. So Clancy didn't want to kill him just yet, thank God. Why not? No silencer, that was why, and this was not the time for gunfire.

Then Miles realized Clancy wanted him alive so he could carry Sam. He wanted two hostages. *Then he'll kill me once he's gotten us away from here.*

Miles didn't even blink. He tried to

213

unfreeze his muscles and his heart after the immense jolt of fear that had shut him down for a moment.

"Wake up the boy, Mr. Kettering. I won't ask twice."

He did, lightly stroking Sam's cheek, speaking quietly to him, telling him not to be afraid, everything would be all right.

Sam's eyes opened, focused on Clancy. "You're a bad man," Sam said, that little voice strong.

"Hello there, you little brat. Too bad you're so valuable, I'd sure like to twist off your head. You got Beau killed, and I'm going to have to pay you back for that."

"Why do you want him so badly, Clancy?"

"I just might tell you some day," Clancy said. "Not that I necessarily believe it." He took a couple of steps back to stand at the end of the bed, his gun aimed directly at Sam.

"Don't even think of trying anything, Mr. Kettering, or I'll shoot the boy. Believe me on this. I ain't got nothin' to lose here. Both of you get up now. You might as well put some clothes on, Mr. Kettering, it's pretty cold out there. The kid's just fine in his pajamas." He fell silent, watching them. "Hey, I wonder if those deputies are croaked yet. Shouldn't be long if they aren't already. We just might take their car, what do you think?"

"Why would you do that? How did you get here?"

"Never you mind about that."

Miles said, "Sam, I want you to get out of bed real slow. Stand over there, okay?"

"Papa —"

"Do as I say. Everything will be all right, I promise you that."

Clancy laughed under his breath. He watched Sam slide away from his father, off the side of the bed. He stood there, in his red pajamas.

"Hey, Mickey Mouse, those are neat," Clancy said. "Now you, Mr. Kettering. I want you to be real careful. You see where I'm aiming now? Right at the kid's head. I'll kill him if you force me to."

But would he really? Miles didn't think so. Whoever had hired Clancy wanted Sam too badly, but he wasn't about to take the chance. Miles eased out of the covers and swung his legs over the side of the bed. He was wearing only his boxer shorts. The air was chilly. Slowly, he stood. Clancy threw him his jeans. He pulled them on, fastened them. He held out his hand. "My sweater's over there."

Clancy tossed it to him. When he had it pulled over his head, Clancy said, "No shoes. I don't want you trying to make a break for it. Now, put your hands behind your neck."

Miles laced his fingers behind his head.

"Okay, now, you walk out of here first, Mr. Kettering. Sam, you follow your dad. Do it, now. Keep walking. Kid, you behave yourself."

He doesn't want Sam dead, Miles kept thinking. Everything hinges on his taking Sam alive. But why? All Miles needed was an opening, a small lapse on Clancy's part, and he could take him. He held himself ready, listened to every breath Clancy drew, realized he didn't breathe easily because he was so heavy, and he was hurt. Just how badly, Miles couldn't guess. He watched Clancy's gun, watched how it remained aimed at Sam's head.

Miles walked slowly down the hall. He barely heard Sam's steps behind him because he was wearing a nice thick pair of Katie's socks. They were nearly to Katie's bedroom door.

This is easy, Clancy, so easy. You can relax a bit, can't you now? You've got us.

They reached the living room in utter silence. Moonlight showed through the front window that wasn't boarded up. Not much, but enough so no one would trip over anything.

Slowly, Clancy motioned Miles to move aside. He grabbed Sam's arm and dragged him toward the front door.

"Papa —"

"Shut up, you little varmint!"

He held Sam with one hand, realized that he couldn't turn the dead bolt with a gun in his other hand, and stood there a minute, wondering what to do.

"Come here, Mr. Kettering. I want you to open that door or I'll hurt your kid."

He pulled Sam back against his stomach.

Miles walked to the front door and unfastened the locks.

"Open it."

Miles opened the front door. The night wind rushed in, cool, sharp.

"Put your hands behind your head and walk."

Miles stopped at the edge of the wide porch that wrapped around the house, touched his bare toe against a rocking chair leg.

"Well, go on down. We'll check out those cops, see if they're dead yet. Then we'll take their car. I still can't believe that damned sheriff ruined my van."

"How did you get back here, Clancy?"

"I already told you, that ain't none of your business, buddy. Walk down those damned stairs!"

Clancy had to know that he was running out of time. Miles had to see exactly where Sam was before he moved. Clancy and Sam were just in his peripheral vision behind him, just off to the right. Clancy had his arm around Sam's neck, held him tightly against his side.

On the second step, Miles yelled, "Drop, Sam!"

Sam went limp and dropped to the ground. In the same instant Miles turned and kicked out, his foot crushing Clancy's injured arm. The gun went flying.

Clancy screamed even as he grabbed Sam by his neck and lifted him off the ground, twisting, holding him away from him. Miles kicked again, this time in the middle of his chest. Clancy dropped Sam and went flying back, grabbing his chest, unable to breathe.

At that moment, Katie came through the open doorway, barefoot, her SIG Sauer in both hands in front of her.

She yelled, as she crouched, "Hold it, Clancy!"

"I've got him," Miles said, and she saw

that he was smiling of all things, an awful smile that held raw hate and triumph.

As he moved toward Clancy, he yelled, "Katie, check the deputies. There's gas in the car, hurry!"

Miles smashed his palm into Clancy's nose, and brought his knee up hard into his crotch.

Clancy screamed and went down onto his knees, holding himself. Katie literally jumped over Clancy and went flying off the porch, and Miles winced as her bare feet struck stone and gravel, but she didn't slow. She jerked open the passenger's side door and pulled the deputy out onto the ground, then ran to the driver's side, and dragged the other man out as well.

Clancy, still bent over, staggered to his feet, his eyes on Sam, who was on his hands and knees, scooting backward toward the edge of the porch.

"It's okay, Sam." Miles jumped toward him and slammed his fist into Clancy's jaw. He felt the skin on his knuckles split, but it felt good, sending this monster into oblivion with his bare fist. He watched him fall senseless, then turned to see Katie bent over one of the deputies, listening for a breath. Sam was sitting on the edge of the porch, huddled over, not saying a word.

"Mama?"

"It's okay, Keely," Miles said. "You stay in the house, okay? Your mom will get you in just a minute. Don't move, Keely. You, too, Sam, go inside to Keely. Katie, do I need to see to the other deputy?"

Before Katie answered, she saw that Clancy was down, not moving, not even moaning and was lying on his side, facing the house. She didn't have any cuffs and couldn't leave Cole here, possibly dying. It was okay, Clancy was down and out.

"Miles, you got him good. Hurry!"

Miles kicked Clancy just to make sure he was really unconscious, and pushed his gun in his pants. "Come with me, Sam. We've got to help the deputies."

Katie raised her head a moment to say, "Cole's not dead! He's breathing!" before she moved over to the other man. Miles was aware that Keely was standing over her mom, just as Sam was standing next to him. He quickly looked toward the porch. Clancy hadn't twitched. "Sam, run inside and get my cell phone and bring it to me."

When Sam handed Miles his cell, he punched 911. A short time later, they heard sirens loud in the still night.

The paramedics immediately covered

the deputies' noses and mouths with oxygen masks. "It looks to me like that was close," said Mackey. He cocked a brow at Katie. "I'd call this a crime spree, Sheriff. You're really keeping us busy. You and the kids okay?"

"I think so." She pointed to Clancy. "For a fat guy, he moves as quietly as a cat burglar. I have no idea what sort of shape he's in, though. Mr. Kettering didn't pull any punches. But he's alive, and that's the important thing. Now we'll find out who hired him. We'll need you all to transport him once we've got you a police escort."

"Nuts," Mackey said. "The jerk must be just plain nuts."

Wade showed up not five minutes later, jeans pulled over his pajamas, his shirt hanging open. "Jesus, Katie, you got him! By damn, you got the bastard."

"Actually, Miles got him. He's got some good moves. Go cuff him, Wade."

Miles was elated and exhausted. He walked to the children who were both sitting on the edge of the porch, went down on his haunches and pulled them both against his chest. He kissed Sam, then Keely, again and again. "I'm so proud of you both."

"I want Mama," Keely said against Miles's armpit.

"Let her do her job, then she'll be over here. You just hold on to me, okay?

"Sam?"

Sam burrowed closer.

"Sam? You all right?"

Sam didn't say a thing. He didn't even blink when Clancy staggered to his feet, knocked Wade off the porch, jumped onto the driveway, and disappeared into the darkness.

Katie cursed a blue streak, and ran after him. Miles leaped off the porch after her. Both of them were still barefoot. Miles heard Wade cursing, couldn't make out his words.

Then dead silence.

He heard a gunshot.

Then more dead silence.

19

Miles watched Dr. Sheila Raines from across Katie's living room speaking quietly to Sam. He wasn't moving, wasn't meeting her eyes. His small hands were restless, pulling on his jeans, scratching his elbow, punching one of the sofa cushions.

"He's hardly spoken a single word," he said to Katie, who was sitting next to him, holding Keely in her arms, the little girl was sprawled out, asleep. Miles barely got the words out. "Too much has happened to him, just too much. And we still have no idea who is after him, and why. And that's the biggest mystery: why go through all this misery to get ahold of one little boy? Twice now they've come after him after he escaped them. Twice! And tonight Clancy came after him all by himself, and he was wounded. It makes no sense at all to me.

"If his kidnapping was for money, then why was there no ransom note? They had almost two days, surely that was enough time to make their demands known to me." He paused a moment, streaking his fingers through his hair. "I was certain it was a pedophile who'd taken him, but no, that isn't the case, and I thank God for that. And I'm as certain as I can be that no one, not even the crooks I caught when I was an FBI agent, would want revenge against me this badly. And if someone did, then why not just shoot me? That would be easy enough to do. Why then, for God's sake?

"Jesus, this whole thing is over the top. And look at Sam, silent, his eyes blank like he's really not here, like he doesn't want to be here because it's too scary, and he has all this terror locked inside him."

Katie touched his shoulder. "It's a terrible thing, what he's been through," she said. "But you know, Miles, even with the short time I've known Sam, I know he's resilient. He's a very strong little boy. Be patient. Sheila is very good. Have some faith.

"Now the motive. There is one, you know that, Miles. There always is. It's just not obvious to us yet, and just maybe we wouldn't necessarily understand it, but there is a motive, obviously a very strong one to the person or persons who had Sam kidnapped, given all the lengths Clancy and Beau have gone to. We'll keep digging and we'll find it, I promise you."

It was as if he hadn't heard her. "And it's not over," he said, still looking toward his son, "not by a long shot. Clancy is dead, and with him the name of whoever is behind this. But they're still out there, I know it and you know it, Katie. And they'll try again, you know that, too. Why stop now?"

"To be honest," Katie said after a moment, "I don't think Clancy would have said a word. Didn't you tell me that you were certain he planned to kill you after he had Sam again?"

Miles nodded. He began rubbing Keely's foot in its bright pink sock, so small, just like Sam's.

"Even so he still wouldn't tell you who hired him to do this."

"No." Miles happened to look down. Katie was still barefoot, wearing only jeans and her nightshirt with *Benedict Pulp: Non-fiction* printed across the front.

He looked down at his own bare feet and saw several cuts. He hadn't even noticed until now. He'd see to them, but not yet, not just yet. Her feet were cut, too. Who cared about feet? He looked again at Sam and Dr. Raines. His boy wasn't moving. He just sat there, looking at nothing in particular, moving his hands.

Savich and Sherlock arrived ten minutes later. Both of them hugged Sam, met Dr. Sheila Raines, then left them alone again.

Sherlock said, "You guys tell Savich what happened while I take care of the bloody feet in this room. You got a first-aid kit, Katie?"

Katie looked at her, face completely blank. She repeated, "First-aid kit?"

"Yes, so I can clean up your feet. Both you and Miles."

Katie blinked, reminded of the cuts on her feet, and shook her head at herself. "Yes, in the kitchen, in the cabinet above the fridge."

A few minutes later, Sherlock looked up to see Katie walking gingerly into the kitchen.

"Where's Keely?"

"I gave her to Miles. I think it helps him to hold her. It's bad, Sherlock, Sam isn't speaking at all. But I trust Sheila, she's got a gift, particularly with kids. She's able to clue right into what they're feeling — their fears and where they're lurking, and how to lessen them. She's really good. Plus I've known her all my life. She's loaded with common sense —" Katie's voice caught and tears filled her eyes.

Sherlock looked at her a moment, put down the first-aid kit she'd just pulled down from a top shelf, and held out her arms. "Come here, Katie."

Katie walked into her arms. It was silly, really, particularly since she was bigger than Sherlock, but it felt good to be held, to know that Sherlock understood what she was feeling, it made a difference. She whispered against Sherlock's hair, "I've killed two men — two — since last night. I've been sheriff of Jessborough for three years now and I've never shot anyone before. Our idea of local crime here is shoplifting and maybe twenty-five DUIs a year. Mainly we herd Mr. James's cows back into his pasture, pull Mr. Murray out from under the tractor that fell on him, tug Mrs. McCulver's rat terrier off the postman, and keep traffic smooth on the Fourth of July. I've never seen a murder or a kidnapping, at least not here. This is a peaceful town. Now this."

"I know," Sherlock said, stroking her hair. "I know it's been a shock, not only to you but to all of us. But you did exactly what you had to do to end it. You saved Sam, I mean you really saved him. Just think about what would have happened if you hadn't been with Sam. Do you think now that you had a choice? In either case?"

Katie shook her head against Sherlock's face.

"Good. Now, I expect Sam to always be there for you. He owes you his life. He can push your wheelchair or help you dodder around when you're old and drooly."

Katie laughed, despite herself. "The image of that," she said, straightening, "makes me want to both laugh and cry."

Sherlock cupped Katie's face between her hands. "The realization that you, no one else, just you, put an end to someone's life — you have to just look at Sam to know you did the right thing when it counted."

"Have you ever killed anyone, Sherlock?"

"No, I haven't, but I wanted to once, real bad. Someday I'll tell you about Marlin Jones. Dillon has, and he told me it dug right into his gut. There was one time he wasn't sorry at all, when he shot a real madman, Tommy Tuttle. But you see, he got over it because he realized that a law officer has to be able, intellectually and emotionally, to get the job done." She paused a moment, and looked disappointed. "I'm really sorry we weren't here to help you take care of Clancy."

Katie smiled. "Yeah, I wish you'd been here, too. He managed to break the locks on the back door, came right up the stairs and I didn't hear him. None of us believed it could happen. Do you know that Clancy actually got into the bedroom where Miles and Sam were sleeping? A fat guy who's quiet as a mouse — that's scary. The deputies didn't see or hear him either, even when he snuck up on them. He had both Miles and Sam out of the house before I heard them." Katie wiped her hand over her eyes, blew out a breath. "Thanks, Sherlock. I'll be okay, I promise."

"I've known you for only a very short time, Katie, but I am very certain of one thing: You're a good person and an excellent sheriff. Now, it's after midnight, your feet are a mess. Come on, let me fix you up. Dillon needs rest, but that won't happen until he's satisfied that everything's under control."

Katie, trying for a stab at humor, said, "Maybe I can be an excellent patient, too?"

"We'll see about that," Sherlock said. She smiled up at Katie, who was five foot nine if she was an inch, took her hand, and walked her back to the living room.

Once she had a bowl of hot water, soap,

towels, and the first-aid kit, Sherlock was ready. She sat on her knees in front of Katie, holding her ankle firm. When she finished washing each foot, it was time for the iodine. "Hold still, Katie, this is probably going to sting."

The word *sting* wasn't all that accurate, Katie thought as she swallowed two full-bodied curses, because Keely would have heard her curse, even in her sleep.

"Sorry. No more stingy stuff, just the bandages," Sherlock said and put the iodine back into the kit.

As Sherlock bandaged her feet, Katie said quietly, "I couldn't believe how Miles kicked the bejesus out of Clancy. He knows karate well." Katie looked over at him as she spoke. "I've never learned a martial art, and after watching Miles, I want to."

Sherlock said, "Martial arts is grand as long as a gun's not in your face. Miles and Dillon used to work out together a lot. Not so often now, maybe once a month they get together. Miles has been so tied up with his new military contract and trying to get all the bugs out of the new guidance system design for the army. He's really quite talented. Dillon said he could fly anything that had at least one wing."

After a moment, Sherlock added, "Miles was in the FBI, you know."

"Yeah, he told me," Katie said, looking over at Miles, who'd moved to Katie's big rocking chair, as she spoke. He was holding Keely in his arms, his cheek resting against her head, slowly rocking, all his attention on his son. She supposed she was seeing him with new eyes now. There was no particular expression on his face, but she knew he was fighting his fear for his son. He was hurting, bad. He was holding her daughter carefully, but he never looked away from Sam. It was as if just looking at him, concentrating only on Sam, he could somehow help him.

Savich was sitting next to him, leaning forward because of his back, his hands between his legs, saying nothing. He was just there with him, and that was good.

Sherlock said, "After Alicia died, Miles just retreated, I guess you could say. It was tough for all his friends to see it and not be able to do anything about it. I never really knew her, but Dillon said she was bright, always upbeat, and smart as a whip." Sherlock looked over her shoulder at him, and said thoughtfully, "Dillon also told me that Alicia sometimes did things he didn't understand, things over the top, like she'd be terrified if Sam even got the mildest cold. Once she freaked out when Sam had a slight fever. She stripped him down, examined every inch of him before she wrapped him in a pile of blankets. When Miles tried to calm her down, she lost it, screamed at him to leave her alone.

"But that doesn't matter now. What's happened to Sam would lay any parent nearly flat. Miles is holding up well, but I'll tell you, Katie, I've never seen anyone so scared as when he discovered that some-one took Sam."

"I can't begin to imagine that fear," Katie said. "Thank God, I've never had to face it."

"I pray that I won't have to either." Sherlock peeled the wrapper off a Band-Aid and gently wrapped it around a cut on the pad of Katie's foot. "It's got to be a parent's worst nightmare. You know some-thing? I'm glad Clancy is out of the pic-ture, dead or alive. Finally. I'm glad you just got it over with. Do you believe for even an instant that he would have stopped? I can see him breaking out of prison to come after Sam again, no matter what. My God, he came two times. What would make someone do that?"

Before Katie could say anything, Miles

said, to no one in particular, his voice pitched low, "Clancy said he didn't necessarily believe it."

"Believe what?" Savich said.

Miles shrugged. "I asked him why he wanted Sam so badly and he said someday he just might tell me, and then he added that he 'didn't necessarily believe it.' It sounded like someone else believed something about Sam, but Clancy didn't agree with it, or wasn't sure about it. I'd swear now that he looked baffled when he said that. Like it was something unbelievable, which makes no sense at all to me. I don't know of anything weird or unusual about Sam at all."

He looked over at Sam again, who was now holding Dr. Raines's hand. She was closer to him, too, and he was leaning into her. It looked like she was getting through to him. He felt a jolt of helplessness that he couldn't be the one with Sam, that he wasn't the one Sam was leaning against, listening to.

He looked up when Sherlock came down on her knees in front of him. "No, you won't do this yourself, Miles. You've done enough. You just sit there and let me clean up your feet. Don't rock too much or you might kick me on my butt. Now, I've fin-

ished with Katie, if you want a recommen-
dation."

Miles said, without hesitation, "Katie,
are your feet better?"

"She put iodine on all the cuts and they
stung for a bit, but yes, now they're better.
Trust Sherlock."

Miles smiled down at her. "She's always
been a rock, just like her old man. I'd trust
her to make doubly sure I'm really croaked
before she lets anyone pull the plug."

"That really makes me feel special,
Miles," Sherlock said, and patted his knee.

"Okay, that was a bit much," he said to
Katie. "I'd trust her enough to play net in
tennis doubles. How's that?"

"Not as dramatic," Katie said. "How
good are you, Sherlock?"

"She's a killer," Savich said, and smiled
at his wife.

Sherlock just grinned. "Now, hold still,
Miles. Goodness, you've got big feet.
What, size twelve?"

"Just about."

"Well, you've got a big body to support,
so that's okay."

"What size does Savich wear?"

Sherlock patted his arch. "A twelve."

Katie stretched out her long narrow bandaged feet in front of her. "Well, I'm nearly

234

five-ten, not all that much shorter than you guys. Maybe someday I can wear a twelve, too. Just three sizes to go."

Savich watched his wife putting Band-Aids on Miles's feet when he wasn't watching Sam and Dr. Raines. He wanted to move from the chair to that very comfortable sofa to relieve the pain in his back. He also wanted some tea. He took everyone's order and went to the kitchen. He saw Katie start to follow him and held up his hand. "Nope, you just sit there and let those size nines recover. If you abuse them, they just might never grow. I'll find everything, and I won't make a mess."

Dr. Sheila Raines, holding both of Sam's hands, said quietly against his temple, "Your papa is so scared I think he's going to start howling at the moon."

Sam gave her a long look and said, "Clancy's not going to come back anymore, is he?"

20

That stopped the show for about thirty seconds. Then Sheila answered him. "No, he's not, and that's a very good thing. He was a criminal, Sam, and criminals shouldn't be allowed to terrorize us. What do you think about him and Beau being dead?"

Sam thought about it, bit his lower lip, shot a look toward his father, and said at long last, "It's just that one minute he was yelling and then . . . he was just . . . gone. There was this gunshot, and he was dead, just like my mama. I'm not glad my mama's dead."

Oh dear. At least Sam was talking, thank God. Sheila leaned her forehead against Sam's and said not an inch from his nose, "Trust me on this, Sam. Your mama's in heaven and I'll bet she's kicking up her heels that you're okay. All the angels are cheering and I bet you there's even a big smile on Saint Peter's face.

"As for Beau and Clancy, they're probably so deep in Hell that the Devil doesn't even know where they are."

Sam thought about that, pulled back and smiled at her. He said, his little boy's voice sounding strong again, "Next time Mama talks to me, I'll ask her if she's heard anything about Beau and Clancy."

"That's a great idea. You can tell the sheriff what your mama says."

Miles wanted to shout when he saw that smile and heard Sam's words. He had no idea what Dr. Raines had said to get Sam speaking again, but she'd done it and he owed her forever.

He said, "Sam, would you please come over and hug me? I'm really on the shaky side. You'd better hurry before I fall over. I don't want to drop Keely. You don't want me to do that, do you?"

Slowly, Sam slid off the sofa and walked to his father. He stood there a moment, his hand on his father's knee, and he patted Sherlock's shoulder. "Hi, sweetie," Sherlock said, and kissed his cheek. "Just look at your father's poor feet. You want to put on this last Band-Aid?"

With great concentration, Sam went down on his knees beside Sherlock and smashed the Band-Aid down. At least it covered most of the cut.

Miles picked him up and settled him on his other leg. He held both children close and began rocking slowly. He whispered against Sam's ear, "You are the bravest boy I have ever known. I am so proud of you."

Sam released a long breath and settled against his father's shoulder. "Don't drop me, Papa, Keely's not as heavy as I am."

"No, she's not. But you, champ, are all muscle and bone. You just settle in, Sam, and I won't complain."

Sherlock rose and stepped back. She looked down at Keely, whose head was tucked into Miles's neck, then at Sam, whose eyes were already closed as his father rubbed his head.

Dr. Raines said after Sam had settled in for a while, "It's not over yet for him, but this is a good start." She rose. "Mr. Kettering, I would like to see Sam tomorrow morning, if that's okay. About ten o'clock?"

Miles looked over at Savich, who'd just walked into the living room, carrying a tray. He nodded. "Yes, that would be fine, Dr. Raines. We'll be there."

"Please call me Sheila."

"Thank you, Sheila. You got him to talk again. I'm very grateful."

"He's already out like a light. Good. Sleep, that's the best thing for him right now." She lowered her voice even more.

"There may be nightmares, Mr. Kettering. Sam had to retreat inside himself for a while, to protect himself, you understand, to close off the horror of what happened. I coaxed him out again, made him pay attention, but the thing is, he really wanted to come back. Being with Keely will help, and with you, of course. He's a strong little boy, you're right about that." She turned to Katie, waved her hand to keep her seated. "No, don't move, Sheriff. In my medical opinion, you should stay off your size nines."

"You're a shrink, Sheila."

"Yeah, but I did think once about becoming an internist, and then I decided I'd rather sleep at night. It's been a pleasure to meet all of you. Perhaps we'll have time to speak more tomorrow. Katie, Miles, try to keep Keely with Sam, okay? My guess is that she's more important to him right now than any of us."

Sheila laid her hand on Katie's shoulder. "If you want to talk to me about things, I'm there for you, don't forget it. It's been a horrendous few days for all of you, but the bottom line is that Sam's safe. By the way, I've always loved that sleep shirt, *Pulp Nonfiction*. Your dad gave it to you, right?"

"Yes, shortly before he died. Thank you

239

for coming and helping, Sheila. I owe you."

"Not this time you don't. Would you look at Keely. I swear she's grown and I saw her just a week ago."

Dr. Raines didn't stay for tea, saying it was well after midnight and she would be jumping off her ceiling if she got any caffeine into her at this hour.

Savich said as he set the tray down on the sofa side table, "I just spoke to Wade, Katie. He got Clancy to the medical examiner. He sounded really impressed this time with how you got Clancy. Since I didn't know any details, I couldn't tell him much about it. Would you like to tell me exactly what happened so I'll know how close I was?"

Katie looked closely at the children to make sure they were asleep before she closed her eyes a moment, and leaned her head back against the chair. "Clancy jumped off the porch, I ran after him. He didn't get far. He was wheezing when I caught up to him. I told him to freeze and, you won't believe this, he started laughing at me, said I wouldn't shoot him like I did Beau because if I did, I'd be a real sorry bitch, said I'd be taken down if I shot him, he promised me that.

"When he caught his breath, he ducked behind a maple tree. I think he knew I didn't want to shoot him, that I wanted to know who he was working for. Unfortunately, I got too close and he charged me. I heard Miles coming behind me, but I knew he wasn't in time. I tried to aim for Clancy's knee, but when he hit me, my SIG jerked up and I got him squarely in the chest. He just stood there, staring blankly at me, as if he couldn't believe that I'd actually shot him. He tried to reach out for my gun, but I took a step back and he just collapsed. He was dead, Miles checked him, too, just to make sure. It was an accident, really. I'm sorry, guys, I wanted him alive."

Sherlock said, "As I said before, I for one am vastly relieved that Clancy is dead. I don't think he would ever have stopped. Now we need to find out who's behind it."

Savich handed each of them a cup of tea. "This is excellent tea, Katie. I was prepared to make do with a tea bag."

"I've always loved Darjeeling," she said. "My mom gave me my first cup when I was about ten years old. I've never looked back. Bless my mom, she replenished my stock just last week."

Mundane things, Sherlock thought, looking from Miles to Katie, to help them put some of this fear behind them. She thought of Sean, her own beautiful little boy, and shivered. Sometimes, the littlest things, silly things really, were just what you needed to remind you that life was coming back to normal, that life was usually just fine, thank you.

Savich carefully rose and straightened his back as best he could. "Sherlock and I will be heading back to Mother's Very Best now. If you guys need anything, call us. Otherwise we'll see you here in the morning."

For the second time, Katie and Miles went to bed, Miles with Sam sprawled over his shoulder, Katie holding a sleepy Keely, who whispered, "I wanna sleep with you, Mama."

"I was just thinking the same thing, sweetie. You won't hog the bed, will you?"

Keely gave her a big grin. "I like to sleep sideways, Mama."

Katie was smiling until it hit her again. She'd shot two men in two days, shot them both dead. Odd how it all felt rather distant now. She no longer felt that debilitating shock that had slammed through her earlier. Now she felt strangely detached. Was it because she'd done something that made her not quite human? No, that was the wrong way to look at it. She set her jaw. She would face this, she would settle it in her mind, once and for all.

21

When Katie woke up early the following morning, Keely wasn't in bed with her. She jumped out of bed and came to an abrupt halt just inside the living room. There, lying on their stomachs on a blanket, were Sam and Keely, watching cartoons, the sound turned down low.

Katie looked down at her feet. For that panicked moment, she'd forgotten her sore feet. Then she thought of Miles. If he woke up he'd be wild with panic when he saw Sam was gone.

She didn't say anything, just ignored her throbbing feet, trotted to the guest bedroom, and stuck her head in. Miles was lying on his back, the covers pushed down to his waist, his chest bare. One arm was above his head, the other hand rested on his belly. His dark hair was standing on end, witness to an uneasy night, and his face was dark with stubble. He was sleeping deeply.

She looked at the alarm clock on the bedside table and saw that it was only just after six o'clock. Let him sleep.

She stood there a moment looking at Sam's father, really looking at the man she'd come to trust and admire in just two days' time, then grabbed a couple of blankets from her bedroom and went back into the living room.

An old Road Runner cartoon was playing, but the kids weren't watching it. They'd both fallen asleep. She turned off the TV.

She pushed the kids apart, marveling at how utterly boneless they were, just like cats. They didn't stir at all. She got down between them, and managed to get the three blankets over them. She put an arm around each child and drew them close. They snuggled in. She smiled as she closed her eyes, holding their small bodies close and safe.

An hour later, Miles woke up, realized that Sam wasn't there, and came running into the living room. There was the sheriff of Jessborough lying on her side, her hair out of its French braid, loose and long, draped over the pillow. She was spooning Sam and Keely was spooning her, and all three of them sound asleep.

For a very long time Miles stood in the doorway, looking at them, then looking at the sheriff holding them, and knew to his gut that everything was changing. He'd felt frozen inside since Alicia's death, but no longer. He turned and walked into the kitchen, made some coffee and pulled out his cell phone to call his sister-in-law, Ann Malcolm. He had called her Sunday morning, to reassure her that Sam was okay, but hadn't had time to tell her much. He'd trusted Butch Ashburn to keep her informed. He wasn't planning on telling her much this time either because there was no reason to upset her with it all. He didn't want to be on the phone anyway. He wanted to be lying in that living room holding Sam.

"Hey, Cracker, it's me, Miles."

She yelled into his ear: "It's seven o'clock on a bloody Monday morning! It's about time you called again, you bastard!" Miles smiled and she was off.

Miles held his cell phone a good two feet from his ear until he heard her running down. Then she started firing questions at him. He pictured her in his mind as they talked. She was wearing one of her gorgeous peignoir sets, no doubt — that's what she called them, honest to God. Whereas her sister, his wife Alicia, had always had both feet a bit off the ground, and a song always on her lips, she'd worn flannel pajamas. Cracker was a part-time estate lawyer, with a big mouth and a sharp brain. She loved Sam, and that was the most important thing.

"Yes," he said, breaking in at last, "everything is okay now. I'm okay. Sam is okay. There's lots to tell you, Cracker, but you're going to have to wait for the unabridged version. Hey, do you know anyone in Jessborough, Tennessee?"

"Me? I've never even heard of Jessborough, Tennessee. What's going on, Miles?"

"That's another reason I called. I thought we'd be coming right back, but not just yet. Sam's seeing a local shrink, and I think she's really good. She came over last night after there was more violence."

Cracker nearly lost it. *"Violence? What damned violence? Are you nuts, Miles? Bring him home!"*

When he could talk over her, and assure her again that they were safe, Miles said, "I'll keep you posted. Please, Cracker, don't worry. Now, I need you to work closely with the FBI — Agent Butch Ashburn was here but he wanted to get back, to get to the bottom of this."

"This sheriff . . . what's her name?"

"Katie Benedict. She's good, Cracker, really good. She's quick, has a solid center, and she's got guts. She's got lots more, but that's a good start. Like I told you, she saved Sam."

"Is she like the woman sheriff in Mel Gibson's movie *Signs*?"

"Well, maybe, only younger. She's really together, like that sheriff was."

"Okay, that's great, but Miles, I want you to bring Sam home. I miss him, you know?"

"I know. Sam is talking to a shrink right now, so that's one thing keeping us here. Plus the sheriff has a little girl, Keely. She and Sam are really tight. Dr. Raines believes Keely is very important to Sam right now. I'm not about to risk Sam's progress by separating them. And the thing is, Sam's probably just as safe here as he would be back home. So, for the next couple of days, I'm keeping him here in Jessborough. Have you thought of anything more that could help?"

"No, but the FBI are checking out all your employees, which takes a good long time. They've spoken to everyone — all the neighbors, all Sam's teachers, even the postman. Give Sam a big kiss for me,

Miles, and tell him I miss him like mad."

"I will. Take care. I'll call if something happens. Hold down the fort. I'll call Conrad at the office, make sure everything's running smooth, so don't worry about the business."

He got Peter's voice mail. When he slipped his cell back into his pocket, he looked up to see Katie standing in the kitchen doorway. She had socks on her feet and a loose shirt over jeans. She'd pulled her long hair back into a ponytail. She looked fresh and scrubbed. He himself wore socks to protect his Band-Aided feet, jeans from yesterday, and his shirt with two buttons buttoned. He smiled. It felt good.

"Cracker?"

"Yeah. She's my sister-in-law — Alicia's sister. She's lived with us ever since Alicia died. She's really Sam's surrogate mother."

"Where'd she get the name Cracker?"

"She nearly blew off my foot on the Fourth of July, got called Firecracker, and that came down to Cracker. She's a brick. I trust her even though she's a lawyer, only part-time since Alicia died. The kids still asleep?"

"Yeah. I woke up, saw that Keely wasn't with me in bed, and nearly had heart failure. I found them both in the living

249

room sleeping. They must have been watching cartoons with almost no sound. I checked you, got some blankets, then went back to the living room. What would you like for breakfast, Miles?"

"You checked me?"

She nodded. "I knew if you woke up and Sam wasn't there, you'd be scared, but you were sleeping so deeply I decided not to wake you. Now, what about food?"

He remembered pushing the covers down, and he'd awakened with the covers down, which meant she'd probably seen him sprawled on his back, wearing only his boxer shorts. He hoped he hadn't had a hard-on. Then he found himself wondering what she'd thought. No, that was nuts.

"Food, Miles," she said.

He blinked. "You know, I haven't thought about food for what is it, three days now, ever since Sam was taken. I'm starving."

"Good, then bacon and eggs it is. Crispy and scrambled?"

22

After Sam's meeting with Dr. Raines, Miles still wasn't sure what the best place was for Sam. What made it easier was that Sam didn't want Keely out of his sight.

Miles knew that Katie was as flummoxed as he was. He couldn't move to Jessborough and he couldn't very well take Keely back with him to Colfax, Virginia.

Because Miles wasn't about to let Sam out of his sight, that meant he also kept Keely with him, and that meant she was out of kindergarten for the moment, cleared by Katie with Keely's teacher.

Needless to say, Keely was pleased about this. Miles and the kids parted company from the other adults after lunch at Molly's Diner on Main Street, after munching on the best meatloaf east of Knoxville.

It was a beautiful day, sunny and clear, with a slight fall nip in the air. He took them to the small Jessborough park, located just a block from Main Street, bordered with trees so outrageously colorful you just stood there marveling at them. In the middle was a big swing set for the kids.

Katie went to her office to brief Wade and all the deputies on the situation. She'd no sooner gotten into her office than Agent Glen Hodges appeared in the doorway. He had his arms crossed over his chest, shaking his head at her.

She sat down behind her desk. "Good morning, Agent Hodges."

He gave her a small salute. "Hi, Sheriff. You're amazing, absolutely amazing. You took out both bad guys."

"Yeah, well, I didn't really want to, and you probably know Clancy practically admitted he was working for somebody else."

"We'll find out who that somebody is," he said. "I spoke with Butch Ashburn. He gave me a rundown. Now I'm thinking I should go interview the McCamys."

Katie smiled. "Admittedly, I'm just a backwoods sheriff, but Agent Sherlock and I have already been to see them. I'd appreciate it if you'd let us deal with the McCamys."

He wasn't happy about that, but he nodded.

"What I'd really like you to do is come along to the briefing I'm giving to my deputies."

He wasn't happy about this either, but on the other hand, Katie wasn't very happy with him. When he left for the department's conference room, Katie called Wade in.

Wade always walked like a guy on the prowl. He was two years older than Katie and he'd wanted very much to be elected sheriff, but the truth was, the powers in town owed a lot to the Benedict Pulp Mill, and so Katie was the one to get the nod. Wade had been a deputy to the old sheriff, a good old boy named Bud Owens who'd believed computers were for wussies. When he'd finally retired, he'd told everyone he wanted Wade. Unfortunately for him, Wade didn't have Katie's education, or her experience as a cop in a big city. Certainly her desire to be sheriff equaled or surpassed Wade's. Her cop experience had been in Knoxville, for two years, and that's when she'd met Carlo Silvestri, who turned her life upside down. For one year, her life had been one screaming crisis after another. Then Carlo's father had come and they'd both left Knoxville.

Katie had taken stock, realized she was a cop to her toes, and what she really wanted was to be sheriff of Jessborough. It was what she needed, too. She loved her work.

It had helped her get through the worst of her father's illness, the devastating and inevitable march of Alzheimer's, which had turned him into an angry stranger before killing him.

She watched Wade, her eyes half-closed. When she'd had enough of his fidgeting around, she said, "Well, Wade, would you like to continue working with Agent Hodges for as long as he remains here?"

"Well, sure, I'd really like that, Katie."

"Thing is, I don't really trust him to tell us stuff, to give us everything we need to know. Can I trust you to keep me filled in?"

She saw it in his eyes. Wade wasn't good at deception, not like she was. She was so good that when she was in Knoxville, they wanted to put her in undercover operations. She just smiled at him and waited.

He said, one eyelid twitching furiously, "Of course, Katie. After all, I work for the Jessborough Sheriff's Department."

"Well, actually, Wade, you work for me. I am the Sheriff's Department."

He flushed, blood rushing to his cheeks. He got all stiff, but he wasn't stupid, and he knew he couldn't cross her openly or she just might fire his ass.

"Yeah, I work for you."

"Okay, you're now my liaison with Agent Hodges." She sat forward, her eyes hard on him. "Listen to me now, this is important. Don't be impressed just because he tells you something. Make sure you know everything that's going on, you got that?"

After he'd assured her he understood, he sauntered out of her office, more enthusiasm in his step.

Katie followed him after a minute. Conversation stopped when she came into the small room. She walked to the head of the table and stood behind a small lectern, her hands clasped in front of her. "There are just eight of us this morning. Nate and Jamie are at home recovering." She looked around the conference at her seven deputies, all of them looking excited and important. She wished she had a basket of candy to hand out to them, they looked so much like school kids. Linnie, her dispatcher and assistant, had already handed out coffee.

She introduced them to Agent Hodges, then went through events chronologically. It took her a good fifteen minutes. "Do you have anything to add, Agent Hodges?"

He didn't, though he wanted to. The problem was that Katie had been thorough, and thankfully, Agent Hodges had the grace to say, "No, you've covered things quite nicely, Sheriff."

"Okay, now here's what we're going to do. I found out that Hester Granby is the church secretary at the Sinful Children of God. I want Wade to get the names of the members from her. He'll split them up and each of you will go interview as many church members as you can today. If you find out anything at all interesting about church operations or either of the Mc-Camys, leave me a message on my voice mail. Don't forget now, we have to be nice. Remember that we have no evidence to connect the McCamys to the kidnapping, it's just that they're our only lead. You already know some of their people, but the majority aren't local. That should give you a head start at least."

Deputy Cole Osborne said, "Sheriff, how will we know if we find out anything significant?"

"You're smart enough. Listen carefully, anything you hear that might sound the least bit off, that's what I want to know about."

After she'd dismissed them all, and said fond good-byes to Agent Hodges, she pulled Deputy Danny Peevley aside. He was the best-liked of all her deputies, just about magic with people. His mama would say that he could get the onion to peel off its own skin. "I have someone real special I want you to speak to, Danny. His name is Homer Bean and he lives in Elizabethton. He owns the Union 76 gas station. I saw Bea Hipple yesterday at the church and she called me, gave me Homer Bean's name. She said she liked Homer, and he'd been unhappy with Reverend McCamy. That's all she knew. Mr. Bean left the church about six months ago. Find out why, Danny. Find out what he thinks of Reverend McCamy."

Once Katie's door closed, she sat down at her desk actually happy to have a chance to look at the three active cases Linnie had left for her to review. Three cases very nearly constituted a crime spree for Jessborough. One DUI — Timmy Engels was at this moment still sleeping off his drunk in the only cell that had a soft cushion. One assault case — Marvin Dickerson was in back in a cell for beating on his wife, Ellie. Katie would keep him locked up until Judge Denver saw him at an arraignment on Wednesday. And she would speak to his wife again, beg her to press charges. But she wouldn't, she never did, so the best Katie could do was keep the bastard locked up as long as she could.

And one last case: shoplifting — Ben Chivers, a kid whose parents were so poor, it broke Katie's heart. And the fact that they were usually passed out at night after drinking themselves blind didn't help matters. *I made you give back that Snickers bar you stole, Ben; now what am I going to do with you?* She closed her eyes and mulled that one over.

Then it came to her and she smiled. It was worth a shot. She picked up the phone, spoke to Mrs. Cerlew, who owned Emmy's One-Stop Grocery, named after her suffragette grandmother. That was where Ben had ineptly lifted the Snickers bar. When she hung up, she grabbed her hat, and stopped by Linnie's desk. "I'm off to see Ben Chivers. I know he's in school, but I'll just get him out of class. It'll make his reputation if the sheriff comes to see him, don't you think?"

"He'll strut," Linnie said, then shook her head. "That's a bad situation, Katie. Those folks of his, all they do is lie around drunk and bitch."

"I've got an idea," Katie said, gave Linnie a small salute, and drove her truck to the local middle school.

Savich looked up to see Sherlock tuck

her cell phone back in her shirt pocket. They were in their bedroom at Mother's Very Best. He was still sitting forward, trying to ignore the constant throb in his back, working on MAX.

"What did the medical examiner have to say?"

"Clancy," Sherlock said as she bounced up and down on the bed a couple of times, "was stronger than a bull, ate like a pig, and had arteries clogged all the way to his ears. Katie's bullet killed him. Nothing more, nothing less." She eased off the bed, smoothed down the covers and walked to her husband. She leaned down and kissed his mouth. She felt the immediate hitch in his breath, and stood again. "About all we can do is play with my hair rollers," she said, a wealth of disappointment in her voice.

"Where are they?"

Sherlock laughed. "You've been working on MAX all afternoon. What have you got?" She affectionately patted the laptop as she spoke. At least Dillon didn't have to worry about the math teacher killer case since Jimmy Maitland had told him to chill out until he was better.

"I've been reading about Reverend Sooner McCamy. He's fifty-four years old, born near Nashville, Tennessee, went to Orrin Midvale Junior College, married and divorced once, no children. He sold cars at the Nashville Porsche dealership, and did very well financially. Then he quit and moved to his rich aunt's house here in Jessborough. He hasn't done anything since then to earn money, I guess because he didn't have to. He married Elsbeth Bird of Johnson City nearly ten years ago when she was only about twenty-four and he was forty-four. He didn't become a preacher until about six years ago."

He tapped his fingertips together, frowned down at MAX, who was humming placidly.

"He's married to Elsbeth four years before he finds his calling?"

"Apparently. But when the calling hit him, it hit him hard. Suddenly he's the founder and leader of this pretty strange-sounding church, the Sinful Children of God."

"He didn't go to a seminary?"

"Nope."

"Hmmm. What did his aunt die of?"

Savich's back was throbbing like the very devil.

She hated seeing the pain in his eyes. "You're taking a pill, buddy, no arguments."

After he'd swallowed the pill, she made him sit for a few minutes until his back stopped throbbing. He said, "Let's see about that aunt. She died something like six months after Sooner married Elsbeth. They both lived with the aunt in that lovely big house that his aunt, Eleanor Marie McCamy Ward, inherited from her husband. Ah, do you have Katie's cell? Ask her."

Katie answered immediately and listened. She said, "That's an excellent question, Sherlock. I'm in the middle of a delinquent problem right now, but I'll get back to you."

When Sherlock hung up, she said, "Katie will check it out. We're having dinner tonight at Katie's mom's. You can tell each other what you know about Sooner McCamy and she can tell us all about Aunt Eleanor Marie. Do you want Agent Hodges to come?"

"Sure, the more we compare notes the better. I think Miles is still with Sam and Keely, even though Katie's mother volunteered to watch them."

"But Miles didn't want Sam out of his sight."

"You got it. I told him to come here —"

There was a knock on the door, then

Sam's voice, "Uncle Dillon! Aunt Sherlock! We're here."

Savich slowly rose, because he knew the pain would knock him on his butt if he moved too fast. He took a handful of Sherlock's hair, kissed her — lust, pain, frustration in that kiss. "I want to do something with those big hair rollers later."

She said against his jaw, "I've been thinking that just maybe we can figure something out that won't hurt you too much."

That perked him up.

23

They went to Katie's mom's for dinner, a large ranch-style home built in the sixties located in the middle of Jessborough on Tulip Lane. She'd lived there for twenty-nine years with her husband. Now, she lived with two canaries, three King Charles spaniels, and an aquarium, temporarily empty. She was serving a huge tuna casserola that the kids would love, Minna Benedict had assured Miles, when she met him at the front door.

"Is that the same as a tuna casserole, ma'am?" Miles asked her.

"My granny called it a casserola and that's just the way it is around here. Hello, Dillon, Lacey. And who are you, sir?"

"I'm Agent Glen Hodges, ma'am."

She shook his hand. "Welcome, all of you. Please, call me Minna. Ah, and the beyond-perfect specimens of kidness — Sam and Keely. Come on in, and let me give you each a big hug and an even bigger chocolate chip cookie, fresh out of the oven."

"What about us, Mom? Just look at Dillon here. The man's back is hurting bad. He could probably use a cookie about now."

Minna Benedict was not quite as tall and slender as her daughter, but she had thick red brown hair even more lustrous than Katie's. She said, "All right. One for each of you, and two for Dillon because of his back. Come in, come in, don't dawdle. There's enough time before dinner. Dessert is always better than dinner any day of the week, isn't it?"

After the three King Charles spaniels had finally calmed down, their silky ears stroked by every adult and child, and the canaries were quiet beneath their night sheets, everyone trooped into the small dining room. To Miles's surprise, Sam took one bite of the tuna fish casserola and didn't stop until he downed two helpings and three of Minna's homemade biscuits. He and Keely had their heads together throughout the meal.

"Let me tell you one good thing I did today," Katie announced to the table at large.

Sherlock waved her fork. "Out with it, Katie, we need to hear something positive."

"I had a boy steal a Snickers bar from a local grocery. His family's poorer than dirt and both parents drink. I went to the middle school, pulled twelve-year-old Ben Chivers out of class and offered him a deal. He works for Mrs. Cerlew at the grocery three hours a day after school. She pays him minimum wage for two of those hours, then he works free for the other hour. Mrs. Cerlew is all for it, too. If he does well for a month, she'll keep him on and pay him for the full three hours, three days a week."

Miles's head was cocked to the side. "That's very good, Katie. This way the kid doesn't have to go into the juvenile system."

Katie shuddered. "Something I like to avoid at all costs. He's not bad, just helpless. This will give him a sense of worth, and a bit of money. I told him to keep his new job to himself as long as he could, or his dad would hit him up to buy some cheap wine."

Minna said, "But of course old Ben would. Now, Katie, Mrs. Cerlew doesn't have an extra dime, so I'll just bet that you're subsidizing his wages, aren't you, dear?"

Katie gave her mother a tight-lipped frown and didn't say anything.

How, Miles wondered, could a sheriff, on a small-town sheriff's pay, afford to subsidize a kid's wages? He was chewing his tongue he wanted to ask so badly when Katie's mom said, smiling, "After the settlement, Katie saved Benedict Pulp mill, and a lot of local folks' jobs, and every so often, she helps folk here in Jessborough, mainly the kids."

"This is my home," Katie said very quietly. "Actually, you could have pulled the mill out of trouble yourself, Mama." She added to everyone at the table, "She's an excellent manager, something Dad just wasn't. Now, that's enough." She looked down at the last bite of tuna casserola on her plate. "Keely, you want one more forkful?"

Truth be told, the very large tuna casserola and the platter of biscuits were memories in fifteen minutes.

Miles sat back and folded his hands over his stomach. "That was delicious, Minna. Thank you very much for letting us come."

"Well, I put up with you adults just so I can get my hands on Sam and Keely. Now, who's ready for coffee and apple pie?"

Savich said, "May I give you my mom's e-mail, Minna? You can give her your recipe for the casserola and she'll give you hers for Irish beef stew." He grinned at his wife. "Then Sherlock and I can bid good-bye to our waistlines."

After Minna assured the adults that both kids were lying in front of the television, glued to *Wheel of Fortune*, Katie set down her cup of coffee, pulled out a file and said, "Eleanor Marie McCamy Ward was only sixty-three when she died of a fall down the front stairs. The ME's report showed that her neck was broken and that the broken bones and internal injuries were consistent with such a fall. Neither Sooner nor Elsbeth apparently were at the house at the time of the accident. He didn't preach his first sermon for five more years, then he was invited to the Assembly of God over in Martinville. Six months after that, he established the Sinful Children of God here in Jessborough. He started with only a dozen or so worshipers. There are now a good sixty in the congregation. He's what you'd call a natural."

"He was an accomplished car salesman," Savich said. "It makes sense that he'd be a natural as a preacher. Minna, do you know anything more about Reverend McCamy?"

"I remember Eleanor told me that Sooner had been an intense, quiet boy, self-sufficient, very into himself, but when he spoke, he was always so sure of himself that people believed what he said. She said he wasn't a happy man, understandable with a bad marriage and living in that big city selling those ridiculously expensive cars. She was quite religious herself. She prayed he would find what he was meant to do in life before she died."

"But she didn't live long enough to see him become an evangelist," Sherlock said.

"No, she didn't," Minna said. "Her death was a shock to all of us. She was a fine woman. But evidently Sooner did find his calling. He's very much admired and respected by his congregation. He's a big part of their lives. Whether that's healthy or not, I won't speculate."

Katie looked directly at Sherlock. "Do you think Eleanor's fall down the front stairs might not have been an accident?"

"Let me ask another question first," Sherlock said. "Was Eleanor McCamy Ward just really well off or was she rich?"

"We could check the probate records, but everyone knows she was worth quite a bit at her death, say, maybe around five million. So, yes, I'd say she was rich."

"And Sooner McCamy inherited everything?"

Katie nodded, sighed. "I wasn't living here at the time, but I remember thinking that her death was awfully convenient for Sooner. But of course, no one could prove anything. You guys met him. He certainly looks the role of the stern country preacher, doesn't he? Dark, brooding, his eyes boring right into your soul."

"You wonder how much of it is for real," Miles said, then rose and went off to check the kids. He returned in a moment.

Katie said, "I suppose Sooner could have killed his aunt."

"Yes," Savich said, nodding as he sipped Minna's delicious Darjeeling tea. "But a push down the stairs was taking a chance. It doesn't guarantee a broken neck. If Sooner did kill her, then he probably saw the opportunity and took it without thinking it through."

Katie said, "You're right. It's not at all a sure thing, she could have come out of it with a sprained ankle."

"You know," Sherlock said after her last bite of apple pie, "I think I'm in need of some more local religion. Katie, do the Sinful Children of God meet during the week?"

"Oh yes," Katie said. "But not on Tuesdays, that's their day off."

Savich said thoughtfully, "I think a better idea is for me and Sherlock to take the kids and go visit Reverend and Mrs. McCamy. You'll know I'll be looking real close to see his reaction to Sam. And I want to know if Sam's ever seen him before. Do you guys think that's a good idea?"

Minna frowned. "If Reverend McCamy is somehow involved in Sam's kidnapping, is it wise to stick Sam right under his nose?"

Sherlock thought about that for a moment, then said, "Absolutely nothing will happen to Sam with Dillon and me with him, that I can promise you, or else we wouldn't even consider taking him over there. Just seeing how Reverend McCamy reacts when confronted with Sam, well, that could give us lots of information."

Miles said, "Minna, these two are the best, don't worry. I'm not. On the other hand, I just might hide right outside the front door, a big stick in my hand."

Katie was grinning as she said, "I agree that just maybe something will pop. After all, Beau and Clancy are no longer in the picture. If the McCamys are involved, they've not had time to recruit more out-of-work criminals."

Late Tuesday morning, Savich and Sherlock, with both Keely and Sam in hand, knocked on the McCamys' front door.

"Who lives here, Uncle Dillon?"

"Two very interesting people I think you kids might like meeting."

"I'd rather watch cartoons," Keely said and laced her fingers with Sam's.

Sherlock said, "We're going to have lunch with your mom, Keely, and your dad, Sam. So that means you need to hang out with me and Uncle Dillon for a while, okay? I doubt any cartoons will be playing in this house, so you'll have to be patient."

"She means she doesn't want us to whine," Keely told Sam, who nodded, then asked, "Where's my dad?"

"He had some calls to make, you know, Peter Evans at the plant. He said he needed you guys out of his hair for a while."

"He always says that," Sam said, "but then he says he can't wait to see me again."

Savich smiled. "That, Sam, is what's known as a parent's curse."

Elsbeth McCamy came to the door after another minute had passed. She stared at the two agents, then she stared at the children.

"May we speak to you, Mrs. McCamy?" Sherlock said. "Forgive us for bringing the children, but we were the only two free adults."

"Yes, of course. Do come in. Reverend McCamy," she called out, "two FBI agents are here and they've brought children."

It really was very old-fashioned of her to call her husband Reverend McCamy, Savich thought. But Elsbeth McCamy didn't look the least bit old-fashioned in her tight low-slung jeans and white tube top that left three inches of bare belly showing. She was wearing a belly button ring, a delicate circle of gold. And her Jesus earrings, shining bright in the morning light pouring through the front windows.

Reverend Sooner McCamy was wearing his patented black pants, a white shirt, and a black jacket. When he came out of his study down the hall, he looked harassed. "Elsbeth, I'm ministering to Mr. and Mrs. Coombs."

"The agents would like to speak to us."

"Take them to the living room. I'll see if Mr. and Mrs. Coombs can wait for ten minutes." He raised an eyebrow as Sherlock said, "Ten minutes sounds just fine."

Elsbeth McCamy waved them into the living room. She eyed the children again. "Hello, Keely. Can you introduce me to this little boy?"

"I'm not a little boy," Sam said. "I'm six."

"I see. And what is your name?"

"Sam. I'm Sam."

Sherlock was watching her carefully when she looked at Sam. She saw nothing but an adult being polite to a child.

"No, you're not little at all. I'm Mrs. McCamy, Sam. Welcome to my home. Do you like it here in Jessborough?"

Sam gave this some thought. "Well, those two men who kidnapped me are dead. Maybe things are better now."

"Yes, I hope so."

"We're very sorry about Clancy's death, Elsbeth. The medical examiner finished this morning and he wanted me to ask you if you wanted to take care of the arrangements."

"No, I don't want to. Let Tennessee do it. Clancy had been bad for a very long time." She paused a moment, and looked down at Sam. "Did you know that Clancy was my brother?"

24

Sam stared up at her, then he shook his head. "Really?" Sam said. "Why did your brother take me?"

"I don't know, dear. We haven't been close for many years now."

"I wouldn't want to be close to Fatso either."

"I can see your point."

Reverend McCamy said from the doorway, "So you're Sam Kettering, the little boy who was kidnapped."

"I'm not little," Sam said.

"He's six," Elsbeth said.

"You look pretty little to me," the reverend said, ignoring his wife as he walked forward to stand over Sam.

"You're old," Sam said, staring up at him. "That's why you're bigger than me."

"Do you think Agent Savich is old?" Reverend McCamy asked, not smiling, his dark eyes intent on Sam's face.

"Well, sure, he's even taller than you, but he's really strong. I've seen him and my dad throw each other all over the place at the gym. They punch each other, yell insults, and groan, and then they're laughing."

"Sam's father and I work out together occasionally," Savich said to Reverend McCamy. "Sam, why don't you and Keely check out that fireplace. It looks pretty old and big to me."

Sam said, never looking away from Reverend McCamy, "Did you push your aunt down the stairs, sir?"

There was dead silence in the living room. Bad idea to bring the kids, Savich thought, but on the other hand, you never knew what could shake loose. So much for the kids watching TV in the other room. Savich watched the reverend's face. He was pale, too pale, except for the dark beard stubble, and now, perhaps, he'd paled just a bit more. He looked like an old-time zealot in all that black with those burning eyes of his. He gave Savich the creeps.

Reverend McCamy shook his head. He reached out his hand to touch Sam, then drew it back. "Why no, I didn't. Why would you think I did, Sam?"

Sam shrugged. "I don't know, sir. Some grown-ups do really bad things. Like Beau and Fatso."

"Fatso? Oh, you mean Clancy. Yes, what you said, that's true enough, and you have good reason to know that. But I'm a man of God, Sam. My mission in life is to bring others to Him, to accept how He suffered for all of us, how He atoned for our sins, even Beau's and Clancy's. And He allows some of us to experience His own sacrifice."

"I wish you'd brought Fatso and Beau to God," Sam said, "before they took me away from my dad."

"Well, who knows? Maybe they were thinking about God when they took you. We'll never know, will we? Not all men are capable of achieving anything like goodness. Are you good, Sam?"

Sam didn't say a word, just stared up at Reverend McCamy.

Keely said, "He's a boy, but I think he's a little bit good."

Reverend McCamy said, "You're the sheriff's daughter, aren't you?"

"Yes," Keely said, hugging Savich's pant leg. "You look like a man in one of my mama's old movies, you know, black and white before there were colors. I don't like black and white."

Savich smiled, just couldn't help it, but he saw that Reverend McCamy didn't appreciate the child's wit. There was no change in his expression, but Savich felt something dark and brooding coming over him, something he didn't understand. But all McCamy said was, "Elsbeth, why don't you take the children to the kitchen and give them some lemonade."

Sherlock said, "That sounds splendid. Let me help."

Elsbeth nodded and walked out of the living room, the kids behind her.

"He's scary, Aunt Sherlock," Sam said in a low voice.

"Maybe," Sherlock said. "Sam, what's wrong?"

He'd stopped and was staring at the big staircase. Keely was running ahead behind Elsbeth McCamy. Sherlock leaned down and whispered in his ear, "Sam, what's wrong?"

"I don't like this house, Aunt Sherlock. Can't you feel it?"

"Feel what, sweetie?"

Sam frowned a moment, kept staring at that staircase, then shrugged. "I don't know, but it's kinda scary. His aunt must have fallen down these stairs."

"Yes, she did."

Sam touched his fingers to the newel post, a richly carved mahogany pineapple.

"Do you think Mrs. McCamy really has some lemonade, or do you think she'll just have Diet Coke?"

"We'll see, now won't we?" Sherlock said.

In the living room, Savich remained standing. It was less painful that way. Reverend McCamy wasn't a large man, but he had presence, and that made him appear bigger than he actually was. Savich remembered the bottomless well of madness in Tommy Tuttle's eyes and wondered if there was a hint of the same madness in Reverend Sooner McCamy's dark eyes as well.

"You actually discussed my aunt's death in front of children? Discussed my murdering her?"

"We thought they were watching TV," Savich said. "We should have known better. We're cops, Reverend McCamy, and we had to wonder about the excellent timing of her demise — six months after your marriage to your wife. No illness, just a sudden fall down the stairs and a broken neck."

"My aunt was a very fine woman, Agent Savich. I loved her very much. She took me in when I was blind and couldn't find my way. She listened to me, comforted me, encouraged me to follow my heart. Her death brought me great sadness. But I knew she basked in God's sacred light. She's with Him now, out of pain, for all eternity."

"Perhaps so. But you were still alive, Reverend McCamy, as was your wife. And you were also much richer. I like your house. It's a lovely property."

"Yes, that's a fact." McCamy waved Savich to a sofa. "It's interesting how the living always regard death selfishly, isn't it? A man will grieve, then almost immediately measure what he'll gain from it. Why don't you sit down."

"Perhaps that's true. I'll stay standing. My back isn't very happy at the moment."

"I've never had back problems."

"I haven't either until Saturday night. Tell me, sir, what do you think of Sam?"

His dark intense eyes rested on his face a moment before he said, "Oh, I'd forgotten that you got hurt at Katie's house. The nurses at the hospital were really excited about having an FBI agent laid out there."

Savich arched an eyebrow.

Reverend McCamy shrugged. "It's a small town, and two of the nurses in the emergency room live here in Jessborough. Gossip is rife. Now, that's an odd question, Agent Savich. What do I think of Sam?

Well, he appears to be precocious, a very forthright child."

"You mean just because he repeats what he heard adults say?"

"No, not just that." Reverend McCamy paused a moment, stroking his thin fingers over the wool of his black jacket. "It's that he's somehow above the normal lies and deceptions of children."

"I've heard Sam tell a few whoppers, Reverend. He's a little boy, and that's exactly what one would expect. But the fact that he saved himself, now that's very impressive. He wasn't cowed by fear — and that's amazing for a six-year-old. I suppose you heard the story of how he slithered out of a window in the old Bleaker cabin, and took off, Beau and Clancy after him."

"Yes, I've heard several versions of the tale. All of them strike to the soul." Reverend McCamy slowly shook his head, his eyes on his fingers, which were still stroking his jacket, against the nap. He said nothing more. How strange.

Savich said, "Don't you believe it's quite a coincidence that Clancy was your wife's brother and he brought Sam here?"

Reverend McCamy raised his dark eyes to rest on Savich's face. "Coincidences are random acts that are drawn together by foolish men."

"I gather you are not a foolish man?"

"I am a realistic man, Agent Savich, but yes, like most men, I am occasionally foolish. I believe that our Lord would have us study each random act as it touches us and try to determine how it will enhance our grace. You think my wife and I were involved with the boy's kidnapping, Agent Savich? Just because Clancy was her brother?"

Savich said slowly, not really wanting to look in those black eyes, eyes that somehow seemed to absorb darkness from light, "What I think, Reverend, is that your wife's brother brought Sam to Jessborough, Tennessee, for a reason. You'll have to admit that both Clancy and Beau demonstrated a great deal of motivation. They simply didn't stop trying to get him until they were dead. That, also, is very strange."

Reverend McCamy merely nodded. He raised his right hand and stroked his fingers through his black hair. His hair was thick, long enough to tie at his nape, but he let it hang loose. Stroking his hair was a long-standing habit, Savich thought.

Savich wished he had another pain pill.

"Why do you suppose they did that, Reverend?"

"I really have no idea, Agent Savich."

"When Clancy was at the sheriff's house last night, he said something unusual to Mr. Kettering. He said that he didn't necessarily believe it. Believe what, Reverend McCamy?"

"I have no idea, Agent Savich."

"Clancy also admitted to Mr. Kettering that someone had hired him."

Reverend McCamy shrugged. "Then it seems that someone was paying them a great deal of money to get the child."

"That much is obvious. But the question remains: Why is Sam so important to the one who paid them? What is it about Sam that makes him so valuable, if you will? No ransom demands, no obvious revenge motive, no pedophilia that we know of, so it must be something else. Do you know what the motive could be, Reverend McCamy?"

Reverend McCamy shrugged. "As I remarked, he is a precocious child, but I can't personally imagine anyone going to all that trouble for a precocious child."

"Then it must be something more."

The reverend's dark eyes rested on Savich's face. "I have found that there is always something more, Agent Savich. It is a pity that men are given free will. There is endless abuse, don't you agree?"

"Why do you say it's a pity?"

"Free will allows men to make disastrous mistakes without end; what they should be focusing on is gaining God's grace."

Savich said, "I think the reason for many of men's endless mistakes is a direct cause of their search for God's grace. Witness the history of Ireland, England, Spain, France — men's disastrous mistakes litter the landscape, Reverend, especially in their efforts to focus God's grace on themselves, and to deny all other men's claims to the contrary."

"That is blindness, Agent Savich, and a man's blindness can lead either to his salvation or his damnation. If a man focuses on God's grace and His suffering for us, His creatures, his blindness will last but a moment of time. Ah, here is Mrs. McCamy with some refreshment for us, Agent Savich."

"And how does a man do that, Reverend McCamy?"

"He places himself in the hands of the prophets placed on this earth to guide him."

Elsbeth McCamy closed her eyes a

moment at her husband's words, and slowly nodded.

Savich asked, "Are you one of these prophets, Reverend McCamy?"

He merely bowed his head and turned his attention to the tea.

The tea tasted as dark as Reverend McCamy's eyes, and it was so hot it nearly burned his mouth. Savich didn't like it. He leaned over to place his saucer carefully on an end table, and instantly regretted it. Pain sliced through his back.

"I do think it's time that you left, Agent Savich. Neither my wife nor I have anything more to say to you."

"Thank you for seeing us," Savich said, the pain nearly bowing him over. He needed a pain pill, fast. He shook Reverend McCamy's hand, feeling the firmly controlled strength of the man. He looked for a moment into those intense eyes, eyes that either saw too much or saw things that were not of this world. Savich just didn't know which. But he did know one thing.

Sherlock nodded to both of their hosts, but didn't say anything. She had each child by the hand.

When they were out the front door and it had closed behind them, Savich said,

"Please tell me you have a pain med with you."

"You'll have to swallow it dry."

"No problem, trust me on that."

Once Savich had managed to swallow the pill, and they were ready to go, Keely said from the backseat, "Mrs. McCamy gave us lemonade."

"I didn't like it," Sam said. "It tasted funny."

Sherlock turned to look at him and slowly nodded. "I thought it tasted funny, too." She waited for Savich to get as comfortable as he could with the seat belt, and started the car.

"Let's go see your mama, Keely."

25

"She's with Mr. Kettering," Linnie, Katie's primo dispatcher, told them. Savich smiled and nodded even as she gave a little finger wave to Keely and Sam.

"Tell you what, Sam," Sherlock said, leaning down to Sam's eye level, "why don't you and Keely stay out here with Linnie, just for a little while."

"That's a good idea," Linnie said behind her hand to Sherlock, rolling her eyes. "I think they've got a problem in there."

Keely, who like every kid in the world could hear everything, said to Sam, "If your papa is yelling at my mama, she just might crack him on the head. My mama is the boss here, Sam."

I would agree, Sherlock thought, and said to Keely, "Okay, here's the deal. Your parents aren't yelling, they're just having a discussion," and she hoped it was true. There was too much stress, too much frustration, on both sides.

Inside her office, Katie was saying, "Dammit, Miles, I can't very well arrest the McCamys just because Clancy was Elsbeth's brother. For heaven's sake, you were in law enforcement, you know I can't."

Miles snarled, no other way to put it. "You know they're involved in this somehow, Katie, you know it. There's simply no one else. Maybe it's just Mrs. McCamy. So bring her in and rattle her. No, better yet, I want to talk to that woman myself. I want to face her down."

"Not going to happen. Anything else?" Katie wished she'd French-braided her hair. The banana clip was listing over her left ear.

"What are Agent Hodges and his crew doing?"

"Since they left all the interviewing to us, they're following the money trail — you know, credit cards, church accounts, money transfers, stuff like that."

"Is the TBI going to do anything at all except hassle you?"

Katie said patiently, "The Tennessee Bureau of Investigation has an obligation to see that the sheriff of a town in Tennessee didn't just decide to up and murder two men. They're just doing their job. They won't be too much of a hassle."

"Yeah, right. You've already spent hours with them."

That was true enough, she thought, and she wasn't looking forward to her next meeting with them. So far, they were satisfied that the two killings were justified, but the investigation — being cops, they wanted to know every detail of what was happening. She sighed, saying nothing.

"I want just five minutes with Mrs. McCamy. She's got to be the weak link here."

Katie sighed again. "Listen to me, Miles. The fact is we don't have any evidence yet against either of the McCamys. What's even more to the point is that none of us can come up with a single reason why either Elsbeth or Reverend McCamy would be involved in Sam's kidnapping. Until we have evidence, and a glimmering of a motive, both of them have their rights."

"There's got to be a reason," Miles said, smacking his fist against his open palm. "This is driving me nuts."

Katie dashed her fingers through her hair, dislodging the rest of it from the big banana clip. With fast impatient movements, she twisted it up again and clamped down the clip. French braiding was the only way to keep her hair on her head where it belonged, but she hadn't had time this morning. One long hank of hair was left curling in front of her right ear and she shoved it back. She said, "It's driving all of us nuts, Miles. Savich and Sherlock should be here soon with the kids. Let's hope they've got something to tell us."

Miles looked at Katie straight on. "I'm going to talk to Elsbeth McCamy myself."

Katie grabbed his arm just before he could get to the door, only to have it open in their faces. Sherlock smiled at both of them, seeing all the fear and frustration on their faces. She watched as Katie gently laid her hand on Miles's forearm. "Don't ever shoot unless you're sure you've got bullets in your gun, Miles. The McCamys are suspects, sure, and we're going to try to find out everything we can about them, but until we've turned up something, they get to sit back and watch us. Them's the rules, you know that. Hi, Sherlock. You have Sam and Keely? Are they ready for lunch?"

"I hope you've got something," Miles said and stomped out of Katie's office. "Where are Sam and Keely?"

"Linnie took them to the bathroom," Sherlock said.

Katie said, "Let me go tell my deputies

289

where I'll be." She walked off in her long, no-nonsense stride, half her hair falling down her back, the other half tightly held in the clip.

Miles quickly realized that Savich was in pain. He was standing very stiffly, like he was afraid to move at all, and his eyes were a bit unfocused. Miles said, "Sherlock, you got some more pain meds for the Iron Man here?"

Sherlock saw that Miles was right, even though the one he'd had not more than fifteen minutes ago should have kicked in. It scared her to her toes, she couldn't help it. She touched her fingers to his cheek. "We can't have this. You're white about the mouth, partner." She pulled out a pill bottle, dumped out another pill into her palm, filled a paper cup at the drinking fountain and gave it to him. "Don't even speak to me until you've got it down your gullet."

At that moment, Savich would have taken the whole bottle if she'd given them to him.

"This is a surprise," Miles said, stroking his jaw as he looked at Savich. "He didn't even try to kiss you off."

"No, he's not stupid," Sherlock said as her fingers touched his forearm, willing her fear for him to subside.

Savich liked her touching him. It felt good. And because she knew him well, because she hated his pain, she continued to stroke him.

"He needs to rest, but of course he doesn't get enough."

"Let's have lunch first," Savich said, "and yes, Miles, we've got some stuff to tell you. Don't fret, sweetheart, I'll be okay. These pills work pretty fast." He lifted her hand off his forearm, and lightly squeezed her fingers.

"Dillon, why don't you sit down over here for just a moment?"

"Let it go, Sherlock," and she did, as hard as it was. She wished at that moment that they were lying on the beach in Maui and had nothing more to do than suck mai tais through a straw.

At Maude's Burgers, everyone ordered a thick hamburger except for Savich, who had grilled West Coast swordfish on sourdough bread, which was interesting but had never been close to San Francisco.

"He's a vegetarian," Sherlock said to Katie. "Sometimes, on special occasions like this, he has fish."

"Why is this special, Uncle Dillon?" Keely asked, chewing each long French fry down to the grease.

"It's special because both you and Sam are heroes. And because we're all here together. Sam, it doesn't look to me like you're really enjoying your hamburger."

Sam, who couldn't speak until he'd swallowed the huge bite he'd taken, gave Savich a big, ketchup-smeared smile.

Ten minutes later, when Keely and Sam were eating chocolate chip ice cream, focused on each other and the chocolate chips they were carefully picking from the cones, Savich said, his voice pitched low, "Jimmy Maitland called just a while ago. The math teacher killer hit again, and he wants us back on the investigation. They need fresh eyes and he says we're the freshest eyes he's got. He sounds more desperate than I've heard him in a long while. The media attention had died down after they'd thrashed over the second killing, but now, with the third, they'll have 'serial killer' plastered all over the TV and the newspapers."

Sherlock said, "He also wants us to come back for a press conference at headquarters tonight. We have no choice at all in this."

"There are lots of good people," Savich said, "but when you mix three different police departments and the FBI together and try to coordinate who's going to be top dog, it can get ugly real fast."

Katie said, "I heard that after the second math teacher killing, the politicians started getting into the act."

"They'll want to ban every gun in the universe, including the one the shooter's using," Sherlock told her. "I can just imagine how difficult it is for the local jurisdictions to deal with this, particularly when the politicians are competing for sound bites."

Sherlock sighed, her eyes for a moment on Savich's plate, where more of his sword-fish sandwich was left untouched. "One thing is absolutely true: Everyone is scared. Everyone wants to catch this guy, and the pressure just keeps growing."

"Maitland said that the principals in the high schools in the killing areas haven't put up any road blocks if the math teachers want to leave town for a while," Savich said. "It's rather like closing the barn door after the horses have run out."

"Three people dead," Sherlock said, shaking her head. "Maitland scheduled the press conference late enough so we'll have time to speak to the third victim's husband beforehand."

"So what are you going to say at this press conference?" Katie asked as she sipped her coffee.

Savich started to say he didn't have a clue, but instead he suddenly just got up from the table and went outside. They watched him talking on his cell phone.

"My husband just got a brain flash," Sherlock said, amused satisfaction in her voice. "The last time it happened, Sean was sprawled on Dillon's chest. Dillon grabbed him under one arm and took him to MAX. An hour later, the Detroit cops arrested a man who worked behind the counter at Trailways Bus in Detroit for the murder of three runaway teenagers, all of whom had left Detroit on Trailways. He'd followed all of them and killed them."

"Why, for heaven's sake?" Katie asked.

"He never really said, just cried so hard his nose was running. Even after six months of nonstop shrinks, I don't think anyone ever understood what he was all about. He's locked away now in a state mental hospital."

Savich came back into the restaurant, sat down, took a bite of his fish sandwich, and said absolutely nothing.

Miles said to Savich, "So all of a sudden, your brain just announced — *bang!* — the killer was a counter clerk at Trailways?"

Savich looked blank until Sherlock said, "I was telling them about the Detroit case, Dillon."

He nodded. "The cops had questioned all the employees at Trailways, but they didn't spot this guy as a viable suspect. Well, I'd just been giving it a lot of thought, that's all, and I took a guess. I asked them to follow this guy for three days."

"What happened?" Katie asked, spellbound.

"He picked out our undercover agent, who was really twenty-six years old but looked fifteen, as his next victim. We got him."

"Okay, Dillon, what's the brain flash this time?"

He smiled at Sherlock, then shook his head at the others. "Too soon for me to say. Now, the big question. It's Tuesday, what do you want to do, Miles?"

"I don't know yet, but I guess I need to stay here for a while longer," and he looked over at Sam and Keely.

Savich saw that he was pissed, frustrated, and nearly at the end of his tether. "Both of you," he said, "keep us informed."

Katie became suddenly aware that both

Sam and Keely were all ears, down to the last licks on their cones. "Finish your ice cream, kids," she said, and wiped a bit of chocolate chip off Keely's mouth.

26

At eight o'clock that evening, at FBI Headquarters in Washington, D.C., Savich stood beside FBI Assistant Director Jimmy Maitland, waiting for the police chief of Oxford, Maryland, to turn the mike back over to them. The police chiefs from all three jurisdictions were lined up behind the podium, trying to look confident in front of all the blinding lights and the shouted questions.

Standing beside the chiefs were the three victims' husbands: Troy Ward, looking sad and puffy in a bright blue suit; Gifford Fowler, skinny as a post, standing with a big black Stetson in his hands; and Crayton Maddox, a successful attorney, looking as pale as a ghost, still in shock. He'd managed to dress himself in a Saville Row suit that had to have set him back a couple thousand dollars. Looking at the man now, Savich thought back to the meeting he and Sherlock had with him only two hours before, at his home in Lockridge, Virginia.

He and Sherlock had driven to Lockridge High School in Lockridge, Virginia, an affluent suburb favored by many upper-level government employees. The crime investigators, local and FBI, were still there, and six officers were keeping the media behind a police rope.

Police Chief Thomas Martinez met them in the principal's office and said without preamble, "The janitor spotted a small leak late Monday afternoon, in the boiler room. He repaired it, then said he couldn't sleep for worrying so he came back early this morning, before six o'clock, to see that everything was still holding." The chief stopped and grimaced. "He smelled something. It was Mrs. Maddox, one of our five math teachers. Evidently she'd stayed late to grade some test papers because she and her family were leaving for the Caribbean in the morning. Her husband said he'd talked her into leaving because of the two killings. In any case, she never made it home. Her husband called us around nine o'clock last evening, scared out of his mind. He'd called her cell, gotten no answer. We searched nonstop for her. The janitor found her. Come this way."

It was not a pretty sight. Mrs. Eleanor Maddox, not above thirty-five, two children, and a whiz at teaching geometry, had been shoved in beside the boiler. Because the weather was cool the boiler had fired up, and that was why the janitor had smelled her body. She'd been shot right between the eyes, up very close, just like the other two women.

Chief Martinez said, "The forensic team finished up about three hours ago. The ME said if he had to guess, it was a thirty-eight, just like the other two. He also said that this time, the guy had moved her here after he'd shot her."

"No witnesses?"

"Not a one, so far."

"Not even a strange car in the vicinity?"

He shook his head. "No. I have officers canvassing the entire neighborhood. No one saw a thing. Basketball practice and the student club meetings were over, so there weren't any other students or teachers around that we know of."

Sherlock said, "I guess he didn't want her found right away. What does the husband have to say, Chief?"

The husband, Crayton Maddox, was a big legal mover and shaker in Washington, his forte forging limitless access to politicians for lobbying groups willing to pay for the privilege. Exactly what that meant, Mr. Maddox didn't explain, and Savich, cynical to his toes, didn't ask. It was nearly six o'clock in the evening, but Mr. Maddox was still wearing his robe. There were coffee stains on the front of it. He was wearing socks, no shoes. He looked like he'd been awake for a week, and none of those waking hours had been pleasant.

Crayton Maddox said, "I called all her friends, all the teachers she worked with, I even called her mother, and I haven't spoken to that woman in nearly two years." He stopped a moment, tears choking him, and stared at Savich. "God, don't you see? This just isn't right; it shouldn't have happened. Ellie never hurt a soul, not even me, and I'm a lawyer. She planned on working until we left for the Caribbean, even though I tried to convince her to stay home, not take any chances. Why did he kill her? Why?"

Savich had no answer. "I know you've already spoken to Chief Martinez, and he'll give us all the details. We're here to ask you to join us at a press conference in a couple of hours at FBI Headquarters. I know you'll want to hear about all that's being done and it would be helpful to us if you came. I think it's important that the world see victims' families, see what devastation this sort of mindless violence can cause. Mr. Ward and Mr. Fowler, the first two victims' husbands, will be there. Will you join us, Mr. Maddox?"

Crayton Maddox bent his head and, to Savich's surprise, didn't ask a single question. Then he said, "Did you know that I called Margie, my assistant? She was here before seven o'clock this morning. She knows everything, that's what I told Chief Martinez, everything about both me and my wife." He paused a moment, glanced down at his Rolex, then out the living room window. "Good God, it's dark outside." He looked up at them. "I'm usually about ready to come home from my office at six o'clock in the evening. Ellie always got home around four o'clock. She wanted to be here when the kids got home."

They heard crying from upstairs, a woman's soothing voice. The children, Sherlock thought. There'd been no children involved in the first two killings. Why had the killer changed?

"My mother-in-law," he said, glancing up at the ceiling. "Margie called her and she was here in ten minutes. I guess we'll have to start speaking again." He stood, all hunched forward, like he hadn't moved in far too long. "I'll be at your press conference, Agent."

Assistant Director Jimmy Maitland

nodded to Savich, then stepped to the podium. He spoke of the cooperation among the three police departments, spoke of the activity by the FBI at the crime scenes, and repeated the hot-line number for any information on the killings. He finished his words to the roomful of reporters with "And this is Special Agent Dillon Savich, chief of the Criminal Apprehension Unit of the FBI."

Most of the reporters knew who Savich was. Jimmy Maitland barely had time to shut his mouth before several reporters yelled out together, "Agent Savich, why is he killing math teachers?"

"Since all the victims are women, do you think it's a man?"

Savich stepped up to the podium, said nothing at all until the room was quiet, which was very quickly. He knew many of them were jotting down descriptions of him and of the grieving husbands. He said, "Mr. George, you asked why is he killing math teachers, and Mr. Dobbs pointed out that all the victims have been women. Yes, we believe the killer is a man. As to why he's doing this, we have some ideas, but it's not appropriate to discuss all the possibilities with you at this stage in the investigation."

"Is the guy crazy?"

Savich stared thoughtfully at Martha Stockton of the *Washington Post*, who had the reputation of being something of a ditz, but this time she had stripped away the nonessentials really fast. "No, I don't think he's crazy in the sense that he's frothing at the mouth and out of control. He seems to have planned these killings well enough that so far there are no witnesses. Why he's doing this, we don't know yet, but I will tell you this: We will find him. We are spending hundreds of man-hours speaking to fellow teachers and former students. We are leaving nothing to chance.

"Now, I would like to introduce to you some of the family members affected by these tragic killings. These are the widowers of the murdered teachers, Mr. Ward, Mr. Fowler, and Mr. Maddox, whose wife was found just this morning. I believe Mr. Ward and Mr. Fowler wish to make a brief statement."

Mr. Eli Dobbs of CNN yelled out, "Excuse me, Mr. Maddox, but your wife was just murdered. How do you feel about standing up there with Mr. Ward and Mr. Fowler?"

That show of crassness was par for the course, Savich thought. He raised his hand. "We will take a few questions later. This is a time of grief and shock for these gentlemen. You might consider their circumstances before you ask your questions."

Troy Ward stepped forward and grabbed the edges of the podium. "I want to thank all those who have sent me cards and e-mails. The police are doing their best, I know, and I just want to thank everyone for their support and their thoughtfulness to me and my wife's family at this terrible time." With that, he stood back from the podium, his eyes on his shoes.

"You didn't call this Sunday's Ravens game, Mr. Ward," Eli Dobbs said. "What are your plans?"

Troy answered, but without the microphone in front of him, the reporters had to strain to hear him. "I'm planning to announce the game this Sunday. My wife would have wanted life to go on, as best as I can manage."

Gifford Fowler took his turn at the podium. He said simply, "My wife was the love of my life. I miss her every moment," and he also thanked the public. He didn't step back, though, and looked like he wanted questions.

"Mr. Fowler, we've been told you're

going to speak at the Rotary Club this Wednesday."

Gifford Fowler said, "They said they wanted to show their support, to share their time with me for an evening. I am very grateful to them for inviting me."

Savich cut it off, stepping back to the podium. He wasn't about to have Mr. Maddox in front of this group. His loss was too new, his control too tenuous. Besides, the world had seen them up close and personal. It was enough.

"Have your computers been of any help yet, Agent Savich?"

"Is MAX going to stand up there and announce the killer?"

There was laughter.

Savich smiled. "MAX is a tremendous tool. But here's the truth: Crimes are solved by good old-fashioned police work. And that's what we're doing, as fast and as hard as we can. Thank you for coming."

When it was all over, Savich gave Sherlock a small salute, then turned to speak to the three widowers. "I thank you for coming. I think it makes a difference. Of course there'll be more questions. I will be in touch with each of you. As soon as we know something, we'll let you know."

He shook hands with all of the men,

then watched them closely as they trailed out, following an agent through the rear door.

Sherlock took his hand and said in a whisper, "That was quite a performance. Do you think it was worth it?"

He turned, cupped her face in his hands, and said, "I think so. We'll see."

Later that night, back home in Georgetown, Sean was asleep on his father's shoulder after helping his parents eat a late dinner of his father's pesto pasta. Sherlock said while she heated some hot water for tea, "Miles called. Dr. Raines is still seeing Sam. Miles thinks it's best to keep him with her for a while longer. Also, he can't imagine separating Sam and Keely just yet."

"I can't imagine it either," Savich said. "Sam is probably as safe there as at home, and Katie has a couple of deputies around him whenever she or Miles can't be with them. I'll bet he'll get Katie to take him to see the McCamys."

Sherlock nodded. "You're probably right. And right now, I can't imagine Sam being away from Keely either."

"Yeah," Savich said slowly, as he watched her pour his tea into his favorite

Redskins mug, "and I was wondering how Miles would do away from the sheriff."

Sherlock shrugged. "Two very strong people slapped together in a mess like this . . ."

"Yeah, but let's keep out of it, Sherlock. Neither of us has a clue as to what will happen between them, if anything."

"The children are very important to both of them," she said. The phone rang and she turned to answer it. It was Agent Dane Carver, to catch Savich up on his case in Miami.

On Wednesday morning Savich was so stiff and sore, he knew he had to do something. Walking on the treadmill sounded like just what he needed. He'd forgotten all about Valerie Rapper. But evidently she hadn't forgotten him. She was there at the gym, waiting for him. Did the woman have spies? Her timing was incredible.

He raised an eyebrow at her. "It's ten o'clock in the morning," he said.

"I sometimes like to work out in the mornings. I saw you on TV last night, Agent Savich," she said, looking over at him as she pressed in ten minutes on the treadmill next to him. "Those poor husbands, I guess you really wanted to remind the public how horrific all this is, and that's why you showed them off."

Savich grunted again. His back was sore, but the walking was helping to loosen it up a bit. Sherlock had bandaged him up really well, knowing he wouldn't do anything too stupid, but since she'd been muttering under her breath at the time, he wasn't sure.

"What's wrong? You're moving like you're hurt. What happened?"

There was real concern in her voice. He looked over at her and said in his mildest, most unthreatening voice, "Nothing's wrong. Just a pulled muscle."

"I thought you were moving a bit stiffly on television last night."

"I'll be just fine." He looked pointedly down at the book he was reading.

"Would you go for a cup of coffee after you're finished working out? I'm buying."

He smiled. "Thank you, Ms. Rapper, but I'm married. I don't go out for coffee with other women even if they're offering to pay."

She laughed. "Sure you can. It's no big deal. I'm not going to seduce you, Agent Savich, it's just a cup of coffee, a bit of conversation."

He shook his head. "Sorry."

"Perhaps it's time for you to loosen up a bit, have just a bit of fun. I know, I know, what fun can you have over coffee? It's possible, I swear."

Savich said, "You've probably seen my wife here at the gym — red curly hair, big blue eyes. She's also an FBI agent. Her name's Sherlock."

"That's ridiculous."

"What? Hair? Name? The fact that she's an agent?"

"Her name," she said, looking into the mirror behind Dillon Savich. "Her name is ridiculous."

"Rapper's pretty funny too."

She stopped in her tracks. "Yes," she said slowly, "perhaps it is." She looked at him again, but he couldn't begin to read her expression. She punched the stop pad, stepped off the treadmill before it stopped, and walked away. She said over her shoulder, giving him a profile that she knew was superb, "You just think about having coffee with me, Agent Savich, all right?"

She was gone before he could answer.

27

It was a beautiful Wednesday morning. Katie looked up at the blue sky with its fat scattered white clouds, and followed them to the ever-present wall of mountains just off to the east. They were covered with maple, poplar, beech, and sugar maples in gorgeous reds and bright yellows and golds, the pines and firs holding to their green. Even the browns looked lustrous, magical, a magnificent palette of colors. There was simply no more beautiful a spot in the world than eastern Tennessee in the late fall. It was about fifty-five degrees, just enough nip in the day for her leather jacket. She breathed in the delicious smell of leaves mixed with the smoke from wood-burning fireplaces. Moments like this made Katie wish she could put off winter, with its frigid winds and snow and stripped-down trees.

She kept the engine running as she watched Miles lead Sam and Keely to Minna's front porch. He leaned down, spoke to both children, and touched each of them — Sam's arm and Keely's hair. They both hugged him, then ran to Keely's grandmother when she opened the front door. Chocolate chip cookies, Katie thought, remembering her excitement when she'd been a kid. She watched the two deputies take their positions, guarding the house with Sam and Keely in it. She made another sweep of the area. Nothing out of the ordinary.

Sam seemed just fine to Katie, thank God. This morning he groused and complained, just like Keely, when Katie had given him oatmeal and not Cheerios, an excellent sign. Miles hadn't helped when he'd looked at the oatmeal, blinked, and said he'd always thought oatmeal was good for making grout, but not eating. The kids had laughed, and Katie, just smiling, waited, until he took a big spoonful, rolled his eyes and said, "This is the best grout I've ever eaten. Here, Sam, take a bite of this." And Sam had said he loved it, and tried to roll his eyes just like his dad. There'd been laughter at the breakfast table, and that had felt very good. She'd also found herself smiling at Miles for no good reason she could think of.

Sam would see Sheila again today, in the early afternoon, but Sheila had told her and Miles that Sam talked more about Keely now and how he'd stuffed tons of leaves down her shirt. He talked more about Jessborough and Mrs. Miggs at the quilt shop who gave the children peppermints than he did about his kidnapping or about Clancy and Beau. It was a good sign, a very hopeful thing. Sheila was sure he wasn't holding back. He was a resilient little kid.

He was more than that, Katie thought, much more than that, especially to her, and that wasn't particularly wise. She got out of her truck and walked up the driveway. All was clear.

When Miles joined her, he said, "I doubt they'll even give us a thought. Your mom is the best, Katie." He paused a moment, drew in a deep breath, reached out his hand to touch a vivid gold maple leaf and said, "How much longer will it look like God's country around here?"

"Another two, three weeks, at most," she said. "Then the storms start coming. We have snow mostly in February and March. And that's beautiful, too. But right now? This is perfect."

He walked automatically to the driver's side of Katie's Silverado, then stopped, frowning.

"No, go ahead and drive." She tossed him the keys.

He saw the lock box on the floor in the back that held her rifle, the rifle she'd used to save Sam.

He said as he fastened his seat belt, "Those two deputies, they're good?"

She nodded, feeling exactly what he was feeling. "Cole and Jeffrey will really keep their eyes open. They both saw what happened at my house when Clancy and Beau went down, so they know this is way out of the ordinary. They're so wired, in fact, I told them to stick to decaf. This was the first time either of them had been involved in any real violence professionally."

"What kind of training do your deputies get?"

"They all have a ten-week training course at the law enforcement academy in Donaldson, near Nashville. My people have also taken courses at the local junior college — Walter State, you know, law enforcement and judicial courses. Wade is trying to get so many courses under his belt that, well, never mind."

"Is he the one who might be trying to get your job?"

She gave him a sunny smile. "No chance of that."

Miles liked that smile of hers, and the mouth that made those smiles, and that gave him pause. He didn't have to move the seat back much at all. He looked over at her, an eyebrow arched. "What do you mean they haven't seen violence? Violence is part of their job, isn't it?"

Katie laughed. "Jessborough isn't Knoxville or Chattanooga. The toughest thing any of them has had to do here in the sheriff's department of Jessborough is round up Mr. Bailey's cows after they were spooked by a low-flying crop duster in August. This is a small town with very few bad outside influences. No hard drugs, just some pot our locals grow, and an occasional still deep in the hills, which is kind of a tradition around here. Most people consider that good clean fun." She paused a moment, looked out the window, and said, "We had nothing but peace here until this happened. I have ten deputies, all of them men. The testosterone has been flowing madly since I got Sam on Saturday."

"Linnie is some dispatcher."

"Yes, she's excellent, knows everyone's problems, knows about all their relationships, even the illicit ones. She's the backbone of the department. I would seriously consider hurting anyone who tried to take her away from me."

She directed him to the big Victorian on Pine Wood Lane. As he looked at the house, realized who lived there, he felt his insides chill.

Her hand was light on his forearm. "We will be professional about this, Miles. Do you agree?"

He nodded. "I swear I won't tie up either of them in their playroom."

"Good."

"But I was thinking I'd like to see what they've got in there."

"You into whips and handcuffs?"

"Not that I know of." He looked thoughtful, grinned at her, and said, "I promise not to drop-kick them out one of those big front windows either."

"Good," she said again. "We got some new cards to play. If we do it really carefully, something might pop."

Katie pressed the doorbell, heard a light footfall. A few moments later, Elsbeth McCamy answered. She looked just like she always looked: hot. It always amazed Katie that she was with Reverend Mc-Camy, who was so dark and serious and intense, his entire being seemingly focused inward on the state of his soul. Every word out of his mouth was a paean to his God, and to his notions that men should be victims of His love. Victim of love — what a strange choice of words, but now it had a new meaning to her.

Katie looked at the woman standing there in tight jeans, a red spandex top, and the Jesus earrings and remembered the sex room upstairs with that padded wooden block. She wondered what his congregation thought of Elsbeth, but truth be told, she'd never heard anything that indicated anyone thought them mismatched or that a sexpot like her shouldn't be a preacher's wife. Like nearly all people in Jessborough, they never caused trouble.

Katie nodded but didn't extend her hand. "Elsbeth."

"Hello, Katie. Why are you here?" She wasn't looking at Katie, she was studying Miles Kettering, a perfect eyebrow hiked up. "You were in church on Sunday."

"Yes."

"You're the boy's father."

"Elsbeth, this is Miles Kettering, and yes, he's Sam's father. We would very much like to speak to you and Reverend McCamy."

"Reverend McCamy is ministering to two of his flock," Elsbeth said. "Mr. and

Mrs. Locke. They're in his study. I don't expect him to be free for another half hour or so."

"May we speak to you until he's free?"

It was quite obvious she didn't want to let them in, but she couldn't think of a reason to keep them out. Grudgingly, Elsbeth stepped back.

"This way," she said. "I'm making some brownies for Reverend McCamy. They're his favorite. Where is your son, Mr. Kettering?"

"Sam is at the sheriff's department, supervising all the deputies."

Elsbeth laughed. "He's a cute little boy. Is Keely with him?"

"Oh yes," Katie said. "They've become inseparable." Now, why had Miles lied about Sam's whereabouts?

"It's comforting to know what we get for our tax dollars, isn't it?"

Katie said, "I'm sorry about your brother."

"Are you really?"

"Yes. I'm a sheriff, not a killer. I can't imagine Reverend McCamy liking brownies."

"Why ever not? He has quite a sweet tooth."

Katie shrugged. "Somehow I think of

him as always being too above all of life's pleasures, immersed in his work —"

"His calling," Elsbeth said, frowning. "It's not his work, it's his calling. God chose him above all others to lead the common man to Him."

"Not women, too?"

"Of course," she said, her voice cutting. Then she lowered her voice as if someone were trying to overhear. "God has granted him His grace, he is God's messenger, so special that God gave him the beauty of suffering."

Miles said, "What do you mean 'suffering,' Mrs. McCamy? How can there be beauty in suffering?"

"It can be a gift to us, Mr. Kettering. Reverend McCamy likes his brownies with pecans, lots of pecans."

When Katie and Miles were settled at the kitchen table with cups of coffee in front of them, Katie said, "I heard a rumor, Elsbeth. I'd like to scotch it and so I figured the only way to know the truth is to come out and just ask."

Elsbeth turned, a can of cocoa in her hand. "What rumor?"

"That you and Reverend McCamy are thinking about leaving the area."

Elsbeth nearly dropped the can. "Goodness, where did you hear that, Katie?"

She was aware that Miles was wondering what she was up to. She just smiled, sipped her coffee, and wondered if indeed Reverend McCamy had been seen going into a real estate office in Knoxville. She said as she watched Elsbeth's hand shake as she measured a teaspoon of baking powder into the mixing bowl, "You know rumors — they're talked about everywhere but don't seem to begin anywhere."

"Well, it's wrong. Of course we're not leaving. Reverend McCamy is very happy here, despite that nasty televangelist over in Knoxville. That miserable man happened to find out that Reverend McCamy was approached by the producers on the cable station, and now he's trying to make everyone believe he's the spawn of the Devil, the bastard."

"What's this bastard's name?"

"James Russert, a real tacky individual, right up there with most of the others who bleat on TV and collect millions of dollars from gullible people."

And Reverend McCamy's congregation wasn't gullible?

Katie had seen Russert, a loud, blustering Bible-thumping TV preacher she turned off as fast as she could.

Elsbeth looked around at them, a big chocolate-covered spoon in her hand. "We've heard that you're harassing our congregation, talking to them at work, following them home. It's disgraceful, Sheriff, disgraceful."

"We're conducting an investigation, Elsbeth. Be sensible, you're up front because Clancy was your brother. Naturally you're part of the investigation."

28

Elsbeth waved that spoon at them, sending some of the chocolate flying. "I want you to leave us and our parishioners alone, or we will find a lawyer who will stop you! Do you understand me?"

Suddenly, she calmed again, shrugged, then turned back to the brownie bowl. She said over her shoulder as she measured more cocoa into the cup, her voice calm again, under control, "Neither I nor Reverend McCamy know anything about this. We have told you this repeatedly. Reverend McCamy loves God. More importantly, he is beloved by God and all those who bask in His grace. He doesn't speak ill of anyone."

"He doesn't speak ill of sinners?" Miles's voice was so mild he surprised himself.

"Regular sinners — our local sinners — they know they're in trouble. They know they need Reverend McCamy to help them rise above their sins."

Miles asked in that same mild voice after a moment of silence, "I understand that

Reverend McCamy believes women need more assistance than men."

Elsbeth McCamy paused a moment, then in a sharp angry movement, pulled a bag of pecans out of a cabinet and dumped the whole bag into a bowl. "Well, not exactly, but we let our righteous men guide us. Reverend McCamy is very serious about every member of his flock leading the sort of life that will grant him God's grace. As for the women of his flock, we know it was Eve who tempted Adam to abandon God's commands, and so it is women who must bear her sin."

What to say to that? Katie and Miles sat in silence, watching Elsbeth mix the ingredients together. She was humming under her breath, comfortable with what she was doing.

How, Miles wondered, watching this woman mix brownies, how could this very strange, very beautiful woman be involved in the kidnapping of his son? But Clancy was her brother. He couldn't forget that, ever. Miles said, "My son was kidnapped for a reason, Mrs. McCamy. Perhaps you could tell us what this reason is."

She nearly dropped the bowl to the clean pale cream tile floor. Katie held very still, her face not giving away that she wanted to punch Miles. Talk about rushing fences. She saw Elsbeth's face, just as Miles did, and it was as obvious to her as it was to Miles that Elsbeth McCamy knew something. It would have been obvious to the postman. Katie realized then that Miles's unexpected question had shocked her into giving at least that much away.

Elsbeth picked up a wooden spoon and began to vigorously stir the brownie batter. She was stirring so hard he could hear the pecans crunch against the sides of the bowl.

Elsbeth walked to the oven and turned it on, still saying nothing at all. She returned to the kitchen counter and continued beating the brownie batter. There was raw fury in every whip of the spoon.

Her Jesus earrings caught the sunlight from the kitchen window when she turned suddenly. "I want you both to leave. I've been polite, but this is police harassment and —"

"Elsbeth, what are you doing in here?"

She turned very slowly, picking up the bowl as she did so, and holding it in front of her, as if for protection. Now that was odd, particularly since it was Reverend McCamy's voice, her husband's.

"We have visitors who were just leaving.

I'm making brownies for you," Elsbeth said.

He came into the kitchen, those dark intense eyes fastened on that brownie batter, but he said nothing to his wife. His eyes passed over Katie, stopped at Miles, and he said, "You are the boy's father, aren't you?"

"Yes, I'm Sam's father. Miles Kettering."

Reverend McCamy didn't approach him, and Miles was glad. He didn't want to shake the man's hand. He appeared to be studying Miles, and thinking hard.

"I have wondered," Miles Kettering said, "why you have named your church the Sinful Children of God?"

Reverend McCamy said, "Because of the first sin, Mr. Kettering. A sin so grave that Adam and Eve were forever cursed and forced to suffer for what she had done." He paused a moment, looked briefly at his wife, then at Katie. He stepped over to the counter and ran a finger along the edge of the brownie bowl and licked off the batter, closing his eyes a moment. Well, Katie thought, that was certainly one kind of bliss. Then his eyes snapped open and he seemed once again the prophet ready to condemn the sinners. He said. "It is written to woman in Genesis: 'Your desire shall be for your husband, and he shall rule over you.' It is a pity your husband left you, Katie. He took away the focus of your life."

"I cannot tell you how pleased I am about that," Katie said and smiled sweetly at Reverend McCamy.

Miles thought the man was mad.

"A husband is woman's shepherd," Reverend McCamy said, his dark eyes resting hard on Katie's face. "Without his guidance, without his support and discipline, she will fall into sin and be struck down."

Katie looked this time as if she wanted to leap on Reverend McCamy, but the flash of murder in her eyes was gone in an instant. She even smiled. "I see you love brownie batter. I do, too. Could I have some, Elsbeth?"

Miles wondered just how long Reverend McCamy had been listening outside the kitchen. Had he been afraid his wife would give something away?

Miles said, "You probably heard me asking your wife why her brother kidnapped my boy."

Reverend McCamy didn't acknowledge Miles's words. He said, "Suffering draws us closer to God, even a little boy's suffering, if it is God's divine will."

Katie said, "I don't understand, Reverend McCamy. How can a little boy's suffering conform to God's divine will? That makes no sense to me. Do you mean that God wants everyone, including children, to suffer?"

He whispered, his eyes on Katie's face, "You misunderstand. I'm speaking of our conforming to the Cross of Christ. It is written: 'Whoever does not bear his own cross and come after me, cannot be my disciple.' It is man's highest gift to suffer for the love of God, to suffer so that he can come closer to a union with the Divine. Of course, only a very few of the blessed ones are granted such divine grace."

"What do you mean conforming to the cross?" Katie asked. "As in one should want to be crucified? That would please God?"

Miles could tell that Reverend McCamy wanted to lay his hands on Katie. To bless her or to punish her because he thought she was blaspheming? He couldn't tell.

Reverend McCamy said, all patience, so patronizing that Miles imagined Katie standing up and smacking him in the jaw if she weren't so focused on what she was doing, "We must embrace suffering to lead us ever closer to God, and in this suffering, there is greatness and submission. No, God does not wish us to be crucified like him. That is shallow and blind, meaning nothing. It is far more than that, far deeper, far more enveloping. Very rarely God's grace is bestowed on a living creature and is manifested in the imitation of Christ's travails on the cross."

Katie said, never looking away from Reverend McCamy's face, "You said that God doesn't want us to nail ourselves to a cross in imitation of the crucifixion. What then is this gift bestowed on so very few?"

Reverend McCamy said, "How long does it take for the brownies to bake, Elsbeth?"

"Thirty minutes," Elsbeth said. She never looked her husband in the face, nor did she look at Miles or Katie. She slipped the glass dish inside the oven, then turned to the sink to run water in the batter bowl.

Too bad, Katie had *really* wanted a taste of that batter. It was time to push again, time to maneuver him where she wanted him to go. She said, "These individuals who imitate Christ's suffering, who and what are they? How are they selected? And by whom?"

Elsbeth whispered, "Don't you understand? Reverend McCamy is one of the very few blessed by God's grace, who is blessed by God's ecstasy in suffering."

Reverend McCamy looked like he wanted to slap her, but he didn't move, just fisted his hands at his sides.

Katie said, ever so gently, her eyes as intense as Reverend McCamy's, "You're speaking of Christ's wounds appearing on a mortal's body. You're saying that Reverend McCamy is a — what are they called?"

"Stigmatist," said Reverend McCamy.

"And you're a stigmatist, aren't you, sir?"

He looked furious that she pushed him to this, and Miles realized in that instant that she indeed had, and she'd done it very well. For a moment Reverend McCamy didn't say anything. Katie knew he was trying to get himself under control and it was difficult for him.

Katie said, "Homer Bean, one of your former parishioners, told us that you'd told a small group of men one evening about being a victim of God's love, about being a stigmatist."

Reverend McCamy said without looking up, "Since they have told you, then I will not deny it. Once in my life I was blessed to have the suffering of ecstasy with blood flowing from my hands in imitation of the nails driven through our Lord's palms."

Katie said, "You're saying that blood flowed from your palms? That you have actually experienced this?"

"Yes, I have been blessed. God granted me this passionate and tender gift. The pain and the ecstasy — the two together provide incalculable profit to the soul. I have kept this private, all except for those few men in whom I once confided."

Katie said, "And how is it you were chosen for this, Reverend?"

"You must recognize and accept the divine presence, Katie. You must believe that it is too overwhelming for mankind to fathom, that it must be the expression of ultimate faith. Thus the godless have sought to belittle this divine ecstasy, to trivialize it, to turn it into some sort of freak show. But it isn't, for I have had my blood flow from my own palms."

Miles said, fed up with this fanatic, his strange wife, and the damned brownies in the oven, "This is all very fascinating, McCamy, but can you tell me why Clancy and Beau kidnapped my son?"

It was as if someone flipped off the light switch. Reverend McCamy's eyes became even darker, as if a black tide was roiling up through his body. He shuddered, as if bringing himself out of someplace very deep, very far away. He said, "Your son is one of God's children, Mr. Kettering. I will pray for your son, and I will ask God to intercede." With that, Reverend McCamy turned and walked out of the kitchen. After a moment, they heard him call out, "Elsbeth, bring the brownies to my study when they're done. You don't have to cool them."

She nodded, even though he was no longer there. "Yes, Reverend McCamy."

Katie said to Elsbeth, "Sam is a wonderful little boy. I will not allow him to be taken again. Do you understand me, Elsbeth?"

"Go away, Katie. Go away and take that godless man with you."

"I'm not godless, ma'am. I just don't worship quite the same God you and your husband do."

When they were driving away from that lovely house, Miles said, "That was excellent questioning. I just don't know what it got us."

"I don't either," Katie said. "But I discovered I could pry him open."

"They're in on this, Katie."

"Yes," she said. "I think so, too."

Miles slammed his fist against the steering wheel. "Why, for God's sake? Why?"

29

Sam and Keely were playing chess, loosely speaking, given that Keely had had only two lessons. Katie had a No-TV rule during the week so the house was quiet, with just a soft layer of light rock coming from the speakers, and an occasional ember popping in the fireplace. The air felt thick, heavy. Another big storm was coming.

"No, Sam," Keely said, "you can't do that. The rook has to go in straight lines, he can't go sideways."

"That's boring," said Sam, and moved his bishop instead because he liked the long diagonal. The only problem was he stopped his bishop in front of a pawn, which Keely promptly removed. Sam yelled out, then sat back, stroked his chin like his father did, and said, "I will think about this and then you'll be very sorry."

Keely crowed.

"Killers, both of them," said Miles, happy to see Sam acting like a normal kid again.

Katie and Miles were seated on opposite

ends of the long sofa, doing nothing but sipping coffee and listening to the fascinating chess moves made by two children whose combined age was eleven.

Two deputies, Neil Crooke, who got no end of grief for his name, and Jamie Beezer, who did a great imitation dance of Muhammad Ali in his heyday, were outside watching the house. When Neil called to ask if he could go unlock ancient Mr. Cerlew's 1956 Buick for him since he'd locked his keys in it, Katie said go, but get back as soon as possible.

She excused herself a moment, and came back into the living room with a plate of brownies in her hands. "They're not homemade like Elsbeth's, but I'll tell you, the Harvest Moon bakery can't be beat."

Miles took a brownie, saying, "You think they're better than the ones Elsbeth McCamy made?"

"We'll never know, at least I hope we won't. Kids? Can the chess battle stop for a brownie break?"

When the plate was empty, in just under four minutes, Miles sat back and laced his fingers over his belly. He stretched out his legs, crossed them at the ankles, and leaned his head back against the sofa. He said as he closed his eyes, "It's Wednesday night. I've known you since Saturday. Isn't that amazing?"

Katie slowly nodded even though she knew he couldn't see her, and said, "We're sitting here like two folks who've been sitting here for a very long time." Except for the SIG Sauer tucked into the waistband of her jeans and the derringer strapped at her ankle.

That was sure the truth, Miles thought.

Katie stared at the glowing embers in the fireplace that periodically spewed up a mist of color. "It seems much longer," she said after a moment. "It seems natural."

He opened his eyes and turned his head to face her. "I can't stay here indefinitely, Katie, although I'm becoming fond of your microwave and your teakettle. The oatmeal was pretty good, too. But the bed is too short, and Sam snores on occasion." He stopped, and sat forward, his hands clasped between his knees, staring at the rag rug Katie's grandmother had made in the thirties. "This still isn't over, Katie. What am I to do?"

Because Katie didn't have an answer for that, she looked over to make sure the kids were occupied. They were on their stomachs, their noses almost touching the chess pieces. She said, "The meeting with the

McCamys — you did good, Miles, asking Elsbeth that question point-blank. At least we know for sure now they're involved — Elsbeth's face gave it all away. She's not good at lying. She'd lose her knickers in a poker game."

Miles said quietly, "All right, they're involved. Tell me why a preacher would have Sam kidnapped."

"Okay, let's just cut to the bone. Reverend McCamy had Clancy and Beau kidnap Sam, told them to take him to Bleaker's cabin. To wait? Why? Well, I suppose, so he could make arrangements."

"For what?"

"We don't know yet, but if that's the case, there has to be a reason, one that makes a great deal of sense to the McCamys. You know, Miles, there was something else Homer Bean mentioned. He said something about Reverend McCamy wanting a successor. No, wanting a *worthy* successor."

"If that rumor about seeing Reverend McCamy in Knoxville at a real estate office is true, and he is planning to pick up stakes, then it would be logical, I suppose, that he'd want to find someone to take his place with all the sinful children. But what does that have to do with Sam? Sam's a little young to be anyone's successor. Just last month I told him for sure that he'd be my successor, but he couldn't take over until he could spell guidance system."

Katie smiled at that. Miles watched her scuff her toe against the carpet and leaned toward her as she said, "Bits and pieces, Miles, that's what we're gathering. Soon it will all come together. We're close, I can feel it. I do wish that Agent Hodges would get back to us on the McCamy personal bank transactions and the church's books."

"Since he had trouble getting a warrant, he said it wouldn't be until tomorrow."

"There's something else. It's Reverend McCamy. I've known him a long time. This is the first time I've seen him come close to losing it. He was out of control a couple of times."

"If they're behind Sam's kidnapping, they have to know that it's just a matter of time before everything collapses."

"Check!"

Sam came up on his knees, shook his fist, and shouted, "You moved the queen like a knight, Keely, and that's cheating!"

Keely punched him in the arm, told him she was tired of chess, and got her favorite board game out of the cabinet, The Game of Life. In the next moment, they were rolling the dice and laughing, fighting over the rules, which neither of them really understood.

Miles said, "You've done an excellent job with Keely."

"And you with Sam. Can you imagine learning chess from a five-year-old who's had only two lessons?"

"I gather you play?"

"Oh yes, my father gave me my first lesson when I was about Keely's age. There are a couple of old guys who sit out in front of City Hall playing chess, probably been there since the Depression. I've never had the nerve to challenge either of them."

He laughed and said in a voice that was too good an imitation of Reverend McCamy's, "It's a pity your husband left you and you lost your focus."

She laughed, too, but it was forced since she really wanted to spit. "Can you believe he actually said that?"

"You handled him very well."

"Maybe, but Elsbeth still didn't let me taste the brownie batter."

Miles looked at her straight on. She'd French-braided her hair again, and a few tendrils had worked loose to curl around her ears. He really liked that French braid, and those tendrils. She was wearing her usual oxford shirt and jeans, and scuffed low-heeled boots. "I saw a cream-colored straw hat on the coatrack by the front door. Do you ever wear that hat?"

"Oh yes. To be honest, there's just been so much happening, that I haven't thought of it. I'm lucky to remember my coat."

"Eastern Tennessee is a very beautiful place, Katie."

She nodded. "Yes, it is. It's the mountains, really — always there right beside you, going on farther than the eye can see. Then you'll look at this incredible hazy blue glaze over the Appalachians. You know, I've always found it strange that people think we're country bumpkins, living out here. But the fact is, we aren't exiled here. We look up and see more stars than any city person can ever hope to see, and you know what? We actually sometimes feel the urge to talk to strangers. You've seen the cows, the dairy farms, the rolling farmlands. We're rich here, Miles, more than rich, we're blessed."

Miles studied her face as she spoke. "Yes, I can see that." He paused, looked toward the kids, then said, "I won't be here in the winter, Katie."

"No," she said slowly, "I don't suppose you will."

He slashed his hand through the air in frustration but he kept his voice low so the kids wouldn't hear. "Usually I ask a woman I'm interested in to go out to dinner, maybe a show in Washington. Yet here I am living in a woman's house and I've known her for what — four days?"

"I'm the sheriff, that's different."

"Is it?"

She made a restless movement with her hand, then smoothed out her fingers along her thigh. "You know what's funny? My husband never lived here."

He let her sidetrack him, it was safer. "What did you do with the jerk?"

She turned on the sofa, tucked one leg beneath the other, and leaned toward him. "The jerk's name is Carlo Silvestri, and he's the eldest son of an Italian aristocrat, and you're right, he's a jerk all the way down to his Ferragamos."

"An Italian aristocrat? You're kidding."

"Nope. His father is Il Conte Rosso, a big shot who lives near Milan, into arms manufacturing, I believe."

"How ever did you meet an Italian aristocrat?"

She gave a really big sigh. "I still feel like

I should punch myself in the head for being so stupid. Carlo and two of his buddies were visiting Nashville. They wanted to see Dolly Parton's breasts, one of them told me, so they drove east. When they landed in Knoxville, one of them, a Frenchman who must have thought it was Le Mans, was speeding like a maniac on Neyland Avenue, one of Knoxville's main streets. I stopped them after a bit of a chase. The idiot had been drinking and nearly went over the guardrail into the Tennessee River."

"So you hauled his ass off to jail?"

"Yeah, I did. Carlo decided he didn't want to leave when his buddy got sprung. He said he fell in love with me when he saw me clap on the handcuffs. It was a whirlwind romance, I'll tell you that. I was twenty-four years old, he was thirty-six, and I knew he was too old for me, knew the last thing he could ever do was leave Italy for good and live in Tennessee, but none of it mattered. I stopped thinking and married him. It didn't matter that he was a spoiled egotist, too rich to have a clue about what responsibility meant. Women do that, you know. Stop thinking."

"So do men."

"For men, it's lust. For women, it's

339

romance. You can get blindsided by both. I got pregnant right away. The problems started probably about a week later and never stopped. When Keely was about a month old, Carlo's father, Carlo Silvestri senior, Il Conte Rosso, shows up on our doorstep in Knoxville, announces that his son called him to come and save him. I really got a good laugh out of that one. I told Carlo senior that I'd removed his son's handcuffs a very long time before."

"So what happened?"

"Daddy did something that will endear him to me and this town for the rest of our collective lives."

Miles sat up. "What did he do?"

"He offered to buy me off for a million dollars if I would divorce Carlo without fuss, change Keely's name to Benedict — my name — and never contact them again."

"You've got to be joking."

"No, I'm not. I remember I just sat there and stared at him, trying to picture all those zeroes following a one and all those commas actually written out on a check, and wondering: Will they all fit in that little space?

"He actually believed I was playing him, that I was a tough cookie, and so do you know what the dear man did? He actually upped the ante. I'll tell you though, I made sure the money was wired into my account before I agreed. Then both Silvestris were out the door within four hours."

"What was the final buyout?"

"A million and a half big ones. I used it to put my dad's company, Benedict Pulp Mill, back on its feet, which guaranteed a lot of folks around here continued employment and thereby, truth be told, got me elected sheriff of Jessborough. I'm the first woman sheriff of Jessborough or, for that matter, just about anywhere in eastern Tennessee." She frowned at her boots, then said, "I don't know if they would have elected me without the bribe."

"It was more a by-product of the bribe, wasn't it? It's not as though you're incompetent."

"You're a sweet-talking guy, Miles," she said, laughing. "I'll tell you the truth though, I was the best-trained candidate for the job."

"Wade was the one who wanted to be sheriff, wasn't he? The one you beat out for the job?"

She nodded. "Wade's a good man, but he's never worked on the streets of a good-sized city where there's actual crime."

Sam turned around and said, "Katie, if you're the sheriff, then can I be your assistant?"

"You know, that might not be a bad idea. But you might end up becoming something else, like president, so you just keep playing."

Sam chewed on this a moment, then sprawled back onto his stomach, his nose nearly touching the dice on the game board. They heard Keely say, "If I become president, I'll make you vice president."

Sam nodded. "Okay, that'd be cool."

"I can give you orders all the time and you'll have to listen to me."

Miles sat back, crossed his arms over his chest, and shook his head. "You did good, Katie — the proper use of money. Well done."

"Thank goodness I've had no complaints since I've been sheriff." She frowned. "This is farm and dairy country — lots of cows — and tobacco country, you know, and that means lots of cheap cigarettes and lots of teenagers smoking. I've cracked down on that something fierce."

"How are you doing that?"

"I know most of the teenagers. I see one with a cigarette in his mouth and I take him and his cigarettes to jail. I can't lock him up since it's not against the law, but I call his parents. You'd be surprised at what a screaming mother can do to a teenage boy, even the mothers who smoke. It warms a sheriff's heart."

He laughed at that. "If my mom had ever caught me with a cigarette, I'd have been grounded for a month. Now, as for your mom, she makes good tuna casserola, and she didn't raise a dummy."

She was pleased, and he saw it. "Thank you," she said. "Casserola — what comfort food. I guess that's why she made it for all of us Monday night."

Katie rose and stretched. He was watching her, she felt it, and quickly lowered her arms, slouched forward a bit.

"Sorry, I didn't mean to do that in front of you."

"Think nothing of it."

"I mean, I didn't mean to preen in front of you."

"Maybe that's too bad."

30

"There, that's it. You're going to be a dentist, Sam, and I'm going to be an astronaut!"

Katie came down on her haunches beside them. "Okay, career choices are set, let me tell you that it's nearly nine o'clock. Time for you guys to get to bed."

It wasn't as much of a production as either adult expected, no more than five minutes of whining. After Katie settled Keely in, Miles did the same with Sam down the hall, they traded places, without thinking much about it, and that made Katie frown down at her toes. What did Miles think about tucking her daughter in and being pulled into reading the next chapter of *Lindy Lymmes, Kindergarten Girl Detective*?

She offered to read to Sam from one of Keely's books, but that made him gag — loudly — so she gave him a big hug and kissed his ear. If she wasn't careful, she thought, she'd fall in love with this little boy.

When Miles had gone to bed, she went outside to speak to Jamie and Neil, who'd gotten the cow safely secured. She gave them a thermos of coffee she'd made, checked and locked all the doors and windows, and fell into bed.

The storm hit hard around two in the morning, rattling windows, slapping tree branches against the house. It was time for a shift change in deputies guarding the house. Katie checked on Keely, who was sound asleep, and went back to bed. Katie had always loved storms, and they never bothered Keely, but tonight, Katie was antsy and wide awake. She finally gave it up, went to the kitchen and put on the tea-kettle. She was standing in front of the sink, looking out over the thick stand of maple and poplar trees not more than ten feet from the house, leached of their beautiful colors in the heavy gray rain.

"You got two tea bags?"

She turned around at Miles's voice, well aware that she was wearing only her night-shirt and her empty ankle holster. Even her feet were bare.

Miles walked straight to her, and wrapped his arms around her, trapping her own arms to her sides. When she pushed against him, he immediately released her, but then she simply wrapped her arms around his back. She felt his smile against her cheek, felt the strength of him against her. He was wearing only a pair of jeans and a dark blue T-shirt. She said against his neck, "You feel good," and that was a lie because he felt far more than good. And he made her feel things she hadn't felt in a very long time.

"So do you," and she could hear tension in his voice, hear that he was lying, too.

He was nuzzling her neck, and said against her jaw, "I like a tall woman. We fit together perfectly." And he kissed her.

Katie hadn't kissed a man in approximately two years and three months, and that kiss had been on the wet side with a beer aftertaste. How far back did she have to go for an astounding kiss, a kiss like this one? All the way back to Carlo.

The teakettle whistled, shrill and loud, and they both jumped. He took her arms in his hands, looked at her a moment, and stepped back from her.

"Do you drink your tea straight?"

Katie nodded. She wished the teakettle hadn't been so loud. He'd given her comfort, and so much more than that, and it had felt right, just right. And she wanted more, and she didn't want a teakettle sounding off in the middle of it. Life was strange. She hadn't even known this man before last weekend.

She watched him fetch two mugs down from the cabinet, dangle two Lipton tea bags over the sides of the mugs, and pour the boiling water over them.

He said without turning, "I like the holster around your ankle. It's sexy."

She looked down, saw that her red nail polish was chipped on her big toe. She grinned at him. "You're pretty easy, Miles."

"Not I." He handed her a mug, picked his up, and clicked it against hers. "To us," he said.

What did that mean? She sipped her tea. The wind howled, and the rain pelted hard against the windows like pebbles thrown hard by angry children.

"I get to meet with the TBI again tomorrow," Katie said, and added at his frown, "The final meeting, I hope."

"Do you need any witnesses?"

She shook her head. "They spoke to Glen Hodges again by phone this afternoon, and of course to Savich and Sherlock before they left. I suppose they might want to speak with you, but no one's mentioned it yet. And I have my deputies, all eager to defend me, even Wade, if he has a

clue what's good for him. The TBI investi-
gator checking out everything calls this
case a corker — his word — and he wants
to hang around. I'm hoping he gets a call
from his supervisor to finish things up."

Suddenly Katie heard something, no, it
was more than that. She felt something
dangerous and close. She ran to the living
room window and looked out through the
thick rain. No deputy car was out there.

She didn't hesitate. "Miles, grab Sam,
quickly!"

Miles didn't ask for an explanation,
didn't hesitate. He raced to the guest bedroom to see Sam was sitting up in bed,
half-asleep. "I heard something, Papa. Out
there."

"Come with me, Sam." Miles grabbed
him up, wrapped him in blankets and ran
with him back to the living room. Katie
was there with Keely.

"Sam was awake. He heard something.
What's the matter?"

"I don't know," Katie said. "I don't
know, but something's not right. Danny
and Jeffrey were supposed to show up at
two, but they're not there. We're getting
out of here right now."

"Katie, you're not dressed."

She was losing it. Not good, but her fear

was building. "Hold the kids, let me throw on some clothes. I'll bring you a shirt and your jacket. Oh damn, the kids need clothes, too. Miles, don't let either of them move. I'll get everything."

Two and a half minutes later, both adults were on their knees quickly dressing Sam and Keely.

"We're outta here," Katie said. Miles knew she was afraid and trying hard not to let that fear transmit itself to the children. He also knew she'd give her life for any of them.

Katie smashed her hat on her head, grabbed all the coats, and said, "We're outta here, now!"

Sam whispered as he clutched his father's neck, "What's the matter, Papa? What did I hear? Are those bad men after me again?"

"If they are, I'll knock their heads together, then I'll let you stomp on them, okay?"

"Okay, Papa," Sam said, less fear in his voice, thank God.

Keely twisted around in Miles's other arm to face her mother. "What's the matter, Mama?"

"Shush," Miles said. "We've all got to be very quiet, okay?" He squeezed both children close to him.

Just as Katie fumbled with the dead bolt on the front door, there was a loud explosion behind them that sent flames and heat out at them through the kitchen hall. Someone had tossed a bomb into the kitchen, where he and Katie had been drinking tea not more than five minutes before. Miles automatically turned his back to the heat to protect the children. Katie bounced back, blinked to clear the shock out of her head, and said, so mad she was stuttering, "The house, s-some idiot just b-blew up my damned house!"

There was a crackling of flames behind them.

Katie pulled the door open and ran out. "We're alive, thanks to you," Miles said as he raced out the door behind her.

"Wait!"

Her gun was out, and she was crouched down, making a sweep. She couldn't see anything through the deluge. There was nothing else she could do. She waved them forward. Miles, huddled over the kids, raced after her.

The rain pelted them, soaking them to the skin within seconds, and there were gusts of wind that forced them to bow forward and brace themselves. Katie led them straight to her truck. "Get in, Miles!"

She turned the key in the ignition and slammed the car into reverse, but the wheels spun. The ground had turned to sucking mud in the heavy rain.

The wheels finally gained traction when Katie ripped the truck back in reverse a second time. She barely missed the huge oak tree that was the oldest thing in her yard. Mud was flying from under the wheels, splashing the side windows, but they were free and that was all that mattered.

In that instant there was a sharp ping, like the sound of something hitting metal, and then another.

"Someone's shooting at us," Katie said low, her voice controlled. "Get the kids down, Miles."

He worked both children down into the space in front of the passenger seat. They were holding each other tightly, not making a sound. How much more of this could two little kids take?

"Keep your head down," Katie said, all matter-of-fact. "I'm getting us out of here."

She hit the gas the instant after she shifted into drive, and the truck shot forward. They heard a tremendous explosion that rocked the truck. Katie stopped the truck and jerked around, even as she dialed 911.

"Those bastards . . . my house is on fire!" She got her night dispatcher, Lewis, and snapped out instructions to him. "Get every deputy out to my house along with the fire department. And Lewis, Danny and Jeffrey never showed up at two o'clock to take over guard duty."

"Sheriff, they told me they were just going to be a few minutes late. Some kids busted out both their back tires."

"Yeah, right, some kids," Katie said. "Well, at least they're okay."

When she'd hung up, she said, her voice flat and calm, "Miles, you take the kids to the sheriff's office. Lock yourselves in a cell. Keely, Sam, it will be all right. Do what Miles tells you. I'll be with you as soon as I can."

"Mama!"

Katie didn't hesitate, she was out of the truck, sliding in the mud and rain, running back toward her burning house, her gun drawn.

Where were the idiots who'd fired at them? Surely there was no reason for them to stay now with Sam gone. But whoever had done this had gone over the edge.

Nothing could surprise her now.

She was crouched down, until she was under tree cover again as she made her way to the side of her burning house. She felt the heat billowing off her house, felt a spark strike her hand, and shook her fingers, cursing. She looked down to see her burned flesh. It hurt like the devil, but she had nothing to wrap it up with. She shook her hand to cool it, then knew she had to forget it.

They'd thrown the bomb into the kitchen. Why? To flush them out? The kitchen was the farthest room from the guest room where Sam was sleeping. They'd probably known that. The last thing they seemed to want was to hurt Sam.

It seemed like years passed before she heard the deputies, the firemen. The bombers were gone, no reason for them to hang around since their target had escaped.

Suddenly, she heard another gunshot. At the same time, her cell phone rang. She yelled into the phone even as she rolled to behind a garbage can, "Wade, stay put, that's an order! The moron who bombed the house just shot at me!"

Another shot, this one a good twenty

feet away. She saw Wade coming around the corner, and yelled, "Don't come any closer, Wade! Get more deputies and get down!"

But Wade just kept running toward her, his gun fanning as he ran. Soon, four deputies were there, yelling, running into each other, trying to avoid flying sparks from Katie's burning house.

"All of you be careful," Katie yelled.

Wade was panting when he reached her. He saw the blood on her hand and turned white. "My God, your hand."

"No, I'm all right, it was a flying spark. Wade, take the guys and check in the woods. See what you can find."

Not many minutes later, she slowly rose to see Wade come running toward her through the thick rain. He was shaking his head.

"Nothing?"

"Not a single damned thing. Hell, Katie, this whole thing's so off-the-wall. What do we do now?"

"We search every inch around here and see what we can find." She pointed him to the shards of glass sticking out of the mud. "They dropped that one and broke it, but its brother went through my kitchen window." She looked down at her hand.

Wade pulled a handkerchief out of his pocket and tied it around her hand. "There, that's better than nothing."

She looked up at Wade. "Thanks. At least the bastards didn't follow Miles into Jessborough. They've got to be okay."

31

Miles had got himself under control because, simply, there was no choice. "Your mama will be just fine," he said as he eased himself behind the wheel. "Now, Sam, Keely, I want you both to sit in the passenger seat and snuggle under those blankets."

They were wet and scared, their teeth chattering, and Miles turned the heat on high. "You guys know what? I'd really appreciate it if you'd sing me a song."

The children, bless their hearts, sang themselves hoarse. "Puff the Magic Dragon" had never sounded so good. He knew they were scared, knew they were dealing with it, just as he was, and he was very proud of both of them. Within minutes, he heard sirens, saw sheriff cars, red lights flashing; he pulled the truck off onto a side street while they streamed past, headed to Katie's burning house. Thank God it was raining so hard, the house just might survive.

He was praying Katie was all right as he

scooped both children into his arms, charged through the door of City Hall, veered to the right, where the sheriff's department was housed.

Lewis, the night dispatcher, waved them in. Then the outer door whooshed open again and there was Linnie, running through the doors right behind them, wearing jeans, boots, a huge sweatshirt with an extra-large bomber jacket over it, and rollers in her hair.

"This way," she said and smiled down at the children, just as calm and cool as Katie had been. His own heart was pounding and he wanted to hit something.

The phone rang and Lewis was on it.

"Everything is fine," Linnie said, leaning down to hug both children. "Listen to me now, I don't want you two worrying. Your mama's really tough, Keely, you know that. And Sam, your papa's right here, big and mean, and no one would mess with him. Now, come this way and we'll get you dry."

Sam stared up at his father, his small mouth working.

Miles came down on his knees next to Sam and Keely, drew them both into the circle of his arms. "Linnie's here to take care of you guys. She's going to get you dry and warm."

The kids, pale and wet, just stared up at him, saying nothing. They weren't buying it, and he was trying his very best, dammit.

"Okay, Linnie is going to watch you and keep you company, okay? She's also going to lock this place up tighter than your bank, Sam."

"Papa, you're going to leave us?"

He said simply, "I have to help Katie. Okay?"

"Don't let those bad men hurt my mama," Keely said, and burst into tears.

"I won't let anyone hurt your mama, Keely. I promise," Miles said as he stood up. "You guys, stay with Linnie."

He mouthed a thank you to Linnie, who was gathering both children against her.

"Wait, Mr. Kettering!" She tossed him a cell phone. "Use it. Call us whenever you can, right, Sam?"

"Call me, Papa."

"You got it, kid."

"I'll hug Keely," Sam said. "She's scared." Miles watched his son pull Keely close and pat her back.

As Miles drove back through the heavy cold rain, the driver's window cracked down, he could still hear sirens. He saw the glow of the flames from a mile away. With the heavy rainfall, at least the trees were protected. He pulled the truck up behind one of the deputy's cars and jumped out.

The firemen were hosing down the roof of the house, but even with the heavy rain there was no hope. Katie's house was gutted, and everything in it gone.

Miles threw back his head and yelled, "Katie!"

One of the deputies came running up, panting as he said, "Are the kids okay, Mr. Kettering?"

"They're with Linnie in jail, I mean that literally. Where's Katie?"

"I think she's still in the back."

Miles said, "They shot at the sheriff's truck. You'll probably be able to dig out the bullets, identify them. Are you sure Katie's okay?"

"I heard her yelling," the deputy said. "When she yells like that, she's okay, just real mad."

Miles nodded and ran to the back of the burning house, rain blurring his vision. He swiped his hand over his eyes, and shouted, "Katie!"

"I'm here."

He nearly ran right into her. She was leaning against a sugar maple, tying something around her hand.

"Dammit, you hurt yourself," he said,

then pulled her tight against him, unable to help himself, he was so afraid.

"Nothing bad, I promise," she said, and pulled back to give him the ghost of a smile. "A flying spark burned my hand. It's not bad. The guys who bombed my house are long gone. Wade and the other deputies haven't found anything yet."

"Both of us know where they went," he said. "First, let's get your hand bandaged a bit better. I saw the paramedics out front."

Ten minutes later they were in Katie's truck, Miles driving, headed for the Mc-Camy house.

Katie turned back to look at the devastation of her house. "Gone," she said. "Everything's just gone, including all my pictures of Keely and even her chess set."

"We're alive and that's all that matters. And you've got your hat."

She was wet and dirty, her hair straggling down beneath her beautiful cream-colored straw hat, her hand hurt, but she managed a smile. "Yes, and now I want to face down the monsters who have tried to wreck our lives." She drew her ankle gun and handed it to him. Driving with one hand, he shoved it into the waistband of his jeans.

As he leaned forward to wipe his hand

across the fog building up on the wind-shield, Miles said, "The rain is finally letting up a bit."

Katie said, "It's nearly four o'clock in the morning. Do you think the McCamys will pretend they were sleeping?"

He just shook his head, concentrating on not sliding off the road. "Unless we get lucky, and these guys have gone back to the McCamy house, I don't know what we're going to accomplish tonight."

Katie said slowly, "I've got an idea on how to get us through the front door."

Miles raised an eyebrow, but when she shook her head, he said, "Who have you called for backup?"

Again, she didn't answer. Her hand was throbbing bad now, she was sick to her stomach about her house and so mad she wanted to spit nails. Did she want backup? Sure, you always had backup, always. She just couldn't believe that she hadn't been the one to think of it.

She blew out her breath and dialed 911. "Lewis, how are Linnie and the kids?"

"They're locked in a cell with Mort, the cleaning guy." There was a pause, and Linnie said, "He's teaching them how to play poker. They're distracted and that's for the best. And yes, they're in dry clothes and they're warm. Everything's okay here, Katie. We got this place lit up like Christmas, and there are four of us here, ready to bust heads if those creeps show up."

"Thank you so much for coming in, Linnie. Okay, here's the deal. I want four deputies, Wade in the lead, out at Reverend McCamy's house." Linnie, of course, already knew they were on the way. Katie imagined that she'd spoken to every one of the deputies. "Listen, Linnie, this is very important: Tell Wade not to use sirens. I want a silent approach and I want them to stay outside and search for the guys who bombed my house. Tell them to be very careful." She paused, smiled a bit. "Give the kids a kiss." She flipped her cell off. "Turn here, Miles."

Miles was hunched over the steering wheel, trying to see through the rain and the fogged windshield. "He wants Sam beyond reason or else he would have just given it up. This has nothing to do with money, this has to do with a madman, and what a madman believes."

That sounded simple, and exactly right, Katie thought. She said, "He must be well over the edge now, surely what happened tonight proves it. I wonder who he found to do this on such short notice. It's got to be someone local, maybe someone from his congregation."

"I wonder if there were two guys or just one. The ability to talk just one member into doing something this crazy, much less two guys, boggles the mind. You said he was charismatic. I guess this proves it."

"When you put it like that, I guess one guy makes more sense. Still, we've got to be really careful."

Katie rolled down the window and stuck her hand out. "It's not raining as hard."

"Your hand okay?"

She didn't answer, just pointed to the big Victorian house that had just come into view. "We're not leaving without answers this time, Miles."

32

The only sound they heard when they got out of the truck was the rain and the rustling of wet leaves. It was cold and there was no moon, not a single star, just fat bloated clouds, probably gathering energy for another deluge. There were no lights on in the big Victorian house.

They were wet. Katie's hat was still clamped down on her head, her hair coming out of its French braid, the white bandage on her hand soaked with rain. She could feel her boots squish as she walked.

Katie rang the doorbell, such a mundane thing. There was no answer. She rang it again, then once more. She was smiling, as grim as Jesse Helms if he'd been a judge. Finally, she slammed her fist against the large wooden door.

She kept pounding until, at last, Reverend McCamy's angry voice shouted, "Who is this? What is going on here? Go away!"

The door jerked open. Reverend McCamy, dressed in pajamas, dressing gown, and bedroom slippers, stood there, his face a study of anger and something else, something that was beyond what they could begin to understand.

"Who is it, Reverend McCamy?"

They heard the light sound of footfalls coming down the stairs. Elsbeth McCamy came to stand beside her husband, staring at them.

She was wearing a pink silk robe that came only to her knees; it was obvious she was wearing absolutely nothing underneath. Her feet were bare. Her hair was tousled around her face and tangled down her back, and for once, she wasn't wearing her earrings.

Reverend McCamy, his dark eyes fathomless and sharp, raised his hands to his hips, and stared at them. They stared back. Finally, he said slowly, "What is the meaning of this, Sheriff? Do you have any idea at all what time it is?"

Katie actually smiled at Reverend McCamy, showing him lots of teeth, and waved her bandaged hand in a shooing motion. "Do invite us in, Reverend McCamy. And I think a cup of coffee would be nice too. It's been a hard night."

"No, I'm not letting either of you in my house until you tell me what's going on.

You both look filthy."

"Well, that's true," Katie said. "Naturally, since I've had my house burned down and we've been running around in the rain, I guess you'd have to expect that."

Still, he didn't move. "Your house caught on fire? I'm sorry about that, Sheriff, but it doesn't have anything to do with us. I don't want to give you any coffee. I want you both to leave."

Katie paused a moment. "Well, there's something else, Reverend, something you should know." She waited, letting this soak in, then said, looking straight into those mad prophet's eyes, "As a result of your hiring incompetent help, Sam is in the hospital with severe injuries."

Miles didn't blink.

Reverend McCamy's mouth worked, but nothing came out.

Elsbeth cried out, "What do you mean Sam is in the hospital? What's wrong with him?"

Reverend McCamy whispered, "No, this can't happen. Tell me he will be all right."

"We don't know yet."

"I'm a minister, I will go to him," and Reverend McCamy turned on his heel. "I'll be ready in just a moment."

Katie called out after him, "You're not

going to the hospital, Reverend McCamy. Sam's in surgery. There's nothing you can do. Best to stay here and tell us why you want Sam so much."

Elsbeth said, "You're being ridiculous, Sheriff. We had nothing to do with this. What hospital is Sam in?"

Miles said, "Do you honestly believe we'd tell you where he is? My God, you'd probably set the hospital on fire to get to him."

"I don't know what you're talking about," Reverend McCamy said, but he was backing up, one step at a time. He was pale, markedly so, and it wasn't that he was afraid of getting caught. It was because he was afraid Sam would die. His eyes, Katie thought, his eyes were quite fixed, no light in them at all.

And Elsbeth? Did she realize her husband was mad? Maybe she didn't want to admit it, but she had to know, just as she had to be involved in all the efforts to get hold of Sam.

"My boy isn't expected to live," Miles said, his voice filled with rage. "Because of you, you fanatic bastard, my boy is probably going to die. Do you understand that, you moron? A six-year-old boy is going to die because of you! No one else, just you."

He walked toward Reverend McCamy, one step at a time, staring into those mad eyes of his until he had him backed up against the wall. He put his face right into his, grabbed his robe lapels, and shook him. He screamed in his face, "And you call yourself a man of God?" Miles yanked him close again, shaking him so hard his head lolled on his neck.

Reverend McCamy tried to pull Miles's hands away, but he couldn't. He yelled, "You fool, you conceited buffoon! *Sam doesn't belong to you!*"

Miles felt the man's spittle on his cheek. He pressed closer and yelled back, "He sure in hell doesn't belong to you!"

Reverend McCamy was shaking his head wildly, back and forth. "No! He belongs to God! And God won't let him die, he won't! I must go to the hospital, don't you understand? I must go. I'm the only one who can save him!"

Katie said, "Why won't God let him die, Reverend McCamy?"

Elsbeth said, "No, Reverend McCamy, don't let them fluster you."

Reverend McCamy slipped out of Miles's grasp and dashed past him. Miles let him go. He watched him stumble over a Victorian umbrella stand, sending it crashing onto its side and splitting it open. Two umbrellas rolled out. Reverend McCamy took off running down the long hallway.

Elsbeth stood there in her sexy pink robe, staring after her husband. Katie and Miles ignored her, and turned to run after Reverend McCamy. He tried to slam the library door in their faces, but Miles shoved it back against him. He retreated back across the room where he did his couples counseling. There were three sofa pillows on the carpet. Why, for heaven's sake?

As they closed in, he fetched up against the bookshelved wall, his hands out to ward them off.

Miles stopped in front of the desk, leaned forward and splayed his fingers on the desktop. "We want you to talk to us, Reverend McCamy. We want you to tell us why my son belongs to God."

"No!" Elsbeth shouted. "Leave him alone, do you hear me? Go away!" She turned on Katie, and smashed her fist into her jaw. Katie, focused on Miles and Reverend McCamy, lurched to the side, nearly falling. She saw stars, but felt more surprise than pain. Katie grabbed Elsbeth's arm, jerked her close, and pulled both her arms behind her. She pulled her against her, leaned over, and whispered in her ear through all that beautiful tangled blond hair, "Just hold still, Elsbeth. Assaulting a police officer isn't going to help the Reverend. We're not going to hurt him."

"No, you can't make me —" She moaned as Katie tightened her hold. Her pink silk robe came open.

"Woman, do not show your body to these sinners!"

"We're not looking at her body," Miles said, his attention never wavering from Reverend McCamy. "I'm waiting, Reverend McCamy. Why does Sam belong to God?"

Reverend McCamy's mouth was a thin pale line. Suddenly, he shouted at them, "You're not worthy, you godless cretin! Why God gave such a son to you is beyond me. But His ways are not always clear to those who worship Him. It is not our right to question Him, for we are nothing compared to Him. The Lord showed me that I must take Samuel, to teach him to understand that he is one of God's favored ones. You don't understand, do you? Sam is an ecstatic! He must learn to accept the sublime suffering he once showed as a small child. He will learn to accept it again. He will throw himself into the well of God's mercy and greet this suffering with great happiness because he was chosen by God."

Reverend McCamy walked around the desk until he came right up into Miles's face. "Don't you understand, you fool? Sam is a victim of love — God's love. He has shown the stigmata! He will experience sublime suffering for all mankind, and his suffering will be radiant in its ecstasy. His very soul will know the beauty and sacrifice of our Lord!"

Miles felt as though he'd fallen down Alice's rabbit hole. He plowed his way through all the mad words. He stood back from Reverend McCamy, studying him. "What are you talking about? What nonsense is this? So you think Sam has shown the stigmata? Is that what this is all about? There is no such thing, you fool!"

Suddenly, Elsbeth stiffened, and jerked free of Katie. She ran right at Miles, her fists swinging, screaming, "Leave him alone! Reverend McCamy, they don't understand. They never will. Say no more. Make them leave. They don't belong here. Make them leave!"

"She's right, you'll never understand," Reverend McCamy said, coming around the desk to his wife, reaching out his hands, for what reason, neither Miles nor

Katie knew. Then he slammed both fists onto the desktop. "Sam — it is not his name! His name is Samuel, his biblical name. He can't die! Save the boy, oh Lord, he is part of You, he is Your beloved victim. You must save him!"

Reverend McCamy was shaking so hard that he appeared to be having a seizure. Tears streamed down his face. "Elsbeth is right. Get out, both of you!"

A man's voice came from the doorway. "I can't let you do this to him, Sheriff, I just can't. Back away from Reverend McCamy."

Reverend McCamy screamed, "Are you crazy? What are you doing here, Thomas? Get out!"

Katie turned slowly around to see Tom Boone, a local postman for twenty years, standing just inside the library door holding a rifle on her. She smiled. "Well, I think there walks my proof on the hoof. Is there anyone else getting ready to come through that door? Or was it just you, Mr. Boone?"

"It was just me, Sheriff, and I'm enough to deal with you. I'm sorry, Reverend McCamy, but she's got a gun, you know. It's right there in her shoulder holster. I didn't want her to hurt you. You, Mr.

Kettering, you get away from Reverend McCamy!"

Miles stepped away.

Katie remembered seeing Mr. Boone on Sunday, at the Sinful Children of God. She said, "Do you believe in this madman enough to try to kill me and Keely and Mr. Kettering to get to Sam?"

"I didn't try to kill nobody."

"Just be quiet, Thomas! Go away from here."

"No, Reverend, not just yet. I've got to tell her how it really was, that I wasn't there to hurt anyone, then she'll leave you alone. I did what I had to do, Sheriff, what the Reverend and God commanded me to do."

"What are you talking about, Mr. Boone? God doesn't have anything to do with this. It was this madman who gave you your marching orders. It was this madman who ordered you to take Sam. Didn't you hear what happened to the other two men he sent to get Sam?"

"I heard, Sheriff. You killed them, both of them. You, a woman, killed two men. You're an abomination."

Katie could only stare at him and shake her head. "And just look at what you did. You threw gas bombs into my kitchen and fired at me in my truck. Then you stayed around and tried to kill me again. What were you thinking?"

Mr. Boone, asthmatic all his life, panted hard now because he was scared. The drizzling rain and cold air had gone into his chest, he could feel it, choking off his air. He looked at the man who had helped him before, the saintly man who'd laid his hands on his chest and prayed and had eased his breathing. Thomas had known it was a miracle. He looked over at Reverend McCamy.

"It was God's orders as well," Reverend McCamy shouted. "I promised that you would be rewarded, Thomas. I promised that I would heal your asthma forever, but only if you finished what you started."

Katie asked, "What else did the Reverend here offer you as a reward, Mr. Boone?"

"He promised me that I would be his deacon. I've always wanted that and now I'll have it, and I'll be able to breathe free and easy for the rest of my life."

Katie had dealt with teenage gang members, drug dealers, homicides, and rapes in Knoxville, but never had she heard thinking as bizarre as this.

She drew in a deep breath, and held out

her hand to Mr. Boone. "Have you lost your mind, Mr. Boone? Did you think even once about your mother and your grandmother, what this would do to them? Listen to me. This man isn't holy, he's insane. Do you have any idea what deep trouble you're in? Now, put down that damned rifle."

But Mr. Boone held on to the rifle like it was his lifeline, and perhaps, in his mind, it was. He kept it steady on her chest.

Katie said to Reverend McCamy, "I believe that in Hollywood they would say the jig's up, sir. Is there anything else you'd like to tell me before I take you to my cozy jail?"

"Damn you, Sheriff, why don't you believe me?"

"Of course I don't believe you," she said, warning signs going off in her head because he was losing it fast. "I'm not mad."

"You stupid woman!" He lurched away and ran to the bookshelf behind his desk. He jerked books off the shelf, hurling them to the floor, reached in and pulled out what appeared to be a videotape.

"I'll prove it to you! Look at this tape! This proves what I'm saying! I'm not insane, you stupid woman! It's on this tape!"

"What's on the tape, Reverend?" Katie asked.

"You'll see," Reverend McCamy said, tears still running down his face, his voice feverish, trembling, quite mad. "You'll see. God, through His infinite grace, through His desire to use me to teach others, has brought me this miracle. I saw the miracle and I clasped it to my soul and swore to God that I would bring Samuel to understand and accept God's mission for him in this life."

He shoved the video into the machine slot, turned on the TV and there it was, without his doing anything else. He obviously kept the TV set to video, ready for this tape.

There was a hissing sound from the tape, and then the grainy sound and squiggly lines faded away. The focus wasn't very good, and there was motion because the camera wasn't being held steady. Miles realized that it was a home movie, of sorts. Of what? The camera came to a stop on Sam, a younger Sam, maybe three years old, lying on his old bed in his child's bedroom in their first house in Alexandria, wearing only his pajama bottoms. He was thrashing around, moaning, or delirious. He was heaving, arching his back, his arms and legs flailing. The jerking camera moved in closer. Miles thought he heard a person crying, probably the person video-taping his son. Was it Alicia?

Miles knew nothing of this, nothing. He watched Sam's arms fly over his head, watched the camera zoom in on his fisted hands. Then his small hands opened, slowly.

There was blood on Sam's palms. And it was running down his wrists.

Miles stopped breathing. Blood? Sam had been bleeding? When? Why hadn't Alicia told him?

The woman was crying loudly now, and the camera was shaking so badly everything went blurry, then suddenly, it went to black.

Reverend McCamy hit the "stop" button, but he didn't look away from the blank TV screen. His breath was coming fast and hard, and his dark eyes were glazed. It was almost as if he was in some sort of ecstasy. Miles watched as his hands slowly unfurled, the palms open, just like Sam's had, and now he was panting, shivering, as if he were in that film with Sam, as if his body wanted desperately to simulate what had happened to Sam.

Reverend McCamy whispered as he continued to stare at the blank TV screen, "Did you see? The child, like Christ, is God's victim and God's sacrifice, here to make the world know His power, and through Samuel's ecstasy, understand God's love and His limitless compassion.

"Samuel, in those moments, those precious moments, was as close to God as any of us will ever be in this life."

33

Reverend McCamy stared at the screen, his wild eyes seeing what was no longer there, but was only there in his mind, so deep that he'd made himself mad with it. Or maybe the madness had come first.

There was a moment of stark silence.

Miles didn't move, just said to Reverend McCamy, his voice calm and steady, "You're telling me that you had Sam kidnapped because you saw a video of an obviously sick, delirious little boy, who, for whatever reason, had blood on his hands?"

Katie felt as if someone had smacked her upside the head and she'd never seen it coming. When Reverend McCamy had spoken of the stigmata, she'd thought of it as just another of the ravings of a fanatic, certainly nothing to do with Sam.

What was all this about stigmata? From what she'd read, which wasn't much at all, the people who'd supposedly displayed the marks of the Cross seemed very ill, both physically and mentally. But why was there blood on Sam's hands in the video? Was that his mother taping this? It was obvious Miles didn't know a thing about it. Why in heaven's name hadn't Miles's wife told him about this?

"This must have happened about three years ago, Reverend McCamy," Miles said. "Why did you wait three years to take Sam?"

Reverend McCamy looked suddenly at his wife, and his eyes went even wilder. "Elsbeth, stay back! Close your robe, woman, you're showing your body to these people, to this man!"

"I'm looking at you, Reverend, not your damned wife."

"I'm sorry, Reverend McCamy, I'm so sorry." Elsbeth turned away, frantically tying the sash on her silk robe again.

Reverend McCamy looked back at Miles. "Taking the boy, it should have been so simple, but I hadn't yet seen the boy, and so how could he understand? He managed to escape. Don't you see? God wants the boy to be with me."

Miles said slowly, "I have never seen that tape. I never even knew about it, don't even know who shot it. I don't remember Sam ever being that ill. He was obviously delirious, very sick. Where did you get that tape, Reverend?"

"I won't tell you. You'll hurt the people who gave me the tape, and they were only doing God's work."

Miles rolled his eyes. "Don't be ridiculous —"

"Very well, at least tell us what you were going to do with Sam?" Katie said. "He's six years old, not a toddler."

"I was willing to leave my ministry here, to take Samuel to Phoenix with us. I've already bought property there. It wouldn't take me long to teach Samuel what he is and what he must do with his life."

"Sam is to be your successor," Katie said.

"Of course, I must go see Samuel. *Now*." He was suddenly the leader of his flock, decisive, full of resolve. He stepped back from Miles and shook himself. "I am going to see Samuel. I will pray for him. I will intercede with God to save him. I will lay my hands upon him."

And he turned to walk out of the room.

"Reverend McCamy," Katie said quite pleasantly. "You, sir, aren't going anywhere."

In spite of Mr. Boone with his rifle pointed at her, Katie pulled her SIG Sauer out of her waistband. He said, "Please, Sheriff Benedict, put that gun down."

Katie turned as she slowly lowered her SIG to her side. "Surely, Mr. Boone, you can't think God is ordering you now to kill both me and Mr. Kettering, to go with Reverend McCamy to the hospital and try to steal Sam away again? Don't you realize that you would be sending that innocent little boy into a life of slavery and madness? Listen, Mr. Boone, I can still help you if you don't hurt anyone."

"No! That's not what the Reverend said!"

Reverend McCamy said, "Thomas, they said the boy was injured. How did that happen?"

"I was going to throw the bombs in the kitchen to get them out of the house. It's just that the sheriff was there, and I really didn't want to kill her like that. And then Mr. Kettering came into the kitchen and I believed they were going to fornicate right there, on the kitchen table! I watched them, but you know what? Before anything happened, she sensed something, I swear it, she knew something was wrong. Maybe she saw me, but I don't think so. I was real careful. She yelled at Mr. Kettering to get the kids, that they were getting out of there. They got to the truck before I could grab Samuel. He drove off with Mr.

Kettering, and he was fine."

Reverend McCamy's face turned red with rage, the pulse pounding at his temple. He shook so hard he had to hold on to the edge of the desk to keep his balance. He yelled, "God will strike you dead, Sheriff! You twisted, perverted woman. You lied!"

Katie even grinned as she said to Reverend McCamy, an eyebrow arched, "I'm a perverted woman? That language isn't particularly nice, Reverend."

"Samuel isn't in the hospital! He wasn't hurt! Where have you hidden him? Where is the boy?"

Miles knew he had to keep calm with that idiot still holding the rifle on Katie. He leaned back against a bookshelf, crossed his arms over his chest and said, "My son is safe in jail, Reverend McCamy. I believe four deputies are guarding him and he's playing poker with Mort, the cleaning guy. I'm sure the sheriff will let him out when you show up in handcuffs."

"This is the man you obeyed, Mr. Boone," Katie said. "Take a good look."

"Kill them, Thomas!"

It was obvious to Katie that Mr. Boone finally realized he was in way over his head. He was holding a rifle on a law enforcement officer, obviously so scared sweat was pouring off his forehead, and he looked ready to faint.

"Kill them!"

Mr. Boone started wheezing, bad. He gasped through the precious breaths he was able to draw, "No, Reverend McCamy, I can't, sir. I can't, sir, I know her mother!"

Everything froze for one long moment.

Then, Elsbeth McCamy grabbed the rifle from Mr. Boone's lax hands. She whirled around and aimed it at Miles, who dropped to the floor behind the desk just as she fired. Katie was on her instantly. Elsbeth screamed, trying to wrest the rifle free, but she couldn't. Katie slammed her fist into Elsbeth's stomach and took a huge handful of her gorgeous hair, pulling it until Elsbeth's head was nearly bent back over her arm. She said very quietly against her ear, "Drop the rifle, Elsbeth, or I'll pull out all that wonderful hair of yours."

Elsbeth moaned but kept struggling, trying to bring the rifle up. Katie turned her and kneed her hard in the chest, knocking the wind out of her.

"Leave my wife alone!"

Reverend McCamy lurched forward, grabbed the rifle from where his wife had dropped it on the floor, and ran, knocking

Mr. Boone over a chair in his escape from the library.

They heard him running upstairs.

Miles said, "I want him, Katie. I'll get him."

She started to go with him, but then she looked at him, really looked, and knew he wouldn't do anything stupid. He had a cop's training and a cop's instincts. He'd pulled out her ankle gun. The derringer looked absurd in his big hand, but up close it could stop a man, even a madman.

"Take care, Miles. I'll get help."

She'd picked up her SIG Sauer and motioned Mr. Boone and Elsbeth to the sofa. She pulled out her cell phone and called Wade, who had to be outside by now.

There wasn't time for Wade to even make it through the front door. Overhead, there was a huge explosion. The whole house shook with the shock and force of it.

Elsbeth screamed. Mr. Boone said, wheezing so hard Katie wondered how he could still breathe, "The Reverend's thrown one of the gasoline bombs. Why would he do that?"

Elsbeth ran out of the library. Katie wasn't about to shoot her, so there was no choice but to go after her. As for Mr.

Boone, where could he go? She shouted over her shoulder, "Mr. Boone, go outside where it's safe!"

She ran out into the hallway to see Elsbeth taking the stairs two at a time. Katie stayed right on her heels. She rounded the corner at the top of the stairs and saw Elsbeth running toward the master bedroom.

Katie heard the crackling and popping of the flames before she saw them billowing out of the master bedroom, the hallway carpet already smoking. She had to get everyone out, fast.

Katie headed after Elsbeth. She saw her run into the master bedroom and yelled, "Elsbeth, don't go in there!"

But the woman disappeared into the room.

"Miles, where are you?"

Katie ran into the huge bedroom, saw the door open to the closet, and watched Elsbeth disappear inside.

"Miles!"

She heard a gunshot, not loud, just a popping noise, and she knew it was from her derringer. She started coughing from the incredible heat and the smoke. She grabbed a pillow from a chair and clamped it against her nose.

She saw Miles, breathing hard, standing in the doorway to the sex room, her derringer dangling in his right hand. "Katie, get out of here!"

"Where are Elsbeth and Reverend McCamy? My God, what happened to your face?"

"We need to get out of here. I don't know where Elsbeth is. I had to shoot Reverend McCamy. He's dead, I checked. Come on, I don't want Sam or Keely to be orphans."

But Katie had to try. "Elsbeth! Where are you? Come out or you'll die!"

There was no answer. Katie started to run toward the sex room, but Miles grabbed her hand and dragged her from the bedroom. He was right, she thought, there was no choice. She pressed the pillow she was holding against her face and ran with him down the long hallway. She stumbled on the stairs, and Miles picked her up and pulled her against him to keep her on her feet.

They ran into the entryway where Mr. Boone and several deputies were crowded together, right inside the front door. Katie said, "I see you can breathe again, Mr. Boone. Just maybe you don't need Reverend McCamy's laying on of hands."

"This is one too many burning houses, Sheriff," Charlie Fritz, one of her deputies said. "The fire department wants us out of here right away. Let's go."

Elsbeth's face flashed in Katie's mind. Had she just given up and chosen to die with her husband? No matter what she'd been a party to, Katie didn't want her to be dead. Too many were dead already.

When they were near the road, they looked back to see the beautiful old Victorian lit up from its bowels, turning the black sky orange, spewing flames upward. Its old wood exploded in shards everywhere. It was an incredible sight, as long as you were away from the devastation.

Katie stood next to Miles, aware that his arm was holding her close, for warmth, for comfort, to make the world real again, to right the madness. He said, "Reverend McCamy went into that sex room and pulled a bottle full of gasoline out of one of the drawers beneath that marble altar. He lit the wick and threw it at me. It hit the bed, and the flames shot up in an instant."

"What happened to your face?"

Miles touched his fingers to the slash along the side of his face, from his temple to his jaw. "He pulled a whip off the wall and slashed me with it."

"And you shot him?"

"I tried to grab the whip away from him, but he fought me. I could hear the fire, knew time was growing short, and then he tried to grab the gun.

"I swear to you, Katie, there was madness pouring out of him, and a frenzy that seemed to unleash all the strength inside of him. He was grinning and moaning at the same time. I felt my blood freeze."

"And then there you were with a pillow over your face."

"You never saw Elsbeth."

He shook his head. "I heard her voice, but no, I didn't see her."

"She preferred to die with that man rather than survive," Katie said, shaking her head. She looked up at Miles and shook her head again. "I think we're going to need a paramedic." She began to examine the cut. "It doesn't look at all deep, but no paramedics this time. I want to take you to the hospital."

Wade was standing next to them now. "The firemen are already bitching at all this work, Sheriff. Now you want to piss off the paramedics?"

Miles laughed, he threw back his head and really laughed. He looked up at the burning house. "It's over," he said, "it's finally over. It seems like it's been going on forever — and it's been only days. Amazing."

Katie nodded and smiled at him. She turned to Miles Kettering and hugged him to her.

34

At ten o'clock Thursday morning the rain had lightened to a thick gray mist, mixing into the low-lying fog that crept up the sides of the mountains, blanketing the land.

"Do you really think it's over?"

Keely pursed her lips, looked doubtful. "I don't know, but I sure hope so. Last night was real scary, Sam."

Sam sighed, thought that every night since early last Friday morning had been scary, and leaned in more closely. "Yeah, I know, but your mom and my dad, they took care of us." He sighed again, deeply. "But since everything is over now, you know what that means, Keely."

"Yeah, I know. You're gonna have to leave and never come back."

"I'll tell Papa that I don't want to leave, okay?"

"Do you think he'll let you stay here and live with Mama and me?"

"I want him to stay, too," Sam said, and pulled Minna's soft wool blanket more closely around both him and Keely because it was getting colder.

"If your papa doesn't want to stay, what are you going to do, Sam?"

"I don't know," Sam said finally and he fisted his eyes. "I'm only six. Nobody listens to me."

"They listen to you even less when you're five. I heard my grandma talking to Linnie just a while ago. She told Linnie that your papa and my mama should get married and that would be that."

"What would be that?"

"Well, I guess it means that if you leave, I get to leave with you."

"Oh. Well, that's good."

"Your father would be my steppapa."

"Yeah, and Katie would be my stepmama. That's weird."

"We could fight and stuff and no one could say anything about it." Keely punched his arm, gave him a huge grin, then settled her head on his shoulder.

They were sitting in Minna's porch swing. Since Sam's legs weren't long enough to reach the porch, he'd taken a walking stick out of the umbrella stand that had belonged to Keely's grandfather. Every few minutes, he shoved the stick against the wooden floor to make the swing go back and forth.

"I don't want you to go away, Sam."

"I know and I've been thinking, Keely. Papa isn't stupid. He'll marry your mom."

Keely said, "You're six years old. You don't know if your dad's stupid or not. My mama says this is the most beautiful place in the world. Even if your dad was stupid, he could be happy here. I know, tell him we'll take him rafting on the Big Pigeon River. That's in the Smokies."

"Papa's been rafting before. I'll tell him, but you know, Keely, he's got that big helicopter business in Virginia. Since those bad men took me he hasn't gotten much work done."

Keely pondered this for a while. "I know, tell him that Mama is the best rafter in Tennessee and she'll teach him. Oh, and tell him that Sam Houston taught in a log schoolhouse when he was eighteen. I'll bet your dad will be impressed. Tell him we'll take him there. Tell him he can e-mail to his business."

"Keely, if my papa and your mama got married, what would your name be?"

Keely didn't have an answer to that. Sam shoved the walking stick against the porch floor and the swing swung out widely. They laughed and hung on.

Children's laughter, Katie thought, there

was nothing like it. She and Miles were standing just inside the screened door. Neither said a word and they didn't look at each other. So this was why her mom suggested they take a look at the beautiful hazy fog that was climbing the sides of the mountains.

Miles said quietly as he stepped back, "They look like a Norman Rockwell painting."

It was true, with their heads pressed together, the swing gently going back and forth, but any words Katie would have said stuck in her throat. She nodded and looked toward the mountains, blurred and softened by the fog, like fine smoke. Her mom had told her that looking at the mountains on a morning like this was like reading without reading glasses.

"Even in the winter, when it's so cold your toes are curling under and the mountains look weighted down with snow, they're still so beautiful it makes you want to cry just looking at them. And down at Gatlinburg —"

"Katie, what the kids were talking about . . ."

She turned to face him then. The emergency room doctor hadn't stitched Miles's face, just pressed the skin together using

Steri-strips. She'd told him to rub on vitamin E and there wouldn't be a scar on his handsome face, unless he wanted to look dangerous, and she'd waggled her eyebrows at him. Katie said, "I guess this means you don't want me to tell you about the Great Smoky Mountains National Park."

"Not right this minute, no."

"Okay. You mean us getting married?"

"Yes," he said. "Maybe we should give it some thought."

Katie had firmly believed, up until, say, just four minutes ago, that she'd rather be incontinent than get married again. But now?

"Katie? Miles? I brought some cinnamon nut bread for the kids."

Her mother had excellent timing, Katie thought. She always had, particularly when there'd been horny boys around during high school. She'd given them enough time to overhear the kids talking, enough time to think about it, even say it out loud. They were both smiling when they turned to see Minna coming with a platter that smelled delicious from twenty feet away.

"I'm starving," Miles said, surprised. "I hadn't realized."

"Glad I had some clothes for you, Miles.

Katie's dad was tall like you, so at least your ankles aren't showing. Sweetie, those jeans are nearly white they've been washed so many times, but you look just fine. Now, I'm going to take these goodies to the kids. They're having a hard time, you know."

"Can we have some first, Mom?"

"Sure. Take as many slices as you want. You two just go into the living room and I'll take care of the kids."

Minna waltzed back into the living room a few minutes later, and announced, "Sam and Keely aren't happy campers. I don't envy you having to separate them."

And now, Katie thought, just a touch of the spurs. Katie grinned at her mother, knowing exactly what she was doing. Miles, however, didn't.

"We're not looking forward to it," he said and sighed. He leaned his head back against the sofa and closed his eyes.

Minna said, "Linnie called while you were in the shower, sweetie. She said the TBI is going nuts and they're coming in force today about noon — that was so you could nap a little bit after that long night. Evidently one of the inspectors couldn't wait to see exactly what had happened here in Jessborough, a town, he said, that's never had anything more than some dippy

DUIs and underage smokers in its extremely long life, until now. Linnie said not to worry, that the inspector really sounded excited. She also said the mayor and all the aldermen couldn't wait to see you, to hear every gory detail, I expect."

Katie said, "Oh yeah, Mayor Tommy will probably want a dozen meetings to thrash everything out."

Minna nodded. "Well, it is the most excitement Tommy's had since he caught his best friend making out with his girl-friend behind the bleachers back in high school. You really can't blame him. Nor the aldermen. I'm an alderwoman, Miles, and so I've already gotten a dozen or more calls."

"No," Katie said. "You're right, it's been a long dry spell for Tommy."

Miles called his sister-in-law, Cracker, told her it was finally over. He'd consid-ered asking Cracker if she'd ever known Sam to be ill while Miles had been away, but decided against it. He knew to his soul that if Alicia hadn't told him about taping Sam with blood on his palms, she wouldn't have told anyone else. But she had given it to someone. Who? Perhaps her ancient priest, an old man who'd been kind and was failing physically and mentally. If she gave it to him then he must have passed it on to someone else, someone who'd given it to Reverend McCamy. They would never know now, and, truth be told, it didn't matter. The video was now ashes buried beneath more ashes and shards of burned wood.

When he'd hung up the phone, Katie had nodded. The last thing Sam needed was to have the media proclaiming him the newest candidate for sainthood, or a freak, or a helpless pawn. She could just see a TV guy asking Sam to please try to make his hands bleed again for the cameras. And here was Dr. X, psychologist, to give a historical perspective on the visible stigmata. Or those proclaiming he was a fraud or a victim of abuse, and exploited for it. Thomas Boone could say whatever he wanted, but everyone knew what he'd done, so she doubted anyone would believe him if he talked crazy.

And he'd said more to himself than to Katie, "What else did she keep from me?"

Katie hadn't said anything, merely taken his hand.

They would come up with exactly what to tell everyone, including the mayor and the aldermen, including her mother, but just not now, not when they were both so tired, like they'd been hung out to dry.

She looked over at Miles, a paper plate on his lap, a half-eaten slice of cinnamon nut bread sitting in the middle. He was sound asleep.

She smiled and nodded off herself.

35

Although two days had passed, Katie still felt unanchored, her brain adrift. She'd dealt with the TBI, attended a special town meeting called by Mayor Tommy Bledsoe, of the long-lived Sherman Bledsoes, to explain exactly what had happened. She'd swear that nearly every citizen in Jessborough was present, along with her mother, of course, and all the mill employees who'd been given the day off to hear the details. There was some media — not national media, thank God. She had told all concerned that Reverend McCamy had been mentally ill, that he had evidently seen Sam when he'd visited Washington, D.C., that something about the boy had attracted him and so he'd arranged to take him. She assumed he wanted to raise him, mold him into what he saw himself as being, make him his successor, and that was surely the truth. He had just gone over the edge. It sounded idiotic to Katie, but not as idiotic as the just plain crazy truth. She and Miles had repeated their story so often that Katie imagined she'd be believing it herself soon.

Neither she nor Miles could explain what they'd seen on the video. She wondered if they ever would. She wondered how and why it had happened to a three-year-old boy. Some sort of bloody rash? Had his fingernails pierced his palms? Or was it a reaction to a medicine? More than likely, because Sam had sure looked sick. And Alicia hadn't said anything of it to Miles. Miles was fretting over that, but Alicia was long dead, and Katie knew he'd have to let it go.

She'd even called together the congregation of the Sinful Children of God and told them how very sorry she was that Reverend and Mrs. McCamy had died in the fire at their home. She wove the same tale, telling them that Reverend McCamy had been consumed with getting Sam, no one really knew why, and then told them the scene of his final disintegration, his complete mental breakdown, and his suicide. There was a lot of grief, a lot of questions, but most of them seemed willing to let life move on, fast.

She sighed, thinking about her home. Gone, nothing left at all. She had no idea what she was going to do yet and was still just too tired to think about it coherently.

"I think it's a good idea, Katie, what we talked about."

She jerked up. Miles was talking about marriage, she knew that even though neither of them had said another thing about it since early Thursday morning. She said, "It's a huge thing, Miles, a really huge thing."

"You lost your house."

"Yeah, I was just thinking about that."

"I've got a house, a really big house, and there's lots of room, for all of us. It's colonial. Do you like colonial?"

"Yes," she said, nothing more, and continued not to look at him.

Miles looked over at Sam and Keely, who were sitting on the living room floor, their jeaned legs spread wide, rolling three red balls back and forth between them. They were evidently trying to keep the balls inside their legs.

"You hit it too hard, Sam!"

Sam said, as he batted a ball back to her, "Pay attention, Keely."

"My God, he said that just like I do," Miles said. "This parent thing, it's scary when your kid mimics you. Say yes, Katie."

"Say yes to what, Mama?"

Suddenly both small faces were concentrated on them. Miles shrugged at Katie who sighed and nodded. "Okay, what do you guys think of Katie and me getting married? Not that she's said yes yet. That way you'd be brother and sister and you could stay together." And that, Katie thought, was the primary reason for getting married, and not a bad reason, really. At least both of them would be motivated to make a happy home for their children. Sam would be hers. And that kiss, she'd felt it all the way to her size nines. The man was potent. That made her smile, but it fell off her face pretty fast. Married, after knowing a man a week.

No, not married. *Remarried.*

Katie had sworn she'd never get married again as long as there was enough breath in her lungs to say no. It was simple, really, she just couldn't trust herself to choose wisely. Just look at what she'd brought home the first time — Carlo Silvestri, a weak, spoiled jerk whose father had paid her a million and a half bucks to get out of his life. Hmmm. At least that was a pretty good trade-off. Carlo's father had saved the pulp mill and a lot of people's jobs. And of course, Carlo had given her Keely — she'd put up with a dozen jerks for that.

The fact was, bottom line, that she didn't know Miles well. Not even a complete week, and those days had been filled with nonstop fear and violence and adrenaline rushes so extreme that Katie was ready to swear that her blood sugar had plummeted to her toes because there hadn't been a life-and-death crisis since the McCamy house burned down, its two occupants with it.

What was a woman with no house to do? Marry a man who did have a house? A colonial?

It was funny if you looked at it a certain way. She'd saved a little boy, his dad had come to town, lots of bad things had happened, and now he wanted her to marry him. Truth be told, it was the children who'd started it. She'd wished now that they hadn't heard Sam and Keely talking on the porch, but of course that was what her mother had intended.

Then again, she couldn't forget those minutes in her kitchen. Fact was, she'd wanted to jump him; he'd felt just that good.

Both children were staring from Miles to her and back again. Sam said slowly, "You guys going to get married?"

"As I said, Sam, she hasn't said yes yet. So, what do you think? Keely?"

"Mama, I've given this a lot of thought

and I think it's a really good idea."

"Keely, Miles only told you two minutes ago, not all that much time to think about it."

Keely slid a glance at Sam, who grinned like a kid who'd just copped an early look at his Christmas presents.

"Keely and I talked about it," Sam announced. "And we think it would be okay."

"This is the way to go, Mama. We're right about this."

It was Miles and Katie's turn to stare, both at each other and at their children. Miles said slowly, "How can you be so sure? You kids didn't even know each other existed until last Saturday afternoon."

Both children gave them a look like, So what's your point?

Miles felt pumped, read to take on the world. He knew to his soul that he wanted to do this. "Katie, what do you say? Let's do it. No reason not to." Knew even deeper that making love with Katie, watching her laugh and love his son, was the right thing.

Katie jumped to her feet, startling everyone. "Okay, guys, listen up. This is a huge decision for all of us. I'm going to think just what this would mean before I commit to anything, you hear me? Sam, your father is going to be doing some heavy-duty thinking, too. You and Keely will have to be patient, and not pressure either your father or me into this."

Yeah, right, Miles thought, looking at his son.

SUNDAY NIGHT
GEORGETOWN, WASHINGTON, D.C.

After the most delicious spinach lasagna Miles could remember, sautéed winter squash, and a Caesar salad, hot dogs and chips and a token salad for Sam and Sean, Savich handed Miles a cup of coffee, black, no sugar. "Sit down, Miles. You still look pretty wrung out."

"Nah, not really. Promise me you made the coffee, Savich."

Savich grinned. "Oh yeah. I've taught Sherlock just about everything I know, but coffee still defeats her."

Sherlock called out from the kitchen, "Did I hear my name being maligned?"

"Not at all," Miles called back. "You make a mean salad, all that feta cheese you add makes it really good, but, and I have to be honest here, you just don't have the

406

same knack with coffee that your husband has, which is amazing since he rarely drinks it."

"No one said you had to be honest," Sherlock said, coming into the living room. She handed Savich a cup of tea, fresh-brewed.

"Thanks." He took a sip, closed his eyes in bliss.

"I like your pirate face, Miles," Sherlock said, "with all those little tape pieces. It's sexy."

"You never said my back was sexy," Savich said.

She actually shuddered. "No, but I will once I stop shaking." She added to Miles, "He's much better, but it's going to take another week before he can stretch without worrying his back is going to break open."

Savich and Sherlock sat across from Miles, listening with half an ear to Sean talking a blue streak to Sam, not much of it comprehensible, but Sam seemed to understand enough. He was rolling blocks to Sean, then helping Sean roll them back to him. They were in the designated kid part of the living room, where toys and chaos could reign without adults tripping over a stray ball and breaking a neck.

Sherlock looked sleek in black jeans and

a black lace top, her curly red hair flying about, her eyes blue as a summer sky. Miles saw Savich grinning at her like a fool, sighed, and thought yet again of Katie.

It had been nearly a day and a half since he'd seen her. Those thirty hours felt like a decade.

"They're still getting lots of rain in eastern Tennessee," Miles said. "I'll tell you, it kept me real alert flying out of Ackerman's Air Field, what with the rain coming down so hard. They've got several storms lined up with little respite in between. Katie and her crew were up to their noses in mud and downed wires, not to mention all the accidents, the odd cow bawling in the middle of the road, mail soaked because some kids poked holes in some mailboxes."

"Sounds like she has her hands full, all right," Savich said and leaned forward so Sherlock could lightly scratch around the wound in his back.

Miles sat back and closed his eyes. Things were really bad and he didn't see how anything could get better. His guts hurt. Sam's guts hurt. Cracker kept asking what was wrong with him. He'd stomped around his office at the plant like a wounded rhino even though there were very few employees there to see it on a Sunday afternoon. Then he'd gone back home and stomped some more.

Even though Sam was safe, he sure wasn't sound, but it was really early yet. As for himself, he felt like he'd left unfinished business he wasn't in a position to finish, and that sucked, big time.

Miles muttered something under his breath, his eyes still closed, and Sherlock figured they were better off not knowing what he'd said.

Savich raised an eyebrow at him.

Miles said, "It's been a day and a half, well, maybe a bit more than thirty hours now. Isn't that amazing?"

"Yes," Sherlock said, "absolutely amazing. Now, you're moping, Miles." She lowered her voice just a bit and moved her chair closer. "Sam and Sean are distracted. Tell us what's going on here."

He cocked open an eye and said, "Yesterday morning I asked Katie to marry me and she turned me down."

Both of them stared at him.

Sherlock said slowly, "You're saying you asked a woman to marry you after — what was it? — not even a complete and full week after meeting her?"

"That's about the size of it," Miles said. "Damned woman. What could I do? I even asked her about architecture and she said she liked colonials."

Sherlock lightly laid her hand on Savich's leg. "I've never had much to do with colonials — they're not what you'd call thick on the ground on the West Coast. Fact is, I would have married Dillon after three days, if he'd only known I was alive, colonial or not."

Savich said, "Oh, I knew, I knew." He clasped her hand and said, "You're not remembering things exactly right, sweetheart. You were so cut off from everyone at the time, including me, until finally, you happened to spend that night here, with me, and then . . . Miles has heard all of that story he's ever going to hear."

Miles looked over to see Sean stuffing a graham cracker into his mouth. "I can pretend I haven't heard any of it and you could give me some pointers, Savich." He paused a moment, then said, shaking his head, "Isn't it strange how Sam looks like me and Sean looks just like you?"

Sherlock said, "So much for the indomitable X chromosome." Then she added, "So, Katie turned you down?"

"Yeah, I suppose because it's been only a

week. Too soon, really, just too soon. She wanted to think about it. I guess maybe I agreed with that. I don't think she ever had a gun out of her hand. Strange time. She's really pretty. Did you notice that?"

Savich nodded, smiling, and said, "How long does she want to think about it? Did she give you any hope at all?"

Miles shrugged. "I don't know. We didn't set a time, but I'll tell you, Sam and I aren't doing so well."

"You miss her?"

"Well, yes, and Keely, but it's Sam I'm really worried about."

"What, nightmares? Surely you've got him seeing a child shrink. What does the doctor say?"

"No, no nightmares," Miles said. "It's Keely. He's miserable without Keely. I'm telling you, those two kids bonded instantly. I've never seen anything like it. It was a nightmare separating them. Katie and I both felt like monsters, and there's Katie's mom, looking at us like she wanted to carry the pitchfork as she led the villagers. Sam is speaking to me now, but he's miserable, too quiet — not sulking, just unhappy. I'm beginning to think it's not going to go away."

"It's only been a little over a day,

Miles," Sherlock said.

Savich said, "So what does the shrink say?"

"Evidently Dr. Jones called Dr. Raines in Jessborough and that's why she agreed to see Sam this morning."

"So what did she say?"

"She said I should do anything to get Katie to marry me."

They all laughed. Sam looked up, frowned at them, and went back to helping Sean build a block fort, which wasn't going too well since Sean would yell and give it a karate chop when it got three blocks high.

"So what are you going to do?" Sherlock asked.

Miles sat forward. "You know," he said slowly, "maybe it's time I was a buccaneer."

"What's a buccaneer, Papa?"

"So you heard that, did you?" Sam, holding Sean's hand, was standing next to his father. "He's learned he has to be real quiet if he wants to eavesdrop."

"Tell us, Papa."

That serious, so serious voice. "All right, Sam." Miles lifted both Sam and Sean up onto his lap. "A buccaneer was a pirate who was given permission by his country to plunder enemy ships. They were take-

412

charge kind of guys, Sam, who did things their own way. I'm thinking that it's time for me to take charge. What do you think?"

"You're always in charge, Papa."

Sean burped against Sam's arm, raised his head and said, "Mama, apple pie."

Sherlock laughed, got up, and went to the kitchen. "Apple pie coming up. What would the buccaneer like to have?"

"Just bring me an eye patch."

Sam laughed, the first laugh that had sprung out of that little mouth since they'd left Tennessee.

36

At eleven o'clock that night, Miles landed his plane at Ackerman's Air Field. Thirty minutes later, he was driving the rental car into Minna Benedict's driveway.

It wasn't raining so hard now, but he could tell that it had really been coming down. A low-lying fog had come up, turning everything gray. The mountains brooded, blurred in a soft mist.

It felt like coming home.

He let Sam, so excited he could barely speak, knock on the door.

Minna beamed at them, clearly startled. "Good grief, Miles, Sam! Come give me a big hug, sweetie. You, Sam, not your daddy. Oh my goodness, it's wonderful to see both of you. Miles, your face looks all sort of romantic."

While Sam was enfolded in Minna's arms, Miles looked over her head for Katie. "I called, but there wasn't any answer, Minna. Where are Katie and Keely? Asleep? It's nearly midnight. I'm sorry we're so late. They are asleep, aren't they?"

Before Minna could say anything, Sam said, "We're here because Papa decided at dinner that he had to be a buccaneer. My aunt Sherlock couldn't find him an eye patch, that's why you can't tell."

"What Sam means, Minna, is that I'm here to sling my bride over my shoulder and cart her away."

"I see," Minna said. She straightened, keeping Sam pressed against her side. She gave Miles a big grin. "Well, now, isn't this the funniest thing? Katie and Keely took off in her truck this evening, headed for Virginia."

"*What?*"

"Oh wow!"

Minna smiled at the boy and the man, who, she suspected, would be related to her in no time at all. "Come in, come in. You can phone Katie on her cell. I'm surprised you didn't get her number before you left."

"She wouldn't give it to me," Miles said. "She wanted time to think without my bugging her and without Sam guilting her."

"Doesn't matter. Don't worry, Sam, Keely's been working on her around the clock."

"I told her I'd work on my dad," Sam

said and gave her a huge grin.

"That's my boy," Minna said. "How long will it take Katie to drive to Colfax?"

Miles felt ready to explode. His heart was pounding, his guts were in a knot. "Minna, please tell me exactly why Katie is driving to Colfax. Spell it out for me."

"She was coming to marry you, of course. She told me if you agreed, she'd call me and we'd work things out from this end."

"You're not joking? She's really coming to marry me? She and Keely just hopped in her truck and off they went?"

"That's it, Miles. She's been stomping around here, driving everyone nuts, she's growled at all her deputies, snapped at Mayor Tommy because he wanted every gory detail about everything, three times. What with all the rain and all the problems that's brought, it hasn't helped. She even snapped Linnie's head off, blew a fit at Keely for her less-than-subtle hints, cried at her and Keely's misery, and then she gave it up. Oh goodness, look at you, Miles. I love to see a man who's trying to think."

Miles stood there with his mouth open, just shaking his head. She'd been acting just like he had, which had to mean that she was miserable without him, without Sam.

"Katie's a buccaneer," Sam shouted. "Just like Papa!" Sam whooped, grabbed his father's hand, and started dancing around.

"Why don't I get her an eye patch for her wedding present?" Minna said. "You flew your plane, Miles?"

He nodded, blinking, still getting his wits back together.

"Then I guess you'd best be on your way back home. You don't want her to get there before you do, do you? And be careful, the weather's terrible."

He thought of Cracker and hoped to God she'd let Katie and Keely in the house if Katie beat him back to Colfax.

MONDAY NIGHT
GEORGETOWN, WASHINGTON, D.C.

"We're married," Sam said with a great deal of satisfaction to the group gathered with coffee, champagne, and Cracker's special triple chocolate cake in the living room.

Savich leaned over and ruffled Sam's hair. He said, "Yep, it's all official now, Sam."

Sherlock, holding a sleeping Sean in her arms, nodded. "You and Keely are brother and sister."

"Cool," said Keely, and punched Sam in the arm.

"Well, you can see where my kid stands on this," Miles said as he handed a slice of cake to Cracker, who was still looking a bit shell-shocked.

Sam leaned over and patted her hand. "It's okay, Aunt Cracker, Katie's really nice and she can shoot people dead if they bother you."

Cracker swallowed the bite the wrong way and began coughing. Sam was slapping her on the back, she was tearing up, and Keely handed her a glass of champagne.

"Just what I needed," Cracker gasped and downed the champagne.

"Oh dear," Katie said. "Would you believe, Cracker, that I'm actually known more for keeping our teenagers on the straight and narrow? No kid under eighteen smokes in my town when I'm around."

Cracker took another bite of cake and said, as she closed her eyes in bliss, "That's not gory enough, Katie. Sounds like Sam thinks you're the Terminator."

But Sam and Keely weren't listening to the adults. They were whispering to each other in the corner of the living room, every once in a while sneaking looks at their parents.

Savich stood, picked up his boy and gently laid him over his shoulder. "It's nearly ten o'clock. We accomplished the impossible — got you guys licensed and married, all in one day."

"Thanks to the no-waiting laws in old Virginia," Miles said. "Lucky the circuit court clerk is real good friends with one of the judge's wives." Miles grinned from ear to ear. "One-stop shopping."

"Married," Katie said, and her eyes crossed. "I've known Miles for a week, and I'm married."

Sam evidently heard that clearly. He and Keely both hooted with laughter.

"Not only can she kill bad guys dead, she can even cross her eyes, Sam," Sherlock said. "What more could a guy ask for?"

"Oh yes, Mama," Keely said and crossed her own eyes. "I can do that, too, Aunt Sherlock."

Katie said to Sam, "Are you still going to be happy about this when you do something bratty and I have to nail your hide to the floor? I'm tough, remember, Sam."

Keely laughed. "I told him that if he acted stupid, you would put him up in a tree, like a cat."

"Hmmm," Miles said. "Sam's pretty good with climbing trees, Keely, maybe I should give Katie some pointers."

"I'm never bad," Sam said. He smiled beatifically and sat back in his chair, crossing his arms over his chest.

On that cue, Sherlock and Savich took their leave, Sean giving little snorting snores as his father carried him out.

It was nearly midnight before the kids were in bed, Keely in a lovely bedroom of pale rose and cream connected to Sam's room through a bathroom. Keely just couldn't get over that. Katie heard her tell Sam not to step a single foot into her side of the bathroom or she'd bust him. It didn't matter that her side had the toilet. Sam made sure to stick his toe over to her side before he went to bed.

Cracker had a suite in the large former attic with its curious sloping corners and polished wooden floors. As Katie brushed her teeth, she hoped that Cracker would soon get over the intense suspicion Katie had felt coming off her in waves when she'd opened the door to Katie's knock.

"You're here for what?" she'd said when she'd answered the door.

"Keely and I are here to see Miles. I'm Katie Benedict. Sheriff Katie Benedict." She'd stuck out her hand and had it hesitantly shaken, then dropped.

"You're the one who saved Sam? Oh dear, Miles isn't here. He said something weird about being a buccaneer, gave me a big hug, told me to wish him luck, and off he went with Sam, I don't know where. I guess you must come in." And she'd stepped back and been perfectly pleasant until Keely said, "Mama's here to marry Miles so Sam can be my brother and Miles can be my papa."

The woman looked like she'd been slapped in the face. Speaking through a rictus of a smile, she said, "Little girls say the cutest things, don't they?"

It seemed an eternity ago, yet it had only been the previous evening. Katie brushed out her hair. She started to braid it, then dropped her hands back to her sides. This was her wedding night. How very peculiar that was. Miles was right about the one-stop shopping. They'd plunked down thirty dollars and were in business. During the brief ceremony Sam stood straight and important beside his father, Keely beside her, and everyone else just a couple of steps back. It was a pity that her mother had been fogged in, no flights out at all for the entire day. Minna promised to come in the next couple of weeks. She wanted to give them some time to themselves.

Peter Evans, Miles's right hand at the plant, had looked as shell-shocked as Cracker. He'd been quite nice, no choice, really. The man looked like a linebacker for the Titans, and had hair as red as Sherlock's.

Katie looked down at the plain gold band. Married. She was married again. She'd killed two kidnappers, an idiot former postal employee had burned her house down, and here she was, in Virginia, married. For the second time. She felt very strange, as if her life had taken a one-eighty, which indeed it had.

Her name was now Katie Benedict Kettering. It was weird.

When she came back to the big bedroom after tucking Keely in yet again for the night, making certain the bathroom door was open on both sides, she faced Miles across the length of his bedroom. It was a big airy room with big windows, antique furniture, and a bed the size of the Queen Mary. Katie crossed her arms over her chest, her position defensive, her fight-flight response in high gear.

She couldn't imagine taking off her clothes in front of this man who was nearly a stranger, and also her husband. She already had in a way, not really thinking about it.

"How tall are you?" she asked.

Miles wasn't a fool. He didn't move even a single step toward her. "Six-two, something around there. I'm not planning on jumping you, by the way," he said and grinned like a schoolboy who'd just shot a three-pointer from twenty feet.

Katie shook her head, both at him and at herself. "This is all just so weird."

"But just look at what you've accomplished in the space of a very short time." He tapped off his fingers. "You've known me for this entire week, enough to know I'll make a terrific mate, and you've made our kids so happy they just might not act bratty for another week. Your new last name isn't that bad at all. The best thing is that I really like you, Katie. Really. You looked great in your wedding dress."

"Don't forget the three-inch heels that brought me eyeball to eyeball with you."

"Never." He hadn't seen her in a dress until their wedding seven hours ago.

"I'm thirty-one years old."

"Yeah, I heard you tell the county clerk. I'm thirty-five, which means I've got more experience than you, a really finely honed judgment, and you should trust me completely." He held out his hands to her, palms up, fingers spread. "These are perfectly good hands you're in, Katie."

"Yeah, yeah, you've had more years to learn how to joke around and be an all-around smart guy." She paused a moment. "I haven't really trusted anyone — a man, that is — since Carlo."

"That makes sense, since the guy was such a gold-plated jerk. But I'm me and there's no gold plating about me. I'm not a shit, Katie, believe me. Now, it's nearly midnight on a fine Monday night. I'm exhausted, you're exhausted, and even Keely and Sam didn't complain about going to bed."

"That's a first and likely a last."

"Come here and let me kiss you. Then we'll go to bed and get our first good night's sleep in a week."

Katie looked at the bed, then back at Miles. "I haven't had sex in so long I think I've forgotten what comes after a kiss."

He started ticking off on his fingers.

"What are you doing?"

"Trying to figure out when I had sex last. I've used up all my fingers. This is truly pathetic. Maybe we can figure it out together, sooner or later. What do you think?"

She wasn't thinking anything, her brain was on hold. She tugged on her sleep shirt that showed a buzzard wearing a cowboy hat singing "Howdy, Howdy, Howdy, I'm a cowboy." He'd have liked that sleep shirt to disappear. He really liked those long long legs of hers; he'd really like them wrapped around him.

"Which side of the bed do you prefer?"

She pointed to the left. After he climbed in beside her, Katie said, "Those pajamas look brand new."

"They're my official wedding pajamas."

Miles flipped off the lights. Silence fell. After about five minutes, Katie said, "What are you humming?"

"Just an old buccaneer song."

"Miles?"

"Yeah?"

"How about we try a kiss, and maybe then those wedding pajamas can go back in the drawer."

A younger man, he thought, rolling over to a beautiful woman who was also his new wife, might feel a little nervous, but all his parts that counted were working just fine.

"We'll always have fun in bed," he said against her mouth, "maybe moan and thrash about a bit, and you'll see, our problems won't follow us here. You know something else?"

"What?"

"I swear I'll respect you in the morning."

When he had her under him, those long legs of hers wrapped around his flanks, and she was panting, biting his earlobe, kissing any part of him she could reach, he said, "We're going to be just fine, Katie," and he laid his hands on her then and she would have flown out the window if he hadn't been on top of her.

37

Sherlock heard a shout and turned to wave at Sean, who was running after Keely and Sam. Then Sam turned, held out his hand, and Sean latched on to it, shrieking. She smiled as she said to Katie, "They're really good with him."

"Yes, Sam told me he had to take care of Sean because he was little and ignorant."

Sherlock laughed.

"Keely said Sean would grow up fast enough. Then she said since boys had so much to learn, she'd better start teaching him stuff now. She didn't want to have to wait and cram everything into his head when he was grown up."

Another shout. Katie looked over her shoulder to see Miles throw a Frisbee to Keely. So much laughter. It warmed her all the way to her bones.

Katie said, "It's been two weeks and no

more math teacher murders. Maybe the madman has simply left the area."

"Thank God for no more murders, but I really hope he hasn't left, it would make it that much harder to get the creep. Dillon hasn't said much, just told me he's doing good old-fashioned police work, and then he smiles. We'll see. I'm busy on other cases, so it's really pretty much in his baili-wick. Calls on the hot line have dropped over the past two weeks to only about fifty a day. You wouldn't believe how many man-hours it takes to check just fifty calls, and all for nothing."

"I can't begin to imagine. I never had to do anything like that." Katie shaded her eyes and looked over the park, always coming back to Keely who was chasing Sam, Sean running as fast as he could behind them. She didn't realize she'd stopped walking and was staring at nothing in particular when Sherlock said, "What's up, Katie?"

Katie gave a start. She looked down at the small woman who could give her a real go in a karate match. "Do you fight dirty, Sherlock?"

"Dirty? Hmmm. As in would I do any-thing at all, no matter how rotten, to disarm a bad guy? Oh yeah. Why?"

Katie shrugged. "I was just wondering, that's all. Would you look at this gorgeous day. Can you believe this Indian summer? In early December?"

Sherlock raised her face to the sun that was bright and warm. A crisp breeze rustled through the nearly naked tree branches, ruffled her hair. Winter was lurking just around the corner, but not today. "Thank God, all that interminable rain has stopped. I swear I was starting to grow mold. At least we've got a couple of beautiful days before that snowstorm hits on Monday."

"Mom says it's finally stopped raining in Jessborough. Everything is still soggy, but things are getting back to normal. Do you know what she sent me for a wedding present?"

"A whip?"

To Sherlock's surprise, Katie looked like she would burst into tears. "What is it, Katie? What did she send you?"

Katie wiped her hand across her eyes, and shook her head. "I didn't mean to lose it like that. What you said about the whip — that's funny, but it's just that every time I think about it, how much it means to me and how she knew how much it means. She sent me copies of all her family photos, put them in three big albums. You know I lost everything when the house burned down. But now I have Keely's first five years again."

"Oh my, that was nice of her. Your mom is the greatest, Katie. Sam's a lucky little boy to have such a wonderful grandmother. You said you guys are going back to Jessborough for Christmas? And there'll be a religious ceremony this time for your mom and all your friends?"

Katie nodded. "She didn't want to come here right away. She wanted to give the four of us time to get settled in with each other." Katie sucked in a deep breath. "You know, Sherlock, it just doesn't smell like eastern Tennessee here."

"No," Sherlock said. "Here, there's always the underlying scent of car exhaust."

"No, it's more than that."

"Okay, there's also the scent of politicians, and that's worse than car exhaust. But you know, springtime in Washington is really beautiful, if you just forget politics."

Katie laughed, but to Sherlock's keen ears, it was forced. She said, "Miles mentioned yesterday that as soon as Savich was up for it, they were going to work out together."

Sherlock said, "That'll end up in lots of

insults and bruises. I hope you're good with the Ben-Gay tube."

"Oh yeah, I am. I told Miles you'd take on the winner."

Sherlock looked very pleased at that. "You've been married thirteen days, Katie, which means that you and Miles have known each other for, wow, a grand total of three weeks. Now, how are things going between you?"

Katie arched an eyebrow. "I don't sleep in the guest room, if that's what you mean."

"Well, no, I would certainly hope that you don't. As I told Dillon, Miles is not only a really good guy, he has this marvelous flat stomach."

"So he does."

"And who could turn that down?"

"Not I. And I'll tell you something else, Sherlock, Miles is also the sexiest guy on earth."

Sherlock was too kind to point out the obvious, that Katie was wrong, dead wrong — Dillon was the sexiest guy, period. Anywhere. Maybe she would tell Katie when she knew her better. Sherlock said, her brow furrowed, "I would think that intimacy between two people who really like each other, who are committed to each other and to a family, well, it would help move things more quickly, take away the artificialness of the situation. Hey, you see a guy in his boxers, whiskers on his face, and the embarrassment factor goes down fast."

"It's still tough, both of us dancing around, afraid to hurt the other's feelings or piss the other off or do something that might upset one of the kids."

"And Sam and Keely are settling in together? Or is there a problem?"

"There are kid squabbles, but yeah, they're incredible together. Just this morning, both of them came bouncing in on our bed at six a.m. It felt . . . good. Sometimes I wonder how Keely could not have known Sam all her life. They're very close. As for Cracker, I haven't a clue what's going on in her head. She leaves us alone for the most part, spends lots of time in her attic suite, or is out with friends for the evenings, movies, I think. She's pleasant enough when we cross paths. I really hope she'll start dating, if she's not already."

Sherlock picked a twig off a maple tree and chewed on it. "She wanted to marry Miles, you know."

"I figured that. Still, she's trying to be nice to me. Talk about a shock for her."

"The thing is that after her sister died, she moved in to take care of Sam, which was a great thing for her to do. Both Sam and Miles were devastated and she provided stability. But it's been over two years now and you're here. It's time for her to get her own life."

"And find a good guy that isn't Miles."

"All right, Katie. What's really wrong?"

"If you want the truth, well then, I'm itchy, restless. The first week, I walked every inch of that very lovely house, raked leaves until I had blisters on my palms, spoke to my mom twice a day, played with the kids until I was too tired to stand. Then this last week . . . okay, I whined, not to Miles, to Dr. Raines — my good friend Sheila — in Jessborough. She can take it. She told me lots of things that just depressed me more. She just ended up telling me to be patient, that it'll take time to settle in, and metaphorically patted me on the head.

"As you know, I'm on a leave of absence from the Jessborough Sheriff's Department. And that puts Wade temporarily in charge, and that's okay, don't get me wrong, but —" Katie shrugged, sighed, and continued after clearing her throat once, then again. "Sorry. Of course, both kids started back to school a week and a half ago. Sam was a hero to his classmates. Unfortunately, Keely's a year behind Sam, but she appears to be doing okay. She misses her friends in Jessborough, but she has Sam and that makes up for it. Sam's included her with all his friends, and since he's the big dog among the first-graders, she's in. It's still early, we'll see. That leaves lots of hours in-between to fill up, hours I never before even dreamed existed."

"Katie —"

"Okay, okay, don't hit me. Here's the bottom line for me, Sherlock: I've got to do something real, something worth-while —"

Yeah, like be sheriff again. Sherlock said, "I understand, truly I do. Give it just a little more time, just like Dr. Raines said. Talk to Miles about it — he's your hus-band now, Katie, and that means you're not alone anymore. You've got this big additional brain to add to the mix, and that's good, at least part of the time."

"Now you're going to preach to me about compromise."

"Fact is, you've got to compromise to have a good marriage, and sometimes that's so sucky I want to yell."

434

"Yeah, yeah. All right, I'll talk to him about it, but not just yet. He's working really hard right now."

Sherlock nodded. "Tell me what else Dr. Raines said."

"Wade is doing just fine as acting sheriff. She says everyone misses me and asks when I'm coming back. All I can say is 'We'll see.'"

Katie started shaking her head. "I was even studying a cookbook yesterday." She sighed. "It's so stupid really, but I never thought about what would happen two weeks after we got married, or a month, or a year, or anything. It was just the right thing to do and I didn't consider, you know, what exactly would come after the wedding. I never once wondered how it would be not to have the sheriff's job, to be living in a place I didn't know, not the streets, not the shops, not the people.

"Sorry, I'm whining again. Damn, sometimes it's really hard to be an adult."

"That's the truth," Sherlock said. "No honeymoon in sight?"

"Miles has been working his butt off at the plant. He says there's lots to be done, what with contract issues still unresolved, design problems with the helicopter guidance system, stuff like that. He's missed dinner three times this past week."

"Hmmm," Sherlock said again. "Katie, you guys are going to have to talk about this, you know. Oh, quick, look at that Frisbee throw Miles just made to Sam."

Katie twisted about to see the Frisbee floating toward Sam, watched Sam leap a good foot into the air and snag it. She heard Miles and Dillon laugh. She wondered what they were talking about. Was Miles talking about her to Dillon? Saying the same things about his life that she'd been saying to Sherlock?

Savich was saying to Miles as they both watched Sam leap into the air and curl his fingers around the edge of the Frisbee to bring it in, "I've just about given up on the Redskins this year."

Miles said, "Yeah, it's hard to even turn the games on anymore, it's so depressing. I have this gut feeling about the Raiders, though, we'll see. Wasn't that catch something? Sam's nearly Olympic with the Frisbee. I've been playing with him since he was three."

"I thought I'd start Sean out next year. You might be right about the Raiders. Jerry Rice and Charlie Garner — those guys just don't quit. Does Katie like football?"

"You know, I don't have the foggiest idea

what my wife thinks about football. That first Sunday we just relaxed, what with no Beau or Clancy to worry about, took the kids for pizza and ice cream and fell into bed at nine o'clock. We'll see if she perks up at kick-off time tomorrow."

"Hey, Sean, come back here!"

Savich was off, scooping up his son, swinging him over his head, letting his shrieks of laughter flow over him.

Miles said to Savich once he'd trotted back, Sean under one arm, "I sure like the sound of your Porsche engine. You get it tuned up recently?"

"Oh yeah. God's creation gets checked if it hiccups once. Sounds really good, huh?"

"You know it does. Sherlock was telling me that Sean loves that car, that you've promised to give it to him when he's eighteen."

"Yep, I did."

"By that time the Porsche will be in a museum."

Savich grinned. "How about that? Hey, all you've got left from McCamy is just a faint line down your cheek. It looks like it just might stay with you."

Miles touched his face. "A good thing. It'll fit my image."

Savich smiled. "How's Cracker dealing

with your marriage?"

"Oh, she's fine with it. She's always a brick. No problem at all."

Savich wondered if Miles really didn't have a clue as to his sister-in-law's feelings for him, or if he was just in denial. He sincerely doubted that Cracker was a happy camper with another woman in the house and this one Miles's wife.

Suddenly, they heard a shot, sharp and clear in the still air, not at all close. It was up ahead, near Katie and Sherlock.

For a brief instant they both froze, then Miles whirled about. "Oh, damn! What's happening?"

Savich yelled, "Sherlock, Katie, gunfire! Hurry, get down!"

"Savich, get Sean behind that tree! I'll get the kids!"

There were two more shots in rapid succession, closer to them.

Savich would swear that he felt the heat of that second bullet as it tunneled past his head before he dropped to his knees behind a huge oak tree, Sean clutched against his chest. Sean was crying and his father was shaking so badly he couldn't do anything except rock his boy, holding him close, trying to cover every bit of him with his body.

He saw Sherlock and Katie crouched down behind a square garbage receptacle some thirty feet beyond them. Sherlock was crouched down, looking all around them, waiting. Katie was on her hands and knees, her cell phone out.

He heard a car door slam, but couldn't see where. He whispered nonsense to Sean, heard his boy sob, felt his small body heave, pressed very tightly against his father's body.

God, that bastard could have shot his son. He called out, "Miles?"

Miles's voice was out of breath. "I've got Keely and Sam. We're down, about twelve feet behind you. Is Sean all right?"

"Yes, just scared to his bones, like I am."

Savich heard voices, lots of them, some screams. Not all that many people in the park, thank God, but enough.

Savich was sitting on the ground, his back against an oak tree, rocking Sean back and forth in his arms, holding him as close as he could.

Not thirty seconds later, Sherlock was in his arms, Sean sandwiched between them, and she was whispering against his chin, "Thank God you're all right."

"I'm fine, sweetheart." He sounded all calm again, but he didn't let her go.

Savich heard Katie say, even as she clutched Keely tightly against her, "Hey, Sam, that was the sort of excitement I'd hoped we'd seen the last of in Jessborough, wasn't it? Did you dive behind a garbage can?"

"There sure are lots of bad guys, Katie," said Sam, who was plastered against his father's side, and blinked at her. He shook his head, "There wasn't a garbage can close. Papa grabbed up me and Keely. We were over behind that big tree." He paused a moment, his forehead wrinkled. "Who's after me this time?"

"Someone who heard you were bad," Keely said, and, bless her heart, she reached out and punched him.

"Sam, I don't think anyone was after you this time," Miles said. "You guys okay? Really?"

"You promise, Papa?" said Sam.

Smiling, Miles picked both of them up, then reached out his hand to Katie. Like Sherlock and Savich, they stood close for a very long time, at least until their hearts slowed.

Katie said, "I called nine-one-one. They'll be here any minute now."

Sherlock said, "I spotted a late-model white Camry screech out of here. I got four numbers off the license plate: WT twenty-seven — that's it."

Miles and Savich looked at each other. Savich said, "Looks like the women took care of things."

As for Katie, she needed to get to a bathroom, fast.

38

Nearly three hours later Katie and Miles tucked the kids into their beds. It was only seven o'clock at night, but both Sam and Keely had just folded down, an adrenaline crash.

As they walked back down the long corridor to their bedroom, Miles said, "They're out like lights, thank God. Amazing."

"Yeah. Keely was gone before I read the first page of her story. She only talked a little bit about the shooting in the park."

"Same with Sam, thank God. Did you see Sean fall asleep in his father's arms? A good thing, since Savich wasn't about to let him go. And the worry in Sherlock's face, damn, this isn't good. Why did this happen? For God's sake, we were in the park with the children!"

"Miles —"

"Dear God, I know the kids seem okay right now, but what about tomorrow, the next day? I think it's smart to use a real light touch, making it all seem like an adventure, getting the spotlight off Sam. I sure hope it works. Sam didn't act like he was freaked out again, not like he was in Jessborough. And Keely seemed all right, too." He shuddered. "Somebody after Savich or Sherlock, I guess." He began emptying his pants pockets on the dresser top. "Since they weren't after Sam, it's just got to shove away at least some of the fear, don't you think?"

"Yes, I think you're right. Miles —"

"You know, Katie, I've never seen Savich freak like this before. He was white as a sheet and didn't even want to give Sean over to Sherlock. This asshole trying to shoot him right there in the middle of a park, Jesus, he could have killed Sean. He could have any of us, even Sam and Keely."

"Miles —"

He set his wallet on the dresser, looked over at Katie who was standing by the bathroom door. "Yes?"

"Maybe the asshole wasn't necessarily just after Savich or Sherlock."

"What do you mean?"

Katie slowly slid her arms out of her leather jacket, pulled it down, and let it slide to the floor. She lifted up her long gray sweatshirt and he saw the blood covering her upper thigh. "It could be that the asshole was after me."

He couldn't take it in, just couldn't. He stood there like a block of wood, staring at all that blood. Then his breath whooshed out. "Oh Jesus, oh God, you're hurt." He was at her side in a moment, his face flushed red, his hands shaking. "Why didn't you say anything? You didn't say a single word! I'm getting you to the emergency room. I can't believe you didn't tell me, that you sat through all the questioning with the cops, and didn't say a thing. No, just keep quiet and don't faint on me."

"I won't faint. It's not bad, the bullet just grazed me, on the side of my hip. If you could just help me off with my jeans we could take a look."

"Shut up. So that's why you excused yourself to that public bathroom in the park, that's why you left Keely with me, oh damn." He came down on his hands and knees in front of her and unzipped her jeans. He eased them down real slow and easy. She'd ripped off the bottom of her sweatshirt and wrapped it around her upper thigh. It was bloody, but not fresh blood, he didn't think. "I'm not going to undo it, it might start bleeding again." He got to his feet, helped her pull up her jeans

444

again. "I'll tell Cracker that we're leaving the house for a bit. Stay put, Katie."

While he was gone, Katie took a couple more Tylenol. When Miles got back to her, looked at her white face in the bathroom mirror and saw the Tylenol bottle, he didn't say a word, just picked her up in his arms and carried her out to the car. "It's funny how it hurts more now that I've told you about it. Isn't that strange?"

She was breathing light shallow breaths, obviously hurting even though it was just a graze. Jesus, a bullet had gone through her. He just couldn't take it in. And she hadn't said a word.

Katie appreciated that Miles was really careful when he fastened the seat belt.

"Hang in there, Katie, the hospital's only about ten minutes away." It was hard not to floor the accelerator, but he didn't want her flying forward.

At a red light, he smacked his hands on the steering wheel. She saw the pulse pounding in his neck. He was angry, very understandable. "Okay, I can't stand it any longer. Give me one good reason, Katie, just one good reason why you didn't tell me." His voice was low and perfectly cold, not a bit of inflection. She wondered if he ever yelled.

She felt a sharp stab of pain that held her quiet until it eased.

"Well, are you going to say anything?" Now, she thought, that was close to a yell. She nearly smiled, but couldn't.

She got hold of herself and said, "The children. I just couldn't let Sam and Keely see that I'd been shot. They've been through so much, particularly Sam, I just couldn't do that to them. If I'd been shot bad, Miles, I would have hollered, but it's just not that bad. I figured it could wait until we took care of the kids. I know it was unfair of me to spring this on you."

"Yeah, right, real unfair."

Sarcasm was good, she supposed. She said, "I just went to the women's room in the park, tore off some of my sweatshirt, pulled down my jeans and wrapped it tight around my hip. Really, it looked to me like a flesh wound, the bullet went right through me. I'm not going to die, Miles."

"You'd better not or I'll really be pissed. So would Sam. So would Keely."

"I don't want them to know about this."

He gunned the Mercedes into the hospital parking lot, and swerved into the circular turnabout in front of the emergency room, figuring they'd get instant attention, and so they did.

He held her hand when the nurse pulled down her jeans and untied the strips of sweatshirt she'd wrapped around herself. The piece of sweatshirt that was directly over the wound was soaked with blood. She didn't touch it. Miles was ready to yell when Dr. Pierce came barreling into the cubicle in the next instant, out of breath. "Hey, I hear we got a gunshot wound," he said, and looked down at Katie's hip. "Would you look at that. I heard about the shooting, Mr. Kettering, but they said it had to do with the FBI. They didn't say anyone was injured. I don't understand why she didn't see a doctor right away."

"We'll talk about it later, Dr. Pierce," Katie said. "Please, just clean me up."

"This is going to hurt a bit, Mrs. Kettering." He managed to get the rest of the sweatshirt off the wound, but of course it had stuck and Katie almost yelled at the pain.

But she hung in there, squeezing Miles's hand really hard when the nurse used alcohol to clean off all the dried blood.

"The bullet appears to have gone through the fleshy part of the side of your hip, Mrs. Kettering. You two know, of course, that I'll have to report this."

"Yes, of course," Miles said. "You wondered why we didn't come to the ER immediately. Well, my wife didn't want our children to know she'd been shot and that's why we're here now."

"Not very bright of you, Mrs. Kettering."

"Yeah, yeah, I just bet you'd choose to let your kids see you dripping blood if you had a choice."

Dr. Pierce paused a moment, then slowly nodded. "You're a cop, aren't you?"

"A sheriff. I know when a wound is bad and when it can wait awhile. Nothing to hit here in my hip except fat, and that always grows back without a problem."

Miles said, "Call Detective Raven at DC Metro. He'll tell you all about it. I'll bet he'll also want to smack my wife around a bit."

"Okay. Mrs. Kettering, I can see this hurts. We're going to start an IV, give you some morphine. You'll want to go to sleep on the examination table in just a minute or two. Then I can clean up this wound and stitch you together. I don't think you'll be needing any X rays. Hold on to your husband's hand real tight. That's it."

She sucked in her breath, and it was done. He left her for a moment; undoubtedly he was going to call Detective Raven.

An hour later, Katie was walking slowly out of the hospital, supported by Miles.

"You're going to be okay," he said, more for himself than for her, Katie thought, as he very carefully fastened her seat belt. "The doctor said you were lucky. Now, don't move."

"I won't."

When he was driving out of the parking lot, Katie said, "Thank you, Miles. I know this was a pain in your butt as well as mine, but, well, thank you."

"You're my damned wife. You think I'd dab some iodine on your hip and go to sleep?"

He was angry again. If she hadn't felt so dopey, her brain cotton, she would have laughed. "Where are we going?"

He turned to face her for a moment. "To the all-night pharmacy to get the Vicodin prescription filled. You're to take a couple every four hours for a day or so."

"I really feel fine."

"That's the morphine talking."

"I understand how you would get really upset what with all that dried blood on my hip."

"Don't even start with me, Katie. I am so pissed at you —"

"That's all right, just so long as we keep

449

this from the children."

Miles sucked in a deep breath. "To-morrow, after I'm sure you're up to it, we're going to discuss who might have shot at us. I'll bet that's what Detective Raven is wondering. Count on him coming by tomorrow, along with half the FBI."

"Bring them on, Miles." She closed her eyes and drifted off. She wasn't aware that he'd stopped at the all-night pharmacy. She hadn't awakened when he undressed her and tucked her into bed.

She wasn't aware that he held her hand until he woke her up at two o'clock and fed her two Vicodin. He held her hand the rest of that long night.

The next morning, the lovely morphine was a hazy memory, the pain in her hip all too present. When Miles held out two big pills to her, she took them without a fuss.

"Oh, no," she said, "where are the kids?"

"I'll take care of the kids. It's still early. When they're up, I'll tell them that you've got a bit of a stomach bug and to leave you alone until you decide to appear. Okay?"

"I can tell you're a parent. You're good. Thank you, Miles."

He paced the room in front of her, then turned back to face her. "Katie, I've been thinking quite a bit about this. I think you did the right thing. We don't know how Sam and Keely are going to be this morning, how yesterday's trauma will affect them, but I do know that if they knew you'd been shot, it would be much worse. So thank you. Now see that you heal while I think about how I'm going to keep the police away from you as long as possible."

"I'll be just fine. Say early afternoon?"

She fell asleep ten minutes later with just a pinch of pain in her hip.

Miles stood a moment in the doorway, then looked down at his watch. It was only six-thirty in the morning. The kids would be up any time now. He hated lying to them, but not this time. He hoped they could carry it off. He didn't want to see any more blank pain in Sam's eyes for as long as he lived.

39

At eight o'clock that evening, only three hours after leaving Detective Raven down at Metro Headquarters, Savich came to stand in the kitchen doorway, watching Sherlock wipe spaghetti sauce off Sean's mouth. Sean quickly replaced it with the next spoonful. What with all the excitement, they'd gotten home very late, and Sean was hungry, tired, and really hyped up. As for Sean's parents, they both hoped some of Savich's spaghetti would put him out. Savich said to Sherlock, not taking his eyes off his boy, "Are you ready for something you're not going to believe?"

Sherlock straightened midswipe. "I heard you talking on the phone to Miles. What's going on?"

"The shooter today. It seems he wasn't after me. He was after Katie."

"After Katie? What do you mean?"

Savich didn't say anything for a moment as Sean clattered his spoon to his plate, climbed down from his chair, and made a beeline for his orange plastic ball in the corner. They both, for a moment, listened to him tell the ball that he was going to bounce it, good.

When she looked up at him, Savich said, "He shot Katie."

"*What?* How? But that isn't possible! She never said a word, she never acted wounded, she —"

Savich leaned his head back against one of the cabinets, closed his eyes. "He shot her in the hip and she managed to hide it from all of us. The bullet went in and through. She'll be okay. Miles called from the emergency room while the nurse was getting Katie into a robe. Turns out she didn't say a word about it until after they'd gotten home and put the kids to bed. Then she tells him. He's still so shaken up he could barely speak straight."

"She's really okay?"

"Yes, soon to be out with a smile on her face from the morphine. Just a couple days rest, and she'll be fine."

Sherlock picked up a hot pad and hurled it across the kitchen. It calmed her and didn't make any noise to frighten Sean. "I don't believe this, Dillon. It's ridiculous, just plain dumb. She's wounded and doesn't even let on? No, that can't be right, it can't."

"She didn't say anything because she didn't want the kids any more frightened than they were. If you think about it, you can see Katie's point. It was an adult decision, hers to make, I guess."

Sherlock's heart was still pumping wildly. She threw another hot pad at the wall, calmed herself down. "It was brave of her." She drew in a deep breath. "I hope I would have the presence of mind to do that. But wait, Dillon, if the shooter hit her —

"That means I wasn't the target. Or, I really was the target, and he could have shot at her first, for the fun of it."

Savich straightened, shrugged. "Maybe he, whoever *he* is, just wanted to scare us. At this point, any guess is as good as any other. Who knows, it might have been a random shooting." Neither of them believed that for an instant.

Savich picked up Sean, who was tightly clutching his orange ball, and walked to the front window in the living room. He stared out into the calm dark night. A storm was expected to hit Monday, winter coming with a grand announcement. And the temperature would plummet. Sean dropped his ball, watched it roll under an end table. He then spoke in his father's ear and patted his face, telling him things he understood, like *good spaghetti* — "I think Sean just said he wanted a puppy."

It was so ridiculous that for a moment Sherlock actually laughed and kissed her son's sleepy face.

She saw the strain on Dillon's face, saw the restless movement of his hands, saw the scars on his hands and fingers from his whittling. She knew he'd been caught off guard by the same devastating feelings she had felt when that bullet had come so close to him and to Sean. It made her want to scream and cry at the same time. He said finally, as if he'd been holding the words inside but they now had to come out, "This was too close, Sherlock, far too close. Sean could have been killed."

Of course she agreed. The corrosive fear, the sense of absolute impotence — she nodded but didn't say anything, just moved closer.

Sean's head now lay on his father's shoulder. Savich lightly smoothed his back, cupped his head. She saw a spasm of fear cross his face. He said quietly, "I've been giving a lot of thought today to what I've been doing nearly all my adult life — being a cop. What if . . . what if, because of me, some crazy kills my son? It would be my fault, Sherlock, no one else's, just mine, and it would all be because of what I choose to do for a living. I couldn't live with that, I just couldn't."

"No," she said slowly, her eyes still on his face, "neither of us could."

He plowed forward, the words forcing themselves out of his mouth. "Maybe, just maybe, I should think about another line of work." There, he'd said the unimaginable, and the earth hadn't opened up and swallowed him. It was out in the open now, those words between them, and he didn't say anything else, just let the unthinkable settle around him, and he waited. Sean suddenly lurched up against his palm, and smiled at his father. He patted his father's face again with wet fingers.

Sherlock closed in and put her arms around him, just as they had after the shooting, with Sean between them. Then she began to lightly scratch around the healing wound in his back. They stood there silently together for several minutes. Finally, she raised her face, patted his cheek with her fingers, hers thankfully not wet, and said, "Do you know, Dillon, I agree with you entirely."

He nearly fell back against the window with surprise. "You do?"

"Yes, I do. But the only thing is, you're the best cop I've ever met in my life."

"Maybe, but Sean —"

She nodded. "This was so scary that both of us nearly went round the bend. But, you know, if you just stop to think about it, the solution to this isn't difficult."

His head came up. "What solution?" He sounded irritated, and she was pleased. She could just imagine how deep he would dig in his heels if she argued with him, what with the worry and the guilt, worry and guilt that had nearly felled her as well.

She went on her tiptoes and kissed him, and again hugged her boy and her husband tight.

"Dillon, you're a smart man."

"Yeah, well, what's your point? What's this easy solution?"

She smiled up at him, kissed both him and Sean again, and said, "As I said, you're smart. But here's your problem; you're just too much of a hero, Dillon; you feel too responsible, like you have to fix every bad thing that happens anywhere around you. It's not just your job, it's who you are."

"Yeah, sure, but —"

"No buts. No more. You're a cop, Dillon, one of the very best. It's what you are, who you are. What happened in the park — it was scary, that's for sure, but the fact is there are such things as random shootings. Would you have blamed yourself for being a cop then? I'll tell you, there have been times when I've wanted to take you away to the Poconos, hide you in a cabin, and carry around six guns to protect you."

"And you don't think I've felt the same way about you?"

She gave him a big smile, reached up her hand and cupped his cheek. "I think we're both doing exactly what we were meant to do. I plan for Sean to see us both well into old age. Get over it, Dillon. It's time to move on."

He kissed her, pulled her hard against him again. Sean burped. "But —"

"I know, there's always a but. Let's just work through this one day at a time, all right? You know as well as I do that the time to make a life-altering decision isn't right after a huge scare."

Slowly, he nodded.

"We've worked through everything else that's come along and hit us in the chops. This is different because it's the first time our jobs have come close to Sean, the first time our little tiger here could have been hurt because of what we do. It will be tough, but we'll do the right thing. Don't worry, we'll sort it all out."

"Sherlock?"

She lightly bit his neck in answer.

"You want to spend some quality time with me?"

She was laughing as she licked where'd she bitten. "Can I strip you naked and kiss you all over?"

He swallowed hard, and nodded, looking at her smiling mouth. Sean burped again.

SUNDAY AFTERNOON
THE KETTERING HOME
COLFAX, VIRGINIA

Katie didn't hurt if she stayed still, and that was a very nice thing. On the other hand, she wasn't stupid enough to laugh or make any sudden movements. She was seated in Miles's big comfortable leather chair, wearing sweats with a nice loose fleece top that hid the bandages under the sweats, her feet up on a big ottoman, her legs covered with a ratty afghan Miles's mother had knitted many years before. She was wearing a pair of thick socks, no shoes.

Cracker had taken Sam and Keely to a children's movie matinee so they wouldn't see or hear the cops. Both of them had seemed just fine, thank God, neither suspecting that she had something other than the flu. She was thankfully spared enthusiastic hugs that would surely have brought a moan out of her. She smiled over Sherlock and Savich, who'd just arrived a few minutes earlier.

Miles brought in coffee and tea, and a plate of scones he'd picked up at Nathan's Bakery just down on Cartwright Avenue.

Detective Benjamin Raven said the moment he sat down on the comfortable sofa in the living room, ignoring both scones and coffee, "I am royally pissed, Mrs. Kettering. That was a really stupid thing to do."

To his surprise, she nodded. "I would agree with you, Detective, if I'd been wearing your cop's shoes and not the victim's."

It was Sunday, his buddies were waiting for him down at the sports bar with peanuts, beer, and the Redskins game. Then Mr. Kettering had called. He'd been nursing his snit for a good half hour now and he wasn't about to let go without cutting loose on the woman who'd ruined his day. "You're a cop, Sheriff, yet you pulled this stunt. You've come pretty close to obstructing justice."

"An interesting point, Detective," Miles said, his voice mild, really quite reasonable now that he'd gotten over his own snit. He turned slightly in his chair and winked at Katie before he turned back. "I think it was pretty dumb, too, but we've already discussed why she did it. Can we move on to something helpful?"

Detective Raven shouted at all of them indiscriminately, "Are all you people nuts? Your macho sheriff here could have bloody bled to death!"

"I really prefer macha, Detective Raven."

"Don't you try to jolly me out of this, Sheriff!"

Miles said, "If she'd been shot bad, she would have yelled. She's not stupid." He paused a moment. "You would have yelled, wouldn't you have, Katie?"

"Oh yes. I've always believed you've got to live to fight another day." She stared at Miles, then gave him such a brilliant smile that he blinked.

"Enough already," Detective Raven said at last. He snagged a scone off the plate, poured himself a cup of coffee, and said, "If you guys are through praising this crazy woman, why doesn't somebody tell me who you think fired at you."

Katie said, "I made a phone call back home to Jessborough just before you got here, Detective. Miles told you yesterday about all the hoopla we went through there. I asked about the congregation, about what was going on with them. Nothing, evidently. Interesting fact though. The place has been a disaster area what with all the storms, but once it started drying out, crews went out to the ruins of the McCamy house to start cleaning everything up and dig out the bodies. It's still really slow going. There's no word yet."

Detective Raven said, "You think one of the McCamys survived?"

"No one could have survived in that house, Detective," Miles said.

"Then what's your point?"

Katie said, "I guess maybe I was just surprised that they hadn't cleaned everything up. It's just strange, all of it."

"Basically, we ain't got anymore diddly than we had yesterday," Detective Raven said, rising, and dusting off his jeans. "I've always hated too many possibilities. It sucks, big time."

"Yeah," Miles said, "I agree."

Savich's cell phone played the *1812 Overture*. He held up a staying hand, listened, and when he hung up, he said,

"That was one of my agents. The white Toyota Camry the shooter was driving was stolen two days ago from a Mr. Alfred Morley, in Rockville, Maryland. Right out of his driveway, during the night. He told the local police and they put out an APB on it."

"I don't suppose the car's turned up?" Detective Raven said.

Savich shook his head. "Not yet."

"Well, like my daddy always says, if things come too easy in life, you have more fun than you deserve. Okay, that's it then. Thanks for the scones." He looked down at his watch. "Well, damn, I've missed a good half of the game."

"The Redskins are probably losing anyway," Savich said. "No fun watching that."

40

Savich was depressed, he admitted it. Sherlock was in a meeting when he left headquarters early to stop at the gym. He wanted to sweat out some of the day's frustrations and see what his back could manage. Maybe he'd find someone he could practice some easy throws with.

What he didn't want to find at the gym was Valerie Rapper; her eyes were on him the moment he came out of the men's locker room.

He nodded to her, nothing more, and headed into the big room to stretch. She followed him, stood at the barre in front of the mirrors and did some ballet moves with her toes pointed out. She said, "I've missed you, Agent Savich."

He didn't answer her, tried to concentrate on stretching out his knotted muscles. The stress had left him feeling tight and cold. At least his back wasn't bothering him.

"Would you like me to walk on your back? I'm really very good at it and you look like you could use it."

"No, thank you, I'm just about all set now," he said and left the exercise room. He worked out hard, moving between the weights and the treadmill, aware that she was always near, and it was driving him nuts. When she got on the treadmill next to him nearly an hour later, he knew he had to put a stop to this.

"Ms. Rapper."

"Yes, Agent Savich?" She cocked an eyebrow at him, actually ran her tongue over her bottom lip. He stared at that slip-sliding tongue of hers, not out of overwhelming lust, but amazement that she actually did that. The only thing he knew for sure about Ms. Valerie Rapper was that she had supreme self-confidence. Hadn't any guy ever said no to her? Evidently not.

He said with a touch of humor in his voice, "Why don't you go introduce yourself to Jake Palmer? You see the good-looking guy down there doing bench presses? He's single, been divorced for a good long time, and I've heard he's ready to start dating again. I'm not in the dating market, Ms. Rapper."

"I'm glad you're not, Agent Savich. I want you all to myself."

Her arrogance astounded him, and he was silent for a moment. "I've already told you I'm married, Ms. Rapper. I've got a wife who wants me all to herself. I'm not available. Please, enough is enough. Hey, Jake can out-bench-press me."

She stretched out her hand and pressed the "stop" button on his treadmill. He stared at her as she stepped over onto his treadmill, right in front of him, ignoring the dozen or so people on the machines near them, and pressed herself against him. She went up on her toes, clasped her palms around his face and kissed him, hard.

There was no punch of lust, just shock at what she was doing, and then anger.

He heard a wolf whistle, but mainly there was just stupefied silence. There was a comment, within hearing, about at least taking it to the parking lot.

"Shall we go to that sexy red Porsche of yours?" she said into his mouth. "But you're a big man, Agent Savich. My Mercedes is roomier than a Porsche, so how about we go there instead?"

Savich grabbed her arms, pulled them to her sides, and held them there.

She looked up at him, her eyes on his mouth, and said, "You're really strong. I like that."

"Dillon, why is this woman taking advantage of you on the treadmill?"

Sherlock. He grinned like a loon. He was never so happy to hear her voice in his life. He let go of Valerie's arms and pushed her back, but her lower body was still close to his groin. He heard a whistle and looked onto the main floor of the gym. There was Jake, giving him a little wave. So Jake had called Sherlock. He nodded back and said to his wife, "Hi, sweetheart, I didn't hear you come in."

"No, I can see that it would have been tough given Ms. Barracuda here all over you."

"Actually, this is Valerie Rapper."

Sherlock gave a cheerful smile to the woman who was standing frozen, still too close to Dillon. "Hi, Ms. Rapper. If you don't get your hands, your mouth, and all the rest of yourself off my husband, and step off his treadmill, I will deck you. Then I will put my foot on your neck and I will rub your nose into a sweaty mat. Is that enough of a threat?"

Valerie took a step back, just couldn't help herself, not knowing what to say to that miserable little red-headed monster. She wanted Savich, wanted just *him*, not anyone else. He'd been playing the faithful game — oh yes, a man could be as coy and tease as well as any woman — but it would have ended quite soon. She said to him, "Would you just look at her. I'll bet she dyes all that wild red hair. There aren't any freckles on her face, and that means a dye job. It's not even well done. I can see roots."

Savich said, "I can assure you that all that wild red hair is quite natural. I'm her husband, I've got the inside track on this."

"Dillon," Sherlock said, "that's a tad indelicate. Ms. Rapper, not all redheads have freckles. Now, please remove yourself or I will take action in the next couple of seconds."

Valerie waved this away. "You know if she weren't here, you'd be pulling me out of this wretched gym in no time at all."

"Do you really think so?" Savich inquired, and a black eyebrow shot up a good inch.

"Of course I do! This is ridiculous. Don't you know who I am?"

Sherlock said, head cocked to the side, "A pushy broad with an embarrassing last name?"

"You little bitch, back off! My father is the CEO and major stockholder of Rapper Industries. I am his daughter."

"Fancy that," Savich said, looking impressed, his mouth smiling, but his eyes hard. "Actually, when you said he was your father, I figured you just might be his daughter."

"I could buy your dumb-ass FBI with my trust fund!"

Now this was interesting, Savich thought. "How ignorant of me. I hadn't realized who you were. Just imagine, the daughter of the famed Mr. Rapper. Now that I realize you're very rich as well as very beautiful, it makes all the difference. Don't you agree, sweetheart?"

Sherlock, her smile still in place, nodded. "It sure does. It makes me realize it's time to bring out my big guns." She pushed Dillon out of the way and stepped up right into Valerie Rapper's face, making three of them on the treadmill. "I don't suppose you know who we are, do you?"

Valerie Rapper blinked. "Of course, you're a couple of unimportant little cops. So what?"

"If he's so little, then why do you want him?"

"I was referring to you. I saw him on TV.

I saw those women reporters looking at him. Go away now."

Sherlock didn't touch her, even though she badly wanted to. She said, not an inch from Valerie Rapper's face, "Oh no, he's mine. Now, Ms. Rapper, you won't believe my big gun — it's a cannon really. My father is the famous federal judge Sherlock. If I tell him you've been annoying me, why, he could have your father and his entire conglomerate investigated. What do you think of that, missy?"

Before Savich could throw in his own big gun and tell her he was Sarah Elliott's grandson and he controlled millions of dollars in paintings, Valerie Rapper stepped off the treadmill, grabbed her bottle of water, waved it at them. "Both of you are crazy, totally crazy. Judge Sherlock! What a ridiculous name!"

"You should know," Sherlock said.

"Don't you dare have my father investigated, do you hear me?"

"Well, I'll think about it if you leave my husband alone."

"I'll bet you dye everything so he won't guess that your hair isn't natural!"

"Gee, I didn't know that was possible. Thanks for the tip."

"What's going on here, Agent Savich?"

470

It was Bobby Curling, the gym manager. He looked both amused and alarmed. "We got a problem here? These two fighting over you? Since when did you become such a sex object?"

Savich grinned at his wife. "Actually, the three of us were just comparing our antecedents. It's my considered opinion that Sherlock and I come from the better gene pool."

"You're not worth my time, either of you!" Valerie Rapper whirled around. "As for you, Bobby, you can take your cheap club and shove it."

She took the stairs two at a time going down, something Savich had never seen anyone do before. Bobby grinned up at him. Savich gave Bobby a thumbs up. "No problem now, Bobby, everything's cool."

"Yeah, but you guys just lost me a customer."

"Maybe," Savich said. "But we also put on quite a show for everyone else."

"I'd say we're easier to get along with anyway," Sherlock said.

Bobby hunched his huge muscled shoulders, took a last look at Valerie Rapper stomping into the women's locker room. "She sure is pretty," he said, and sighed. "I've been watching her go after you, so I guess in the spirit of keeping marriages together, it's okay with me she's leaving." He sighed again, and turned away. "I'll bet she's really rich, huh?"

"She says she is." Savich turned to his wife, lightly touched his fingertip to her cheek. "Thanks for showing up. Good timing, as always."

"The Special Forces couldn't have moved any faster than I did getting here. I'd hug you but you're sweaty. Oh, who cares?" She plastered herself to him and whispered against his neck, "When I saw her pushing against you, I have to admit I nearly lost it. I wanted to heave one of the bicycles at her or throw her over the railing or knock her beautiful capped teeth into her tonsils."

"You were the model of restraint," he said, hugging her.

She cupped his face between her hands, pulled him down, kissed him hard. "Thank God you're so sweaty, I can't smell her on you. We're a pretty good team."

He looked down at her. "From the time I kicked your SIG Sauer out of your hand in Hogan's Alley, I knew we would be."

She bit his neck, which tasted like salt. "I called Lily. She came dashing over to watch Sean. You want to go rescue your sister?"

"Nah. Lily's always complaining that she doesn't get him to herself enough. Let's give her another hour. Now, I've got to shower. Maybe we could stop off at Dizzy Dan's and get a pizza. We could take a couple of slices home to Sean and Lily. They've both got a big pizza tooth."

Sherlock laughed. "A little kid and he loves his pizza with artichokes on it." She grinned up at him. Yes, everything was under control. "Let's do it. We'll get you the Vegetarian Nirvana, which sounds scary to me."

"Only Sean and I truly appreciate pineapple and broccoli," he said.

"You got that right. Me, I'm pure carnivore," she said, and bit his neck again.

41

Agent Dane Carver said, "Glad you guys made it in time. He just made his move, see him? He's over there by the side of the house, trying to hide in the shadows, but he's just too damned big. I was just on my way after him."

Sherlock said, "Would you look at that bulky wool coat he's wearing. He looks like a huge black bat."

"Let's have a closer look," Savich said. Dane gave Savich his infrared glasses and Savich saw him clearly, skulking to the side of the small 1940s cottage using the oak trees as cover.

Sherlock said, "Did you get her name?"

"Ms. Aquine Barton, single, longtime math teacher at Dentonville High School. She's in there alone, Savich."

"Okay, Dane, hang back and call the cops when I signal you. We're going to let him heave himself over the windowsill into the cottage, then we'll get him. I don't want him getting close to the teacher. Just close enough so it's the final nail in his coffin. Just keep your fingers crossed that he doesn't try anything stupid, and keep your gun ready."

Savich, Sherlock on his heels, ran bent over, SIG Sauers drawn, to the front of the cottage. "We're being cowboys," she said to the back of his black leather jacket.

"Not really. This guy's not going to give us any problems once we confront him. Keep down and stay behind me."

"Sometimes I hate it that you're the boss."

He grinned into the darkness as he eased the lock pick into the front-door keyhole.

It took under three seconds. The lock released and the front door slid open with just a push of his toe.

It was utterly black inside. The air smelled like jasmine, so much jasmine your nose felt stuffed with flowers.

They paused, listening. They'd watched him jimmy the window into the dining room, not more than twenty feet away from where they were crouched over in deep shadows by the front door. It was lucky he hadn't tried to go right in through a bedroom window. That, they couldn't have allowed. They walked lightly, pressing themselves against the wall in the hallway, listening to him try to get through the window. How he could get in without awakening Ms. Barton neither of them could imagine.

They heard him land hard on the dining room floor.

"That's it," Savich said and ran lightly into the dining room.

Savich said, quietly, but clearly, "You can stop now, Troy. It's all over."

Troy Ward's head jerked up. He recognized Savich's voice even though he couldn't see him clearly.

He yelled at the top of his lungs, "Get away!"

As his voice echoed off the dining room walls, they heard a woman yell loud enough to make the crystals on the chandelier over the dining room table dance. "You little creep! How dare you come in here to rape me! Just look at you, all dressed in black like some sort of gangster, sneaking into my house, landing like a brick on my dining room floor! How's this, you nasty little pervert!"

There was enough light coming through the window to see Ms. Aquine Barton bring a huge old iron skillet down on Troy Ward's head. Troy's finger jerked the trigger on his gun in reflex, and a bullet slammed into the lamp on Ms. Barton's sideboard. It exploded, sending shards of glass flying all over the room.

"Get down, kids!" Aquine Barton yelled even though there were no kids around. "Just look what you did, you little creep! That was my mama's lamp." She leaned over Troy Ward's still bulk and kicked him in the ribs with her bare foot. Then she looked up, saw two more shadows, heard them breathing hard, and flipped on the light, skillet raised high. "Two more of you?" She waved that skillet toward them. "You just come here and I'll lay you flat, too."

"Ms. Barton? Please don't hurt us. I'm Agent Savich and this is Agent Sherlock. We're with the FBI. Please don't slam us with that skillet." He pulled out his shield and flipped it open.

She looked them both up and down, then checked out his FBI shield. "A woman's got to protect herself. Had this skillet under the bed for a good fifteen years now. First time I had to use it. Who is this nasty fat little man anyway?" She waved the skillet very close to Troy Ward's head. "What is all this about? What are you doing in my house at midnight? I have school tomorrow, you know."

"The man you just flattened, Ms. Barton, is the math teacher killer," Sherlock said. "And you brought him down all by yourself. Thank you very much."

Ms. Barton stood there, staring down at Troy Ward, then back at Savich. "I know who you are now. This man was one of the widowers, standing behind you, Agent Savich, on that podium. I remember thinking he really needed to go to the gym, maybe even sleep there, no food. When was that press conference? A couple of weeks ago?"

"Yes, ma'am," Savich said. "You've got a very good memory."

"But his wife was the first one killed. Oh, I see. It was him all along, the scummy little jerk." She kicked him with her bare foot. "But why was he here?" Her dark eyes widened and she whispered, "Oh my goodness, he was here to kill me, to make me his next victim, wasn't he?"

"We wouldn't have allowed that, Ms. Barton," Sherlock said. "We were right with him all the way. We just had to wait until the moment he stepped into your house. Then we were prepared to arrest him. By catching him here, we've left no way for a lawyer to get him off. There was never any danger to you. I was looking forward to taking him in myself, but you didn't give me a chance, you just bonked him on the head and laid him right out."

Bless Sherlock, Savich thought. She was excellent at distraction.

"I see now. You boobs set me up." Ms. Barton crossed her arms over her chest, still holding the skillet.

A schoolteacher who had obviously heard better lies than Sherlock's.

"Yes, ma'am," Sherlock said. "But you're a heroine, ma'am. You've made things safe for math teachers again."

"Well, yes, I suppose I have," said Ms. Barton as she fussed over her knee-length nightgown.

Dane appeared in the doorway, out of breath. "You got him, Savich?"

Savich grinned and waved toward Aquine. "No, Ms. Barton here brought him down with her trusty iron skillet."

"Holy shit, ma'am," Dane said. He stared from Troy Ward back to her, and gave her a fat smile. "You did a fine job."

"You watch your mouth, boy."

"Sorry, ma'am, I guess the shock made me forget my manners."

"Well, I'll tell you, I've taught nasty-mouthed little high school boys for nearly thirty years now. There isn't anything I haven't heard."

Troy Ward groaned. Aquine kicked him. He shuddered, fell still again. She said, "I see what you had in mind now. You just wanted me standing in a corner, fluttering my hands, all helpless, right?"

"Yes, ma'am," Savich said, smiling. "We're the law. We're paid to hit people, occasionally. But you know, it doesn't matter who brought him down in the big equation of life. You got him, and that's just fine."

"Agent Savich, I'll just bet you got yourself smacked when you were in high school."

"Only a couple of times, ma'am," Savich said. "I was always really good in math, though."

"How did you know he was going to come after me?"

"We didn't know, ma'am. I was never certain that it was really a serial killer, I couldn't afford to be. I had all three widowers at the press conference with me so everyone watching could get a good look at them. Maybe someone would call the hot line with something on one of them. After the conference, I had both Mr. Ward and Mr. Fowler followed. Then, only Mr. Ward here because I was almost sure he was guilty, but I needed more proof, and would you look at this — he landed right in your dining room. Ms. Barton, this is Agent Dane Carver, he's the one who's been keeping a close eye on Mr. Ward tonight. He called us here."

"Hello, Ms. Barton. Aren't you cold, ma'am?"

It was in that moment that Ms. Aquine Barton realized she was standing in front of three people wearing only her night-gown. She pointed the skillet at Troy Ward. "You don't let him escape, Agent Savich, and I'll get a robe on and turn up the heat in here."

They barely had time to turn Troy Ward onto his back before she was back, belting her long purple chenille bathrobe while somehow keeping a grip on the skillet.

Troy groaned, his eyelashes fluttered and he stared up at Savich. "You bastard. How did you know I was here?"

"I think the more relevant question is what you're doing here, Troy. It's kind of late to be paying a social call, don't you think? And you didn't even use the front door. Now, coming through a dining room window makes things look a little suspect, don't you think, Troy?"

"I didn't want her to hear me."

Sherlock said, "You landed a little hard, Troy."

"I'd say so," Ms. Barton said, "I can hear a boy playing with a paper clip at the back of the class room. You sounded like a hippo trying to squeeze into a water bottle."

"Bastard. I want my lawyer."

"I'm not a bastard, you nasty little man. I'm a teacher."

"Not you, you stupid woman, him!"

Savich said, "You know, that's why I didn't call you in for a chat. You're too smart, Troy, for me to talk you into confessing, aren't you? Yeah, I'll bet you would have kept your mouth shut and demanded a lawyer. And I did wonder if I would have ever gotten enough to send you to prison for three murders and one attempted murder. So we just watched you. Thank you for climbing right in."

"I'm at the wrong house. I didn't mean to be here. It's all a mistake. I want my lawyer."

"Yep, a big mistake, I'd say. Agent Carver here followed you to the library this afternoon, saw you perusing local yearbooks. He figured you'd spotted your next victim. Fact is, though, even if we hadn't been doing our good old-fashioned police work, you picked the wrong math teacher."

"No, that's a lie. But why did you suspect me? What was there about me that made you suspicious? I can see it on your face. There was something you latched onto, wasn't there? But what? I'm a professional sports announcer, what could have made you suspect me?"

Savich saw that Aquine Barton was holding her iron skillet just a little tighter. He gave her a slight shake of his head. He said, "I was in an accident several weeks ago, Troy, and they loaded me up with morphine. I was remembering our conversation, but in a morphine haze everything's different. Maybe some hidden connections come bursting through, things that I'd picked up that you hadn't actually said to me."

"And just what did you pick up on, you bastard? That I wasn't like you, because you were just like all those other moron jocks? You knew I was different, didn't you?"

"I listened to you call some of the Ravens game on Sunday. You were very good, just the right mix of play calling, commentary, and sweet silence."

"Yeah, I'm the best, but it's just not enough, is it? You're just waiting to tell everyone, aren't you?"

Savich said, "That Smith and Wesson thirty-eight of yours, Troy. Turns out when I spoke to your wife's sister, she remembered your owning a gun a long way back. A revolver, just like this thirty-eight you brought here to Aquine's house. I know there are lots of thirty-eights in the world, Troy, but the thing is, now we'll get to test yours. Do you think we'll find a match?"

"I want a lawyer."

"You'll get your lawyer. But you might as well know we found where you bought the gun way back in 1993 in Baltimore. A small gun shop owned by a Mr. Hanratty on Willowby Street, downtown. He keeps excellent records. I'm sure your lawyer will show you a copy of the sale."

"Sounds like you better just fess up, Mr. Ward," said Aquine, who now was sitting on a dining room chair, the skillet in her lap.

"Like I said, Ms. Barton, Troy here is really smart. You know, I kept worrying about motive, Troy, just couldn't understand why you'd murder your wife, even if she found out you were gay."

"I'm not gay! That's a lie! That's not a motive either."

"No, but she wasn't just going to tell the world about your being gay, Troy. I think some people already knew that and didn't really care. What she was going to tell the world was that you trade in child pornography, and that you just couldn't allow."

"You can't know about that, you can't, unless — you hacked into my computer without a warrant? I'll sue your ass off, Savich! That's against the law!"

"You're right, it is. But you know, I have an agent in my unit by the name of Ruth Warnecki, and she used to be a D.C. cop. She has lots of snitches. One of them called her, told her he'd seen you on TV and knew he'd also seen you one night buying some kiddy porn on the street over on Halloran. I went there, and guess what, Troy? We found a witness who recognized your photo, said he'd seen you pay to go into a live shop with little kids parading around naked. Now, I can't prove yet exactly what went on in those shows, and if we find out who the owners of that nasty little business are, we'll nail them right along with you. But how much of that did your wife find out about, Troy? Did she even know you were gay?"

"I want a lawyer. None of that crap means anything. Witnesses are paid off all the time. I don't know anything about child pornography. Leave me alone."

"You know, Troy, we really don't need your cooperation, not after you huffed your way over the windowsill and landed in Ms. Barton's dining room with the murder weapon in your hand. That's what I'd call catching the perp dead to rights. You're a murderer, Troy, a vicious, cold-blooded murderer, and you're going down for it. All the way down. You got anything else to say?"

"I want a lawyer," Troy Ward whispered and pulled his legs into his chest.

Dane Carver hauled Troy Ward to his feet, read him his rights, and cuffed him. They left Ms. Aquine Barton with a fine story to tell the press and her students.

42

Katie was sore, but she wasn't about to lie in bed and have the kids wonder if there was something else going on other than a brief bout with the flu. She showed up at the breakfast table, trying to stand straight and not limp. "Okay, I'm making waffles this morning. Miles, do you have twenty minutes?"

He really didn't, but he leaned over and kissed her. "Sure. I've never had your waffles, Katie."

"It's the best thing Mama makes," Keely said. "You're lucky. She doesn't make them often."

Miles grabbed Keely and tossed her into the air. She was his daughter, he thought, an amazing thing. She was laughing, and Sam joined in, hoping he was next. Miles, not about to let him down, swung him up and around, too, nearly crashing into the kitchen table.

"Did I hear *waffles?*"

"Aunt Cracker! That was a neat movie yesterday. And the pizza was yummy."

"Sure was," she said, reaching out and ruffling Sam's hair, then touching Keely's hair. "See kids, Katie is just fine today. It wasn't the full-blown flu, was it, Katie? Something not quite so bad, thank God, maybe just something you ate that didn't agree with you."

"Could be," Katie said. "Thank goodness it was nothing much, whatever it was."

Katie made the largest batch of waffles ever, Miles fried up bacon, and Cracker made the coffee. The kids laughed and argued and ate until Katie thought they'd both be sick.

Forty-five minutes later, Katie dropped Keely and Sam off at the Hendricks Elementary School, with its attached preschool, only four blocks from their home. The last thing she wanted to do was go back to the house and pace and worry and wonder and make herself nuts. So she started driving. Even though she rarely saw them, she knew her two bodyguards were following her, two FBI agents assigned to protect her after the shooting in the park on Saturday, whenever she left the house.

Funny thing, but she was certain to her toes she was the one the shooter had wanted. Not Savich, not Sherlock, certainly not Miles. But who was it? She couldn't think of a single person. For an instant, Cracker's face flashed in her mind. No, that was impossible, surely. She decided to call her mother when she got back to the house. Talking to her mother always made her feel better. She wished her mother were with her right now, but no, that could be dangerous.

It was very cold, well below freezing, the sky an iron gray, the wind stiff. Snow was predicted by evening, the weather prediction of the first winter storm only a day late. It would stick and the kids would have a blast.

She turned the heater up a bit, and kept driving. She drove past Arlington National Cemetery, a place she'd first seen when she'd been not more than five years old. All those thousands upon thousands of grave markers had touched her deeply as a child, though she hadn't completely understood what they meant. Now, as an adult, all her own worries disappeared in the moments she stared over those fields of white crosses. So many men, she thought, so many.

She drove around Lady Bird Johnson Park, then headed across the Arlington Memorial Bridge that spanned the Potomac. The water below was a roiling gray, moving swiftly, and looked so cold it made her lips tingle. She turned at the Lincoln Memorial when she saw the sign to Roosevelt Memorial Park. She'd first come here as a child, long before the memorial had been built, her small hand tucked in her father's as they walked along the famous Cherry Tree Walk on the Tidal Basin near the national mall. She'd brought Keely here when she'd been a baby, just after Carlo was out of her life, with her mother and father.

She shivered. It was getting colder. She turned up the heater again. The sky looked like it would snow much earlier than this evening.

She parked her Silverado in the empty parking lot at the memorial, and looked around. There was no one here, no killers, no tourists, no workers, just her. She decided to walk through the memorial once again.

One started at the beginning, since the memorial was organized chronologically, and divided into four rooms, which really weren't rooms since it was all outside, each room representing one of Roosevelt's terms in office. There were quotes, displays, and waterfalls everywhere. The place was so huge you could wander around until you dropped, but Katie didn't browse. She found herself walking directly to the third room, depicting Roosevelt's third term, where the waterfall was much larger and much louder. There, just to the left of the waterfall, was a large sculpture of FDR, and beside him sat his dog, Fala. Katie's dad had loved Fala, loved all the stories told about the little black Scottish terrier, who'd even had his own comic strip. She stood looking at the huge sculptured cape that covered Roosevelt, listening to the hammering of the water crashing against huge loose chunks of granite. She'd heard that the waterfalls froze sometimes in the winter. With the way the temperature was plummeting, she imagined it wouldn't be long before they were silent, frozen in place.

Her mind flashed to her father lifting Keely in his arms, pointing to Fala, telling her a story about how he'd performed tricks on demand. How he'd wished he'd been old enough back then to go to Washington to see him in person. Oh Lord, she missed her father, wished he'd gone to a doctor earlier, but he hadn't, just like a damned stubborn man, her mom had told her, and burst into tears. Not that it would have made much difference.

There were memories, she thought, that touched you throughout your life. She had to keep hoping that all of Sam's terrible memories would be tempered with the laughter and joy of experiences that were sweet and good.

She looked at the statue of Roosevelt and said, "If you had lived any longer, would you have announced to the country that you were willing to be president for life? And would the people have elected you?"

She half-expected an answer, and smiled at herself when the crashing water was the only thing she heard. Then there was something else, footsteps coming up behind her. She didn't turn. She thought it was one of her bodyguards, come to check on her, and that was comforting. She stood there, wishing something made sense, wishing she was back in Jessborough, with Miles and Sam and Keely, all of them, in her house that had been magically rebuilt, her mother smiling as she came from the kitchen, carrying a tray of cinnamon buns. She craved another evening filled with tuna casserola and laughter.

She nearly jumped straight into the air when a voice behind her said, "There you are, the little princess."

Katie froze.

"That's right, just stay right where you are. Don't move a muscle."

Katie didn't even consider a twitch.

"All right. Turn around and face me."

Katie slowly turned.

"Surprised to see me, Katie?"

"Yes. Everyone believes you're dead."

Elsbeth McCamy shook her head. "They won't for much longer. I hear they've nearly dug all the way through the ruins of my beautiful house. They'll soon find just one burned body, not two. Poor Reverend McCamy, not even buried yet, left under all that rubble, all that rain pouring down on him. No! Don't you move, Katie Benedict!"

Katie held utterly still.

"I know I shot you on Saturday, but here you are, walking around this ridiculous memorial. I just couldn't believe it when I saw you leave that big fancy house of yours this morning, looking all chipper, herding those children off to school like any good little mother."

Suddenly, she started shaking, and the

gun jerked in her hand. "Dammit, I shot you! Why aren't you dead like you're supposed to be?"

Katie heard hate and despair in her voice. And a bit of madness. She said, "It appears you're not a very good shot."

"I practiced, dammit, practiced for a good week before I hunted you down in that park!"

"People watch TV, see lots of violent movies, and think that when you fire a gun you kill someone, but it's just not true. No matter how good a shot you are, it's difficult to hit what you're aiming at. Don't feel too bad, you didn't miss me. You shot me in the hip." Katie lightly rested her hand against her upper thigh. "It aches a bit, but I'll live."

"I'm only two feet away from you now, Katie. When I shoot you this time, you'll die."

That was surely the truth. Where were her bodyguards?

"I had to stay back in the park since you were with those other federal agents, and that new husband of yours. You really landed on your feet, didn't you, Sheriff? Nice big house, husband kissing your feet, so much money you must think you've died and gone to heaven."

"Actually, I really didn't think of it quite like that," Katie said. Where were her bodyguards? Probably close, they surely couldn't have lost her coming through the memorial. There wasn't another soul around. Maybe they didn't want to intrude on her when there was no one here to threaten her?

"I wanted servants, but Reverend Mc-Camy only wanted God, and me. Always God first, me second. He didn't want servants to come into our home and intrude on his privacy. So I did everything myself, even made brownies. How he loved my brownies. I made them from scratch, stirred together all that chocolate and chocolate chips and pecans, but I didn't eat any. He didn't like any fat on me, said it would be a sacrilege.

"Do you know that he studied his palms and his feet every single day? He prayed until his knees were raw, offered God everything he had, probably including me, if He would just bring back the sacred stigmata one more time. But God didn't answer his prayers."

"The story from Homer Bean was that Reverend McCamy had experienced the stigmata when he was a child. Did you believe that?"

Elsbeth McCamy nodded. "Of course. It's all he could talk about, all he could think about. He would picture it, envision it happening again over and over in his mind, but it never did. He was furious with his parents for not recording it for posterity — to show to his congregation, to prove he wasn't like those crooked loud-mouthed televangelists, that he was blessed by God himself."

"I've given it a lot of thought, Elsbeth, and do you know what I think?"

"If I don't shoot you dead right this minute, I guess you'll tell me."

Katie stayed as still and small as she could. "I don't think Sam suffered any holy stigmata. I think it was some sort of rash or exanthem, something brought on by his illness. I don't think it was blood on his palms."

"His mother believed it was blood. For God's sake, she videotaped it! She could probably smell the blood. You can, you know. Smell blood, that is." She shook her head, bringing herself back from some memory. "She gave the tape to a senile old priest whose sister recognized its value and knew a member of the Reverend's congregation. That's how it came to Reverend McCamy. Who are you to question any of

496

this? You're just some hick sheriff."

"Let me ask you this, Elsbeth. Was Sam the only child like that Reverend McCamy had ever heard about, had ever tracked down?"

Slowly, Elsbeth nodded her head. "Yes, but that doesn't mean anything."

"I suppose it doesn't. I'm surprised and pleased that you managed to escape the fire, Elsbeth."

"I doubt you'll be pleased much longer. If I'd burned to a crisp with Reverend McCamy, you wouldn't be looking death in the eye."

"How did you get out?"

Elsbeth McCamy shrugged. "We had a little . . . playroom at the back of the closet. There's a door that leads down from there and out of the mud room. Reverend McCamy was dead, I knew it, and I didn't want to die with him, and so I got out of there really fast."

"That little playroom, I saw it once."

"That's impossible. No one ever saw it."

"Well, yes, I did. Agent Sherlock and I looked around your house once because we thought Clancy was there. I can understand why Reverend McCamy wouldn't want servants hanging around to find it by accident. I'll admit I was really surprised

497

that Reverend McCamy was the sort of man who tied his wife down and whipped her."

Elsbeth McCamy looked blank a moment, then she threw back her head and let out a high wild laugh, and that laugh blended in with the crashing water and sent puffs of cold breath into the air. Katie was ready, only an instant from jumping at her, when Elsbeth's head came back down, her laughter cut off like water from a spigot, and she whispered, "I want to kill you anyway, Sheriff, so please, come at me, please."

"Why did you laugh?"

"Because you're so wrong about us," she said. "Just like his damned aunt Elizabeth. I know that she snuck in there when we were building the room, looking, poking about. She believed Reverend McCamy was crazy, that he abused me and that I loved it, that I was a pathetic victim. But you're all wrong. Before I shoved that old busybody down the stairs, I told her what we were going to use that room for. I told her why Reverend McCamy was having it built, and how much he needed it. He gave himself over to me when we were in that room, and he forgave himself for his faults for a few moments at least, when he was strapped down on his belly over that fur-covered block of wood and I whipped him, whipped him until sometimes the whip cut through and brought blood. And I could smell it. He dedicated that blood to God, and prayed that God would reward him with the return of the sacred stigmata."

"Those vials in that cabinet. What did you use those for?"

"Reverend McCamy used them to help him mortify his flesh, help him transcend the pain of giving himself over to God, pain that was both corporeal and spiritual. He cried in that room, not from the pain, but from how exalted he felt in those moments when the whip split his flesh and his blood flowed off his body onto that beautiful marble altar.

"But you ruined our life, Sheriff, destroyed everything. I've thought of nothing else but killing you since my husband died."

Now! Katie dived and rolled, hoping that Roosevelt's sculpted cloak covered her, and jerked her derringer out of its ankle holster the instant she stopped rolling. It was nearly worthless at any distance at all, that little gun, but if you got close enough, it could kill.

Elsbeth fired, one shot, then another and

another, all three of them striking the sculpture, ricocheting off, sending stone shards flying. Katie stayed down, protecting her face.

Elsbeth yelled, "Come out of there, Katie Benedict! You deserve to die for what you did! That statue won't help you!"

Katie stuffed herself tighter against the sculpture. "Don't come any closer, Elsbeth, I have a gun. Do you hear me? I don't want to shoot you, but I will if you force me to. Give it up. Toss the gun over here. There are bodyguards here, two of them, FBI agents. They heard the shots. You don't have a prayer, just give it up!"

Elsbeth suddenly appeared around FDR's huge cloak. She stopped not three feet from Katie, smiled down at her. She didn't see the small derringer. "You're lying to me again, Katie. You don't have a gun. You're expecting your precious bodyguards to ride up like the cavalry and save you. But there won't be time for that." And she laughed again. It made Katie's skin crawl, that laugh.

"You know something?" Elsbeth said, nearly choking. "I wish Reverend McCamy could see me now."

"I could tell he was proud of you, Elsbeth."

Those beautiful blue eyes lightened a moment with pleasure. Thank God, Katie thought. Maybe she'd bought herself some time. That big Beretta was pointed right at her head.

Elsbeth McCamy blinked, looked momentarily confused, then shook her head so hard her ski cap fell off. "He was my dearest mentor, a great man who had God's ear and made me scream with pleasure when he made love to me. And you sent him to his death."

As she flexed her finger around the trigger of the Beretta, Katie brought up her derringer and fired its two shots point-blank into Elsbeth's chest.

Elsbeth stumbled backward, but she didn't go down. "My God, you shot me! You miserable bitch, I won't let you kill me like you did my husband!"

Katie threw herself at Elsbeth's knees. She heard a gunshot close to her head. She could smell her singed hair burning as she used all her strength to shove Elsbeth down.

The front of Elsbeth's coat was drenched with blood now. She raised the gun and fired toward Katie again, wildly now. Katie rolled into Elsbeth, pushing hard against her legs, throwing her arms up to dislodge the Beretta. She knew that at any moment a bullet would smash through her flesh.

There was a single shot, only one. Katie, her arms still pressing against Elsbeth's knees, looked up and saw a frown of faint surprise on Elsbeth's face. The frown was frozen in death. Slowly, she fell backward, landing hard. Katie jerked back and leaped to her feet. Her hip burned, and her heart was pounding.

She looked down at Elsbeth McCamy, surely dead this time, her eyes open, staring at nothing at all. Her beautiful hair spilled around her face. She looked very young, innocent even, without any evil or madness about her, just lying there on the ground, the front of her coat soaked with blood and the back of her head ruined.

She heard the sound of the cascading water and the wind whipping between the monuments. And her own harsh breathing, so deadened with relief that she couldn't move.

She heard running feet. Katie turned to see the two FBI agents, panting, their guns still drawn. "You okay, Katie?"

"Yes, I am, Ollie. I'm very glad you came when you did. That was an excellent shot. I'm also very glad that you're both all right. I didn't know if she'd killed you."

Agent Ollie Hamish shook his head, looking embarrassed and angry at himself.

Agent Ruth Warnecki patted his arm. She said to Katie even as she nodded over at Elsbeth, "She did something much smarter than try to kill us. She came right up to us, knocked on the window, and when Ollie here rolled it down, his hand on his gun, mind you, she told us she was your sister-in-law, that she had to speak to you about Sam, and she promised to keep a sharp eye out for anyone suspicious. We didn't think anything of it. You'd think after all our years of being suspicious of anything that walked on two feet — but she was so believable, so young and nice-looking. We bolted out here when we heard the shots."

Ollie Hamish pulled out his cell phone and dialed. "Hello, Savich? We're here at the FDR Memorial. You'll want to get down here real fast. You'll want to call Detective Raven, too."

"And Miles Kettering, please," Katie said. She looked again at Elsbeth, then slowly sank down to the ground, clasped her hands around her knees, and bowed her head.

43

Detective Raven rose. "You guys like to live on the wild side, don't you?"

Katie couldn't move because Miles was holding her so tightly against his side she could barely breathe. "Oh yeah," Katie said. "I live for excitement. This time though, I think I'd like to just lie in the sun for a good long while and not think about anything but my husband's beautiful body."

"Hmmm," Detective Raven said, startled. "Not just yet, okay? There'll be more questions, more discussions, particularly with the D.A., so check with me before you go off to find a nice white beach."

When he was out the door, whistling, Katie realized that Miles was holding her even more tightly and he was shaking. She was surprised, somehow, despite everything that had happened. She lightly touched her fingers to his face. "I made a small joke, Miles, just for you. It's over now, really, it's all over."

He pulled her so close she could hear his

heart pounding against hers. She raised her face and kissed him, and was kissing him a second time when he said into her mouth, "When I got that call from Savich I was so afraid I nearly passed out. Here we've been worried about the kids, and I guess —"

"I know. We've been so worried about them that we didn't stop to think about how all this was affecting us." He was still shaking. She kept holding him tight, kissing him until she felt him relax a bit. She smiled. "Do you want to know something, Miles?"

"No, not unless it'll make me want to sing and dance. I can't take any more bad stuff for a while." He pressed his face against her neck. "Don't tell me, Keely wants Sam's room."

"Oh no, we've made hers even more girlie girl now and I don't think we could get her out if we tried. Just maybe, I hope, it is something that will make you want to dance and maybe hum a tune."

She could feel his mouth grinning against her. "Okay, Cracker's found a boyfriend and is moving out this afternoon?"

"Could be, but she hasn't said anything to me about finding a guy and moving. Nope, it's something else entirely."

"All right, tell me."

She said slowly, her voice dead serious now, "When I was facing Elsbeth and I knew she could raise that Beretta and shoot me just like that" — Katie snapped her fingers — "I knew for sure the last thing I wanted was to never see you or Sam or Keely again. I guess the bottom line here is that I love the kids and I love you, Miles."

He was silent as a tomb, didn't so much as flinch. He didn't do anything at all. She couldn't even feel his heart against her chest any longer.

She fidgeted, tapping her fingertips on his shoulder. "Miles?"

"Yeah?"

"Does that make you want to dance and sing?"

More silence, heavy winter silence.

"Miles? If you don't say something, I'm going to have to toss you on the floor and sit on you."

"That might be a good start," he said and bit her earlobe.

She pushed away from him to see him grinning like a thief who'd just lifted Bill Gates's wallet.

"Sit on me, Katie, do whatever you like. I don't want to sing or dance right this minute, what I do want to do is strip you naked and do everything I can think of to your injured body."

"My very serious declaration makes you horny?"

"Let me tell you what it makes me. I'm going to very gently help you upstairs to the bedroom, and then I'm going to feast. I'll set the alarm for about the time Sam and Keely come home from school."

As he carried her up the stairs, just like Rhett Butler, he whispered in her ear, "I love you, too, Katie."

Since Miles didn't set the alarm, when Sam and Keely came running into their bedroom, they stopped in their tracks and looked at each other. They looked at their parents, sound asleep, Katie on top of Miles, the blankets, thankfully, drawn up to their ears.

"Hey, Papa, why are you home this early?" When Miles mumbled something, and waved a hand at them, Sam and Keely jumped onto the bed, laughing.

Epilogue

"Hey, Sheriff, where you been? You'll freeze your butt out there."

Sheriff Katie Kettering pulled off her gloves and tossed her cream-colored straw hat onto the small table next to Linnie's station, given to her by Sam for Christmas after her old one was destroyed in November. "It's cold but the butt isn't frozen yet," she said, rubbing her hands.

"Perfect shot. You sail that new hat as good as the old one, Sheriff," Linnie said. "You're really late. What's up?"

Katie shrugged. "Mr. Turner's rottweiler, Sugar Plum, chased Benny Phelps all the way to Molly's Diner, where he barricaded himself in, much to everyone's enjoyment."

Pete Margolis, one of the firefighters from next door, here to steal some of Linnie's coffee, said, "Oh well, Benny's the

508

new postman and Sugar Plum just doesn't know him well enough yet. What are you going to do about it?"

"When I took Sugar Plum home and explained the problem, Mr. Turner gave me some of Sugar Plum's treats. Benny can try tossing them to her when he delivers the mail."

"After a week of the treats," Wade said, "she'll probably want to deliver mail with him."

Linnie said, "Mayor Tommy called, now he's begging. He wants you to talk to some reporters from Knoxville, help put Jessborough on the map."

"He just doesn't give up, you have to give him that. Tell him no way, again, Linnie."

"He also wants to know Miles's time-table for moving the plant here. He's all ready to shove it through the county planning commission, and he needs the plans for the plant. He said it should sail through, given Kettering Helicopters Inc. won't be sitting any farther than fifty yards from the Benedict Pulp Mill."

"I gave Miles a real good deal on the price," Katie said.

"Mayor Tommy's rubbing his hands together about all the new jobs he'll get credit for."

Katie said, "Tell Tommy that Miles will be here tomorrow. He can talk to him then."

Deputy Neil Crooke stuck his head around the corner. "The toilet in the men's room needs work, Sheriff."

"Call Joyce over at City Hall. She'll take care of it."

Wade said, "Oh yeah, Billy Bob Davis was hitting on his wife again, but when I went over there, she just snuffled and said she'd run into the door. There was nothing I could do."

Katie rolled her eyes. "You know what, Wade, why don't you and I go out to their farm and have a little chat with Billy Bob. Maybe if we rub his nose in some of the manure out there, it'll help him listen better."

Wade grinned and grabbed his leather jacket. "Sounds like a plan. I'll follow you out there."

Katie bundled up again, planted her straw hat on her head, and headed out, sucking in the sweet cold air. She walked to her newly repainted Silverado, all the bullet holes and dents finally repaired. She smiled toward the thick fog-covered mountains. She could reach out her hand and touch them, nearly. She hummed as she revved the powerful engine. She drove slowly down Main Street, making sure none of the snowdrifts would cause any problems. She waved to Dr. Sheila Raines, running across a well-plowed Main Street after her cat, Turpentine, black as sin and easy to see against all the snow. She saw Dr. Jonah Flint wave to Sheila, then eagerly join her to go after Turpentine. Hmm, something just might be going on there.

She was still humming forty minutes later when she had her knee on the small of Billy Bob's back, pressing his face in the dirty snow in his backyard while she told him what was what.

She heard one of the Gibsons' dairy cows moo loudly into the bright blue sky. She heard the Benedict Pulp Mill's noon whistle.

It was a perfect day in the most beautiful place on God's earth.

About the Author

Catherine Coulter is the author of the bestselling FBI suspense novels *The Cove*, *The Maze*, *The Target*, *The Edge*, *Riptide*, *Hemlock Bay*, and *Eleventh Hour*. She lives in northern California.

You may write Coulter at PO Box 17, Mill Valley, California 94942, or e-mail her at readmoi@aol.com. Visit her website at www.catherinecoulter.com.